Love and Honor in the Felgenland

Join us here to learn about our books: https://woodenhookstudios.com

Edited by: Alane Kochems

Love and Honor in the Felgenland
A Story in the Felgenland Saga

By
Eric C. Holtgrefe

Wooden Hook Studios

To my wife, your love and support made this possible.

To my children, your motivation carried this project to completion.

To my parents, thanks for all that you've done, and the things you've taught me.

Colossians 1:12

"Sergeant Weimar, check out the cliff three hundred meters forward and be advised there are hostiles sighted in your sector," Max's lieutenant, named Nordlinger, said over the command channel, the C-channel. The C-channel was a closed network between the lieutenant, Max, and the other squad leaders. Max raised his hand and waved a signal for the twelve Assaultmen in his squad to form a battle line. All eyes were on his one-hundred-and-eighty-two-centimeter frame. The four teams began to break up into a 'V' on Max's position. The Assaultmen wore ceramic-metal battlesuits and helmets for protection from small caliber weapons. The line of Assaultmen moved forward, covering the sector.

Max's regiment had been in the contested star system of Llande 21185 for over two years. The regiment had been fighting in space, on moons, and planets. Max had been planet side on Llande 21185 C—called Nakdong by the locals—for fifteen months. This was officially his last patrol. The patrol's mission parameters were to capture or kill the region's remaining anti-Union partisans and Terran militia.

Max tried to focus, but his mind wandered. Soon, he'd be off this dust ball. He was slated for some relaxation time on Lochiel when he rolled back into the base. After Nakdong, he was sure to get a promotion. The Union had officially declared war against the Terran Directorate. Since the war escalated to a total conflict, Max knew he'd get new stripes or officer's acorns. Rank escalation would be coming fast to everyone. Lieutenant Nordlinger had even recommended Max to attend the military academy at Stoneglen.

"Yes sir," Maximilian von Weimar returned over the C-channel to his officer. Max and his squad were part of the First Stahlburgh Rifles of the Assault, the ground forces of the Felgenland Union's military. Max watched as his fire team leaders, Corporals Andreas, Marko, and Tobias, shepherded the "FNGs," Assault slang for "Frightened New Guys," into the formation. Everyone needed to get back to base. Then Max would be off for R&R and, afterward, the home world—Stahlburgh. Max returned to the task at hand. All future thoughts would require him to finish this last patrol.

Max watched the terrain rise; the enemy could place weapons up high and rain down fire on his squad. Max started to worry. So far, the patrol had gone well—not running into partisans or Terran militia. His unit had been reinforced before the patrol, and he had complained to his superior, a color sergeant named Bannerman, over-babysitting a bunch of 'green' Assaultmen, especially on this his last patrol. FNGs had a habit of doing things backward. Doing things backward often killed someone.

Max motioned for Marko's team, Fire Team One, to advance to the left. A small track continued up a hill to a sheer cliff face. Marko and his team would sweep the trail and inspect the top of the cliff. Max's team was holding the center of the line, along with Andreas's team, while Tobias and his team would sweep out to the right.

Max's peripheral vision caught movement on the top of the cliff face to his left; he said over the squad channel, "Left, check left!"

The squad's helmets spun leftwards; a team of Terran militia appeared on the ridge above them. Marko flung a handful of drones into the air, and the squad's battle network immediately started generating a tactical map of the terrain. Within a moment, Max saw the map appear as a little window on his heads-up display or HUD, which was projected on the faceplate of his helmet.

"Fire Team One's got this!" Marko said as he oriented his fire team towards the left. Max called up a drone camera feed. The team of Terran militiamen was setting up a heavy weapon. Max's HUD identified the make as an Arm-nikov, a more powerful version of their AN-2347. The gun was terrible news for Max and his squad, as the hassium rounds could rip through an Assaultman's battlesuit and keep on moving.

Max said over the squad channel, "Push forward, Marko!" On the feed, Max watched in horror as the militiamen finished the work on the heavy weapon. Max could see that Marko's fire team was too far away to return fire on the heavy gun. Within seconds, the placed AN-'47 started firing at Fire Team One. Max and his men dropped to a prone position. Max could see the tracers from the heavy weapon glow all around the Assaultmen as the Terran militia swung the gun in a wide arc to suppress the entire Felgenlander squad.

"Hang on, team one," Max said over the squad channel. He watched the drone feed as the Terran heavy weapon tracers came around, moving their bead of fire to Marko's fire team. Max watched in frustration as hassium projectiles from the deadly Terran gun began shredding the Assaultmen in Marko's team.

Max was about to utter a command, but Andreas's and Tobias's teams began to crawl forward. Andreas's team moved forward a few meters and began to return fire.

"Fire Team Two covering," Andreas said. Max assessed Fire Team Two's position; the Assaultmen were at the bottom of the cliff face. The spot was safe from Terran fire but couldn't do much to retaliate against the enemy either.

Tobias's team went from crawling to crouching to running. "Fire Team Three, go wide. We'll try for a flank," Tobias said to his men. Max checked the drone feed. Team one was down. The Terrans were reacting to Fire Team Three's attempted flank, and Max could see the line of tracers arcing toward Tobias's Assaultmen.

Max and team four took that moment to stand and rush to where

Andreas's team was positioned. As he ran towards the cliff, Max slung his weapon and snatched a grenade from his waist. Skidding to a stop by Andreas, Max pulled the pin and flung the grenade upwards. Max checked his throw on the HUD; the camera showed the grenade making a high parabolic arc before dropping right on the Terran heavy weapons team. The grenade turned into a crimson flower of super-thermal plasma. The bloom engulfed the top of the cliff. The remaining teams continued to lay down covering fire. Max waited for the smoke to clear. Once the dark cloud had dissipated, the camera showed nothing remained but ash.

Max scanned through the various drone feeds, looking for other hostiles. He studied the horizon and then looked up at the cliff's top. Looking skyward, Max noticed parachutes opening.

"Parachutes!" one of the FNGs stood and shouted into the channel.

"Stay down," Max said in caution. He didn't want the FNGs standing to gawk while another potential enemy could surprise the entire squad.

Max switched to the C-channel and said, "Hey, lieutenant, I see 'chutes close to our position. Can I get a sit rep?"

"Just getting the word now, Weimar," Nordlinger said, "confirmed, those are friendlies, repeat those are friendlies."

"Aye, sir," Max said as he watched momentarily as the parachutes floated over the sector. Max grew frustrated as he saw his FNGs sitting there, waiting for orders from him. They should have been spreading out and watching for hostiles. "Perimeter check! Someone check Marko's fire team," Max said over the squad channel. Max's squad jumped up and went about securing the landing zone, or LZ. The medic, an Assaultman First Class named MacGregor, checked the lifeless bodies of Marko and his fire team. The Terran weapon had cut the Assaultmen down mid-charge. The medic looked up from the carnage, shaking his head. Max tried not to think about the loss as he prepared the LZ for the dropping platoon.

After thirty minutes, the new platoon was staged and ready for action. As Max's squad maintained overwatch, an officer moved toward where Max and his men were spread out. The officer moved through the terrain like he was taking a Sunday walk, and Max suspected he was fresh from the Academy.

"Staff Sergeant Maximilian von Weimar reporting, sir," Max said. The ensign's helmet instantly synchronized with Max's, establishing a private point-to-point comm channel.

"The infamous Maximum Carnage," the ensign said to Max. The officer used one of the *Noms de guerre* the local press had given Max. "You've gotten quite the reputation. I'm Ensign Mike Barrington, Second Stahlburgh Rifles. Our orders are to relieve you and your squad."

"Thank you, sir," Max said, hiding his embarrassment at being called that stupid name.

"One moment," the officer said. Barrington was pressing his hand against his helmet. The ensign tried to push the tiny ear bud further into his ear canal. Max wasn't an officer and was not permitted to listen on their comm channel—the O-channel; however, Max could hear faint O-channel chatter bleeding into Barrington's communication with him. The sound was fuzzy and indistinct.

Max suspected even in the ensign was having trouble making out the chatter.

"Aye, aye, Colonel, I will bring him and report immediately," the ensign said, his voice clear over Max's point-to-point channel.

"Pritchard, get over here for guard duty. Pike, you take over Weimar's squad—get them ready for load up and evac," the ensign said, over his squad channel to his Sergeants and the point-to-point with Max. Max suddenly realized that the green officer had forgotten to switch off their private channel.

"Sir?" was all Max could muster. He wasn't sure why he was being relieved.

"Oh, Staff Sergeant, I'm under orders to take you to a field court martial conducted by Colonel Kuhlemeier. Please surrender your rifle to Sergeant Pritchard," the ensign said.

"What are the charges, sir," Max asked. As Pritchard came over, Max handed his rifle to the sergeant. Max was utterly clueless about why he was getting a field court martial. Marko's team had died, but Max felt confident in his actions during the fight, and Marko's team had gotten spectacularly unlucky. Max was sure there was nothing criminal in any of that.

"I don't know, Staff Sergeant. Sergeant Pritchard will escort us to the Colonel; he gave me a direct order."

Sergeant Pritchard, Max, and the ensign moved as quickly as they could over the broken two kilometers of the sector. They marched towards the center of the landing zone. Max saw the dark shape of the command tent rising as the internal automaton elevated the structure. As the peak of the command tent stopped moving, three battlesuited officers walked from behind the structure and entered while two Assaultmen followed and then moved to guard the entrance. Max, Pritchard, and Barrington approached the tent. "Ensign Barrington, with prisoner and guard."

"Barrington, enter with your prisoner," the stern voice of the colonel said through a speaker over the tent entrance. Pritchard, duty completed, turned to walk back to his squad. Max and the ensign entered the tent. Entering, Max noticed an auto-table was in the process of unfolding and rising to full height. The three officers were opening chairs to sit behind the table. Max's HUD labeled the officers Colonel Kuhlmeier, Major Jones, and Lieutenant Nordlinger, Max's commander. Max turned his head as another officer entered; the HUD labeled the newcomer Lieutenant von Huegel. Von Huegel carried a ceremonial saber, the sign of guilt or innocence.

"Barrington and prisoner, remove your helmets," Kuhlemeier ordered. Max flipped the quick release, and his helmet came off.

"Ensign Mike Barrington, will you stand in for the Procurator of the Defense," Kuhlemeier asked.

"Sir, I've only done this once before," the ensign said quickly.

"Once is enough. Now, yes or no?"

"Yes, Colonel, sir," the ensign said.

"Lieutenant Wilhelm von Huegel, will you stand in as the Procurator for the Union?"

"Yes, sir," the Lieutenant said, "and, for the record, my experience away from the battle lines is assisting the Judge Advocate General. I have also aided magistrates at the shire level as a legal researcher."

"Thank you, Lieutenant," the colonel said at the unwanted exposition.

"Have you, Barrington, and you, Huegel, ever won a case in civilian court," the colonel asked, "The code of military justice is explicit—justice can't be done if one side has more experience than the other."

"No, sir," the men responded in unison.

"You both have been instructed at the academy in the regulations involving a field court-martial and have attended the minimum of at least one court-martial?"

"Yes, sir," the men responded. Max was unsure what the charges were against him, but Kuhlemeier would run the court-martial by the book.

"Then," the colonel said as he rose, "by the authority granted to me by my commission in 2330 Anno Domini and by the Union Parliament, under our first Protector, Karl the Great, I now invoke this field court martial. I am charged with the authority of this field court martial by our current Protector Raimond—Allfather save him!"

All assembled said, "By His grace," in unison. Max anticipated severe charges from the court martial as the colonel and the presiding officers took their seats.

"Now, to the charges, the accused, one Maximilian von Weimar, holding the enlisted rank of staff sergeant, is now charged with fraud, waste, and abuse of Union property," the colonel said, looking at a tablet, "How does the accused plead?"

Max shook his head 'no' to the ensign, who said, "Not guilty, sir."

"Noted. Present your case, von Huegel."

"Mister von Weimar," the lieutenant said, "on your enlistment forms, you state you grew up in Glasgowburgh, in the county of Freiherr von Huegel, my uncle. On the forms, you listed your father's name as Frank and your mother's name as Maria; your age seventeen—a legal adult in the Union."

"Colonel, I object," the ensign stated. "The Articles of War state that the Procurator for the Union must make a case based on facts that pertain to the accusations against the defendant. Lieutenant von Huegel has yet to provide evidence demonstrating that Weimar is guilty of anything."

"Noted, but I will allow the lieutenant a chance to continue, provided he makes his case more expediently," the colonel said.

"Sirs, I say to you that Maximilian von Weimar is a fraud. He has enlisted under a lie and is not worthy of continued duty by falsifying his age, family, and name."

Max rolled his eyes at the lieutenant's statement. Barrington looked quizzically at Max. Max knew the officer needed an explanation and motioned to speak with him.

"Colonel, might I have a short recess to discuss this with my charge," the ensign asked.

"Granted, we'll step away, Barrington, for propriety," the colonel said. He and the officers on the court martial then stood and clustered at the far end of the tent. The lieutenant waited a moment and joined them. Max and the ensign stood out of earshot for their discussion.

"What's going on, Weimar," the ensign whispered.

"Sir, the lieutenant is right. I lied on the forms. My surname is Fraser. Weimar is my mother's maiden name. Eleven years ago, I was underage—sixteen—when I joined the Assault. I lied about my parents's names because my father and I don't get along. I ran away after a fight with my father—in hindsight, the argument was stupid. Running away, I couldn't ask for permission to join up—my father detested the military—so yes, I lied to get in."

Barrington nodded, but Max softly continued, "Everyone knows that if the Assault decided to prosecute all the boys who lied on their enlistment forms, there wouldn't be enough of us to go to war. Yet, here we are."

"Wait, something doesn't add up here, Max," the ensign said, "Colonel Kuhlemeier has a Judge Advocate General's aide-de-camp, and the rest of the court martial has sat silently on what feels like a court of the star chamber. This must be political."

"My guess, sir, is that my father has rattled someone's cage at high command or in Parliament."

"He some sort of lord, Max?"

"Yes, sir, his full name is Kenneth *Graf* Fraser of Gilbraith-on-Heather, known locally as the Earl of the Bonnie Dundee."

"Wait, Max! You're one of the descendants of the 'First Earls' of Stahlburgh?"

"Yes, sir," Max said, "Technically, I am the second son of the earl —the spare."

Barrington shouted, "Colonel, we'd like to change our plea."

The colonel turned from the small huddle and said, "Go on."

"Sir, after a brief discussion with my charge, I'd like to enter a plea of Not Proved."

"That is a guilty plea—does the accused agree to this? I will warn the accused that I can condemn him to a firing squad if he cannot offer a mitigating statement," the colonel said sternly.

"Yes, sir," Max said. Max perceived why Barrington had changed the plea; Max would admit his guilt, and, in exchange for cooperating, the colonel would slap him on the wrists for punishment.

Men who lied on their enlistment forms could be shot. Mainly, they were reduced in rank, and the whole affair was considered a clerical error. Max watched the officers file back and take their seats behind the table. Lieutenant von Huegel stepped forward and turned the ceremonial saber on the table. The point of the blade was aimed right at Max to signify his guilt.

"Accused and his Procurator, attention," the colonel said. Both Max and Barrington snapped their heels together.

"As presiding officer, I, Colonel Kuhlemeier, declare that the judgment of this court-martial is a verdict of 'Not Proved.' Mister Fraser must now make a statement to guide the court on his sentencing."

"Yes, sir," Max said, "court-martial, I joined the Assault under a false name—and under the legal age of enlistment. However, I have always conducted myself with the honor and dignity of an Assaultman. Whatever my name may be, I hold the Allfather, the Union, and the protector dearer than my own life." Max stood ramrod straight, waiting for his sentence. He prayed Barrington's gambit would work, and he'd be back with his unit soon—minus a stripe or two on his uniform.

"Thank you," the colonel said. "Under the Articles of War, I have the option of levying a punishment as harsh as death by firing squad; however, as these crimes were reported outside of regular channels and there are extenuating circumstances surrounding Mister von Weimar, or rather, as he should be properly known, Mister Fraser..."

At hearing his rightful surname, Max interpreted why the forged enlistment documents were an issue. Max prayed inwardly that the worst hadn't happened. He felt his stomach churn, and he asked the Allfather for him to escape the coming nightmare with a quick hanging. He felt hot despite the cooling unit on his battlesuit.

"In light of the accused's good conduct and excellent service record," the colonel's voice returned to Max's ears, "we levy a punishment of discharge from service on this day, the seventeenth of March twenty-three-fifty-three Anno Domini, along with forfeit of all campaign pay. The accused will be transported back to Stahlburgh, where he will assume his rightful name and title as the *Graf* or Count of Gilbraith-on-Heather, known by the populace as the Earl of the Bonnie Dundee."

Max felt the blood rush to his face. The tent began to spin. That his father might have passed away was not shocking, but Archy? The last he had heard, Archy was alive and well. Why was Max now the earl?

With the sentencing completed, the colonel said, "Your grace, the protector thanks you for your service and sends his condolences on the death of your brother, Archibald, and your father, Kenneth." Max tipped forward. The shock of his brother's death and inheriting something he had never wanted made the now earl fall.

"Barrington to your charge." The colonel's voice rang in Max's ears as he fell. The ensign scrambled to catch Max, but his tumble had surprised the assembly.

The ensign lifted Max's unconscious form and carried Max to the transport. Unconsciously and unknowingly, Max was on his way back to his home world, Stahlburgh, and back to the region where he grew up, the Sheeplands. Max had left his home as a poor runaway. He was returning as a lord, the head of one of the most ancient families in the Union.

Part One

Inheritance

CHAPTER ONE
Homecoming

"Ah, the Bonnie Dundee," Max said to himself, "just as I remember the old pile... what a dung heap." Max had just crested the small hillock from the town and the train station and saw the estate before him.

"This estate is your birthright," a heavily accented voice said from the brown burnt grass below.

"The red-headed Cormac speaks," Max said, smiling. His eyes tracked to find the speaker. Max looked around, but instead of finding Cormac, he noticed three broken windows in the large, stately house. Finally, looking to the grass below, Max saw the huntsman, wearing brown and blending into the terrain.

"You mean the gray-haired Cormac," the huntsman—Cormac Munro—said, moving across the lawn as Max descended to the same level. The two men met, and Max stretched out his hand. Cormac stood slightly shorter than Max, with gray hair and a tanned, leathery face. The huntsman's pale blue eyes twinkled as he met Max's outstretched hand with a grip that almost brought Max to tears.

"Cormac!" Max said, welling up with emotion and a little pain at the handshake.

"Aye, lad, you've been gone too long. I was headed up the *Cruach Mhòr,*" Cormac said, pointing towards the most prominent peak on the estate with his rifle, "if you're up for the trek, we could go together, for old time's sake." Max nodded, dropping his rucksack and stripping off his uniform jacket. He was sure the gear wouldn't walk off. Moving across the lawn, both men approached a hill, climbing silently. After a hundred meters, their pace slowed, each watching for the game. Max would pause and turn an eye on the scene far below them. The house looked terrible, worse than Max had remembered. The manor was missing glass in windows and shingles on the roof, and the entire façade needed a new coat of paint. When Max looked from the house, he noticed that the lawns and gardens were abysmal, too.

"Been a good year. The herd has grown," Cormac said, stopping momentarily and breaking into Max's observations. Max noted that the huntsman was detached, although Max had no idea why.

"Uh huh," Max said, climbing up where Cormac had stopped.

"Kenneth's gout hadn't allowed him to hunt as much as he had in years past," Cormac said brusquely, "Archy did his duty, but he didnae have love for the hunt. Hunting was your great love. Too bad you weren't around, Max." Max merely nodded. As Max joined Cormac, the huntsman angrily continued his near run up the mountain. Cormac suddenly stopped and pointed.

"There," Cormac said, looking sharply, "that'll be himself, the Pompous Trousers."

"Huh?" Max said as Cormac handed him his rifle. Max looked through the site on the rifle as Cormac whispered, "See his fur. Archy thought they looked like trousers, and since the stag was so proud, we called him the Pompous Trousers."

Max sighted on the deer. A gentle squeeze and the stag would be mounted over whatever shambles of the fireplace remained in the manor below.

"I can't," Max said, suddenly very sad at the thought of his brother, "my heart isn't in the mood."

"I suppose once you've hunted a man, our game just isn't that exciting," Cormac said with disapproval, taking the rifle gently from Max's hands. Max felt cut to the quick by Cormac's rejection. What was worse was that Max was unsure why the huntsman seemed so angry.

"Yeah, something like that," Max said, looking over the vista.

"The funeral was beautiful, lad," Cormac said, a tear in the corner of the rough man's eyes, "Fionnula, Archy's intended, was there. She laid the wreath on the lawn below, over the memorial marker. I played on my pipes, and Meg recited some of Robbie Burns's work. Kenneth... Well, he went downhill immediately. He was almost too sickly to attend the service. He went out with us anyway. The chill was in the air, and the day was full of rain."

"Thanks, Cormac," Max said, strangely icy, as if everything was just a bad dream. He would wake up and fall out of a bunk on a ship or barracks. He'd be yelled at by an officer or another sergeant or shot at by a Terran, but Archy would be safe, alive, and assuming his rightful place as the earl.

"You should have been there," Cormac said, raising his voice angrily.

"I think things worked out better by me staying away," Max said, "the last words father said to me was I wasn't fit to bear the name Fraser."

"I didn't know that, laddie," Cormac said, his face showing pain at hearing Max's statement, "Archy dying was a shock to us all, lad."

Max nodded. The statement was as good as a spoken apology from the huntsman, who said, "I wish I could have been there, Cormac. How did he die?"

"His hover-truck had gone off the side of the road to the northeast, you know, the one that track leads across the back of *Cruach nan Caorach*," Cormac said, his voice cracking.

"Aye," Max said, seeing the huntsman's pain in telling the tale.

"We found where he missed his turn," Cormac said—which Max rightly inferred to mean Cormac found the scene, "There were skid marks near the road that went over the edge. He must have been going at a bloody great speed. The ruts Archy left in the track showed that he took the turn too fast. The skirts must have shredded on the impact with the guard rails as the debris was everywhere."

Max nodded, watching as Cormac's eyes continued to water.

"The truck skidded out and went into free fall over the side," Cormac continued, "We were about to go after where it landed, but a mountain blizzard came down upon us. The snow was terrible, and we had to wait a week for the weather to clear. When we found the impact site, Archy's body was a scene from a nightmare."

"If someone had let me know," Max said, "I would have raced back. They would have let me—I had leave accrued."

"Kenneth fell ill from all the searching," Cormac said, "I suggested sending a message to you, but he wouldn't allow me. He held the whole mess against you like you leaving cursed Archy. The old man then caught pneumonia and perished a fortnight later, but what killed him was Archy's death. We buried Kenneth next to your mother's grave over on the north side of *Glen Gorm*."

"And Archy?" Max asked. He felt the warmth of his tears on his cheeks. The whole thing was real, and Archy was well and truly gone.

"You are walking on him," Cormac said, "he had always wanted to be cremated, like the Prophet. We spread his ashes all over this mountain."

"Well then, the mountain is sacred ground now," Max said, wiping his eyes and nose with his sleeve.

"Aye, it is, lad. I suppose you'll be heading back to the Assault now. With the war on and no one knowing where you were, your Aunt May challenged the succession. She stated your cousin Hector was the rightful heir. Hector bragged about how the clan will confirm his title."

The succession conflict made Max pause. He had never liked his aunt or her brat of a boy, Hector. May had run off and married a woodcutter against Max's father's wishes. For years, May and Kenneth didn't even speak to one another. When May's husband died, she and Kenneth reconciled. Then, she and Hector moved into the Bonnie Dundee. Max remembered those days. He and Archy were just boys, but the tension between Hector, May, and the rest of the family had been tremendous. Hector did not get along with Max and Archy. As a result, Kenneth sent Max and his brother to boarding school. After a few years, even though they lived in a home with over fifty rooms, his aunt and father began constantly sparring. Finally, Max returned one Christmas to discover that May and Hector had moved out. May had departed after some choice words with Kenneth. Then, they relocated to the family's home in the capital. Kenneth sent for Archy and Max. Max lived in the Bonnie Dundee until he left for the Assault.

"What makes Hector think he has a claim?" Max said, returning to the present.

"Well, he's made a great boast about your inability to assume your duties with the war on and you being in the Assault. Hector says that either in name or deed, he'll be taking over."

"Aha," Max said.

Cormac continued, "Hector's attitude hasn't gone over well with the retainers or the village. You may have been gone a dozen years, but the retainers and villagers all feel the estate is yours by rights. You know how the folk of the county are about their rights."

"I do, like that boxing day when those old pensioners came up the drive with that old stag carcass?" Max said with a laugh.

Cormac nodded, and Max continued, "Those two cottagers were arguing loudly about who owned the dead stag. The snow came down all around them. You were a sight to behold when you finally came out of your house and told them that the earl wouldn't see them until after Boxing Day. I wish you could have photographed their faces when you said that. Both of those old geezers were insulted that you had said their case wasn't of high importance after they spent hours convincing each other that the possession of the carcass was the most important thing in all the Union."

Cormac laughed and said, "I remember those fools. They ended up splitting the deer. One got the head for a trophy, and the other the backside for his supper."

"By the Allfather, I am glad to be back, old friend," Max said. Max moved to look at the scene below. The stately home stood flanked by run-down gardens, which in turn were framed by fir trees. From up on the mountain to Max, the estate looked idyllic, perfect, and peaceful.

"How long are you sticking 'round for, lad?"

"Oh, I dunno," Max said with a smile, "eighty or ninety years, Allfather willing."

"I'm no young fool, laddie," Cormac said, his voice gruff like an old dog's bark, "If you aren't serious, I'll never speak to you again. But, if you are going to stay, I will back you. No more getting wild hairs and running off, though."

"Won't happen... They booted me out, Cormac. I could beg my way back, but you know..."

"You're a Fraser, and you have more honor than that. Aye, I understand."

"Something like that, yes," Max said.

"Well then, welcome home, lad," Cormac said. Then, with a conspiratorial wink, the huntsman said, "Time to let your cousin know he will be waiting many years for his title."

"With pleasure," Max said, "that little turd always used to steal my sweet roll, you know, the ones the cook Old Jean would make?"

"Aye, the best cook in Sheeplands, she was. Her like won't be seen in Stahlburgh for many a generation," Cormac said as the men slowly trekked down the mountain. The huntsman was more relaxed in his pace, and Max suspected that Cormac took a longer way down. Max figured Cormac wanted to give him more time to reconsider his decision to stay. When the land leveled out, the two men picked up the pace and reached the edge of the grounds west of the manor. The *Holstensonne* was dipping under the horizon behind them, and the lights flicked across the breadth of the first floor. Inside the house, Max saw many people's silhouettes.

"What's all this Cormac?"

"One of Hector's parties, Max. He throws one every other night, and his guests are draining the whisky reserves at a murderous rate."

"Why every other night? Why not every night?" Max asked. The question was out of curiosity since Max wouldn't put anything past his cousin.

"I don't believe Hector's constitution could withstand a party a night, lad," Cormac said with a hint of malice.

"Wait, Cormac! He isn't holding court in the wee hours of the morning as Father did?"

"If you mean the wee hours of the afternoon, well..." Cormac said, but Max cut him off.

"Cormac, what do the barons and the squires think of all that?" The men approached the house just as night came. The bright lights inside flooded out over the grounds, obscuring details outside.

"Think of what, young man?" a gruff codger said. Max's eyes adjusted as he looked away from the light streaming from the large windows. A group of old men was next to the house's west entrance. Some sat while others stood in the once proud decorative garden. Even overgrown, the hedges concealed their presence, as Max had easily missed the gathering. The old men sat conspiratorially together outside of the party. Max guessed the codgers felt some bit of duty to attend Hector, the heir presumptive, yet they weren't comfortable inside with the rest of the guests.

"Watch your tongue, Finn," Cormac said sharply, "That is the earl you are speaking to."

Max's eyes had just adjusted to the darkness when someone shone a flashlight in his face.

"Och! That was no Hector," one old man said as he turned off his torch.

"I ken that Gillis," another said. The codgers—like all the folk of the Sheeplands—were apt to carry a flashlight or torch, just in case.

"Well, who is he," another asked. Max was blinded again as someone else shone the light in his face and then turned the torch off.

"I dunno who that is," another spat.

"I'm Maximilian Fraser."

"*Graf* Fraser of Gilbraith-on-Heather," Cormac said to the old men, "This is Earl of the Bonnie Dundee to you lot!"

"Little Max?" one of the men said. Max waited. He expected another light to shine on his face. Thankfully, Max could almost make out the number of the assembled group now that his low-light vision was returning.

"You should all rise the presence of your earl," Cormac said protectively. Max knew the huntsman jealously guarded his status as the earl's chief retainer and would make these men hop—if they didn't respect Max properly.

"Welcome back, your laird-ship," the errant baron said. Max could make out the baron's form, standing in respect.

"Thank you, you're Mungo, right?" Max said. He had hastily remembered the name of one of the seven barons who owed his family loyalty.

"Ye-yes, your laird-ship," Mungo said to Max, then turned to his companions with a hint of pride at the recognition and said, "By the rood! He remembers me."

"Now, if you'll excuse me, I must attend to my cousin's guests," Max said. He moved away from the group of old men, night vision regained, and then stepped into the western cloakroom of the stately home. Max immediately noticed his jacket and rucksack were neatly stowed in a cubbyhole, out of the way of all the people.

"Meg will have done that, lad," Cormac said, noticing Max's head turned toward the stored gear.

"Better in here than out in the garden where the dew would have gotten over it all," Max said, pulling his uniform jacket from the hook and throwing the garment on. Max and Cormac then exited the cloakroom into the grand corridor.

The grand corridor ran east-west across the home and was approximately sixty meters long. Next to the cloakroom where Max and Cormac stood were the stairs to the library, while at the far end was the main foyer with the house's grand staircase. The corridor was almost five meters wide yet full of guests. They stood in clumps throughout the hall's sixty-meter length. Max attempted to skirt the small groups of guests as he and Cormac made their way across the width of the stately home. Finally, Max and Cormac arrived at the door that led to the foyer area with the grand staircase.

"Right," Max said to Cormac, pushing the door to the foyer open, "Time to make some unwanted guests very unhappy."

Max stepped through the door, and Cormac shouted, "The Earl of the Bonnie Dundee, Maximilian *Graf* Fraser of Gilbraith-on-Heather."

Max felt the immediate hostility from the crowd as the music stopped. Now, all eyes were on Max. Max walked forward a pace, and the guests parted around him like a drop of soap in oil.

"Good evening," Max said, "this party is now over. My servant Cormac will help you into your coats and escort you to your vehicles or, if you prefer—a taxi."

Many guests began a queue to leave and struggled like sheep at a market to move to safety. Max watched bemusedly as they attempted to go. He was about to move on to another room when a man of about twenty-four or twenty-five appeared. The drunk man had reddish brown hair and light brown eyes and stood at the same height as Max.

"I'm sorry, but you will have to leave," the man said as he staggered towards Max, "as rightful heir and trustee, I determine who stays on my land or…"

The man stopped mid-sentence and stared awkwardly at Max, "I say, I must be really drunk, or you look almost exactly like my dead uncle Ken."

"Hector, you remember Maximilian?" Cormac asked the drunk. Max had suspected the drunk was Hector and was relieved by Cormac's confirmation. The last time the cousins had seen each other, they were boys.

"Cormac, what are you on about? This can't be Maxie since Maxie is in the Assault, and with a war on, they never will let him go. Now, since he's away, I'm in charge. You heard what the Campbell fellow said, 'Mind this place like a good lad,' and no one could confuse you for a lad, you old goat. He was speaking to me."

Max felt his face flush during the discussion. Max finally lost his patience with his cousin's behavior and said, "Hector, you have five minutes to apologize, or I'll have Cormac throw you and this rabble out into the gutter."

"How dare you, sirrah!" Hector puffed up, swaying, "I am a member of the landed gentry and a regent. I will not be spoken to in such a manner…"

Max halted Hector's rambling with a quick punch to the nose. Hector fell backward and landed with a satisfying thump. Seeing violence inflicted on their host, the guests redoubled their efforts to shuffle out the door. The message was clear: the party was over.

Cormac smiled at Max and said, "Welcome home, your grace!"

CHAPTER TWO

Earl's Court

Max awoke, thrashing against the pathetic mattress that was his father's old bed. Max wanted to return to his old room, but in the interim of eleven years, Kenneth had Max's bed taken down and put into storage. By rights, Kenneth's old bed was Max's now, although Max suspected the mattress was as old as his father had been. Aside from the poor mattress, the bed frame was sturdy and, barring a coat of varnish, still serviceable. Max suspected the frame was original to the house, but that mystery was for another time.

Max sat up briskly and was rewarded with a sharp headache. He then felt the remains of the intoxicating effects of the single malt Felgenland whisky that he and Cormac had shared before his bedtime. Max then realized he would probably have to confront his cousin and Aunt May today about the usurpation of his title. The conversation would become an ugly affair, with accusations and recriminations. While not fond of his cousin and aunt, Max didn't want them as enemies either.

Max stood and paced to the window, hoping to open it and get fresh air. He looked out over the glen. The clouds hung low in the sky, touching halfway between the glen and the mountain tops. He leaned his head out the window to take in the whole expanse of the view. From his waist up, he stood visible across the countryside in his night clothes.

"Mungo, Gillis, the earl is *awake,*" a gravelly old voice below the window gasped. Max turned his head to gaze below him. A gaggle of old men sat huddled under the window, like a gathering of geriatric Romeos from a Shakespeare revival. The old men wore the traditional dress of the Scots of the Stahlburgh Sheeplands: Tam o'shanter with a long-speckled feather, a knit wool sweater, a full plaid, and wool socks barely visible above a study calf height boot.

Max looked at the gathering and said, "What do you all want?"

"Your magnificence, we are here for the court," one of the old men replied.

Max pulled himself back inside and said, "Egad, they *want me* to hold court."

Energized by the request, Max changed into a set of older bib overalls and a cable knit sweater. A far cry from the traditional dress of the geezers below his window, but Max felt the clothes were a better costume for any potential activities he would be duty-bound to today. He checked his appearance in a full-length mirror in the corner of his new room and made his way out and to the kitchen. In the kitchen was a pot of coffee, still hot, and Max didn't hesitate to grab a quick cup. Max suspected someone, most likely his sister or the huntsman, must have brewed the pot for him. Max then proceeded across the kitchen to the grand corridor, then eastward to the doors to the great hall.

Max threw open the doors to the hall and was disheartened by all the trash strewn on the twenty-by-fifty-meter floor. Max also noted a thick layer of dust on the sills and other flat surfaces. The banner of the Frasers lay on the floor and covered in dirt. Max deduced that all the trash must have been generated from the parties his cousin had hosted. The garbage would have to go, and Max would need a large dumpster to haul the refuse away.

In disgust, Max kicked most of the debris away from the large tarp that covered an imposing piece of furniture at the far end of the hall. Finding a space to stand, Max pulled the tarp, revealing the tall throne underneath. As he tidied up, the old men perambulated into the hall.

"He's using MacLeod's stool," one of the old men exclaimed as Max pulled the tarp away. The old man was giddy. The old squire was the dictionary definition of giddiness.

Max hadn't planned on sitting on the stool but took heed to the suggestion and plopped down on the throne. The seat was an ancient Steelwood chair crafted, allegedly, for the pirate MacLeod—the discoverer of Max's homeworld—Stahlburgh. Max mused on how the Frasers had come to possess the chair. Max realized the possession was probably unintentional as he sat on the chair. Very quickly, Max lost feeling in his buttocks. The numbness was replaced with an almost dull, aching pain climbing from his butt and into his lower back. Max was shocked by the agony in his lower extremities. He'd sat on metal railings that were more pleasurable. Max wiggled and tried to lean into the chair's backrest, yet relief for his bottom wasn't achieved.

"Only the hardest truest Fraser can abide that chair, your magnificence," one of the squires said as Max sat. Max smiled grimly. He knew a test when he was presented with one. All the old men's gazes snapped to Max, scrying if Max could endure MacLeod's stool. Max knew they were determining his weaknesses, especially after his cousin's behavior. The old men wanted an earl much like the legends, and he had to be rigid, uncompromising, and just.

"Thank you, but I am not here to discuss seating. Please present your clan, given name, title, and case," Max said. The faster the court was over, the faster he could move to a more comfortable seat and complete the old men's test.

"Court so early, I should have expected that," Cormac said in a low grumble. The huntsman had appeared from behind the throne, coffee mug in hand. Max looked up over his shoulder to Cormac with a smile. Max noticed the huntsman was also paying the heavy price for consuming the bottle of whisky in celebration of Max's vow to stay last night.

"Your magnificence, I represent Clan MacLay. I am Donal, Esquire, presenting a most serious case. My neighbor, Squire Tavish MacNee, has been lumbering out my land these past twenty years," Donal said. Max tried to look impassive, but the case was almost as old as he was. Max suspected Kenneth had ignored this quarrel for lack of a good solution or indifference.

"My laird," and even older Tavish MacNee spoke, "Tis my land, Squire Donal MacLay moved the Union surveyor's stones during the last survey—twenty years ago. The stones were moved three kilometers to surround a copse of Steelwood trees. Then MacLay laid claim to the trees so I cannae lumber them. I have ignored this insult and lumbered the trees anyway."

Max remembered tall, proud trees as he recalled seeing them when he climbed the trail with Cormac yesterday. The trees stood out from the pine forest around the demesne of the MacLay off to the northern edge of his estate. Max realized the conflict was significant because the trees were a rare and valuable export from Stahlburgh. Woodworkers prized the boards the trees would make throughout the galaxy. The wood had a tight grain, few knots, and was of extreme hardness and durability. Max looked at the Steelwood chair he sat on and back at the squires. The lumbering and sale of the wood could cover operating costs for his estate. Max was tempted to seize the trees as was his right as headman. Max reasoned that a percentage of the profits should have returned to him by rights as the earl. Max made a mental note to see if the sums of money had been paid and to check the estate accounts after court.

"That's my land. I didnae kick the stones," Donal said. He puffed himself up and pulled a dirk from his boot. MacNee wasted no time and pulled a knife from his waist. The two old men began to circle each other. Each one was looking for an advantage before they attempted a strike. Max tried not to laugh. The scene was comical.

Max sobered when he considered, at their ages, the men had more of a chance to hurt themselves, the onlookers, or Cormac.

"That's enough," Cormac shouted, "are you here to gain the earl's judgment or fight like schoolboys?"

The old men stopped circling, and Max saw Cormac's scolding chagrined them. Other, equally aged squires quickly separated the two belligerents. Max sighed in relief as the old combatants put their blades away, bowed, and said, "Apologies, lairdship."

Max decided the feud wasn't worth more years of indecision and said, "I now judge that MacLay is the rightful tenant. As my tenant, he will take half the profits for the next ten years. In addition, MacNee will repay MacLay for ten years to offset past losses. MacNee will have perpetual lumber rights at a reasonable price set by MacLay. Furthermore, the earl's rent will remain in the hands of the MacNee while he repays his neighbor, next case." The old men nodded in agreement. They all claimed the decision was straight out of the Bible, and Solomon could not have done any better.

"The wisdom of the earl has no bounds," Squire MacNee said, bowing, smiling.

"A decision that shows his justice and mercy," Squire MacLay said, giving Cormac a wink and a sly grin. Max nodded and inwardly smiled, yet another test from the old gaggle. A test his judgment had passed. Max suspected the gathered codgers had plotted—probably —the test outside his window.

"Sire, your barons wish to perform the ceremony of homage," Cormac said, reading from the note one of the elders had handed him. Max quickly recalled the county had seven shires. By tradition, the order of precedence of the shires was Eagill, Inverkailor, Monfieth, Carmoille, Breakin, Aberleemnay, and Cairnbahan. A local council administered each shire, represented by a member of the Union's Parliament and overseen by the baron.

If Max wished to act in a shire, he did so in concert with the barons. Any action taken by the earl without the consultation of his vassal would show a public lack of confidence. A baron on the receiving end of that massive loss of face could fan the fires of rebellions and start a blood feud.

The blood feuds and open warfare, Max hoped, were in the past. Max suspected that these days, barons would settle their grudges in a higher court, like the ones in Balquihidder or even the Union capital, the *Bundstadt*. Max wasn't keen on a legal fight either, as the attorney fees could break the accounts of an old estate, like the Bonnie Dundee. Max returned to the court and let the worries about legal cases lie for another day. The barons had lined up in a row. Five august old men stood, each waiting to be presented. The last time he'd seen this ceremony, Max was a boy. One of the barons died and was replaced by an heir, who swore this oath to Kenneth.

"Baron Gillis of Eagill, Chieftain of the Clan Ross on the Knockburn," Cormac said as the chief retainer.

Gillis approached, took a knee, his joints cracking, and said, "Allfather bless you and keep you, my liege. As the appointed man by our protector—long may he live—Me and mine will follow your banner in war and plow your fields in peace."

Max had a moment of panic before he remembered the traditional response he needed to give. The words popped into his mind, and he said, "By the Allfather, our Union, and the protector, I will defend you from trouble. Uphold your rights and privileges as they were in times of our grandfa'rs—are now—and will be in the days of our sons." Gillis smiled in delight, grunted as he stood, and then moved next to Cormac to signal his allegiance.

"Baron Mungo of Inverkailor, Chieftain of the Clan Haldane of the New Highlands," Cormac said in the introduction of the large old man.

Mungo bowed low, rather than knelt, and said, "Allfather bless you and keep you my liege. As the appointed man by our protector

—long may he live—me and mine will follow your banner in war and mine out your ore in peace."

Max repeated the response, satisfying Mungo, who nodded and then took his place next to Cormac and Gillis.

"Baron Donalbaan, the elder of Monfieth, Chieftain of the Clan MacLeod of the late-comers," Cormac said.

Donal, the white, stood smiling. That Donal was known as the white amused Max. Max imagined that Donal's sons, and perhaps grandsons, must also have white hair. The man was so old. Donal's leathery face smiled. His eyes sparkled with a youthful fire as he agilely knelt before Max.

"Allfather bless you and keep you, my liege. As the appointed man by our protector—long may he live—my clan, as scions of the great MacLeod of the Stars, offers you our swords in war and our cunning in peace, and that we show our true faith to the Union. May always my kinsmen hands alone hold your banner and our pipes lead your forces to war. Your enemy's blood is our wine and their bones our bread," Donal said, the centenarian reciting the phrase from countless repetitions throughout his long life.

Max nodded and repeated the traditional response. Max watched as the old man went over and picked up the Fraser banner, reverently brushing the trash and dirt from the flag. Donal then moved to stand next to his peers, behind the earl, while holding onto the banner.

"Baron Duncan of Carmoille, Chieftain of the Clan Duncan of the Bogs," Cormac said. He and Duncan both gave each other a surreptitious smile, and then Duncan approached the earl. Duncan and Cormac were about the same age, and Max had heard stories of the two men's exploits, some famous and others infamous.

"Allfather bless you and keep you, my liege. As the appointed man by our protector—long may he live—Me and mine will follow your banner in war and trade your goods in peace," Duncan said and bowed low.

Max repeated the response. Duncan straightened, winking at Cormac, and took up station behind Max, next to his friend. Max looked at the row. Only one baron was left, yet he still needed two other vassals.

"Baron Eoin of Aberleemnay, Chieftain of the Clan Fraser from the Little House of Lovat," Cormac said. Eoin nodded at the introduction. He approached Max on the throne and placed his hands above Max's.

"Allfather bless you and keep you my kinsman and liege," Eoin said, "As the appointed man by our protector—long may he live— you make us proud to be a Fraser. We keep the traditions showing the little brother will follow the elder to war and support the Fraser traditions in peace. By your marriage, we wish to see our bloodline kept strong! To protect you, we guard the passes from enemies and keep the glens free of all dangerous beasts. We believe in the old proverb, 'Strength is the only reward for the strong.'"

Max remembered the many times his father mentioned Eoin and their common kinsmen. Max knew that the earl had a unique response to this barony as long ago, the barony had belonged directly to the earl.

"My little brother, the Clan Fraser stands united against all enemies. The house of the earl will defend you from trouble and uphold your rights and privileges as our common ancestor did in the days of old Scotland, during the age of chaos when we were rescued by the great MacLeod who brought us here and will be in the days of our sons," Max said, "brother stand at my right hand, steward to this great house and the Allfather's blessed land."

The old men cheered and clapped heartily. Max blushed. He had remembered the phrasing perfectly. Whatever tests had been enacted today, Max had passed them all. Max felt a pang of regret at never reconciling with Kenneth as Max thought his father would have been proud of his responses today.

With tears in his eyes, Eoin said, "The last time that oath was spoken to me was almost fifty years ago, and I am proud to see my kinsman remember the rights and traditions of the clan."

"If there is no other business, I petition the Earl of the Bonnie Dundee to close our session," Cormac said.

Max waited for any new business. All were silent, and he said, "I now declare court adjourned."

"Allfather preserve the earl and our Protector Raimond, first of his name," Cormac said. All the gathering, except for Max, stood and said, "Long may they live!"

The old men queued to shake Max's hand informally. Many of the squires gave Max a pat on the shoulder as a sign of approval. Max stood and stretched as the old men, some satisfied and others happy with the court, began filing out of the large doors of the house.

Max watched them go, suspecting their destination—the local pub. Max turned and said to Cormac, "I need to look at the accounts. I'm worried that Hector hasn't been collecting the rent or paying the bills."

Cormac chuckled. Max and Cormac left the great hall via the grand corridor. The men briefly crossed the corridor, entered the main foyer, and went up the grand staircase in the front of the house.

"Cormac, where were the Barons of Breakin and Cairnbahan? Why were they not at the court," Max asked Cormac when the men arrived outside the small hallway entrance to the library. Upon opening the door, Max again beheld the library's beauty. The library was five meters tall, floor to ceiling. Shelves of books lined the walls. The room was famous in the Sheeplands for containing the most extensive physical collection of books on Stahlburgh or even the entire Union.

"The Baron of Breakin, Geordie Stewart, is too busy chasing the Baroness, Isobel Douglas, of Cairnbahan to do much of anything these days," Cormac said, slightly irritated.

"And the baroness?"

"She's a handful," Cormac said grimacingly. Max laughed inwardly at the thought of the baron chasing the baroness. Judging by the ages of his barons, Max assumed Breakin was chasing Cairnbahan in a matching set of wheelchairs.

"Cormac, any idea how Archy and my father worked the estate's accounts?"

"Whoa, lad, you're exhausting my knowledge on this topic. From what I remember, your father trusted physical accounting books. The only argument he and Archy ever had was about the ledgers. Kenneth couldn't fathom Archy's methods for accounting. Archy used some fancy programs on the estate's server farm," Cormac said, pointing to the terminal in the antique, ornately carved computer desk in the library.

Max walked over and sat at the terminal. He pushed a switch and interfaced with an older version of a popular Terran virtual desktop. Max looked through the digital accounts. He had two setbacks for every success at translating Archy's numbers. Max would attempt to cross-reference the physical books to the virtual books. Max found the physical books another story entirely. Kenneth's ledgers were fiction, with numbers not based on supporting documentation. In frustration, Max resorted to pulling up the bank's copy of the estate's operating accounts. Maddeningly, the records from Gilbraith Savings Trust had no bearing on the physical or virtual books.

The bank stated the estate had a balance of one hundred and twenty gold dragons, eighty silver griffins, and thirty pfennig. With that overall figure, Max attempted to cross-correlate the number to Archy's digital accounts or Kenneth's physical book. Max grew increasingly frustrated bouncing between bank, book, and program without successfully balancing the records. Max's patience ran out as he leaned over—for the twentieth time—to recheck one of the lines in the physical ledger. Turning his elbow, he bumped the ledger off the desk and onto the floor. As the book hit the floor, all the bills Kenneth stuffed in the front pockets spilled over the library.

Max stood up and began chasing the papers. As he knelt to collect the first article, he saw a repair bill for the estate's farm equipment with one hundred gold dragons and fifty silver griffins cost. Max frowned. The money requested was a princely sum, equivalent to the purchase price of one of his poorer shires.

Max looked around for Cormac and realized that the huntsman had left Max at some point. Max assumed the huntsman was off to do one of his many duties. Max pushed the paper back into the book, carrying the ledger to the desk to continue his fool's errand. He continued to work but was interrupted by a soft mezzo-soprano voice.

"Hello, Soldier," the woman said, putting her hands around Max's eyes.

"Hi Meg," Max said. His sister was being his sister, and he wasn't in a good mood to deal with her teasing. After two days of being a ghost, Meg—Max's sister, finally appeared to say hello.

"Did you miss me," Meg asked, removing her hands from Max's face.

"Of course, where have you been the past two days," Max said crossly.

"I meant the last eleven years," Meg said, "You never wrote, you never called Archy, Cormac, and I constantly checked the obituaries to see if your name was there."

Max sighed, "You know why I left and couldn't write."

"I see," Meg said. Max shook his head and tried to return to the bookkeeping. Meg pulled out her lipstick, applying an extra thick coat of red to her lips. Max was too intent on the books to see the mischief that was about to occur.

"Welcome home, bro," Meg said with a kiss on Max's cheek. Max felt the gobs of lipstick slide down his cheek where Meg kissed him. Max prayed for patience, as he had endured Meg's trick previously at every Christmas and Easter reunion. After his bratty little sister began wearing makeup. She would coat her lips and kiss his cheek.

"Look, Maxie is wearing makeup," Meg said with an evil giggle.

"You are such a child," Max said as he attempted to wipe the lipstick off his cheek. Meg continued her evil giggle, watching her brother annoyingly scrubbing at the bright red lipstick on his face. Even though the lipstick had been removed, Max continued to rub until his fair skin was bright pink from the friction. Meg put her hand to her mouth to compose herself, her prank following the same pattern. Max was satisfied that Meg's anger had been lessened.

In frustration, Max paused his scrubbing and said, "I'm at an impasse, so I'll have to ask. Do you know anything about the estate's finances?"

"No, sweet brother," Meg said, "I'm only the part-time cook and housekeeper. Money is all on you, boys. After all, a female cannot inherit the estate, or so says a bunch of old codgers—err, I mean— our clan elders."

"Drat," Max said, dejected. After fighting the bookkeeping of his predecessors, Max wasn't up for a discussion on the injustice of the title and the estate's inheritance.

"That bad?" Meg said, looking with a measure of pity on her favorite brother.

"Worse, Archy and father seemed to have differing accounts of the accounts. I'm beginning to believe these ledgers are just competing fiction sets."

"Maybe I can have Andrew come over and take a look?" Meg said, biting her bottom lip, as she did when nervous. Max could see the hopeful look in her eyes. She wanted to talk about Andrew, whoever that was.

"Who is Andrew?" Max said, absentmindedly rubbing his eyes

and leaning back in his chair.

"My fiancé," Meg replied with a smile, "the Baron of Loch Urqhart, over in the County of Gilmerton-over-the-Torboultoun."

"Those folks are the MacDonald's vassals," Max said. The Frasers were vassals of the Campbell clan. The Campbell and MacDonald clans had an ancient blood feud that went back to old Scotland. Both clans had happily continued that feud in the diaspora, adding more unforgivable acts against one another, all in the days before the protector. When the protector came, he ended all of the blood feuding. Still, both clans, their vassals, and their allies held to the rivalry and were always quick to condemn the other clan for any aggression—real or perceived.

"Should I ask Andrew to come over?" Meg asked, pushing Max.

"No, I won't have anyone who follows the MacDonalds here, and I certainly don't want a MacDonald's help," Max said, snapping at his sister. Max didn't want help. He didn't want to be the earl!

"Fine," Meg said, visibly angry at Max's irritability.

"Well, as the earl, I won't bless your marriage. You might as well cancel the wedding now," Max said, escalating the conflict. The annoyance of Meg's statement on the clan laws, the frustration of the books, and his anger at inheriting an estate mired in mismanagement had broken Max's reserve.

"You don't have to, sweet brother," Meg said, the bitterness in her voice unmistakable, "Father gave me his permission on his deathbed."

Max saw the beautiful day outside the stuffy library behind Meg. The sight of a cloudless sunny day, which Max was wasting, pushed him over the edge.

"How dare you take advantage of a sickly fevered old man," Max said. While Max had no love for his father, Max was raging at the thought of Meg asking for permission to marry a rival clan on Kenneth's deathbed. Max imagined the sickly old man passively accepting Meg's demands without understanding.

"He was quite lucid when he died, you jackass," Meg replied, her fury unchecked, "if you were here, you would have seen why father consented. You know, he was right about you before he died!"

Meg's statement hit Max hard. Max sat there staring. What if Meg was right? Max felt terrible. On his absence, Meg was correct. He hadn't been around. Max had let his anger and frustration over the inheritance, the estate's poverty, and the accounts' confusion cause a needless quarrel with his beloved younger sister.

Meg rushed out of the library. Max wanted to stop her but decided that a wounded Fraser woman was like a crazy bear. Max took a deep breath and knew that mending fences had to wait. Meg would eventually cool down, and Max could seek forgiveness as always.

Alone once again, Max returned to looking into the finances. His attention wavered, and he kept looking out of the extensive library window. Max stared out towards the mountains. After a few minutes of staring, Max saw Cormac appear leading a hunting party. Max noted they were headed toward the trail that led up to the range's peaks.

The party stood, rifles in hand, waiting for the huntsman's signal to begin the ascent up to the high stalking grounds. Max desperately wanted to leave the library and join them. Looking at the mess before him, Max reasoned that the finances had carried on these years without him. Another day or two wouldn't bring ruin to the estate. Max rushed to power down the tablet and close the desk.

"Best to go shoot a deer," Max said, "then I will have all the meat I need for a while." Standing and heading towards the library door, Max suddenly felt relief at the decision to stop work and leave the library.

CHAPTER THREE
Queen Amang the Heather

Max's temper had dissipated as soon as he stepped outside the library. Max had walked through the house and to the exit for the estate manager's office. The office was a small squat building inside the "U" that was the foundation of the great house. Inside the manager's office was the gun vault with the manor's hunting rifles. Max eagerly pulled out his old hunting rifle and two magazines. He made his way westward around the north side of the house and, slinging the rifle, trotted towards the hunting party.

Cormac, ever watchful, saw Max coming and said, "Hurry up, laddie. Otherwise, we will leave without you."

Max quickly joined the half dozen men in the stalking party. The men were all his age and wore black armbands around their upper arms.

"Cormac, what is up with the black bands?" Max asked, noticing the armbands.

"We're going on a hunt," Cormac said, "we figured that if we bagged a deer, we'd donate the meat to the soup kitchen in Archy's name."

Max understood the gesture. Archy was always racing to help others, and several hundred kilograms of venison would go a long way to those in need.

"Ah, just so, and here is your armband, my lord," said one of the men. He handed a black band to Max.

"Thank you," Max said, "and your name is?"

"Geordie Stewart," Geordie said, "Baron Breakin to the common folk and... adventuresses."

The gathered chuckled at Geordie's comment. The baron was a man in his early thirties, not the image of an ancient baron that Max had expected. Breakin stood a few centimeters taller than Max, with light brown hair over his pale face and coppery brown eyes. Geordie wore a hunter's outfit of a tweed homburg hat, brown jacket, brown pants, and calf-high hiking boots like the others in the hunting party. Unlike his companions, the Baron's outfit all bore designer labels. Max figured the hunting costume was about ten griffins, the cost of a luxurious business suit.

"I missed you at court this morning," Max said. Max wanted to make sure that Geordie recognized he was the earl. Max was unhappy about the lax way Hector had run things, and he determined Geordie would realize Max was a different man.

"I'm sorry, old chap," Geordie said with a smile, "I'm used to being a gentleman of leisure—Kenneth wasn't much to crack the whip, I'm afraid."

"I expect your oath, Breakin," Max said. Geordie at first looked insulted, but then he smiled.

"By Jove," he said, "you believe in these pensioner ways."

"Your oath," Max said. Max would not let his vassal duck or shame him for his command.

"Geordie, just give Max the bloody oath," Cormac said. Cormac was impatient to get going. Max noted that Cormac was also tired of the game Geordie was trying to play.

Geordie knelt on the grass and said, "Allfather bless you and keep you, my liege. As the appointed man by our protector—long may he live—my clan and I will follow your banner in war. We will brew your ale and distill your whisky in peace."

"By the Allfather, our Union and the protector, I will defend you from trouble and uphold your rights and privileges as they were laid down in the days of our grandfathers—are now—and shall be in the days of our sons," Max replied.

Geordie stood up, brushed his trousers off, and said, "Don't worry yourself, old chap. The clan's distillery gives me plenty of rights and privileges. After all, mine is the most popular whisky in the Sheeplands."

"Oh really?" Max said. Max wanted to be cross with Geordie, but he couldn't. Instead of appearing boorish, Breakin came across like a cartoon of a country squire.

"Of course, I own the *Royal Neep*. The whisky has sat at the protector's table. The Pentothian delegation ordered six merchantmen full of the stuff. I believe you have a cellar full of my reserve, or well, you did—before Hector, the lout, showed up."

Max stifled a laugh. For all the games with the oath, Max found Geordie's characterization of Hector put the baron on the better side of Max's nature. An impatient Cormac said, "Let's get moving. My watch shows almost noon. At this rate, we'll be coming down the mountain at midnight."

The party began the trek up the mountain, Geordie regaling the others with his tales of adventure. He was an interstellar playboy with fantastic homes in the capital, the *Bundstadt,* and Laplace on Newton in Tau Ceti. After several minutes of constant talking, Max tuned out Geordie's tales. To someone who had never left the Sheeplands, the stories might have been exciting and unbelievable, but Max had heard—and experienced—similar adventures in his decade-plus years in the Assault.

As the party climbed to the large plateau that was the stalking area, Cormac gave the baron the evil eye. Geordie shut up. From here on, the party would need to be quiet if they wished to see a deer. The consistently variable weather started to cloud up, and an ominous cloud came over the mountain's peak. The cloud drifted down the peak, moving lower. Within minutes, the party was surrounded by a thick, impenetrable fog.

Max lost sight of the hunting party as the cloud settled on the plateau.

"Cormac, Geordie," Max called out as the fog descended.

"One moment," Cormac said. Max tried to determine where the huntsman was by his voice. The glens were picking up the huntsman's voice, and the echoes confused Max.

"This way," Cormac said. Max couldn't determine where the huntsman was. Cormac's voice seemingly echoed from both the left and right. Max was completely disoriented. He wasn't sure where the rest of the hunting party was. Max decided to pick a direction and move a few meters, calling out where he suspected the party was. Cormac's responses grew fainter. Max changed direction and moved a few meters on another heading, calling out again. Max didn't fear being lost, but he was concerned the others would needlessly worry over losing him. After all, Max had been tramping these mountains since he could walk. Cormac's voice was so soft that Max realized the party had moved to another part of the mountain.

Max knew the hunting was over. Cormac wouldn't allow anyone to shoot in the fog, and there was no way to determine where the projectile might end up. Max smiled. Cormac prided himself on being a safe guide, and the huntsman knew the stakes on these mountains. The barons of Cairnbahan had for ages had their sheep loose in the range, at ease with their sheep grazing even if Cormac's hunting expeditions were out.

Max heard a loud baa close to him through the fog. "Thinking of the sheep must have summoned one," Max muttered. He moved towards the sound, the mist dampening his face. The terrain sloped down sharply, and Max realized he was heading down the side of the plateau. He hoped that he might clear the fog by moving down in elevation.

Max trod down into a high glen. The mist, which had stubbornly hidden the vista below, suddenly parted and revealed a small clearing. The clouds formed a roof around the dale, and Max looked and saw the large flock. The sheep almost crowded out the vale, but the vision among the sheep stopped his heart.

She was the most beautiful woman he had ever seen. The shepherdess wore long golden blond hair in wavy ringlets, which blew in the gentle breeze. Her fair face had clear blue eyes that scanned the flock, nervously seeking anything out of place. She wore a white colored blouse and a long Douglas tartan skirt with the hem obscured by a sheep. He stopped to stare at her. Max moved towards the woman. He was standing there, gawking awkwardly.

"Hello," Max roared as he approached. He didn't want to appear weird or strange or startle such a beautiful woman.

"Hello yourself, good sir," the shepherdess said, her soprano voice rang out in the glen. Max felt his heart race. He wanted nothing more than to ask the woman her name. Max was young when he left, barely noticing women when he enlisted. He had been involved with chance encounters with the female of the species, but nothing serious. Max had never even fallen in love. There wasn't time nor inclination. Max had felt that a combat infantryman in the Assault wasn't a good match for a woman. No Felgenlander father would bless a marriage to his daughter with the potential of her becoming a widow so high.

Max contemplated that with the war on, those ideas may be changing. Max realized that, as earl, he could ideally court or even marry. The promise of falling in love drove Max forward to the shepherdess. Max decided to ask her to have a cup of coffee with him.

"Do you often bring your sheep up here," Max asked instead. His nerve had failed him. Max, the brave Assaultman, did not have enough courage even to ask the woman her name! Max worried about what her response would be. She might be married or reject him.

The shepherdess smiled politely, making Max self-conscious, then said, "I often come up here when I watch the herd for my uncle. He's away now, on business for the Barony of Cairnbahan."

"You live in Cairnbahan? Perhaps I could visit you? We could go for a coffee or a pint, whatever you prefer," Max said. He felt like a passenger in his own body, his mouth blurting out the words uncontrollably. The shepherdess smiled and then looked at the armband Max wore.

"You're in the hunting party Cormac was bringing up, aren't you," she asked.

"Why yes, we're culling the deer in the name of Archibald Fraser. Did you know him," Max asked.

"I knew of him. He was several years older than I was, but everyone knew of Archibald. He was the earl's heir after all," she said, "Since you knew Archy, you must be some rich squire's son. I am surprised you have a moment for a poor shepherd's daughter. Rich squires and their sons have never impressed me much."

"Why not?" Max said. He was suddenly very hurt by the young woman's rejection.

"From what I've seen, the earl and his friends care little for anyone that doesn't carry a title. A man that believes—like Robbie Burns —'*The rank is but the guinea's stamp, The Man's the gowd for a' that*,' I could love a man like that with all my heart," she said.

"Oh," Max said. He wasn't sure how to reply. The shepherdess had seemingly rejected him by association. An awkward silence ensured.

"I'm sorry," the shepherdess said, as the flock began to move on over the glen hills, "I must stay with the sheep."

"Aye," Max replied to the woman, and then he said, "I suppose you must."

The shepherdess and her flock then moved down the side of the mountain and were gone. Max sat there for a moment, trying to collect his wits. He hadn't even asked her name, and her perception of the earl shocked Max. Sure, Hector had been terrible, but his tenure was short. Had Kenneth, Max's father, been absent from his duties?

"There you are. The fellas were getting worried about you," Cormac said. The huntsman appeared above him on the elevated side of the glen. Max turned and began his ascent to reach Cormac. The fog, continuously variable, had lifted. Max stood on the same level as the huntsman. He asked, "Cormac, do you know…" Max then hesitated. The question he was about to ask felt silly as he played with the query. Max was going to finish asking if Cormac knew the name of the blond shepherdess Max had just encountered. The more Max thought about the question, the more unbelievable the meeting seemed.

"Know what, lad?" Cormac asked, breaking into Max's thoughts.

"Never mind," Max said. He and Cormac began walking up the trail. After ten minutes, the two men arrived at the spot where Max had lost the party. The others nodded as he joined them, while Cormac went out in front of the group as scout. Max watched the huntsman hike a few meters forward, disappearing over the side of the mountain.

"There you are, old chap," Geordie said, visibly worried, as Max joined the group, "The fog came on us, and I turned around to ask your opinion about the war. That was when we realized you had gone missing."

"I'm fine, Geordie, well, except for being waylaid by Venus and some sheep," Max said. The men started laughing at the ridiculous statement.

"Max," Geordie said, "that is almost as good as Archy told us when we were stalking two years ago. He was lost in a fog much like this one, and when we met up with him, he swore that he had been drinking moonshine with King Brian of the Leprechauns. We almost believed the tale as Archy's breath smelled of the stuff. Then Cormac told us of the hip flask that Kenneth kept up near the summit—for emergencies, of course."

The men stopped laughing, and their faces grew wistful. The baron produced a small whisky flask, saying, "I going to toast Archy and Fionnula with this flask at their wedding, but a drop now seems more appropriate."

The men took turns passing the flask around and all toasted the memory of Archibald Fraser.

"I say, you should hold a gala or fête," Geordie said, changing the painful subject of Archy, "I know the old duffers around here prefer their courts and whatnot, but us younger chaps would prefer a proper ball. With the war on, the ratio of men to women up here in the Sheeplands is like one chap to a dozen ladies, all of whom are locked away like Rapunzel by their overprotective fathers."

"That's a good suggestion," Max said. Max was about to expound on the idea when Cormac returned over the ridge. The group hustled to catch the swift huntsman. Max looked at the men as they began to hike forward and asked, "With the war on, why aren't you all serving?"

"I did my time," Geordie said quickly. He pulled up a trouser leg, showing off a metal lower leg.

"I lost my leg when the *USTC MacAlasdair* was attacked over Asimov in HD 260655. The Allfather was with me, though, and I got out of the transport and was rescued by a true Valkyrie, a woman named Sternfahrer. She was the skipper of the *USWC Advantage.* The gloriously beautiful captain and her sultry amazons ferried my companions and me back to Stahlburgh. Upon arrival home, I was ministered to by many beautiful doctors and nurses who, after wearing down my poor body, gave me a medical discharge and sent me back to Breakin. Thankfully, since I am fabulously wealthy, I've got a biotic leg growing in the best organics lab. The cost was legendary, but with the new leg, I'll be ceilidh dancing with the best of them."

Max listened as the others told their story. Max understood why they were not serving or serving the war in some capacity. On the trek, Max began to feel the effects of the whisky. The liquor and the feeling of camaraderie for the men in the hunting party was a balm on his bruised heart.

After a few minutes of trekking, Cormac said, "Well, I had hoped the weather would give us some respite. There is no use in wasting any more time. Let's head in." As if on command, the clouds closed in on the group. However, the visibility wasn't nearly as far as Max's encounter with the shepherdess. On the slow descent, Max mused how he found Geordie to be a bore and braggart on the ascent. After sharing some stories and a little whisky, he had changed his mind about the baron. Max looked over his shoulder. Geordie continued to regale the company with his exploits in interstellar dating. Max suddenly believed that Geordie was using his fanciful tales to hide something in his past. Max stopped for a moment, pretending to catch his breath, and as Geordie walked by, Max noticed the baron had an almost imperceptible limp. Geordie was finishing his tale as the group reached the Bonnie Dundee, and he said, "While I was in the house of ill repute, I was complaining to one of the courtesans and said, 'Pardon me, madam, but I believe the fee was too high.' To which the courtesan replied, 'I no the madam, bub, I am just the nookie lady,' and the Terrans claim we are the uncivilized!"

The men laughed at the punchline, and Max joined in their delight. All of the stress of the day had evaporated. Max groaned inwardly, trying to forget that the books, his dealings with his cousin, and his fight with Meg would need solutions.

"Breakin, I am bored. Take me home," a young horse-faced woman said. She wore a tartan dress with a high collar, and her brown hair was tied bowstring tight into a bun at the top of her head. Helen looked like a female Geordie. She started tapping her foot impatiently.

Geordie comically rolled his eyes to the men and said, "That is my sister, Helen. She likes to visit Meg. Helen is a sensitive soul…" Then he turned to Max and said, "To be frank, I wasn't quite sure about you at first, my liege. I imagined you were one of those stiff shirt types pining for his pensioner days. But after our hunt, your company has been an honest pleasure. Feel free to call me at Stewart Castle whenever you'd like."

Max gripped Geordie's hand, shook, and said, "I shall, and please call me Max. The Bonnie Dundee will always welcome you, Geordie."

"Breakin!" Helen said impatiently, interrupting any further conversation.

"Duty calls," Geordie said, leaving the men. The others wandered away as Geordie departed the gathering, leaving Cormac and Max alone.

"I've got a bottle of the old Fraser whisky if you're interested, lad," Cormac said as he and Max stood on the broad lawn surrounding the Bonnie Dundee.

"Sure, I'm not expected, and after the fight I had with Meg, I doubt there will be dinner waiting for me."

"She'll calm down, lad," Cormac said as the two men walked across the lawn to the small croft that housed the huntsman. The pair stepped inside the croft and into the kitchen. Max maneuvered around the cozy room until he sat at the small table that sat in a nook. Cormac walked over to a cabinet and produced two small glasses. Expertly, the huntsman poured four fingers of whisky into each old-fashioned glass and then placed one in front of Max while gently depositing the other glass in the spot across from Max at the two-person table.

"What did you want to ask me, lad?" Cormac asked as he slowly eased himself into the other chair at the table.

"Cormac, I saw someone today..." Max began but was cut off by Cormac.

"You saw a lot of folks today, lad."

"No, no, I saw a woman. She was up on the mountain, herding sheep."

"I'm not sure who that would be. Usually, Angus goes up there with one of the flocks. What so special about this woman?"

"She was the most beautiful woman I have ever seen, Cormac. I asked to see her, but she said something about me being a rich man and she, a poor shepherdess, and how rich squire's sons don't impress her, and Robbie Burns..."

"She sounds like a right 'Queen amang the Heather,' lad. I'm sorry she said things wouldn't go anywhere. Plenty of fish in the sea and plenty of whisky, too."

Max drained the Scotch. He was just a few paces from the house, an easy walk home. Max poured another four fingers of whisky. He wasn't motivated to deal with his problems. Tonight, he just wanted to drink them away.

CHAPTER FOUR

Blood and Whisky

Max woke from a deep black sleep. He rolled over onto his back and spat out the grass that, curiously, was in his parched mouth. He sat up. His chest was damp from the cold, wet ground. Max grabbed his head. His skull throbbed, and his body hurt. He was chilled and sticky all over. Why was he sleeping on the front lawn again? Max looked around, his senses returning. Whisky and the devil had made him sleep in the garden overnight.

"I have to stop drinking with Cormac," he said to himself with a croak. He stood up and stretched. As life returned to his body, Max realized that, sadly, the lawn made a more comfortable bed than his father's old mattress. Max attempted to shake off the hangover as he trundled into the house. Most of his clothing was wet and muddy, making Max look like a ditch digger rather than an earl.

"Ah, there he is, Hector," his aunt said as Max entered the house. She stood in the foyer, lying in wait for Max's return.

"Good Morning, May," Max said, his head ached. Max was not able to tolerate his aunt and cousin this morning. He attempted to move through the main foyer and into the formal dining room, shaking off his relations. Max could smell the bacon and sausage in the air, and as he cleared the main hall, he saw where Meg had chafing dishes lit. The dishes were prepped and waiting for the hot breakfast Meg was cooking. May and Hector doggedly followed Max. The long table in the formal dining room had two spaces at its head and foot. May moved to take the seat traditionally belonging to the lady of the house, the rightmost space at the head. Since Max was the earl, the seat would have been left vacant for Max's wife.

"You see, Hector, that is how a gentleman greets his relations," May said, sitting in the chair. May had the typical Fraser features, stark, high cheekbones, and the distinctive nose and lips she and Kenneth shared. She wore her silver hair in fashionable Union style and sat ramrod straight in her best blouse, complete with a woman's ruffle tie in a Fraser tartan. May was armored and ready for battle.

"You are correct, Mother," Hector said, following Max and seating himself, "I have let the country air go to my head, and my manners have suffered."

Hector and May had rehearsed this dialogue. May was to play the proper adult, and Hector the chastised child. Max hated that the family games had started so early this morning. The discussion between aunt and cousin made Max's head hurt even more. He tried to keep his best poker face on, but he was constantly reminded of his bad luck as he sat in the earl's seat. Max was not comfortable in the earl's place. Sitting in his father's spot felt odd. Max had always sat on the left-hand side of the table as the second son, being the useless spare.

"Maximilian, I am sorry I haven't made an appearance sooner," May said, continuing the farce, "I should have realized in your time of need that you would need a maternal figure to aid you. After all, there are so many responsibilities for you, and you are, after all, just one man."

As if on cue, Hector said, "Why yes, Max, I could help you with the books and running the estate."

Max tried not to scowl as he looked at the vultures beside him. He knew the game they were playing. His aunt and cousin would slowly, bit by bit, take over the running of the estate—if he let them. Of course, May and Hector would take over in the guise of helping. Max was sure that once the proverbial camel's nose was in the tent, the rest of the ugly beast would follow. May and Hector would then plunder the accounts and decimate the meager remaining resources of the estate. When their mismanagement would bring everything crashing down, May and Hector would conveniently have some issue that forced them elsewhere. Max would then be left with an even greater mess to clean up. When they, hypothetically, made their getaway, May and Hector might be vindictive. If they decided to 'get even,' they would contact the Parliament, specifically, the upper house, the House of Dynasts. Max remembered there was a department that audits the great estates for cases of fraud and mismanagement. As urged by Hector and May, The auditors would find the mismanagement and then counsel the earl's liege—the Grand Duke Alistair Campbell—to replace the earl. Max would have the title stripped, and the inheritance must be redetermined. Then, smartly, Hector would appear. He would be the logical choice since he had brought the fraud and waste to the Parliament.

Max frowned inwardly. Hector as his heir was a horrifying thought. Hector technically wasn't even a Fraser! The resulting chaos when Hector assumed the title of the earl would be horrendous. Max guessed that Hector and May probably hadn't thought that out in their schemes.

"Why thank you, Hector, but I would hate to keep you and your mother away from the family house in the *Bundstadt*," Max said, returning to the conversation. Max tried a weak flanking maneuver.

"Oh, dear boy," May said, "we sold the house when your father died. We knew the estate would need our help."

Max realized his flank was countered but was saved from uttering something stupid by his sister. Meg entered, pushing a cart containing the large breakfast reserved for when people sat in the formal dining room.

"Here you are, Earl Max," Meg said, on cue, scooping eggs, Terran bacon, blood sausage, beans, and a cooked tomato onto his plate. She filled his coffee and gave him a small glass of premium Eisenwald orange juice. Meg then did the same for Hector and May. The interruption and appearance of food were enough, and Max's cousin and aunt began shoveling the food into their mouths, using the appropriate utensils.

Max paused and placed his hands together in silent prayer. He thanked the Allfather for Meg's interruption and the food. He prayed that either Hector or May would choke on the breakfast, so they would have to rush to the hospital and leave him alone for the rest of the day. Finishing his silent prayer, Max looked at the breakfast but didn't feel hungry. He was thankful for the pause and placed tiny morsels in his mouth to restrict any attempt at speech.

Meg finished her servant duties and made her plate. She then sat at her traditional place at the table, second on the left side. Max looked between Meg and May, wondering how Kenneth and May had developed such a poisonous relationship. Max then realized that his previous conversation with Meg was the start of something similar. Max resolved not to repeat history. As much as he had been upset with Meg's upcoming nuptials, perhaps he had judged the affair too quickly. Max decided to close the rift between his little sister, someone who was his best and only friend for many years, from growing. Max began his attempt to repair things with Meg.

"Meg," Max said, "I was thinking about what you said yesterday, and perhaps Andrew *should* come over to look at the books. I'm sorry I spoke in haste about your fiancé. He should stay for dinner when he comes over, as he will be part of the family."

Meg, who had been reserved while serving breakfast, suddenly beamed in joy. May coughed violently as Max's statement must have caught her off guard. Max looked between the two women. Meg must have gotten an earful from Hector and May about Andrew and his loyalties. Max patted himself on the back internally. He killed two birds with one stone. He repaired his relationship with Meg and angered Hector and May by encouraging Meg rather than scolding her.

Hector frowned and said, "But Andrew is a lackey of the MacDonald! He cannot enter our clan lands! I won't allow him to set one foot inside this house."

"I didn't realize the Flemings owned this land," Max said to Hector, whose family name was Fleming. Max wanted to disabuse Hector of the notion that he would ever own the estate.

"Oh, Max," his aunt said, her tone insincere, "I suppose you didn't know, but Hector is Fraser now. He legally changed his name when he reached majority."

Hector sat with a smug grin on his face. Max inwardly cursed. He had over-extended his lines, and now the enemy was upon him with a fury. He quickly thought out the situation. A name change wouldn't necessarily mean anything to his vassals and kinsman. The clan structure was a fluid and often fragile construct. Hector and May would have to gain approval from many tradition-bound old men for the gambit to work. Max saw that May and Hector had been plotting their little coup for quite some time. Meg broke the silence and said, "Auntie, I believe the Earl of the Bonnie Dundee and Fraser Chieftain has spoken, and so my intended is welcome here at the Bonnie Dundee." Max could have squeezed the breath out of his sister. She rallied the reinforcements, and the battle was not yet lost.

"Oh, sweet child," May said. Those few syllables put Meg in her place. Meg wasn't a child by galactic standards. Meg was twenty-five standard years old. However, the Union had lived in peace and prosperity for almost one hundred years. The Felgenlanders had seen an enormous gain in life expectancy with that peace and prosperity. To the long-lived codgers who crafted the dating and mating mores, Meg was just old enough to be considered an adult.

Her aunt's barbed comment exposed Meg's unmarried status,

youth, and inexperience. Max could see his sister's face turn red in anger. May had countered their surge. Meg's arguments were killed in action.

Max sensed his forces crumbling against May and Hector's onslaught.

"Meg's point is still valid, May," Cormac said as he stood at the kitchen door. "Max is the earl, and the earl decides who comes, stays, and leaves."

May frowned. She had not expected the huntsman to comment. May could not easily dismiss Cormac. Although May was a Fraser by birth, blood, and upbringing, Cormac was the chief retainer of the county and had tremendous utility as the chief huntsman.

May folded her hands. She had done all she could to sabotage Meg. In retaliation, she gave Cormac a stare that showed her displeasure. Max noted that his side was turning the tide of the family battle. Now was the time to finish this little intra-Fraser skirmish.

"Well, Meg, I suggest you get Andrew over here quickly. I need the books in order, and I'd like to meet him before the Installation Ball and Clan Gathering," Max said. Meg squealed excitedly at the mention of a ball and her fiancé's visit and said, "Andrew and a ball! Oh, Earl Maxie, you're the best!"

May looked deflated. Max had ended her current plans. Hector sat deep in thought, tallying the pros and cons of the recent development.

Cormac laughed at Meg's reaction and said, "I need to practice on my pipes." The huntsman promptly left the dining room. Max stood and pushed his chair away from his half-eaten breakfast, stretched, and said, "Well, I am off to discover what money the estate holds, and then I will require your help, May, and yours too, Meg, in planning the ball."

"How may I help, your grace?" Hector said, like a lost child. Max suddenly felt sorry for Hector. Max pondered and considered that Hector was in a far-off estate, living an unaccustomed life, without friends, and in the company of family that were more like strangers.

Max thought quickly. He needed to give something to Hector that wasn't too important to the estate. His mind instantly made up. Max said, "Hector, I need you to help Cormac mark the land for the tents and the highland games. I'm relying on you to make this as flawless as possible. Now, I'm off to the Library."

Hector nodded eagerly, and Max turned to walk into the kitchen. He wanted to put some distance between his family and himself. He went through the kitchen and found the side stairs that led up to the library on the second floor. Max climbed the stairs, and as he did so, the reproduction of John Graham, 7th Laird of Claverhouse, 1st Viscount Dundee, known in old Scotland as the 'Bonnie Dundee,' appeared. The portrait hung on the back wall of the second story of the grand corridor, almost covering the entire space. The painting was placed strategically so anyone entering the state apartments would see it.

Max recalled from his youth the many times his father had dropped the fact that the house had been named in Graham's honor. Max had heard, by family legend, that one of the Frasers had followed the Bonnie Dundee in the ancient Jacobite rising of 1689 and most likely died fighting alongside the Bonnie Dundee.

On the wall, next to the extensive reproduction of the first Viscount Dundee, was an oil painting of his father, Kenneth, at Max's age. Kenneth stood in traditional Fraser formal wear in the painting, his full plaid bearing the ancient Fraser tartan. Looking at the portrait, Max saw Kenneth had his left hand resting casually on his ceremonial dirk while Kenneth's right hand was propped up against one of the library's bookshelves. In the background of the painting, Max could see the image of his mother as she looked on at Kenneth. Max looked at her for a moment. She, too, looked young, much younger than when he had last seen her as she lay dying when he was a little boy.

Max suppressed a tear as he looked at the painting. His mother had the same sad, soulful, loving look she always wore in his mind. His father seemed stern and disapproving while staring back at him through the painting. Max felt the painting was almost like a view screen where he could talk to their shades.

"You never taught me how to be an earl, father. I am sorry we never were able to resolve our differences. If you were here, I'd ask you why I seem to be surrounded by people who seek to usurp me, why I seem to be the only one who cares if the estate goes up in flames. This wasn't supposed to be my job, Archy..." Max trailed off. He didn't know what to say about Archy. His parents still stared back through the painting with the same faces. Max decided to give up on communicating with the dead and attempt to communicate with the finances. Stepping into the library, Max knew the portrait would have to be removed for a picture of Max.

Max cleared his mind as he sat at the computer again. He began to trace through the numbers, attempting to connect them. Time must have flown because Max felt like he had just sat down when a soft voice said, "Excuse me, your grace."

Max checked the large clock in the library. His 'short time' was almost forty-five minutes. Max stood and looked at the man. He was a little taller than Max, wearing a brown tweed suit, his thinning light brown hair was neatly combed, and the man was freshly shaved. Max stood, approached, and said, "You must be Andrew."

"Aye, your grace, Baron Andrew Urquhart of Loch Urquhart, Clan Urquhart," Andrew said, presenting his hand for a handshake. Max took Andrew's hand and gripped the palm tightly. Andrew did not flinch and returned the grip with an equally firm shake. So far, so good, Max thought, evaluating Andrew.

"Please, Andrew, call me Max," Max said, releasing the clasp.

"Aye, Max. Meg mentioned you were in the Assault. I brought over a hard copy of the paper in case you hadn't seen the news," Andrew said, presenting the paper. The hard copy bore the coat of arms of the city of Gilbraith-on-Heather on the left side with the words, *The Sheeplands Gazette* in bold on the masthead with 'First in the Sheeplands and Second to None!' as the motto.

Max looked at the headline in the paper. The story said, 'Assault Advances on Nakdong!' Underneath the large headline was a picture of Max's old commander, Lieutenant Nordlinger, holding the Union flag. At the top, another headline also said, 'Lion of Llande captures enemy headquarters on Nakdong!' with a picture of a corporal named Wulfjaeger. The corporal had led a squad to capture some high-ranking enemy soldiers.

"Thank you, Andrew," Max said with a smile, "The officer in the main picture was my former commander."

"Well then, I'm pleased I brought the paper with me, Max," Andrew said. Max observed Andrew was a quiet man. Max would have to carry the conversation.

"Meg said you were good with accounts," Max said, "do you mind looking at the books?"

"I'm a licensed accountant, Max," Andrew said, then awkwardly, he continued, "I know there are old rivalries between our lieges, but I'd be most pleased to help you out. The Urquharts of Stahlburgh have always respected your clan."

Max nodded and then joked, "You may lose that respect after you marry Meg."

"Doubtful, a woman of the gentry who will cook and clean, she's worth a barony," Andrew said.

Max raised his eyebrow at that statement. Not many barons wanted their wives to lift a finger with a pot or broom.

Andrew noted the expression and said, "My clan isn't rich, but we aren't poor either. Aside from a title, we have more kinship with the middle classes. I work as an accountant, and my father was a medical doctor. Meg and I expect our children would be in the professions or the trades."

"I'm not someone to argue the alternative," Max said, "I was an *enlisted* Assaultman after all."

"Yes, I had forgotten that fact," Andrews said, "Now let me see these books."

Andrew produced his tablet and began accessing the records. Together, both men scoured the accounts, trying to correlate the figures and find some record of income and expenditures that matched. After what seemed to Max like hours, they were interrupted by Meg delivering sandwiches and tea.

"Freiherr von Huegel," Andrew said in shock, looking at the expensive tea, "my favorite. This must have cost a fortune, dearest!"

Meg blushed and said, "A girl needs to spend her pocket money on something. How goes the books?"

"At this point, just start over. These accounts are useless. Plus, from the number of bills I've seen, the estate has been delinquent in payments," Andrew said as he began banging numbers into his tablet. "Making the best guess I can," he said, "You have seventeen golden dragons, twenty-five silver griffins, and fifty copper pfennigs. That's the total of the estate's treasury. You seem to be taking in around two dragons a month."

"That's good, right?" Meg said she was eager to see the estate on a sound footing.

"No, you are spending five dragons a month," Andrew said with a frown, "Also, your clan gatherings cost around ten dragons an event. At this rate, you're broke in three or four months. I've seen this sort of thing a lot. Your estate is primarily agricultural. Agricultural estates have relied on Union exports to make ends meet. With the war on, exports are down. The estate's finances suffer from those economic forces."

"What if I economize, ride out the trough? I don't have to spend all that money, right?" Max said.

Andrew shook his head and said, "You can scrape by if you economize more, but that's the rub: you are just scraping by. The house will need maintenance, and every time something breaks, you will feel the hurt of the cost. From the amount of bills present, I'd say that Kenneth has been losing money for years. The loss hasn't been drastic, just a death by a thousand cuts. Max, you must throttle back your expenses and increase the estate's income. Otherwise, the estate is bankrupt."

"What happens then?" Meg asked. She looked worried at the word bankrupt.

"That depends on what the earl's liege will do," Andrew said, "My liege, Angus MacDonald, is the Great King of the Skye Isles. You'd think being a great king would make a difference since the Angus could afford to have a less profitable vassal. Sadly, Angus is a skinflint and would declare the bankrupt estate forfeit. In no time, Angus would install a new crony and work the forfeiture to make up the deficit. The rents would go up, and the people would find all sorts of levies and fees tacked on to their goods."

"Huh, I've never met my liege, Alasdair Campbell," Max said, "From what I remember from Father, the Campbell is a fair man. I'm guessing Campbell would act similarly. The high peerage expects results. With the war on, they cannot afford mismanagement in their fiefs. The old protector never liked inefficiency, and I have no clue how the new one feels."

Andrew nodded to Max in agreement. Max was barely better than the nobles-in-title who lived in apartments and collected no rent. Max wasn't among the great lords who owned scores of counties, acres of land, and hundreds of industries.

"When is the happy day?" Max asked, changing the subject. The estate was his concern. He wished his sister happy and focused on her future.

"After the feast of *Dienstantritt*, if you have no objections?" Meg said, naming the celebration of the beginning of the Prophet Malcolm's mission. The feast was a celebration belonging to the Union's state religion, and *Dienstantritt* started in the middle of May, which was considered the most traditional time for a wedding.

Max realized that Meg was still worried over his reaction to her nuptials. Max hadn't meant to be so mean. Meg was his little sister. Max chose his words carefully. He didn't want to come across as overbearing and overprotective. Max said, "A lovely time for a wedding. Will you be married here on the estate? Or in the village chapel?"

"We were hoping to have a Catholic ceremony in the church by the loch," Meg said, worried about Max's reaction.

"You aren't a Stater?" Max asked Andrew—in astonishment. Most Felgenlanders belonged to the state religion, or as the Terrans called it—the Felgenland Central Christian Orthodoxy.

"Afraid not," Andrew said, "I'm Centauran Catholic, no offense to the protector, but we believe the Pope is the head of the true church. My family has kept the faith since we came to Stahlburgh, even though, at times, our faith has made people shun us."

"I've converted as well, Max," Meg said, "Andrew took me to mass, and I decided to be baptized after that. I was so moved."

As shocked as Max felt, he had served in the Assault with folks of all creeds. However, Max didn't know many Catholics. He tread carefully because he didn't know what to say. He decided that asking questions was safest.

"Can I attend your wedding?" Max said. Max remembered that some non-state religions had strict policies on who could attend their ceremonies.

"Of course!" the couple said in unison. Max smiled. He'd be invited to the ceremony, at least.

"I was hoping you'd give me away," Meg said, "I had asked Cormac, but he seems to believe that honor belongs to you."

"Of course, I'd be honored, sis," Max said. Meg then gave the earl a bear hug. Andrew smiled and shook one of Max's hands that dangled out of the iron squeeze of his intended.

"Oh, I'm so happy!" Meg said, "Now, I must plan this investiture ball. We've got to find a lady for you, sweet brother, maybe one with fabulous wealth to rescue the old pile here! Oh yes, the dynasty also must go on! We don't want Hector or May ever running this place."

Andrew nodded at Meg's statement. Meg then released her grip on Max and began pacing, tapping her mouth with her index finger. Max recognized the telltale signs of a Fraser woman constructing a Machiavellian plan.

"A ceili... No, that won't work. Max is not that good of a dancer," Meg said, ignoring that her brother stood paces away, "A fancy ball? No... Max wouldn't remember all the names, and then there would be a fight over who he'd need to dance with..."

"Huh? What are you on about?" Max asked. Meg ignored him as she continued to think. She stepped back and forth, finally stopping. Meg said, "Well, dear sweet, brilliant earl, we need an event where you can meet the folk without much pressure. That would be awful if you forgot a baron's female relative's name! A slip-up like that might cause a feud!"

Max nodded. He hadn't considered the complexities of who he'd have to dance with. Max's mind returned to the shepherdess. She was the one he wanted to dance with.

"Wait, I have an idea! A masquerade! Yes, yes, yes!" Meg said.

"Huh? What?" Max said.

"You know, a masquerade—where everyone is in disguise! See, no pressure! You'll be in camouflage. We will all be concealed!"

"Brilliant Meg! You always have the greatest ideas," Andrew said, "I could go as a unicorn, and you the pure maiden who tames me."

Meg smiled at her betrothed and said, "Down, boy! This isn't about us. We're a lock! This is about Max!"

Max merely coughed at the couple, reminding them he was present.

"What should Maxie go as?" she said, "He needs to look extra handsome and macho so the ladies line up to marry him!"

"He can be a black knight!" Andrew said with a smile.

Max laughed out loud. Of course, a rival clan would see the Earl of the Bonnie Dundee as a black knight or brigand.

"Sounds fantastic. I can be a black knight," Max said, "now, let's continue until we head down to dinner. I need to get a set of proper accounting books together. The ball will need to be paid for, after all. Meg, see to our supper, and Andrew, please see to my books."

"I told you, Andrew," Meg said, "Max was destined to be the earl since he is so bossy."

"Don't worry, dear," Andrew said as he opened up an accounting program on his tablet, "soon we'll be away from here. The commendations won't be as majestic, but the roof won't leak either."

Max watched as Andrew opened a new accounting ledger and began copying figures the men had determined to be truthful. Andrew stopped ever so often and queued up the ledger in a print job so that if anything happened, there would be a hard copy version of the figures. Max was thankful for his future brother-in-law's help. He was most grateful that the hard and soft copies would match.

CHAPTER FIVE

Preparations and Invitations

The end of March came and went. Max felt time flying away as he looked at the calendar. The date circled on his digital calendar showed, 'April 3, 2353'. In about a week, the gathering would begin, and that first night, the tenth of April, was the day of the investiture's masquerade ball.

Max reflected on how the family had pulled together. Hector and Cormac were able to get all of the necessary tents and bleachers needed for the games assembled. May and Meg, on the other hand, caused more headaches than help. The women were proverbial rams running down the hill, crashing head-first into each other. Meg would plan for a red backdrop with a white tablecloth, and May would choose the opposite. Max suffered the most, as there was no compromise between the two women. They would run to Max, screaming that their way was right and the other's was wrong.

Max would retreat to the library like he did today. He looked down at his handiwork on the ornate desk. He had just signed another invitation to the masquerade ball. He placed his signet on the outside of the invite to seal the envelope. After the wax cooled, he looked at the addressee. This invitation went to the mysterious Isobel Douglas, the Baroness of Cairnbahan. The mysterious Baroness Douglas had yet to make a correspondence with Max or an appearance at the Bonnie Dundee. Max had been on the estate since the twenty-fifth of March. The baroness had missed almost two weeks of court without even a note to her earl.

"I'm done with women," Geordie said as he appeared in the library and slumped into one of the recliners beside the ornate desk.

"Hello yourself, Breakin," Max said as his vassal entered. Geordie had become a friend to Max. Someone with Max could discuss things and not worry there was a hidden agenda. The man was a veteran, wealthy, and not a social climber, although his stories pretended otherwise.

"I tell you, that Douglas woman!" Geordie said in frustration. Since the hunt, Geordie was continually visiting Max. All Max had heard from the man for the past week was the joy of his new leg. Max held his doubts because sometimes he could see that the leg still gave Geordie problems. Today's conversation was going to revolve around women, though. Max felt that was a more positive discussion for the baron.

Geordie looked at what Max was doing and said, "What do you have in your hands there, old chap?"

"Invitation for the baroness," Max said with a smile. He was rewarded with Geordie turning red in anger. Max hadn't meant to annoy his friend, but he could tell Geordie was tired of Isobel Douglas. Max placed the invitation into the post bag. He or another household member would put the bag out for the post carrier before the morning pickup.

"I had invited her to the ball, and of course, she turned me down," Geordie snarled.

"Why?" Max asked, preparing another invitation.

"She said that we could be no more than good friends, and she wouldn't limit her options at what would be, according to her, 'the premier social gathering on this side of the Sheeplands.' Can you believe the nerve of the woman, Max?"

Yes, Max could believe that Isobel felt that way. Everyone under fifty looked forward to the masquerade, where social standing, traditions, and etiquette wouldn't get in the way of a good time.

Max also had gotten an earful from Geordie about how Isobel kept him at arm's length, and Max had to be careful after he had politely suggested that Geordie cast his nets elsewhere. Geordie did not react well to the suggestion.

Max phrased his response and said, "I understand where she is coming from, but no worries, she'll be hanging off your arm—unknowingly, of course—since the event is a masquerade. As Stahlburgh's most eligible bachelor, she'll be unknowingly be drawn to you."

"No, no," Geordie said, "You were right. I'm done with her, with a ratio of twenty women to one man here. I shall have my pick of the ladies. There are many fairer, younger, more agreeable women in the county."

Geordie then went on to discuss how he would woo his new paramour. Max half listened. On dating, he considered Geordie an organic white noise machine. Max prepared the current card he had in front of him for mailing. Max looked at the note, suddenly realizing he held Geordie's card. Max merely handed the invite to the baron, who opened the envelope, marked his attendance, and promptly returned the note to Max. Max then put a check in the column and one number in the guest list under the row for Geordie.

"If only all the invites were as easy," Max said to himself.

"What was that?" Geordie said.

"Nothing, please continue. You'd send her to the *Bundstadt* for a spa weekend, is what you were saying," Max said, not missing a beat. Geordie continued with a smile. Max's eyes wandered out to *Cruach Mhòr*, where he had met Geordie. Max felt like he had known Geordie for years, though they had only known each other for less than a fortnight. At the thought of the hunting party, Max suddenly remembered the shepherdess.

"Geordie, do you know who tends the flocks up on Cruach Mhòr?"

"One of the men from Cairnbahan, I believe. Why?"

"Never mind," Max said. Max then printed out a poster for the ball. The posters would go up across the village and into the countryside. Max had successfully argued for including the common folk at the masquerade—not every earl's wife had been of noble blood and bearing. Secretly, he hoped that his mysterious shepherdess would attend. If she were as adamant about wealthy squires' sons and the earl, then she wouldn't show. Max's secret hope was she would show up anyway.

"Well, I'm off, old chap," Geordie said, "I'm being fitted for my costume. I've decided that Sir Galahad suits me, just in case you are wondering."

"A perfect choice," Max said, standing. Geordie stood, extending his hand for Max to shake.

Max shook Geordie's hand and said, "Best of luck. I need to check on the catering and supervise the cleaning crews. Hector's parties have made a terrible mess."

"Good luck and farewell," Geordie said, "I shan't keep you. I'll let myself out."

"You as well, and thanks," Max said, and the two men separated. Max went out the hallway entrance, and Geordie exited the library near the stairs. Max trod through the small hallway and out to the second floor of the grand corridor. Looking westward, he could see the reproduction of Viscount Dundee and the portrait of his parents. Max moved north to the corridors with his bedroom.

Entering the large master suite, Max spied a large package on his father's decrepit mattress. Max crossed the room to touch the package longingly. Max wanted to rip the plastic off and unroll the contents. It was his new mattress. However, the presence of workmen in the room prevented Max from unrolling and flopping on the mattress. Max had auctioned the old frame to help pay for the ball. A collector bought the antique, and the workmen would break down the old bed frame for transport. Once removed, Max would install the new mattress on a wider—modern—frame, with a hopeful expectation of a decent night's sleep.

"That woman!" Meg said as she stormed into Max's room, startling Max and the workmen, "There you are! You have to do something about her."

"What did she do now, Meg?" Max said, looking skyward for some help from the Allfather.

"I've already hired *Harmony in the Heather*. They are from Andrew's barony, play traditional music, and... are... amazing! But May said they were too uncultured for the ball. She hired an orchestra. We can't afford an orchestra, Max."

"I'll talk to her, don't worry," Max said, hoping to diffuse the situation.

"Thanks, Max, that woman makes me so mad. Oh! I've got to run. I've got a fitting for three potential wedding gowns, and the seamstress is coming to measure me for my ball gown."

Meg dashed out and down the stairs before Max could even say goodbye. The chaos in the house was starting to ratchet, and there was a week to go.

"Maximilian!" May's voice shrilly called for him.

"Here, aunt," Max said, against his better judgment. May shouted for him again, and Max left his room and proceeded down the state apartment stairs to see two sets of florists standing next to May in the north vestibule.

"Yes, Aunt May?" Max said as he presented himself.

"You need to choose," May said, "I've hired Herr Schildt from the *Bundstadt* to deliver flowers, whereas Meg has hired Mister MacInnon here from the village for the same task."

Max could guess which vendor was the more expensive. He would have to side with Meg on this one, which meant he'd need to side with May on something else. Otherwise, he'd be playing favorites. The delicate balance that had come to pass between Meg, Hector, May, and Max was implicitly underwritten by Max's being impartial about all of the May-Meg conflicts.

"May, you should know that we always support the local vendors here at the estate. Herr Schildt, here is a few griffins for your trouble," Max said.

The florist accepted the bills, bowed, and said, "*Danke,* if you ever need me, your aunt has my card."

"Well, Mister MacInnon, I expect the order to be filled and ready at the appropriate time and date," May said, her tone demanding and cross.

"As I said to Miss Fraser, we'll have the lilies ready on time the day before," MacInnon said as his rival departed.

"Lilies will not do," May said, "we will need Martian orchids and Venusian roses."

"Och! I told you, Ma'am, I cannae get those in time," MacInnon said, "We are a patriot shop that only supports flora that can be grown in the Union."

May looked at Max as if he could make the man cough up the flowers.

"Work the flowers out with Mister MacInnon, May," Max said. He then changed track, "What about you hiring an orchestra?"

"They are the local philharmonic," May said, "I know Meg hired that group, Heather Fields or whatever, but I remembered your father's love of the philharmonic. I believe you, as the earl, are one of the board members. What did you say? We should support the locals."

Max was hoisted on his own petard and would have to support May on the philharmonic, even though the orchestra would be more expensive.

"I'll tell her to cancel her musicians. Look, I have to go to the great hall and supervise the workers installing the dance floor. Can you handle things here?" Max asked his Aunt.

"Yes, I'll manage, dear boy, I always do," his aunt replied, appeased by her newly won victory. Max slid past her and moved down the corridor into the great hall.

"Max?" a man's voice said, "Max, I haven't seen you in twenty years."

"Ewan?" Max said, shaking the man's hand and embracing him, "Ewan Fraser, so good to see you, cousin!"

Ewan was one of Max's extended relations, a nephew of Baron Eoin of Aberleemnay. The last time he and Ewan had seen each other, they were both in short trousers. Ewan had reddish brown hair, blue eyes instead of Max's brown, and the same nose and lips all the Frasers shared. Max looked to Ewan's guest, a man of about forty.

"This is George Reynolds from Sol," Ewan said.

"I'm surprised they let you come here, with the war on and all," Max said, "I'm Max."

"I'm a refugee, and I'm really from Mars," George said with a distinct twang to his accent, "Ewan has been good enough to put me up with his family."

"Pleasure, George! Ewan, how are Molly and the children?" Max shook George's hand and then turned to his cousin.

"They keep busy running our tourism agency on Eisenwald," Ewan said, "Molly sends her regrets. She wishes she could be here, but she is working. Someone has to mind the travel agency. Max, I'm sorry for showing up early, but I wanted to arrive before the rest of the clan to claim my room and something close for George."

"No problem at all, Ewan. Now, if I remember, your room was the red one, with the armor stand outside, right?" Max said, searching his memories for the room where he and Ewan used to play.

"The one exactly," Ewan said with a smile, "I think the blue room will suit George. The room is one door down the hall from mine, so he won't get lost while looking for me. You know how confusing the house can be for some."

"Yep," George said, "Ewan has built up this here shindig so much I had to see things with my own eyes. He told me there is going to be a whole passel of Frasers tomorrow."

"Yes, I figured he'd need some commentary on our traditions," Ewan added.

Max nodded, "I'll lead you to your rooms. After you're settled, I'll ask Cormac to bring up your luggage shortly."

Max took the two men on a mini-tour through the manor. They climbed the stairs to the state apartments, then went down the passage into the grand corridor. There, they stopped so Max could point out Viscount Dundee's portrait and that of his parents. He opened the red room. The room hadn't been used, and a stale smell hung in the air. Entering, Max decided to fix the odor. Ewan was one of his favorite cousins, after all.

"I'll open a window to air the room out," Max said, wrestling open a stuck window. After a bit of tugging, he had all the room's windows opened, and the smell withdrew.

"Now, on to the blue room," Max led George down the hall and opened the blue room's door. The room's bright blue paint glowed as Max entered the chamber.

"That's some serious blue, hoss," George said as he entered, but the Martian smiled as he looked at the room. The neon blue was supposed to evoke an Eisenwald beach scene. Unlike the red room, the air in the blue room was pleasant.

"No smell, though," Max said, "I'll let you get comfortable as well, George. Let me know if you need anything." Max checked his watch. The watch face showed half past noon. On cue, his stomach growled.

"When you are ready, lunch will be in the kitchen. Ewan knows the way, George," Max said as he turned to leave the room. Before leaving the wing, Max popped his head into the red room and said, "I'll leave you now, Ewan. I'm sure you are tired after your trip. There's lunch in the kitchen. You should take George on a tour of the grounds afterward."

"Thanks, Max. If you have a moment later, I'd like to speak with you privately," Ewan said. Max nodded and waved. There was too much to do to stop. He then left the corridor with the red and blue rooms, entering the grand corridor's second floor. He then went down the grand staircase and through the foyer and the formal dining room to the kitchen. Cormac was lighting gel canisters under the serving dishes in the kitchen.

"Meg said to keep the food she prepared for us warm," Cormac said, "I got caught up helping Hector set up the main pavilion on the games field, so I am behind schedule. Did you meet up with Ewan?"

"Aye," Max said, "He's in the south wing with his friend. You'll need to haul up their luggage. They are getting comfortable after their trip and will need a change of clothes."

"I'll do it after lunch," Cormac said, "Also when I saw Ewan, he asked to go fishing tomorrow with his friend."

"Do you have the time?"

"Ah, no," Cormac said, "but that's never stopped me."

Max smiled, piling his plate with lamb chops from one of the serving dishes. He bit into one. The lamb was offset with a strong mint flavor. Cormac put the lamb chops and some fried potatoes on his plate, covering everything with some gravy from the chops.

"I almost forgot, an express courier delivered a reply letter from one of the guests," Cormac said, giving Max an envelope addressed to him in calligraphy.

"Wow, ornate and quick. I sent that card out this morning by post. The response shows a lot of work," Max said.

"Well, the masquerade has been the talk of town now for almost a fortnight. I noticed that the return address is Douglas Hall," Cormac said. Cormac began eating a chop as Max flipped the card over and back. Cormac devoured the food on his plate as Max stared at the card. The card was ornately addressed to "His Grace, the Count of Gilbraith-on-Heather. The Earl of the Bonnie Dundee." Max smiled and noted the return address and an ornate seal, which showed a mountain flanked by an "I" and a "D."

"The envelope smelt of wildflowers," Cormac said, taking another bite of lamb. Max did not know which was stranger—the speedy response from the mysterious Isobel Douglas—or that his huntsman was sniffing his mail.

Cormac noticed the look Max had given him and said, "Well, aren't you going to see what she said, lad?" Max nodded, proceeding to break the seal and open the envelope.

"Looks like she will be attending without a guest," Max said.

"She's a handful, lad," Cormac warned.

"You've said that before," Max said, watching as Cormac stacked his plate in the sink, "Don't you have more envelopes to sniff?"

Cormac chuckled, grabbed another chop by the bone, and heading off, he said, "Aye, and luggage to haul and lots of other work to do. I'll see you later."

Max waved as the huntsman left the kitchen through the rear door. He looked again at the response, puzzled that the Baroness was so eager for the masquerade yet so reluctant to come to offer her loyalty oath. A loud crash pulled Max away from his thoughts. Max dashed from the kitchen to see what new mayhem had occurred.

CHAPTER SIX

Masquerade Ball

The moon, *Eisenwald,* shone bluely and brightly as the orb rose above the horizon. A cool April breeze swirled across the Bonnie Dundee's entrance. A large bonfire was buring on the lawn. On the south side of the blaze, Cormac's fingers tapped on the chanter as his pipes wailed. He played a pibroch as he marched forward. The huntsman was in full Sheeplands finery. He wore a Tam o'shanter with quail feathers, a Prince Charlie jacket, and full plaid with the ancient Fraser tartan. When the tune ended, he proclaimed, "The forty-seventh gathering of the Frasers has commenced." Cormac then marched to the house's entrance, his bagpipes softly whining as the pipebag slowly deflated.

After weeks of preparation, the gathering had begun. Tonight, Cormac would act as master of ceremonies, allowing Max to mix and mingle incognito with his guests.

The great hall's doors stood open, showing the newly installed dance floor. Max and the others wandered inside. When he entered, the orchestra of the Gilbraith Philharmonic began to play a waltz. May and Meg appeared in disguise, performing crowd control and keeping the entranceway clear. Max watched as May and Meg would each match a man and a woman and then gently herd them out on the dance floor. Looking at the great hall, Max observed a mass of dizzying colors. Men and women wearing disguises were spread over the large room. Max walked to the bar, which had yet to attract a crowd at this early evening hour.

Standing at the bar, Max debated his drink. Max watched as a woman in an aquamarine dress and mask came up to order. The woman ordered a local red wine, and the barman efficiently poured her a glass. She accepted and moved back into the crowd, not even glancing at Max. Max turned to order when a costumed knight approached.

"Aha! A black knight," a flamboyantly costumed man said to Max, "I hope you dare not cross blades with me, for you will lose. I have defeated your green brother, as I am Sir Galahad!"

"Biased old stories, I always believed a black knight would triumph," Max replied, shaking Galahad's hand.

"*Royal Neep*, sirrah," Galahad said to the barkeep. The barman poured four fingers of whisky and handed the drink to Galahad. Geordie wore a full mask with the visage of an ancient crusader, with plastic armored plates covering his dark gray tailored suit.

"Any intelligence on who is who, Geordie?" Max asked. Max, too, wore similar fake armor over his—insignia-free—Assault dress uniform. Max should have gotten an outfit tailored, but he didn't have the time or the funds. He made do with the uniform and the plastic armor. Max looked in the mirror before the ball to confirm his outfit was generic enough to pass at least for one night.

"Haven't the faintest, old chap," Geordie said, "I spotted a lovely young woman in a pink gown. I think I shall pursue that venture."

"Good luck," Max said. Geordie nodded, grabbed his whisky, and disappeared into the crowd.

"*Primus* Ale," Max said to the barman, finally making his choice.

"*Schwartzbier*, please," a young woman in a russet gown said. She wore a mask, veil, and headband complete with antlers. Her costume was meant to represent some ancient deity. Her dress was modest, only showing a hint of skin around her décolletage. She wore a russet and silver choker around her neck. Her mask covered her upper face and was coppery brown. Her hair was hidden from Max's view by a coppery brown veil. The veil was held in place by a brown cloth band that sprouted two large deer antlers. She wore russet silk gloves, in which she gracefully accepted the beer.

"Diana, I presume?" Max guessed, leaning forward to talk to the woman as the barman served his drink.

"That's a good guess, but I am not Diana. I have been mistaken for her even by foolish mortals in antiquity. I am *Abnoba*, the Gaulish forest and river goddess. Fear not, roguish black knight, tonight I hold no hatred for anyone who mistakes me for Diana," Abnoba said, smiling.

Max felt a flush of embarrassment, which was thankfully hidden by his mask. Covering for his mistake, Max placed his drink on the bar, bowed, and said, "Of course, I should realize the wise Abnoba would recognize me. The color of my armor and puckish nature have prompted tales far and wide."

Abnoba laughed and placed her drink on the bar. She then curtsied.

"I won't say too much right now to spoil the unmasking, but where I live, a specific black knight is one of my clan's heroes," Abnoba said, "Although we call him something different."

"Where is that, wise Abnoba," Max asked. Abnoba quickly sipped her drink and responded, "Close enough. Do you live nearby, sir knight?"

"Aye, I live very close too," Max replied after retrieving his drink and taking a sip. He then put his pint closer to Abnoba.

Max was about to ask another question when the goddess Sophia —his Aunt May—appeared. May wore a white half mask, silver wig, and white Grecian-inspired gown. Max blushed as he noticed that May's dress was too low-cut for a woman her age. Max, unfortunately, could not say anything about May's gown at the moment—unless he wished to divulge his identity. Max and Abnoba turned their heads to see what Sophia needed.

"Now, this is a ball, and you two *must* dance with each other," Sophia said. Max marveled at how his aunt could make an ultimatum sound so enticing. Usually, May was a harpy, but she blossomed at a ball.

"Shall we?" Max asked Abnoba, motioning her towards the dance floor.

"I'm not that great at waltzes," Abnoba responded. Suddenly, the band switched to a slower song.

"I promise not to step on your toes during the slow foxtrot," Max said with a smile. Abnoba nodded as Max offered his hand, leading her out onto the floor. Max looked down, occasionally, at their feet. He was careful to keep his plastic-looking sabatons away from the hem of Abnoba's dress and the pointed russet tips of her shoes.

Max's concern over stepping on Abnoba's toes eased as he did his best to follow the dance steps. The couple began dancing together in time with the music. Max was enchanted by Abnoba. He led her around the slow circuit others were making on the dance floor.

"Have you lived here a long time, sir knight?" Abnoba asked. Max could smell her perfume—full of wildflowers and vanilla. Max could feel the warmth of Abnoba's skin through her dress. He fretted about where he placed his hand, keeping his grip firmly on the small of Abnoba's back. He wanted to maintain his hand's neutral position. If he strayed too far up or down, she might take offense.

"Yes and no," Max said, pushing his concerns from his mind, "I've recently come home from the war. How long have you lived here, goddess?"

Abnoba smiled radiantly and said, "A girl could get used to that address. But to answer your question, I have lived here most of my life, except for my secondary schooling when I went to St. Brigid's Academy just outside the *Bundstadt*. Were you really in the war?"

"Yes, goddess," Max said, "I was a sergeant in the Assault."

"In a volunteer unit, sir knight? Most men here left and formed the Seventy-eighth Sheeplands Volunteer Rifles."

"No, I was in one of the line units commissioned by the protector himself," Max said. Abnoba's mask lifted slightly in surprise. Sadly, Max did not get a better look at the wearer's face. The music crescendoed, and Max spun Abnoba around a corner on the dance floor.

"You must have seen horrors on the battlefield," the goddess said, returning to Max. Abnoba's question on another's lips could have been considered offensive, but the goddess's statement seemed genuine, and that disarmed Max.

"Aye, I had a fire team cut to pieces in my last action. War is hell, goddess, like the old Terran general said," Max replied, having a sudden vision of Marko and his team being butchered.

"I detest the slaughter. Many of those who left have already given all for the Union," Abnoba said. Her voice was soft and sad. Max suspected she lost someone close, so he tried to bolster her spirits.

"Despite all the slaughter, this war is just, goddess, we were attacked..." Max said but was cut off by Abnoba.

"No, do not misinterpret what I said, sir knight. The alternative to the war—a Terran boot on our throats—justifies the bodies we throw into the charnel house. Those who have died have made a true sacrifice. I only wish victory would come without the further loss of a Felgenlander's life," Abnoba said, her soft tone turning to steel.

"Now, you sound like my old commander," Max said with a soft chuckle, following the music and spinning his companion around.

"Can you tell me his name? But only if his name wouldn't reveal your identity—just yet. After all, there is something romantic about a masquerade," Abnoba said.

"Lieutenant Frank Nordlinger, he just planted our flag on Nakdong," Max said. He was proud of his lieutenant, even though they weren't particularly close while serving together.

"I read about him in the Gazette!" Abnoba said with a hint of surprise, "What an honor to serve under such a man."

Max was about to respond when a soft announcement came over the microphone.

"Please switch partners," Aphrodite said. Max smiled and remembered that Meg had, at the last minute, changed her disguise to match her aunt as a deity.

Max watched as another man took Abnoba's hand. Abnoba smiled and waved, but before she could say anything else to Max, she was whirled out of sight on the crowded dance floor. Max wished to stay with Abnoba but was at least comforted that he wasn't the only one missing someone. He realized there was a forlorn unicorn pining for Aphrodite's return.

Max walked to the edge of the dance floor and grasped a waiting lady's hand. The lady wore a gold dress and a golden mask.

"Fortuna, I suspect, may I have this dance?" Max asked.

"A black knight, ugh," said the new partner. The voice was familiar, and Max suspected that he was dancing with Helen, Geordie's sister.

"Listen," Fortuna said, "if you are one of the commoners all dressed up, you may as well exchange me at the next turn."

Max realized that silence was the best response, and as the band switched to a Tango, he eagerly cut in to change partners with another couple. He then danced off, escaping Fortuna. His new partner was a woman who must have been significantly older than he was. Her gown was blue, and she had a fake shepherd's crook in her hands.

"Oh, a black knight, how dashing," she said as he whirled her around.

"Bo-peep, I presume," Max said, "A pleasure to cut in with you, my lady."

Bo-peep giggled like a schoolgirl at Max's chivalric sentiment. She, unfortunately, said nothing else. Max attempted conversation.

"Do you live near here, Miss Peep?" Max asked. For his effort, he was giggled at in response. Max was not that impressed by the woman, and as the music ended, Max politely excused himself.

"One more hour to unmasking," Cormac shouted over the gathering. Max decided to pause dancing and people-watch. He stepped off the crowded dance floor through a small break in the crowd. To his left, near the bar, he saw Geordie holding court with several ladies and a smaller number of gentlemen.

Max turned to look over the dance floor, hoping to see Abnoba. The dance floor was a menagerie of brightly-colored costumes. The dancers were vying for space on the crowded dance floor. Some dancers' outfits were homespun, some were off the rack, while expensive custom boutiques had designed others. People moved in and out of Max's vision. Max smiled. The masquerade ball was a success.

"Did you enjoy anyone's company especially?" Aphrodite said as she glided over and stood next to him.

"Aye, Abnoba's company, but I cannot seem to find her," Max replied to his sister, "I thought you'd be the fair maiden tonight."

"I thought about going as 'the fair maiden,' but I couldn't have May upstage me as a goddess," Meg said.

"So, where is your unicorn?" Max asked. He was trying to suppress a laugh at the entire situation.

"Andrew? Oh, he changed his costume as well. He came as Adonis when I decided on Aphrodite," Meg said, "I told him he didn't need an outfit, and in fact, no clothes at all would be a better costume for him."

Max laughed and said, "That could be awkward. What did he say when you told him that?"

Meg smiled through her half-mask and said, "He expressed his sentiments to me wordlessly and insistently."

"Say no more," Max said, "I can imagine what happened next."

"Well, duty calls," Meg said, moving away, "I've got a mission now: find Abnoba. What did her costume look like?"

"Russet dress with a mask attached to a headdress with antlers," Max said.

"Gotcha, all right, I'm off." With that, Aphrodite was gone.

Max continued his people-watching, scanning the crowd, hoping to find Abnoba. Max eventually gave up and headed to the bar.

"Did you find her?" Max said as his sister crossed his path to the bar.

"No," Meg said, "but I am still looking. I think half of the Sheeplands are here!"

Max watched as Meg squeezed through a group that stood talking and drinking. He attempted to do the same but wasn't given as much courtesy as his sister. Instead of continuing to the bar, Max grew frustrated and moved to the edge of the hall. Max went through the north side door and headed to the eastern gardens. He checked his watch. He had spent over half an hour people-watching.

Soon, Cormac would appear and announce the unmasking. Max hoped he'd meet this second mystery lady, and he could ask her out for a coffee, perhaps with a less disastrous outcome than the shepherdess.

Outside and free of the crowds, Max walked south toward the oversized main doors to the great hall. Max's going was slow as he continued scanning for Abnoba, but he also had to avoid loiterers. Couples and some singletons waited in the gardens outside the great hall as private and public transports collected people. The vehicles would ferry the waiting guests away from the Bonnie Dundee.

Max scanned the waiting crowds to see if Abnoba was there. She was not. Max returned to the great hall's main door and entered, courteously squeezing his way in as others left. Clear of the doors, Max wandered forward, looking around. He decided to head back to the dance floor.

Max felt like his luck with the shepherdess was repeating. He stepped onto the dance floor, feeling forlorn that he hadn't had another chance to talk with Abnoba. Max walked into the center of the dance floor, avoiding all the happy dancing couples. He felt a pang of jealousy at others's good fortune. The emotion was only momentary as Abnoba appeared among the dancers. She walked right up to Max.

"Sir knight, we meet again," she said. Her mask shifted slightly higher as the goddess smiled brilliantly and batted her copper-colored lashes at him.

"Goddess," Max said, his smile shifting his mask, "I am *most* pleased to see you."

"And see me, you shall," Abnoba said, "In moments, we will discover each other's identities. I'm very interested in meeting properly."

"Yes, I'd like to meet the most interesting woman at this masquerade," Max said.

"Oh, will you introduce me?" Abnoba said, misunderstanding Max's compliment.

"I meant you," Max said, "our conversation and dance were the highlights of my evening."

Max noticed Abnoba's exposed cheeks blushed. She said, "I had also enjoyed our dance together. I find meeting new people here in the Sheeplands difficult. With the war, people are leaving, and those that stay don't have your modesty."

Max felt a surge of emotion. He liked this woman. He was going to pay her another compliment when Cormac's voice interrupted.

"Ladies, Gentlemen, please remove your masks," The huntsman said as he stood at the northern end of the dance floor. Max watched as the guests began removing their masks. Max's heart rate spiked as he found the straps holding his mask. He began removing the ties. As his mask came off, he tried to see what Abnoba looked like.

Abnoba's mask was part veil, headband, and upper face cover. The disguise required more effort to remove than Max's simple plastic mask. Max held his mask and watched as blond ringlets peeked under Abnoba's veil. Max agonized over the few moments Abnoba took to remove her disguise.

"By the prophet!" Max exclaimed, "Shepherdess?"

Max looked at the woman in front of him. Apart from the masquerade makeup, she was the woman from his dreamlike experience on the mountain.

The unmasked Abnoba smiled and said, "I should have realized that the black knight was you, my rich squire's son."

Max was going to ask the goddess-shepherdess her name when Cormac approached.

Cormac's tone was rough, and he said, "Isobel, you owe his grace your *oath of vassalage.*"

"Cormac," Isobel said in shock, "this is the earl, Maximilian?"

"Maximilian *Graf* Fraser, Earl of the Bonnie Dundee," Cormac said gruffly, "meet Baroness Isobel of Cairnbahan, the Lady of Clan Douglas of White Mountain."

Max's heart fluttered. The goddess, shepherdess, and mysterious baroness were all the same person, and she now stood before him! Max quickly realized what he should do. He placed the baroness's hand to his mouth, kissing her gloved hand politely, and said, "A pleasure, your excellency."

Max let go of Isobel's hand and caught a grumpy stare from a red-faced Cormac. Isobel held the kissed hand like the appendage was a cherished treasure. She batted her eyes at Max and said, "Your grace, the pleasure has been mine."

Cormac then growled and said more than asked, "Isobel, when will you give your oath to the earl?"

Max was surprised at Cormac's insistence on the demand.

Isobel nodded and said, "Ah yes, the oath. I am willing now

should the earl desire the assembled guests to witness."

"Yes, please," Max said, "Cormac, clear a space."

Cormac shouted for the gathered folks to move and called for their attention. Within a few moments, a small space cleared around Max and Isobel.

Isobel bowed with a deep curtsy in homage, her head tilted upward as she looked at Max and said, "May the Allfather, creator of the universe, bless you and keep you, my lord and my liege. As you are the appointed man by our protector—long may he live—Clan Douglas of White Mountain will follow your banner in war and herd your sheep in peace."

Isobel stood up straight, waiting for Max's response. She again smiled at Max, batting her eyes and then darting a look at the ever-reddening Cormac.

Max said, hand over his heart, "By the Allfather, our Union and the protector, I will defend you from trouble and uphold your rights and privileges as they existed in the days of our grandfathers—are now—and will be in the days of our sons."

Max paused and realized that some could construe Max's oath as a marriage proposal. Max's silence became awkward, and Isobel turned to address both Max and Cormac.

"Are you satisfied, your grace?" she said, breaking the spell.

"Only if you call me Max."

Isobel smiled, nodded, and said, "Aye, Max, and you must call me Isobel." Cormac moved close to Max and whispered, "She's a handful, lad, a bloody handful."

"Shepherdess was what I was calling you before," Max said, ignoring Cormac and giving Isobel a wink. Isobel let out a belly laugh that startled some of the other guests who, the ceremony over, were in their own deep discussions.

"What?" Max asked. Cormac shook his head in disgust and promptly left to attend to the now-dispersing crowd.

"Max, I am not usually on the mountain with the sheep. My uncle or his man, Angus, usually tend the sheep. I was only there that day because Angus was ill from the Martian flu. So, as much as I am a baroness, my clan makes no distinctions when we have chores. My uncle, the ultimate guardian of the flocks, was gone that morning on clan business to the *Bundstadt*. I was only shepherdess for a few days. I'm sorry I haven't come to court. There is always so much going on in Cairnbahan! I was unaware you were accepting oaths of vassalage. Otherwise, I would have found someone from the village to watch the flock—your flock—and I would have given you my oath. In Cairnbahan, the sheep always come first. We have an old clan joke that our shire was called 'the White Mountain' because the sheep blanket the sides of our hills."

"I would like to see your mountain if you'll be my guide, Isobel," Max said.

Isobel paused, and Max grew worried. Was he about to be rejected again? He thought of Isobel's initial rejection on the mountain.

"Perhaps," Isobel said after a pause.

"Is this because I am the earl and not a plowman?" Max asked, feeling hurt from his first rejection.

"No, no," Isobel said, "had I known you were a gallant Assaultman, and from what has been said, a man who sees people before rank... Well, I shouldn't have been so hasty. Just dancing with you, I could tell you were different," Isobel said, smiling.

Max felt he needed to press Isobel more on this guided tour, but he was interrupted by Meg and Andrew. Isobel and Max turned their attention to the new arrivals.

"I see you found your goddess. I should have known Isobel would come as Abnoba. I'm surprised you tolerated the crowds and being indoors for the ball," Meg said. Meg was serious, and Isobel did not seem to react negatively.

"Aphrodite, Megan, that's perfect," Isobel said, "and between you all—I did sneak out for some fresh air for a while. Things got too claustrophobic after Geordie cornered me and began his latest attempt at a conversation about our potential marriage."

Max felt like he had been punched in the stomach. If Geordie, Max's friend, had asked Isobel to marry him, that could complicate things. If Isobel had consented to Geordie's offer, she should have remained the mysterious shepherdess Max had thought her.

"And?" Meg said, instantly reading her brother's discomfort.

"I'll call you later," Isobel said, "Good night, my uncle is waiting outside to take me back to Cairnbahan. The ball was lovely. Thank you for inviting me. I expect I will see you tomorrow at the gathering. I hope we have more time to talk."

"Yes," the siblings said in unison, and Andrew, ever the quiet one, nodded. She turned to go but paused, quickly turned around, and kissed Max on the cheek. She then sprang away, leaving the group. Max's heart leaped, and he could feel the subtle amount of lipstick Isobel's kiss deposited on his cheek.

Max started to feel the effects of the emotional roller coaster he had ridden all night. On the one hand, he had found his shepherdess, but on the other, she could soon be Geordie's wife.

"You got a kiss, bro," Meg said, then obnoxiously she snickered, calling out, "Maxie's wearing makeup."

Meg continued to giggle, but Max didn't care if he had Isobel's lipstick on his cheek. Max decided he would never wash the cheek in question ever again. If the lipstick were the only thing Max would ever have of Isobel's, the stamp would remain a banner for all to see.

"Come on, puppy dog. We've guests to send off!" Meg said, pulling her brother's arm.

Meg and Max strode towards the great hall's main door. May intercepted them before they could position themselves to shake hands with the departing guests. Without even asking, May wiped the lipstick off Max's cheek.

"That will not do, Maximilian," May scolded him, "We can't have the earl have a reputation as a playboy. We are a respectable family, after all."

He was furious at May's statement and forward behavior. Before he could respond, he was approached by departing guests who shook his hand and offered thanks for the ball and their invitation. Max looked around between guests, and as he suspected, Hector was nowhere to be found. Max saw Cormac was just outside the entrance, ensuring guests could drive, had recovered their belongings from the coat check, and had transportation from the property. May floated away, heading towards another part of the house. After her actions with Isobel's lipstick, Max didn't care if May wandered off a cliff.

After a seeming eternity of shaking hands and saying goodbyes, the final guests left. Meg and Andrew then exited, presumably to go to Andrew's home. They were still madly preparing for their wedding. As they departed, Cormac appeared bearing a bottle of whisky.

"Is that the reserve?" Max asked the huntsman as they locked the main entrance and went to the bar.

"No," Cormac said as Max and he stood at the bar.

"Well then, let's not hold back. Break out the good stuff," Max said as Cormac reached behind the bar to produce two clean shot glasses. Max didn't care if he would wake up in the snow. He had found the mysterious baroness, shepherdess, and goddess in one night and one person.

"Are you sure, lad? We still have a lot to do?"

"Why not? The party is over and was a success. Tomorrow, we'll wake up hungover and go to the games, and in the evening, the Frasers will gather and feast. I think I can afford a drink for the hardest-working huntsman in the Union," Max said.

Cormac, visibly exhausted, raced out of the ballroom, returning shortly carrying a bottle of the best Fraser whisky.

"Grab the glasses, laddie, let's get comfortable," Cormac said, motioning Max to follow him. He and Max crossed the great hall, then to the grand corridor, finally ending their journey in the formal dining room. The men moved the chairs from the table and sprawled in the seats.

"Your father distilled this when you were born," Cormac said. He broke the seal on the bottle and started pouring the liquor into two glasses.

"To your health and continued success," Cormac said, saluting his liege. Max raised his glass in return. Max felt bulletproof as the whisky slid down his throat. Whatever fate lay in store for him tomorrow, he knew that today had been a good day. It was the day he learned that the shepherdess's name was *Isobel*.

CHAPTER SEVEN

Games and a Gathering

"Squee!" Meg's voice shrieked as she ran through the Bonnie Dundee. Max's hungover mind couldn't process the sound and nudged him towards consciousness. Meg burst through the door to his room and flopped on Max's bed, jolting him. His head throbbed.

"Weimar, reporting, sir!" Max said, reflexively returning to his days in the Assault.

"*She... said... no,*" Meg said in a loud excited voice.

"Who said what?" Max asked as his mind began to function.

"Wake up, you dolt! She said 'NO.' She rejected him. She's available!" Meg said, shaking Max.

"Who, Isobel?" Max said, bolting upright. The hangover could wait. The previous night's events flooded back into Max's head. Max's heart began to race, and not just because of the dehydration.

"Yes!" Meg said, "She had to leave the masquerade because Geordie kept pressing, and she finally told him that she was not interested in him!"

Max digested this information for a while. He remembered thinking he would have to tread carefully to avoid hurting Geordie's feelings.

"What do you think I should do?" Max asked Meg.

"Send her flowers or a card," Meg said, "If you want to impress her, send her a bouquet of wildflowers with a note that lets her know you had a nice time together." Max looked a bit skeptically at his sister.

"I've known her since we were in primary school," Meg said. "While I am not close to Isobel, I know what she likes. Come on, bro, trust me! I can see this is where Dad really goofed. You and Archy should never have gone to boarding school. I stayed put, and trust me, I know the people here!"

Max moved as if the suggestion was an order from high command. He dropped his feet to the floor. He stripped off his nightshirt and threw a day shirt over his pajama pants. He looked at his sister and the door, signaling he wanted privacy.

"Wait? You are going to get the flowers now?" Meg asked. Her face showed her excitement. She stood up to leave the room and then halted by the door, waiting for an answer from her brother.

"Well, coffee first and then the flowers," Max said, "Provided I can avoid the rest of the Frasers that have descended on the Bonnie Dundee."

Meg stepped out in the hall, poked her head back in, and said, "I have your back, bro. I'll run interference. After all, this is the most noble cause of all: *love*!"

Max rolled his eyes as his sister drew out the word "love." Instead of responding, he pushed her head out, shut, and locked the door. Max then changed clothes, moving from his pajama bottoms to a Prince Charlie Jacket and full plaid of ancient Fraser tartan, along with wool socks, mid-calf boots—and a pair of underpants. Max, fully dressed, left his room and stealthily moved across the house to the library entrance by the portrait of Viscount Dundee. As he approached, Ewan and George met him in front of the reproduction.

"Have a coffee, Max," Ewan said, handing Max a disposable cup, "I happened to grab two when I was down at breakfast. I heard Meg shrieking like a banshee and figured you'd need the cup."

"Much appreciated," Max said, taking the coffee in hand, "what are you two up to?"

"Ewan said he'd explain the hubbub to me, you know, what y'all are up to today," George said with his strange accent.

"Aye, and I'll give George some background on the installation. You have memorized the speech, right?" Ewan asked.

"By the prophet's ashes!" Max swore, "I knew I was forgetting something..."

"Don't worry, the speech is only a paragraph. There is plenty of time to remember your lines before the installation, cousin," Ewan said paternally.

"Come on, hoss," George said to Ewan, "Let's go outside. You can explain these here games to me."

"We'll catch up later, Max," Ewan said as he and George descended the corridor toward the house's main entrance. Max was relieved to be alone. There was no need for an audience to order flowers. He slurped down the coffee and went to his desk in the library's center. Sitting at the ornate desk, he booted up the computer's video application and called the florist.

"Hello, MacInnon's Flower Shop, this is Sara," a young woman said. The computer projected a holographic display with an interior image of the shop, with Sara's upper body behind the counter. The experience gave Max the impression of being inside the shop.

"Hi Sara, this is Maximilian Fraser. I want to order some flowers, with some discretion," Max said. He wasn't sure what others would say about the earl sending flowers to his baroness. He didn't want his attempt to date Isobel to be broadcast far and wide, either.

"Of course, your grace, how can I help," Sara responded. Max realized that Sara's discretion would only go so far, as she had instantly recognized him. The response made him pause, and he decided that if people talked, there was little he could do to stop them. Max wished he could assess Isobel's intentions before the wagging tongues would. He also hated the thought of transmitting his feelings to the entire county.

"To hell with caution," Max said to himself, then to Sara, he said, "Your best bouquet of wildflowers, to her excellency, Isobel Douglas."

"Of course, your grace," Sara said, "Do you want a card sent as well? If so, what shall the card say?"

"Yes, the card should say: Isobel, I had a wonderful time dancing with you last night, Max."

"Perfect, your grace. When and where shall we send the flowers?"

"Immediately, to Douglas Hall in Cairnbahan," Max said. As soon as he told Sara where to send the flowers, Max remembered that Isobel would be at the gathering. There was a chance the flowers would miss her if she were already at the Bonnie Dundee.

"I'll have Duncan, our delivery boy, send the bouquet out immediately. Your account has cleared the funds, and we'll message you a receipt. We'll both show self-restraint about the delivery. We're used to men wanting our secrecy with flower deliveries. But, if you are worried about the gossip, sir, I'd avoid the beauty salon," Sara said with a knowing wink, "Can I help you with anything else, your grace?"

"No, thank you. Goodbye," Max said, thankful for Sara's service, reserve, and information.

"Goodbye, sir," Sara said, severing the connection. Max checked his watch. The watch face declared the time was almost ten hundred.

"Drat, I've got to shave, as well as find and remember the damn speech," Max cursed under his breath. He moved briskly from the library to his bedroom's private washroom. After twenty minutes of shaving, combing his hair, and a final check of his clothing, he was ready to face the multitudes of Frasers, retainers, and onlookers.

Max remembered where he put the speech. He had used the paper as a bookmark in a novel he was reading. He removed the paper from the novel and placed the book face down to hold his place. Now, he needed to cram the speech into his head. Max had barely been a teenager the last time he had worn this attire. He placed the Tam o'shanter cap, replete with a long, speckled feather, on his head and looked in his full-length mirror.

"Now, if I only had a few MacDonalds to fight," Max said with a flex and a chuckle. He then left his room and went down the large, ornate, public-facing staircase at the front of the house. He could see the gathering below as he stepped towards the top stair.

"His Grace, the Earl of the Bonnie Dundee," Cormac announced. Max's extended cousins, uncles, and aunts stood in the great hall. They all clapped as he appeared.

"Good morning! Are we ready to go see some caber tossing?" Max said to the crowd.

"Aye!" the group shouted. The assembled Frasers then filed through the large main house doors. As Max and Cormac exited, Cormac produced his pipes and began to play *Flora Fraser*. The gathering marched down to the fields where athletes stood ready to compete. All that remained was for the earl to give the starting word. Cormac finished his tune as Max reached the stands.

Max ascended to his box above the highland games field. The private box stood out from the stands and displayed the Fraser coat of arms: *Quartered fraises and crowns with St. Malcolm's Cross in an oval in the center.*

The folks who had gathered smiled and waved at Max. Max's head and neck grew tired as he returned the nods. After a moment's climb, he entered the box and sat on a comfy folding chair. His box would be his duty station for the remainder of the games.

Max shouted, "Let the games commence!"

A muscular man hoisted his caber on the field below and began his toss. Max wanted to see where the caber went, but retainers and relations soon blocked his view as they presented themselves to him. Cormac appeared and began organizing the visitors into a proper queue. He hollered, waved, and moved the mass of retainers and relations down and out of Max's sight. As Max waited, he looked at his speech and committed it to memory. After Cormac had organized the visitors, he announced the individuals at the head of the line.

"Alexander Fraser, Squire of the Isle of Saltoun on Lochiel, and his daughter Margaret," Cormac said. Alexander was a decade or so younger than Kenneth, while Margaret appeared to be Max's age. Alexander had gray hair over his blue eyes and tanned Fraser nose and chin. He wore a Prince Charlie jacket, full plaid of ancient Fraser tartan, and knee-high leather boots. Margaret wore a blue sweater and a sash that blended into her long, ancient Fraser tartan dress. She also bore the Fraser features and had shoulder-length brown hair that framed her blue eyes and fair face.

"Earl, the Saltoun Island Frasers wish you joy and a long life on this Installation Day as our chieftain," Alexander said, "and I present my young, unmarried daughter. We are kinsmen separated by at least six generations of kinship. Thus, may I suggest that my daughter seeks a distaff relation for a husband to strengthen the unity of our clan?"

Max wore his best poker face. Margaret was not unattractive, but Max wasn't interested in marrying a cousin. There were also ramifications in accepting the proposal today. But for purposes of honor, Max couldn't rebuff the squire's offer too firmly. Max sat for a moment and then replied.

"Cousin, we know the earl cannot make such choices on a Gathering Day. The honor of the clan and your house demands that the petition be repeated a month after the gathering so the clan may have the chance to mull over this proposition, for the circumstances of my marriage are not entirely in my control," Max said. Max played the offer safe. He was free to marry whomever he wished, yet for clan politics and honor, he'd have to present his betrothed at a gathering.

Recalling the stories his father had told of his courtship to Max's mother, Max realized that Kenneth had done something similar when marrying. The whole dance of presentation would ensure the earl couldn't be coerced or tricked into any agreement without the clan's consent. The entire arrangement kept everything honest, and at this moment, Max was grateful for the provision.

Alexander took this setback in stride as he nodded and said, "Aye, your father, Allfather bless his soul, said the same when my father presented my sister, Mairi."

Max felt pity for Alexander's family for being rebuffed by two generations and said, "I thank you, Cousins, for your gracious offer. Please feel free to call on me at any time."

Alexander bowed, and his daughter curtsied, and they left together. Max checked to see who was next. Cormac would signal to the head of the queue to ascend for their audience. Max was thankful that the meetings would be more private. Taking a moment's respite, Max looked at Cormac.

"Did my father have to deal with this?" Max asked.

"Aye," Cormac said, "He married your mother specifically because had he chosen a Fraser bride, the clan would have taken up arms against each other, brother fighting brother. That he loved a woman of the von Weimar dynasty made the match palatable for the Frasers who would rather see a foreigner as the countess than one of their scheming kinsmen's daughters."

"Well then, next in line, please, Cormac."

Cormac returned to his position. The meetings soon blurred together for Max as a train of Fraser relations, barons, and squires came to wish him well. For every congratulation, there was a request from a supplicant. The supplicants all wanted influence, money, or his hand in marriage. Max looked down at the field. The games had progressed to the hammer throw and the line to see Max was still substantial.

After a pause, Cormac said stiffly, "Her Excellency, Baroness Isobel of Cairnbahan."

Isobel stood outside the box. She wore a tan jacket over a long skirt with the Douglas clan's light blue and green ancient tartan. On her head was a pale blue wool beret, complete with a speckled feather. Max smiled at Isobel, and she batted her eyes back.

"Good afternoon, your grace," Isobel said, "May I sit with you for a while?"

Max straightened up in his seat, gestured to the chair next to him, and said, "Of course, your excellency, please, by all means, join me."

Isobel sat beside Max, and both looked out over the game field for a while. Max looked up from time to time to see Cormac glaring at him.

"I thank you for the flowers, Max," Isobel said. Sitting next to each other, the couple could speak softly with limited worry about eavesdroppers.

"You are welcome," Max said. After the limbo of the previous night, he was ready to take things slowly and cautiously.

After a few more moments of silence, Isobel said, "Look, I don't want to be forced into anything. There are plenty of my kinsman that are pressing me to entertain all sorts of gentlemen."

"I hope I didn't give you the impression that I am forcing you to do anything other than your oath," Max said, worried he had offended Isobel somehow.

"No, and you *deserved* my oath. Besides, Cormac forced that out of me," Isobel said with a laugh. She continued, "I am sure Megan told you, but Geordie had proposed, and I told him no. He didn't listen to me and felt my answer wasn't strong enough for him."

"I see," Max said, "I understand his desire, although perhaps not his methods, Isobel."

Isobel blushed but continued, "I think, perhaps, you don't understand. Geordie and I were practically raised together. He was older, but we were like brother and sister. Our clans, really our mothers, were desperate for us to be a match. When I was just a girl, had he asked me, I would have consented, but then I went away to finishing school in the *Bundstadt*."

Max just nodded, listening. He looked at Isobel and saw a beauty that was more than her charming exterior. He listened to Isobel and realized they were kindred spirits. Of all the fates Max could have chosen when he ran away, he chose the Assault. Why? So he could see the galaxy.

Isobel continued, "When I graduated, I was offered a chance to serve my conscription in the capital as a clerk assistant and personal secretary for the Minister for Cairnbahan, Rosie Douglas-Fairlane, my late cousin. I served my conscription and learned from one of the strongest, most ambitious women I'd ever met. She made me realize there are places far from the Sheeplands and even the Union. I wanted to see those places and explore them. She helped me understand how vast this galaxy is and how small the Union is. After my conscription, I returned to Cairnbahan, and the thought of settling with Geordie, becoming a bairn factory, and never leaving... Well, I didn't like that fate. In the interim, Geordie had developed a reputation. Although, as a man, I suppose that reputation isn't considered a bad mark on one's character."

"I was raised with the idea a gentleman holds to one paramour and does not kiss and tell," Max said.

"Oh well," Isobel said, "here I am blabbering on like a complete idiot."

"Not at all. I do have to ask, if you wanted to see the universe so badly, why come back here, Isobel?"

Isobel looked wistful, then said, "I was going to join the Navy, be one of those interceptor pilots. I was all set to leave, and then my father died. He was the old baron, and I was his only surviving child. The clan had never before had a baroness, and my cousin, Rosie, made an impassioned argument in my favor. She was very persuasive. Instead of seeing the stars, I became the baroness. I returned to take up my father's mantle and run the barony. My uncle, Kensie, helps, but there are many problems in Cairnbahan."

"Is there anything I can do to help?" Max asked. He didn't like the idea of Isobel having problems and felt his duty as earl was to aid his vassal.

"No, Cairnbahan is my duty," Isobel said, "Don't get me wrong, I appreciate the offer."

"Believe me, had you offered to help me, I would not refuse," Max said.

"You're sweet. I don't believe that, though. Still, I thank you for the compliment and the offer," Isobel said, "Again, thank you for the flowers. They cheered me up after what happened with Geordie. Now, I must mingle with the rest of the folk here. Even a troubled baroness has her duties, too."

Isobel stood up and then looked at Max for a minute before she kissed his cheek. She left the box and went down to the highland games field while Cormac looked with disapproval at his liege.

"Really?" Max told his retainer, "What do you have against her?"

"The Douglas women are headstrong. They have no idea what they want, but they'll fight to the death to get what they cannot have. I don't want to see you get hurt, lad."

"I'm a big boy, Cormac."

"That is what I am afraid of, laddie. Now, the games are over, and it is time for the installation. Are you ready?"

Max quickly pulled out his speech and suppressed a moment of panic. If he was not ready now, he'd never be.

CHAPTER EIGHT

Peaks and Valleys

The highland games were over, and Max stood up. He and Cormac descended from his box to the field. As Max moved across the lawn, all eyes were on him. The local priest in his ceremonial vestments trod from the other side of the lawn to meet Max and Cormac in the middle of the field. The reverend was a Fraser named James, and he carried a sizeable ornate gospel of Malcolm. Malcolm was the state religion's founder and prophet. While the Bible was more meaningful, Malcolm's gospel was a very close second in importance. A younger deacon, similarly attired, followed the priest carrying a large claymore. While finally, an acolyte came bearing a ring on an ornate pillow.

The deacon and acolyte flanked the priest, who began softly chanting a prayer.

Once finished with the prayer, the priest spoke loudly and said, "Do you, Maximilian, son of Kenneth of our illustrious Clan Fraser, accept the responsibilities as chieftain of the great clan of Fraser, whose sons turned the first sod on Stahlburgh, and whose daughters spun our world's first wool?"

Max collected himself as he tried to remember the words. Between petitioners, Max had studied the oath. Max had never heard the oath spoken. He used his command voice and said, "By the Allfather's grace and my heritage through my father Kenneth, I promise to defend all of the children of the Fraser from all who wish them ill. I promise by the blood that courses through my veins that I will strengthen our kith and kin. Your needs are my needs, and all who enter my house will receive the clan's hospitality, as was our tradition in old Scotland and is now on Stahlburgh and in the Union. I swear this by the Allfather; Jesus, the Son of Man; and the Holy Spirit, as Malcolm, our Prophet, and our teacher instructed us."

The acolyte presented the ring to the reverend, who blessed the band. The priest put the ring on the littlest finger on Max's right hand. The priest smiled as the deacon then gave him the sword. The priest blessed the sword and presented Max with the large blade. Max took the sword, resting the claymore across his shoulder while holding the hilt. Max was now officially the chieftain and final arbiter of the clan—*the Fraser*.

"Chieftain, I present your clan," Reverend Fraser said. The Frasers, friends, retainers, and guests loudly cheered. Max felt on top of the world. The Frasers, retainers, and well-wishers left the stands and swarmed the field in their desire to head to the feast.

The servants hired for the day began to set up additional seating on the games fields and finalize the buffet under the expansive pavilion on the lawn. Max watched as the high table went up under his Aunt May's repeated and unnecessary guidance. Hector approached Max, extended his hand, and said, "Congratulations, cousin. May your guidance be long and wisdom great."

Max smiled, took Hector's hand, and said, "Thank you, Hector. I hope to see more of the fine help you've provided the clan in setting up this gathering."

Hector's response was drowned out as Max was given a big hug from Meg, and she said, "I'm glad you are back, bro! Congrats! You'll run this place better than dad ever could, Earl Max!"

"Your grace," a servant said, interrupting, "your place is here."

The servant guided Max to the tallest chair at the high table. A plate of food, wine, and a small glass of water sat ready for him.

"Fraser venison, from your land; new potatoes, from the Valley of the First Farmers; and Eisenwaldian wild beans, your grace," the servant said, lifting the lid and presenting Max's meal. Max's stomach rumbled, and he realized that he had only had a cup of coffee all day. To his surprise, his watch read seventeen hundred—dinner time.

Hector sat two chairs to Max's right as heir. The chair immediately to Max's right was purposely vacant. The seat was reserved for the Countess of the Bonnie Dundee, Max's future wife. Seated past Hector was Meg, while on Max's left sat Reverend Fraser, followed by the deacon. Past the deacon on the left was Eoin, the Baron of Aberleemnay, the next Fraser in the order of precedence for the clan.

Max tried to eat slowly, but he was famished. Max worried that he looked more like an Assaultman in a chow hall than an earl at a gathering. Between stuffing his face and drinking, Max was continually interrupted by well-wishers. Upon finishing his venison, potatoes, and beans, Max noticed an angular man in a tan suit waiting for Max's attention. Max thought the man was yet another well-wisher.

"Your grace," the man said, "I am Daniel von Huegel, by courtesy called *Freiherr* of the Barony of Knockhill. I congratulate you today on your installation."

"Why thank you, baron," Max said, a little brusquely, as the man was now disturbing his enjoyment for the next course.

"Oh, this isn't a social call. I'm here on Union Parliament business. My father, James, the Margrave, sent your father, Kenneth, a notice," Daniel said. Max's instincts began to sound an alarm. Something about this man unsettled him. What business did the man have with Max?

"I'm confused. What does that have to do with today's events?" Max asked. He was missing a piece of information in this conversation.

"Oh, I see, you haven't seen the letter," Daniel said, "The margrave sent a physical letter along with the message service notice to your father. My condolences on his passing."

"What letter, what message service?" Max asked, now growing irritated. Max had scoured the server farms and was sure he had found all the critical correspondence. What had he missed?

"Forgive me, my father—The *margrave,* or as you, Sheeplanders quaintly say, marquess—is the Secretary of Dynastic Affairs in the House of Dynasts in the Parliament," Daniel said, "Unfortunately, Kenneth, Allfather bless his soul, was in breach of his oath to his liege. He hadn't raised the levies in over twenty years, and this county's roads and Union highways have deteriorated. If that wasn't enough, other violations have been levied against the old *graf*—or, as you called him, the old earl. I'm here as the secretary's agent to ensure things are corrected. Officially, my position is that of a Union auditor. We auditors work through the hundreds of cases the Secretariat receives every year. Thus, auditors—like myself—are essential public servants. We're the ones who follow these issues through to their conclusions."

Max felt his stomach tighten. The Union auditor stood before him and, by appearances, looked ready to arrest Max at the gathering, all due to a sword of Damocles that his father had kept secret. Max calculated the costs of repairing the kilometers of Union highway. Max's answer was beyond the means of the estate. Roadwork would be big money. Max suppressed his panic, but he wondered how many other things his father had neglected. Did Max owe some fealty or gesture to the protector, his liege's liege?

Max realized he needed to head to the capital, but only if the estate could function without him. However, he would only be able to get the answers in the *Bundstadt*. If Max couldn't find the answers, he would have to assume his seat in the House of Dynasts and fight the charges.

Returning to the man before him, Max wanted to assure the auditor that a new regime would make good on the outstanding issues—given enough time.

"Your Excellency, perhaps we could discuss this tomorrow?" Max said as the family watched the interplay. The others at the table looked stone-faced at the auditor. The family had decided on the affair, and they would support Max. Even Hector looked harshly at the auditor.

"Your grace, my name is *Herr* von Huegel or Daniel. I am only a baron by courtesy," Daniel said with sternness in his voice, "That aside, I would be open to discussing this early tomorrow before I head home to the *Bundstadt*." Max had to give the auditor some credit for being willing to stand firm despite the entire high table giving him the evil eye. The next move was Max's.

"I will see you at nine hundred then. Thank you, *Herr* von Heugel," Max said. The man nodded, turned on his heels, and left. Max's joy was gone. He felt deflated and emotionally spent. Worse, there were still two dinner courses remaining. Max's appetite waned as the duck course arrived and left. His appetite was nonexistent when the final course—a roast pig—appeared. Somewhere between the second and third courses, the *Holstensonne* dipped below Stahlburgh's horizon, and evening arrived. After a few minutes, the plates were removed, and the dinner was over. With darkness, the temperature dropped.

The clan dispersed. Older members headed for the house. Half the younger members moved to the village pub, and the remainder huddled around the just-started bonfire. Isobel came towards Max as he stood gazing into the flames.

"Max, would you like to sit with me by the fire?" Isobel said. Max didn't want to be by the fire. Instead, his instinct was to rush to the library and scour the records again. Isobel's pleasant company could not remove the sour encounter with the auditor or the worries churning in Max's imagination.

"I'd like to..." Max said. Max should have been more excited about sitting beside his "Queen Amang the Heather," but the day's events had utterly drained him of emotion.

"Is something wrong?" Isobel asked. In the firelight, Max could see the worried look on her face.

"Can we take a walk? I promise to return you to the fire," Max said. He wanted someplace private to tell Isobel without the rest of his clan surrounding him. Walking together, alone, wasn't entirely proper, but that was a minor concern Max had on his mind.

"Of course, would you like to head along the loch track? If we walk far enough, you can see a bit of Cairnbahan," Isobel said, "although only the silhouette of the White Mountain will be visible in the darkness."

"Sure," Max said. He set off, and Isobel matched his steps, walking beside him. They walked silently for several minutes while doubts raged in Max's head. Max wondered why the baroness was even bothering. Max might be the former earl soon, and, most likely, Isobel would not want to have anything to do with him.

"What is wrong, Max?" Isobel asked softly. Eisenwald crested over the horizon. Max could make out the worry on her face from the light reflecting on the loch. Max was pretty sure Isobel hadn't heard the conversation with the auditor. Max's heart ached to pour out his soul to Isobel. Max felt so easy with her. Max was surprised at how fast he had come to seek comfort from her presence.

"There is an auditor from the Parliament on the estate," Max said. Max felt a release of pressure, quickly followed by guilt. Max began to worry whether he should have even mentioned the auditor to Isobel. Wasn't the audit his burden as earl—alone—to bear?

"Things might not be that bad," Isobel said.

"I don't know, I've always heard that an auditor's visit is trouble. I've inherited a title that, apparently, my father didn't take seriously.

The auditor charged Kenneth with dereliction because he did not raise the levies nor repair the Union highways. He said Parliament was forced to take action."

"These are the Sheeplands! All roads are in poor condition. What does the Parliament expect? Even with a moderate winter, there would still be potholes from here to Balquhidder-on-the-Angusburn!" Isobel said. Max could see the rage on Isobel's face in the low light. Max felt some relief. Isobel must have heard similar complaints, and she was firmly in Max's camp.

"I think this is more than just roads," Max said. He breathed a sigh of frustration and said, "The auditor alluded to my father having more open issues and complaints. Since I inherited this mess, I am responsible. I suppose I won't be the earl for long. Perhaps I will hold the record for having the shortest tenure as the Fraser earl?"

"That'd be terrible if the Parliament removed you so quickly, especially as you've just started. What would you do," Isobel asked.

"I don't know. Try to go back to the Assault, perhaps. Or, look for work here. I can see the advert in the *Sheeplands Gazette,* 'For employ: one slightly used earl—can act aristocratic.'"

Isobel laughed and said, "I'm always looking for a huntsman." Max saw her face in the twilight. Her smile was barely visible. Isobel continued, "Of course, if the replacement doesn't like me, I may also be out of work."

"That would be Cairnbahan and the county's loss," Max said. Isobel started to shiver. The temperature around the loch was dropping.

Max changed the subject and said, "Let's sit around the fire. I feel much better after talking with you, Isobel."

Max released some of the tension he'd been holding. If Isobel would accept him after only a few hours of acquaintance, others would feel similarly.

"I'm glad," Isobel said, "I felt much better after talking to you at the games, Max. Thank you for just listening to me. I haven't felt like someone has really listened to me in a long time."

"You're welcome," Max said as they walked to the fire. Max felt Isobel's hand close around his as they walked along.

Max had a brief fear of what would be said if he was seen holding hands with Isobel. Max inwardly shrugged. He could be another nobody in the Sheeplands after tomorrow. Then, nobody would care about his love life.

"And here is our host. Perhaps he can answer the question better, George," Ewan said as Isobel and Max appeared. Max looked at the roaring fire. Ewan and George sat next to each other on a log, and a dozen Frasers sat in a circle around the blaze. All eyes went to Max, but Isobel did not release her grip on Max's hand. Max gently squeezed her hand in appreciation.

"What was the question, Ewan?" Max said, escorting Isobel to a log so that she could sit by the fire. Max then sat strategically beside her so that his kilt protected his modesty and he was a polite distance from the baroness.

"Okay, Max, y'all are a dictatorship, yet Ewan keeps talking about how your honcho just got elected," George said with his twang, "So how does a dictator get elected, and how does that work when he runs things?"

"I tried to explain, but then I recalled that the Earl of the Bonnie Dundee is an elector. Perhaps you could explain how the election works better than I do," Ewan asked Max.

"Sure, Ewan," Max said, "George, I wasn't the earl at the election, and I don't know whom my Father supported. So, my answer comes from what I learned in boot camp, where we were required to understand the system. We even had to take a test."

"I suppose that'll do," George said, leaning forward attentively.

"The Protector Raimond—long may he live—actually holds two positions. They are known as the protector and the patron. The protector is the head of government in the Union. He's also the head of our military. The patron is the head of state and the head of my faith, the state religion, which you Terrans call "the Felgenland Central Christian Orthodoxy." Max paused to see if George was following. George nodded his head, not wishing to stop Max from his exposition.

"The patron signs laws, which is essential when politically charged issues arise. If the people vote against the issue, the patron will veto the bill by tradition. This assent (or veto) makes the protector so beloved by the commoners," Max said.

"All right, but why'd he get elected? Shouldn't he inherit?" George asked, "he's a king of sorts, too, right?"

"No, by the Union constitution, the protector can only be selected from the descendants of our first protector, Karl. Those are the *Cognati*—the kinfolk. Also, the election isn't what you think it is. You cannot *campaign* for the position of protector. There are no debates from the contenders. In the recent election, both *Cognati* made their intentions known..." Max said but was interrupted by George.

"Hold on, so only the politicos chose the protector?" George asked, "That sounds like the ancient communists of Earth."

"No, no, not so fast, old boy," Ewan said, jumping in, "plenty of electors are not political. Some are clerics in the state religion. Others are guild masters. The position of elector comes from inheritances from the founding clans, like the Frasers. What you may be confusing are the votes cast by proxies." Max looked at Isobel, and she smiled at him. She sat enjoying the blaze, content to let Max, Ewan, and George talk politics.

"Sure, Ewan, I heard about those," George said, "the Martian press was just going on about the evils of the proxy system in the last election. How the new bigwig had hundreds of votes all sewn up before voting even started..."

"To outsiders, things may seem that way," Max said, interrupting, "The proxies are merely promises of support. Also, proxy rules are only allowed in the first voting round. After that, I'm free to vote for whomever..."

"Now, why in the hell would you give up your vote, even for one round?" George said, confusion clear in his choice of words, "If I were you, I'd keep my vote and my mind to my damned self."

"Like everything in the Union, it is a tradition. Proxy voting helps establish large blocks and support a smaller set of candidates. Of course, there are assurances the contenders offer to the proxy holders. It becomes horse-trading of the highest degree," Max said.

"There gotta be a quid pro quo, so what do you get?" George asked.

"The proxy holders, usually the liege lords, have their laws, courts, and rules. As a proxy, I am stating my desire to remain under the infrastructure my liege has created. Gilbraith-on-Heather uses this infrastructure, and we don't have to pay, directly, for it at all," Max said, "if I were to choose another proxy holder or hold my vote, that's essentially an act of independence. Independent actions like that haven't happened in almost a century."

George's face scrunched up in confusion. Max chuckled and said, "Yes, the voting is complicated, but mainly the proxies are a tradition."

"But, what happens if the new protector passes a law to 'get even,' Max?"

"Well, the protector cannot pass laws. He only proclaims an edict. Edicts aren't laws and are easily overturned by the Parliament and the courts. An edict only has binding power if the Parliament declares an emergency. Again, we haven't done that in many decades. I am not sure the old edicts are even valid. Does that make sense, George?"

"Sounds about right," George said, ending the conversation. Max realized that George probably didn't have a clue.

"Come along, George. With some whisky, we'll have a better chance at making sense of this," Ewan said.

"Fair enough, that hooch y'all make ain't half bad," George said, standing up from his log. George said, "'Night all."

"This way to the house," Ewan said to George, then to the group, "Goodnight all."

The Frasers muttered various responses. Max saw that the political conversation had reduced the crowd around the bonfire, although the flame was still blazing. As Max glanced at Isobel again, he noticed she was still shivering. He thought Cormac had left a few blankets by the woodpile and went to check. Max found one and put the blanket around Isobel.

"Thank you, Max," Isobel said, "You can join me. There is room under the blanket... if you are cold."

"If you don't mind," Max said but hesitated. By old Felgenland tradition, a gentleman sharing a blanket or his plaid with a woman was a sign of marriage for the lower castes.

"Not at all," Isobel said, realizing why Max paused, "because I'm sharing a blanket on a cold night with a friend, nothing more."

As Max slipped the blanket around his shoulders, he caught a whiff of Isobel's perfume—wildflowers with a hint of vanilla. Max felt his heart skip a beat at Isobel's very distinctive scent.

Max moved closer. Isobel teased, "Besides, you'd have to ask my uncle for my hand in marriage before the clan would allow me to share your bed."

In the firelight, Max could see Isobel batting her eyes at him. Isobel's marriage comment caught Max off guard, and he thought to remove the blanket.

However, Isobel wrapped her arm around him, holding him fast.

"A proposition for the future perhaps?" Isobel smiled, "For now, let's just be a boy and a girl sharing some warmth on a cool night."

Max slowly relaxed, realizing Isobel wasn't serious. Max also noticed quite a few other couples snuggled together for warmth. Everyone gathered knew that sitting by the fire was just sitting by the fire.

Max imagined himself no longer the earl. He decided that, unburdened by a title he never wanted. He would have happily put his arm around Isobel. Without a title, he could ask Isobel's uncle for more. Guided by the thought that he might not be the earl much longer, Max followed his impulse and slipped his arm around Isobel. Together, they watched as the bonfire slowly became coals. The others said their good nights and left. Isobel and Max noticed they were alone when the last charcoal went out.

"We should head back to the house," Max said after a few minutes. He wasn't sure where this relationship with Isobel might go. The feelings he had were beautiful and reckless. Max hesitated on how to move forward. He remembered, earlier in the day, Isobel had said she didn't want to be pressured into marriage.

Max wasn't sure what to do next. His heart wanted him to move fast. However, as the earl, the only acceptable course was a proper courtship, followed by a betrothal and marriage. The Felgenlanders expected their nobility to be noble. The nobility were required to be exemplars for the rest.

"In a moment," Isobel said, placing her head on his shoulder, "I understand we need to keep up appearances, but I am enjoying being able to just be a girl with a boy, just next to you, in this silence. I haven't had a smooth tenure as the first Douglas Baroness. My clan, well, are good folk, but they are all headstrong and think they know what my job should be and what my place is. I like that you listen to me. Having someone to talk to is nice. I don't often get to be a person. Usually, I must be the baroness and carry my clan's burdens."

After a few more moments enjoying the night and the silence, Isobel said, "Let's head back. I don't want to trouble you any further. My predicaments are my own, and you have plenty to worry about."

"You can tell me," Max said, a little too impulsively.

Isobel stirred, standing up and taking the blanket from Max, "Okay, but no more for tonight, Max. We've done enough sharing for the time being. You are right. We must head back, where I am the fiercely loyal vassal, and you are my liege."

Max felt conflicted. He wanted to tell Isobel he could be more than that. Then Max remembered that the auditor was coming in the morning. After the visit, Max could be just a discharged sergeant. Max could be everything to her as a nobody—if a discharged sergeant were a match for a beautiful baroness.

"You are right," Max said, detaching from Isobel and standing up, "Would you mind holding hands on the way back?"

"Not at all," she said. She dusted off her skirt and placed her hand in his. Together, they walked back to the house. Max gave Isobel's hand a gentle squeeze at every other step. She responded with a gentle squeeze back each time. After several quiet, blissful moments, they returned to the Bonnie Dundee's entrance. At the main entrance, Max and Isobel separated and said goodnight. Isobel became the baroness, and—for the moment—Max was the Earl of the Bonnie Dundee and Chieftain of the Fraser clan.

PART TWO

EARL

CHAPTER ONE
Interview with an Auditor

Max woke up, but he was still tired. He would wake and look at the clock on the wall every hour on the hour. The clock read eight hundred. Max needed to get up and move. Max suspected the auditor would be arriving shortly. The auditor would want answers. If Max couldn't provide the correct answers, that would be the end of his tenure as earl.

Max reminded himself that the gathering had gone well. The clan accepted him as chieftain. He had also spent some private time with Isobel. Max stopped his wool-gathering and hopped out of bed. After a shower, shave, and a quick trip to the bathroom, he was ready to face the day.

Max dressed in the installation gift Meg gave him: a business suit and brand-new dress shoes. Max looked himself over in the mirror. He looked presentable. Max grabbed the handle, opened the door, and entered the corridor to the state apartments. Cormac stood in the hall waiting, like he was standing guard.

"Coffee," Cormac said, handing Max a cup of coffee. Meg appeared and joined the two men in the corridor. She had hash browns and some eggs on a plate.

"Breakfast," Meg said, handing the plate to Max. Cormac and Meg's behavior reminded Max of the petty officers who would prep the Assaultmen for an orbital drop.

"This isn't a battle," Max said. The statement was said to Cormac, Meg, and himself.

"We just want you to realize we're here for you, and we'll back you," Meg said.

"Aye, lad," Cormac said in agreement, adding, "If there is a fight, we're with you."

"I am going to an interview," Max said, "nothing more." Max gobbled the food and chugged the coffee. With calories consumed, he felt ready to meet the auditor. He, Cormac, and Meg traveled together to the front of the house. They could see a hover taxi outside as they approached the main entrance. The taxi floated to the steps, depositing the auditor. The auditor wore a dark gray suit and carried a small briefcase.

"Good morning, your grace," the auditor said entering, "In case you don't remember, I am Daniel *Freiherr* von Huegel, auditor for my father, James *Markgraf* von Huegel." Daniel used the form of address common in the *Bundstadt.*

"Good morning, Daniel," Max said.

"Now," Daniel said, "if you don't mind, can you show me the estate's records? If you have a private place we can go to, we can start the interview there."

"We'll head to the library," Max said. Then, before he left, he quickly said to Meg and Cormac, "Please take care of any other guests or issues while I am in the interview. Many of the clan members will be leaving today."

"No worries, lad," Cormac said while Meg silently nodded. Max then escorted the auditor from the main foyer up the grand staircase. Ascending, the auditor's long legs gave him an advantage, and Max had to push to keep up with the lean, tall man as the two men climbed the staircase. On the second floor, they stopped, and Max motioned to go to the left. As they did, the portrait of Viscount Dundee was visible at the end of the Grand Corridor.

"Impressive reproduction," Huegel said, pausing to look at the portrait of the Bonnie Dundee, "My mother's family had a similar painting in their *Schloss* on Eisenwald."

"Thank you, Daniel," Max replied. Deciding that business was more important than art history, he said, "Now, the library is here to the left."

Max led the man into the library and motioned for Daniel to sit at his desk. The auditor sat, opening his briefcase and producing a new model tablet.

"I'll need access to your server farm," Daniel said. "I'll download your records. The financial forensics will, of course, take place later. I'll scan and copy the pertinent records now." Max placed his thumb on Daniel's tablet screen, providing the needed authorization for Daniel to access the records. The tablet downloaded the necessary data, loading and processing a plethora of apps and screens. The speed of the procedure was an order of magnitude faster than what Max's tablet could do.

"By chance, what make is that tablet? Its speed and processing power is impressive," Max said.

Max was stuck with the estate's hand-me-down equipment. Something more modern might be helpful—provided he remained the earl.

"Something my cousin makes. A Huegel Tablet version four. I looked up your records and saw you served with Wilhelm, my cousin, on Nakdong," Daniel said.

Max took a seat next to the desk. Max wasn't sure where the conversation was going and decided that a prudent response was best.

Max said, "Aye, he was the Procurator for the Union at my court martial."

Daniel laughed and said, "That sounds like Willie."

The tablet beeped, and Daniel began tapping on it. After a moment, the auditor asked, "Your father never served?"

"No," Max said, "he felt that the enlisted ranks were made up of tinkers and thieves, while the officer class were fools who believed they were ancient knights."

"What a terrible attitude. We all lift this Union on our shoulders, and the military lifts the hardest these days due to the war. I served in the Assault," Daniel said, "I was an officer for ten years. I only resigned my commission when my father became the secretary for dynastic affairs in the Parliament. Running an estate and performing service as a government secretary is tough for one man. Plus, the older estates are less efficient, which makes things even harder for just one man to run. Issues get missed, or forgotten, or even ignored, correct?"

"Yes," Max said, feeling like the auditor was taking the long way with his questions.

"What do you feel about the new protector, Raimond?" Daniel asked. His tone throughout had been casual. So far, the interview had been a discussion, not an interrogation. Max noticed that with every question, Daniel's tone became more serious. The interrogation was about to begin.

"Long may he live," Max said. The answer was safe. Who could argue against a long life for the beloved protector?

"No," Daniel said, angry, "What do you *feel* about him?"

"I served both protectors, old and new, in the Assault. I would do so again in a heartbeat," Max said. Max felt his anger rising. He would not sit in his house and tolerate his loyalty being challenged by anyone. Max stared into Daniel's eyes. If this interview came to a conflict of wills, Max would not back down.

Daniel gracefully broke eye contact, tapped some notes into his tablet, and said, "Well then, I'll mark you down as a regime supporter."

Max felt his anger climb again. Daniel was playing with him. The thought of the interview had plagued Max for almost a full day. Max fumed. If the auditor was going to do something, the man should have the decency to be direct.

Max said, "Look, I don't know why you are here. My father never told me about the issues you mentioned, but rest assured, with enough time, I will fix them."

"Ten dragons, seven griffins, and thirty-three pfennig are my software's best estimate of your finances. You must spend twenty dragons in labor to get the roads up to code. Your tenants' buildings in the village are an eyesore. The Gilbraith constabulary is practically crumbling, as is the train station. All that effort will require you to be present directing the work."

"Yet, you'll have to take your seat in the Parliament. Plus, you'll be required to visit your liege and make your vows of homage. As a peer, the protector may demand your service in the chancellery, or the government may require you to serve as a secretary. What will you do then? You'll need to spend time in the *Bundstadt*. Who will manage the affairs here? Shall I go on? All of the complaints and the state of the village point to someone who has not been managing things well. Your father, may he rest in peace, felt like he could thumb his nose at the protector and the Parliament. I'm here to ascertain how far the apple has fallen from his rotten tree."

The auditor's expression never changed during his speech. He acted like a surgeon, cutting out the tumor before the rest of the body would suffer.

Max and Kenneth had never agreed on anything. Yet, Max was shocked at how his father had recklessly let things go.

"I will recommend one year of probation for your tenure," Daniel said, "I will return. Parliament will expect results. That means flawless roads, renovated buildings, and wealth in the village. Additionally, I expect no further complaints from retainers and vassals."

"Complaints?" Max said, an electric shock flowing through him, "Who has complained?"

Daniel looked at his tablet, avoiding eye contact. Max could see how the man struggled to divulge the information.

"As a peer of the Union, I have a right to face my accusers," Max said as his anger rose. "My rights come from the Allfather, and the Constitution guarantees those rights, whether a man is protector, peer, or peasant."

Max had suspicions about who complained. However, if his vassals had complaints, Max wanted them to come to him and lay out their grievances. Going to the Parliament and around him was poor form.

"Quite right. I will forward the complaints to your messaging service. That way, I have honored your rights and done my duty to maintain confidentiality," Daniel replied. Max nodded, even though he hated Daniel's bureaucratic answer. Max's tablet chirped, and he seized the device. Max opened the document and quickly scanned through the text. Most of the complaints weren't surprising. Hector and May had outdone themselves. There were three pages of incidents.

The one complaint that surprised Max was from Isobel. The baroness had lamented the poor conditions of the Earldom's flock. Isobel's grievance took Max's breath away. Max could deal with Hector and May. He expected their actions. Max felt crushed and betrayed. He never suspected Isobel would complain to the Parliament about him.

"I have drawn up the required paperwork on my tablet. Please sign your probation terms at the bottom. Your signature acknowledges you recognize the issues and will comply with the Parliament's directives to rectify them," Daniel said.

"And if I wish to dispute these complaints?" Max said.

"You may approach my father, the margrave, in the *Bundstadt* or challenge the complaints in an open session of the House of Dynasts. I warn you, sir, that with the war, the Dynasts have been occupied with legislation concerning our necessary victory over Terra. Your concerns may not even get a hearing before the probation ends."

Max thought momentarily and then picked up a stylus and signed the form.

"Thank you, your grace," Daniel said, "remember, I will be back in a year. Now, I'll see myself out. Please have a nice day."

Max watched as the auditor left. Isobel's complaint had taken all the fight out of Max.

"Well, looks like you still are the earl, lad," Cormac said as he quietly entered the library.

"Isobel made a complaint against me to the Parliament, Cormac. How could she?"

"I warned you. She's a handful. She came out here five years ago, taking over for her father, James, rest his soul. She and Kenneth had an instant dislike of each other. At that time, Archy was away serving his conscription with the Campbells. Had Archy been around, he could have mediated the conflict. As time passed, Kenneth couldn't even be in the same room with Isobel."

"With Kenneth shunning Isobel, she complained to anyone who would listen. First, she moaned about how the sheep were being neglected. Then, she demanded Kenneth do something. She wasn't wrong. Kenneth was too busy in the *Bundstadt* in those days, and the county was a distant memory for the earl. Isobel didn't take kindly to being ignored. She escalated the conflict—and went on a crusade against Kenneth. Things got so bad that the Gilbraith village shops barred her from entry. I tried to warn you."

"What do I do, Cormac?" Max asked.

"I don't know, lad. I've never been an earl. I tried my hand at love, but that didn't work well for me, either. I'm sorry. I am not the right person to ask for advice," Cormac replied.

Max sat there, and, eventually, Cormac retreated. Max reviewed the complaints. The complaints that Hector and May had made were petty. Max could quickly fix matters centered around the estate. Some time, money, and skilled labor would resolve them.

"I say, Max, can I have a word?" Ewan said, poking his head through the library door, "I hope this isn't a bad time? However, I did need to speak privately with you."

Max shut down the tablet and placed the device into a pigeonhole on the desk. Max replied, "Not at all, Ewan. What can I do for you?"

Ewan laughed, walking towards Max and taking a seat, "I apologize, but I happened to overhear some of your discussion with the auditor. I think I can help you with at least some of your problems."

"Huh, Okay," Max said, "as you've heard, I'm in a tight spot. What can you do for me?"

"Max, I'll come out and say this directly. Molly and I aren't travel agents. We're Union Special Intelligence Service," Ewan said.

Max nearly fell over in his chair and said, "You're spies!"

Ewan straightened, looking offended, "No, spies sell out their own country. Molly and I are intelligence officers. We met at *the retreat* while going through the evolution to work at *the Firm*."

Max had a passing understanding of spies, err—intelligence officers—from his days as an Assaultman. "The Firm" was slang for USIS. "The retreat" was a clandestine training ground in Stahlburgh's southern hemisphere. "The Retreat" would instruct new recruits on combat tactics, human intelligence gathering, and technical intelligence collection. Max remembered from his Assault days that USIS did both foreign and domestic intelligence work.

"Well, to the heart of the matter," Ewan said, "You might have guessed this, but George is more than just a refugee we're helping. He's Martian resistance."

Mars was the first client state the Terran Directorate had created and the Martian resistance had fought the Terran Directorate for almost thirty years. Max never knew his cousins led a double life, working as travel agents while being USIS officers. Max wasn't sure the life of a spy or an intelligence officer was something he could do, but he was desperate.

"I hadn't, but what does that have to do with me," Max asked.

"*The Firm* needs a space where we can train resistance members. All done under the deadliest of secrecy. The political backlash from the Union training... partisans... would be immense. *The Firm* requires this training ground to be isolated. A place where, if a stranger shows up, the locals will broadcast his presence across several shires. While coming up with a short list of locations, Molly and I debated including the estate. I was a staunch advocate for the Bonnie Dundee, but Molly was hesitant. I suspect you'd understand why she had her reservations. Uncle Kenneth was not the best patriot. He wouldn't agree to have his land turned into a secret training ground in a million years. Working with USIS would have been repugnant to him, but you, on the other hand..."

"Served and are a loyal Union son," Max said, finishing Ewan's sentence, "Fine. Ewan, what are you offering?"

"Fifty griffins a month for usage. We would start bringing in tours, some completely legitimate, others covert. You'll never know the difference, so you'll have plausible deniability. I apologize for the low usage fees. I always say, 'Don't ever expect miracles on a government salary.' However, we'll help with the estate's problems. USIS and the protector have resources to build roads, restore buildings, or raise new ones. *The Firm* can also help politically by portraying this venture as essential to our victory. All secretly inside Parliament's halls. We'll also schedule hunting trips regularly. Resistance fighters need practice shooting at moving targets and all."

"There is a catch here, I am sure," Max said.

"Yes, Max, silence—absolute silence. If there are any issues with locals, *the Firm* needs you to make them disappear before any journos or other busybodies show up, asking all the wrong questions. Can you do that, Max?" Ewan said.

Max did the math. Fifty griffins a month was six dragons a year. If Max added the resources from raising the levies, he'd have enough labor to make the roads passable. Adding the USIS expertise and the scheme might save him.

Max considered the political cover the venture promised and thought his cooperation should put him on the positive side of the ledger with the protector. That small amount of political capital would be helpful in the future. After a contemplative pause, Max said, "Yes, I'm in."

Ewan took his hand in a firm handshake, saying, "I just knew you'd agree! Thanks, cousin! I'll set up the details with George and his group, and then we will get back to you when the tourists will arrive. If all goes well with this venture, and you are agreeable, *the Firm* could support you in building a small spaceport over by Cairnbahan. Molly and I had the idea and drew up some plans. We plotted out an area on the map we thought would be a perfect spot for a landing zone. A small spaceport would simplify the logistics for our little secret."

Max smiled. He hadn't even considered how to get the tour groups in and out of the estate. Building a spaceport by Cairnbahan would stir up new problems, and Max had to deal with Isobel's complaint.

Max nodded and said, "A spaceport. Let me think about that,"

"Of course," Ewan said. Max felt like a small ray of hope had shown through the dark stormy clouds. He stood and said, "Glad to help, Ewan. If you will excuse me, I must handle some internal business..."

"Of course, Max," Ewan said, standing, "I will be in touch."

Ewan and Max left the library. Ewan went to prepare to return to the capital, and Max would find the weasels, his cousin and aunt. The time had come to settle things with his relations.

CHAPTER TWO

Giving Family the Business

"May, Hector!" Max bellowed as he went through the house, combing the halls for his quarry. With every shout, Max grew louder and angrier. Max burst onto his cousin and aunt as they hid in a small drawing room off the staterooms in a quieter part of the house.

"Found you," Max said. His temper was starting to control him.

"Yes, nephew," May squeaked as Max entered. Max slammed the door shut. The loud bang made the duo jump.

"Are you with me or against me," Max said. May's face was like a child caught stealing candy while Hector started laughing, like what Max said was a big joke.

"The question was simple: are you with me or against me," Max said. May just stared. She repeated, "But... but... but..."

Max looked from May to Hector, who just continued to laugh like an imbecile.

"If you are with me, I want your oath on the Fraser signet. No more complaints. No more deception. Or I will banish the both of you! I will drive you from the clan. If I go down, I will sow the fields of this estate with salt. You will never have a hope of inheriting. If you are not with me, I will ensure I am the last Fraser Earl of the Bonnie Dundee. Before they drag me away, I will burn down this house to its foundation," Max said. His throat hurt. He had yelled so loudly.

"But, Cormac and Meg..." May said, but Max cut off her statement.

"Will hand me the kerosene and matches," Max said. After realizing the severe situation, Hector stopped laughing and said, "Can he do that, Mother?"

"He's bluffing," May said, fortified by her son's question.

"Try me," Max said, a deadly coldness in his eyes, "A ship has only one captain. A unit has only one commander. This county will have only one earl. If you think you can do a better job, Hector, petition the clan. I doubt they will reverse their recent decision to install me. Or, perhaps you and your mother can return to the *Bundstadt* and beg the protector for the title. With the war, I doubt he'd choose Hector over me, a veteran. Every press in the Sheeplands would be screaming about the injustice of one who did not serve being installed over a decorated war hero."

"He can't burn down the house, can he?" Hector asked, returning to Max's previous comment. May just looked worn and old. Max was tired of the duo's fantasy. The estate was about to go under, and he needed all hands to keep the old ship afloat.

"I have your answer then. I will begin the banishment process," Max said, attempting to goad the two schemers to react somehow.

"Max, we can't go back," May said, breaking down in tears, "We didn't sell the house. We lost ownership."

"I won't let you burn my birthright," Hector said, turning red and standing up. Max admired Hector's sudden willingness to fight, but if things came to blows, Max was confident he'd win.

"Hector, sit down and be quiet!" May said, snapping at her son. Hector dropped back into his chair—like he was kicked. May's sharp comment made Max realize that May had never scolded Hector. Max's mind rewound events and went back to what May said.

"What do you mean 'lost the house?' The family's house?" Max said, "You received a generous stipend! You could have owned several fine homes in the capital! What happened, May?"

"Oh, Max, losing the house was entirely my fault. The stipend paid for our lifestyle for several years, but then I mortgaged the house to begin spending money I didn't have. After Kenneth kicked us out, I went crazy: hosting parties, getting box seats at the opera, entertaining the high and mighty. For all that mattered, Kenneth, ever the protective big brother, continually increased the monies he gave me, hoping..."

"Things would right themselves before the money ran out," Max said, finishing May's sentence. Max felt like he was finally unearthing how the estate became so impoverished. The books finally made sense. Max knew where the money went and why things had become so mismanaged.

"Yes," May said, "To make matters worse, there was a fire, and the house burned. Not so badly we couldn't live there, just badly enough that the house started to crumble. After several years, the city authorities lost patience with me and condemned the house. By then, Archy was gone, and Kenneth was ill. So, we returned, beggars with nowhere to go. Please, please, sweet boy, you must not throw us out," May said, tears beginning to slip from the corners of her eyes.

"You never told me they condemned the house, Mother," Hector said, looking at his mother in shock.

"How could I? You were absorbed in the gentleman's life. I had hoped to find you a nice débutante with money as a match. We could have rebuilt the house and our lives. Alas! I could never make that happen, my dearest boy," May said to her son. Max felt terrible. He had been so angry at the deceit that he never suspected that May and Hector had their share of troubles. Now, Max needed to heal the wounds. He had a thought. He hoped his idea would reverse the situation.

"Listen," Max said. He tempered his words. He needed to be stern but just. He needed to be their chieftain now. "You two may live here indefinitely under these conditions. First, you may not complain to the protector, the Parliament, *or even the flower shop girl* about the county, the earl, or the estate. If I shackle you to the floor of the wine cellar, you'll bear that as your lot in life. The complaints you've sent to the Parliament have caused me enough trouble. In return for your cooperation, I promise not to shackle you to the cellar floor.

"Second, you both must work. I will ensure the work is within your abilities, but I cannot afford freeloaders! The estate has no money, even less for idle hands. With your work at the gathering, you've shown you can manage events here at the estate. We'll discuss how to further your talents.

"Third, Hector, you must take the pledge. Your drinking has cost this family and your character too much. I can only compel you, so you must pledge to God. If you break your pledge and sneak a drink, you will stain your immortal soul and suffer for eternity.

"Fourth, I cannot afford a lavish aristocratic lifestyle, and as you are both now my wards, you cannot afford one either. No more wild parties, fine clothing, exotic foods, flowers, gifts, or treats!" Max said, finishing his terms.

"I accept and thank you, dear boy," May said, falling from her chair on her knees. Max's anger flashed, and he said, "May, I am no longer a boy. I am your earl. You have my leave to call me Max or his grace, but from now on, I am your liege."

"I'm sorry, your grace," she said. She crawled forward on her knees, head bowed. At that moment, Max pitied her and raised her to her feet. He hugged her. Max then turned to Hector, who hadn't budged from his chair. He was in shock.

"Well, Hector, what is your answer," Max demanded. Max wondered if Hector could ever find his way to manhood or if he would forever remain a boy in a man's body.

"Match me," Hector said, steel in his voice, standing.

"With whom, Hector? Who would have you as you are today," Max asked.

"A minor noble," Hector said, "What about Cairnbahan? She's a baroness. I could marry her." Max knew that even if Isobel were the last woman in the Union, she would never consent to a match with Hector.

"What makes you think she, or her family, would accept the match?" Max said, "A match only happens when the families agree."

"Doesn't matter, you are her liege. Order her to marry me," Hector said insolently.

"You toad," Max said, "You would dare to suggest that I force Isobel to marry you because she *caught your fancy*? You would make me a tyrant to her people so you can play at being a husband?"

Max realized no matter his recent misgivings about Isobel, he felt something substantial for her. His feelings would need to be sorted out later. Max set his mind to the here and now.

"Big talker, earl," Hector said sullenly.

"I see. You choose banishment then. You have twenty-four hours to leave the county," Max said. Hector looked in shock at Max and then May.

"He can't do that, can he mother?" Hector said in disbelief.

"Yes, he can, Hector," May said, "you've made your bed, and now you must live with your choice."

Hector began crying. He knelt at Max's feet and blubbered, "Don't abandon me! My liege, forgive me!"

Max wasn't made of stone. He just wanted peace. Max let Hector cry momentarily, then said, "You must swear to follow me without reservation. My word shall be your law, my command your utmost duty."

"I shall, I shall!" Hector said, tears running down his face.

"Very well, you may rise, my kinsman," Max said, "If you are unwavering in your duty, I solemnly promise to hire a matchmaker of you and your mother's choosing to find a bride who meets your specification. If you choose a woman of means, you will be established with her, and we will only be kinsmen after that. Do you agree?"

"Yes, yes," Hector said. Max had won, and both Hector and May were beaten. However, the win was Pyrrhic. If Max hired a professional matchmaker who could match Hector to a woman he desired, the cost would be astronomical. Max pushed that thought aside, as he was sincere in his offer. May and Hector would no longer be his concern. A matchmaker that could produce such a match—the cost might be worthwhile.

Hector spat on his palm and offered the hand to Max. The gesture was the old way the Sheeplands menfolk sealed a bargain. Max spat on his hand and grasped Hector's hand. Both men shook hands, and Hector said, "Your word is my command, my liege."

"If you break our bond, I will not hesitate to banish the both of you," Max said, "Now, sit. We have much to discuss now that we've settled family business."

May and Hector sat. Max produced a handkerchief and wiped his hand, neatly folding the cloth and presenting a clean, dry square to May. May took the handkerchief and dried her tears. Hector used his handkerchief to wipe his hand and dry his face.

"May, your excellent work with the gathering and the masquerade ball makes me believe we should open parts of the Bonnie Dundee to the public. The house, with all the history and grandeur, would be a splendid place to hold events. I have heard of other stately homes where a line of burghers would queue to pay a fair sum to escort their daughters down the aisle for a wedding. This style of event planning is your forte," Max said. May's face showed her reaction: absolute repugnance.

"Common folk here, in the house and chapel?" May said.

"Aye, we'd get the local carpenters to install several barrier doors to separate the family section from the public section," Max said, "Between Hector and Cormac, we can police the public area for any troublemakers."

"But all of those strange folks in our ancestral home?" May said with disbelief. Max remembered his recent conversation with Ewan. They would need to screen and carefully select their guests.

"No, we will choose who may visit. We will collect references, and the guests will pay handsomely for the privilege of being here," Max said. Max now had to work out how to separate Ewan's special guests from folk who wanted the house for events. A problem for the future, Max decided.

"I just came from discussing using the estate for hunting excursions with Ewan. We need to modernize drastically. The manor is huge, in desperate need of repair, and underutilized," Max said, "Renovations, well placed and planned, will aid our fortunes. As the estate's health improves, we can reclaim rooms for the family side of the house. We'll then move outsiders into guest cottages or consider financing a hotel in the village."

May still wasn't convinced, but Hector interrupted her further protests, "What about me, my chieftain? What will my duties be," he asked.

"Well," Max said, "What about you? What do you feel your skills are?"

"I could run the fishing expeditions, sir," Hector said. Max fought the urge to say 'No.' Hector had little patience for teaching and less for fishing.

"You can start by assisting Cormac on his trips. After he gives you his seal of approval, then you can run the trips. Cormac is the huntsman, and those trips are part of his portfolio. Requiring his approval to do so is fair, agreed?" Max said, masking his real fears behind the need to keep his chief retainer happy.

Hector smiled and said, "Cormac will pass me after a single trip,

I'm sure, sir."

Max was happy that May and Hector had given their word and were working in tandem with the earl, for now. Max had only one item from the auditor's list of complaints: Isobel's sheep concerns. With Hector and May's loyalty promised. Max seized the initiative and said, "Oh, one last item: you will write letters to the Parliament in both paper and electronic format to revoke your complaints. From now on, all complaints come to me. Are we clear?"

"Yes," May and Hector said.

"Good, get to work." Max watched his aunt and cousin leave. Max sat momentarily and reflected on all he had learned today about his father before heading to the library.

Max opened the roll-top desk and picked up one of the old estate tablets. He was tempted to pull up a retail site and order a new device, but he knew the cost was beyond his current means.

He looked at the messages in his communication queue. There was mail from Isobel near the top of the list. The subject said, 'Thank you for a lovely evening.' Max wanted to open the message but hesitated because of Isobel's complaint. Max sat and pondered her behavior. Isobel would spend one moment sharing her soul, and the next, she appeared to be the cause of fire and brimstone raining down on Max.

After last night, Max wanted the two of them to become something more than liege and vassal, but this morning, he was upset to discover she had submitted a complaint about the earl. Max wondered why she hadn't just retracted the complaint when Kenneth died. Max also pondered how Isobel could say in one breath that she didn't want to be married and then take his hand or share a blanket with him—all signs of a desire for courtship.

Also, Max wasn't sure if Isobel was ready for the lengthy courtship process. He wasn't sure he was up to it either. Courting took time and effort. He didn't necessarily have the energy for courting with the estate in such dire straits. Max decided not to open the message. Instead, he decided to get up from his desk and check what Meg and Cormac were doing.

131

CHAPTER THREE

Road to White Mountain

Max left the library and went down the stairs to the first floor of the grand corridor. He then exited from the cloakroom, heading out into the west garden. He was searching for Cormac or Meg.

In the mid-morning sun, the once beautiful gardens were an awful sight. In days past, the east and west gardens with their terraces were twin jewels, with working fountains and hedge mazes where not a leaf was out of place.

"Yet another chore, I need to hire a gardener," Max told himself. He followed the footpath until it became a dirt track and left the main lawn. Max noted the trail was heading up into the mountains. Max had no intention of leaving the estate, but his feet carried him onward.

Max kept thinking about Isobel's complaint to the Parliament. Cormac said the complaint was old. The complaint was referring to arguments between Isobel and his father. The more he pondered, the more the complaint's existence angered him. Max kept asking himself why Isobel hadn't retracted the complaint when Kenneth died. What was Isobel's angle?

"What exactly does she want?" Max said to himself. Max was sure that Cormac was right about her. He took the fork in the trail and climbed up the mountain track. His anger rose as he grew higher in the climb. The *Holstensonne* shone down on Max directly overhead, and he could see Eisenwald's edge just above the horizon. Max noticed the trail had dog-legged into a small glen with a small *shiel*, a mountain hut, on the ridge line. He pumped his legs towards the hut, attempting to excise his rage by burning calories. After a half hour of hiking, he approached the small *shiel*.

"Good afternoon, young man," an older Sheeplander said. The man sat near a small fire inside the hut, which Max could see through the open doorway.

"Good day... Is this your shiel, old man?" Max asked. Max knew he was making a poor start to a conversation, but the question was all he could muster. The hut would be a rental, and Max knew he was the landlord. The structure was on his land, after all.

"No, young man," the old man said, "the lord of this land owns this structure. This hut has stood here providing shelter for several scores of years. No one claims this small house as their own, yet all rest under the roof."

"May I join you?" Max asked from outside the threshold.

"I cannot stop you. Only the earl can."

Max entered the two-meter by two-meter hut. A singular window allowed light to filter in. The hut was warm enough and offered protection from rough weather.

"Are you a sheep herder?" Max asked.

"Aye," the old man said as he gathered warmth in the shed.

"Do you work for the earl?"

"No, not directly, young man."

"Then whose sheep do you watch?"

"I am a Cairnbahan's man. The clan's flock has wandered off down the side of this mountain. I've been cold all day, so I am sitting here attempting to eat my supper in peace."

"Ah," Max said, unwilling to catch the hint, "how many in your flock?"

"Do you always ask so many questions, young man?" the old shepherd said crossly. He produced a bread crust and promptly bit a hunk off to reinforce his desire to be left alone.

"I'm sorry, I only wanted some conversation."

Clearing his mouth, the old man spoke, "I don't make a habit of speaking with strangers."

"Oh right, I'm Max."

Max extended his hand to the old man, who merely looked at the offering. After a moment, the old man said, "I'm Ken. I'm called Ken, the Watcher, by my clan."

Max looked Ken over. He sat cross-legged on the floor in an old plaid and a worn wool sweater. He wore no shoes, and his soles, like his old wrinkled face, were leathery. He sat eating his bread and sipping dark liquid in a small clear flask.

Max stood there for a while. The man finished his meal and said, "Where are you headed, young man?"

"I don't know."

"Aha! There is your problem. You'll never get there if you don't know where you are going. On that note, I say good day to you, Max."

Max watched as the old man left. His anger had propelled him up the mountain, yet he did not know where he was going. Max hadn't even changed clothes. He still wore the new suit and dress shoes he had worn to meet the auditor.

"Huh… I found a Zen master in a hole-ridden plaid," Max told himself. Max looked out of the door and saw the flock of sheep come up over the horizon. His heart beat faster as he expected Isobel to be with them. Instead, Ken the Watcher guarded the sheep.

"Don't stay too long, or the earl will charge you rent, young man," Ken said with a laugh to Max.

"I'd never get rich that way," Max said to himself. He then went out from where the sheep had come, his feet moving him towards the White Mountain of Cairnbahan.

Max wondered where his feet were taking him. The Assault had always given Max the direction he needed. Follow orders, keep your uniform and bunk neat, and lock your heels in a salute when reporting to your superiors.

Max didn't understand how to be an earl. His father never taught him. Kenneth felt that was Archy's destiny. Max was discovering that as an earl, everyone wanted something from him. Meg wanted her brother to be the dashing earl, giving her, the beautiful bride, away at her wedding. Then she'd choose a lady to be his new Countess. Max suspected Meg and his bride would spend their days chatting at high tea and tut-tutting their husbands.

Cormac wanted a strong earl who held all the traditions sacred. An earl who lived in a hunting lodge and had scores of guests over for hunting parties, fishing expeditions, and nature walks. Cormac wanted a green man earl that was one with the land.

May wanted the earl to rely on her, to have her as a temporary lady of the estate. May wanted a position where she could hold balls, pull strings, and find a good match for her son.

Hector wanted the earl to materialize a rich, good-looking wife whom Hector could drink to forget. Hector's earl would entrust every confidence to the lout, forgiving Hector when he ultimately failed in his vassal's duty.

What family wanted was one matter, but what did Max want? Cairnbahan, the White Mountain, came into Max's view on cue. The geography was striking. The mountain had a white-capped peak and a small village on its southern escarpment. Even as far away as Max was, he could see the sheep covering the mountain. Max was so entranced by the view that he didn't notice the sunny day had turned cloudy until the sky opened on him.

Driven by the cold rain, Max hurried to descend the rough track. The rain soaked through his new clothes, but he couldn't do anything but keep moving. After a half hour of hiking, Max came to a gravel trail. After a few more minutes, the gravel turned into asphalt. Once Max was on the asphalt, his pace quickened, and soon he was on Cairnbahan's outskirts.

"Got caught in the rain, eh, mister?" a ten-year-old girl said. The girl wore a white blouse over a sleeveless tartan dress that bore the coat of arms of the local school. She had light brown hair and bright blue eyes. Max looked at the ingénue and judged he could ask her for directions.

"Aye, lass," Max said, "Is there a pub around here where I can dry off?"

"Come with me," the girl said, leading Max. Max wasn't sure what spectacle he made, walking hand in hand with the young girl. Nevertheless, the two went up a street and made a right down another, unmolested. Together, they approached a small cottage where a woman, who looked ten years older than Max, sat on a covered porch of a small house. The woman had straw blond hair and the same bright blue eyes as the girl. She wore a tight black wool sweater and the Douglas plaid on her long skirt.

"Jennie, who do you have here?" the woman asked.

"Mummy, this man is all wet," Jennie said, "I brought him to you so you can help him."

"Hello, I'm Max," he said.

"Jennie, you know what I've told you about strangers," the mother told her daughter. Then, to Max, she said, "Hello, I'm Matilda, please come in."

Max stepped into the cottage's front room. The house was small and tidy. He could see the kettle was on in the small kitchen.

"I'm sorry to intrude. I suppose your husband will be home soon," Max said, feeling like a stranger as he entered the house.

"No, he won't," Matilda said, "he passed away two years ago."

"I'm sorry," Max said with a pause. He then said, "If you don't mind me asking, how did he die?"

"He was killed in action. He was a daring Assaultman, a member of the line—not a volunteer. He took a Terran slug on an asteroid near Protelan," Matilda said, her blue eyes unfocused as she recalled her memories of her husband.

"What was his name," Max asked. He felt he should honor his fellow Assaultman in some small fashion, though he suspected he wouldn't know the man.

"James Douglas, Staff Sergeant in the First Sheeplands Grenadier Regiment, 'the Douglas Own,'" Matilda said. Max knew the regiment. They had fought together, though kilometers apart, on Nakdong. Max had never met the man, though.

"Was he related to the baroness?" Max asked.

Matilda smiled sadly and said, "Aye, we all are, some distant, others close. James was her half-brother."

Max had never thought to ask Isobel about her family. The information reinforced to Max that he barely knew Isobel.

Matilda smiled again, producing a hand towel for Max, and asked, "Did you serve?"

"Aye, I was a sergeant in the First Stahlburgh Rifle Regiment. We are informally called 'The Sons of the Protector.' I signed up where my mother's people came from, a village called Normandy-ober-Donau," Max said.

"That's in the Valley of the First Farmers, right?" Matilda said. In response to Max's nod, Matilda said, "I always got 'P's' in geography in school."

The widow was showing off, saying she got a 'P' for 'Perfect.'

"Well, thanks for the towel. I see the rain has slowed," Max said, breaking the silence.

"You are welcome to a cup of tea," Matilda said as the kettle whistled.

"Thanks," Max said, "but I've got to keep moving. I'm off to the big house."

"Business with the baroness, I'd imagine," Matilda said, "Folks say she's the most eligible catch in the Sheeplands... that is if you listen to such gossip."

His curiosity piqued, and Max said, "Well, the rain is still heavy. I can probably wait a moment and join you for a cup."

"Jennie dear, fetch the *Freiherr von Huegel*. I'll get the pot and cups," Matilda said to her daughter. The daughter, who was in a room over, pretending to read—jumped up and ran to the kitchen. Jennie rifled through the tea cupboard. Max watched as the young girl unearthed the fancy tea tin from where it was buried at the bottom of the cupboard. During her search, the girl had discarded other less costly teas on the floor. Retrieving the prize, Jennie hastily pushed all the boxes back into the cupboard and slammed the door shut. Matilda rolled her eyes at Max over her daughter's actions.

Matilda placed fancy tea cups for Jennie, Max, and herself on the small table beside the cookstove. She then brought out a pot from a tiny recess near the stove. With the teapot, she carried a little ornate milk pitcher and a small basket with three tea balls. Matilda opened the tea ball for Max, and, for his part, Max tried to be sparing with the tea. He knew *Freiherr von Huegel* tea was costly for a poor widow with a daughter. Military pensions went only so far, even with the protector's generous wartime guarantees.

"Take as much as you'd like, dear," Matilda said, noticing Max's reluctance.

"I would hate to rob you of your best tea," Max said.

Jennie laughed and said, "Don't worry, mummy never drinks this unless we have company."

"Silence, you little rascal," Matilda said playfully to her daughter, then to Max, she asked, "Milk?"

"No, thank you," Max said.

Matilda stared blankly into space as she hovered with the kettle. Caught up in memory, she said, "After he enlisted, my Jamie drank his tea straight, said he learned that way in the Assault. He laughed and said that where he'd be on duty, there wasn't always a cow handy for some cream."

Max felt uncomfortable at triggering such pain in the widow. Max reconsidered his first impression of Matilda's age as he studied her. Her husband's death had prematurely aged her. Max wondered if she was considered beautiful in an earlier day, before her husband's death.

"You mentioned the baroness," Max said, searching for another topic of conversation.

"Aye, she's my fourth cousin, Isobel. The village all call her 'the catch of the Sheeplands,'" Matilda said with what sounded to Max like jealousy, "Isobel must have had at least seven men call on her in the last fortnight."

"Tell him about the ball, mummy?" Jennie asked.

"Och... you're becoming the little gossip," Matilda said teasingly to her daughter.

"What about the ball?" Max asked, curious as to what the commoners were saying.

Matilda continued, "Well, rumor is that she dumped the Baron of Breakin and cast her net for the earl himself, all on the same night as the masquerade ball."

Max had never realized how far or how fast the word would travel. He wanted to defend Isobel's behavior but didn't think he could. He worried the village would add him to the tally of "gentlemen calling on Isobel." Again, Max wished things could be more straightforward.

"Huh, the earl, eh?" Max said, trying to dismiss the topic. Unfortunately, Matilda didn't catch the hint.

"Aye, my cousin Betty was at the ball. Betty said the earl is a real dashing charmer and a bold Assaultman. Betty said he was tall with dark hair..." Matilda said, trailing off as recognition came to her.

"Your grace!" Matilda said, eyes going wide, "Forgive me, sir! I didn't intend to gossip!"

"No, no, I asked," Max said, attempting to calm the widow, "Thank you again for the tea. Now, I really must be off."

"Aye," Matilda said, "and if you find yourself again in Cairnbahan, please feel free to call on Jennie and me."

Max nodded, saying, "I shall. Thanks again for the tea."

As Max exited the house, he heard the two women inside screaming excitedly.

Max paused, listening as Matilda said, "Jennie! By the Allfather! That was the earl!"

Jennie, for her part, said, "Yes, mummy! He was nice!"

Max smiled. For all the widow's pain, he had given her a small bright spot in her day—by his presence. He walked through the mist, determined to find the answers to his questions, no matter where things led.

Max followed the track, as all the Cairnbahan trails seemed to lead to the big house. After walking for a few minutes, the large great house of the Douglas rose before him. If he wanted to carve out a future with Isobel, now was the time for Max to discover precisely who the baroness was. Max thought, *would the real Isobel please stand up?*

CHAPTER FOUR

A Drive with a Friend

Max walked right up to the main door of Douglas Hall. Isobel's family home was in much better condition than the Bonnie Dundee. The gardens were neatly managed. Max could see no mold or rust on the ironwork that ringed the gardens. He placed his hand on the door, preparing to knock, and then realized he didn't know what to say or do to gain entry.

"Hi, I'm the earl..." Max practiced to himself, "No..."

"Hi, is Isobel home?" Max said, trying again, "No..."

"Baa!" a sheep said as a flock appeared. Ken the Watcher appeared with the rest of the sheep.

"I see you've found your way," Ken said, "to my niece's door, no less. I can't say you are the only lad who has done so..."

"Ken? Wait, you're Kensie," Max said with a sudden recognition.

"Aye, Kensie Eachan-Khan Douglas. This would be my fine house if I had been born two minutes earlier. Now, how can I help you, young man?"

"I'm here for Isobel," Max said.

"Ah, the direct way. I must warn you that if you intend to take her by force, you are missing your Claymore," Kensie said, "Of course, these days, you'd be better off with a pin rifle. Our village may be upset at a young bravo running off with their baroness—she is well-liked here."

Max blushed at such a bold statement and said, "I meant, I am here to see her."

"Ah, just look?" Kensie said, "I suppose I can support that. The touching is what gets you youth in trouble these days."

Max stammered, "I mean... I suppose I am calling on her?"

"You don't sound certain about that," Kensie said, "are you sure you want to be here, young Max?"

Max took a breath and said a silent prayer to the Allfather that he wouldn't kill Kensie. Then, he decided to restart the conversation and play the proper gentleman.

"Kensie, I, Maximilian *Graf* Fraser, am here to ask your permission to call on your niece, Isobel Douglas, Baroness of Cairnbahan."

Max waited. Time stood still as Max anticipated what Kensie would say. Kensie screwed up his face like he was constipated. Max felt like his heart had stopped. Max was sure Kensie would say no.

"Sure, why not," Kensie said, his features relaxing. The response was unexpected, and Max desperately wanted to ask Kensie to repeat himself.

"If you just press the buzzer," Kensie said, after a pause, "the staff will let you into the foyer. Isobel is a good woman but has been as lost and confused as you are, young Max. Please don't take anything she may say or do too seriously. After her father died, she has been trying to find her way. She wasn't supposed to be the baroness, after all. But that is a story she will have to tell you herself. Again, goodbye, young man."

Max felt his heart restart. Just like that, he had been permitted to see Isobel. Max wanted to feel like this was a victory, but he had too many questions for Isobel. He turned to knock on the door, but Max's courage failed. Instead, he turned around, determined to hike back to the Bonnie Dundee. As he headed away from the house, a hovercar appeared and coasted into a parking spot near the house's broad lawn.

"Max, old chum, long time," Geordie said as he exited the fancy hovercar.

Max was momentarily stunned but said, "Geordie, what are you doing here?"

"Tea, old boy," Geordie said, "I came over for tea with Isobel. Would you care to join us? By the prophet! You look dreadful and wet."

Max weighed several different responses and finally settled on the truth. "I was in the area on business, and I was caught in the rain. I foolishly left my umbrella at the house."

"Let's see if you can borrow at least a shirt or sweater. Now let me inquire if we can enter the hall," Geordie said. Max bitterly wanted to tell his friend why he was visiting Isobel. But after all that had happened that morning, he wasn't nearly as confident about Isobel as last night.

Geordie gently tapped the door with the ornate knocker, and an old housekeeper opened it. "May I help you, young men? You both have been standing on her excellency's front lawn like this was a cattle day in the village," the housekeeper said.

"Hello, Madam," Geordie said, "We are here for tea with Isobel."

"Her excellency is not seeing any gentlemen today. She is suffering from a headache," the housekeeper said. The old woman was of hardy Stahlburgh stock, in other words—*a battle-axe*—and woe to those who would say that to the housekeeper's face.

"Would you please tell her excellency that Baron Breakin and the Earl of the Bonnie Dundee have called," Geordie said. The matronly housekeeper scowled at him.

Max watched as the housekeeper merely shut the door on Geordie's face. Geordie, for his part, shrugged. Max turned and was about to start his trek back when Geordie said, "Tell you what, old chap, let me give you a ride back. You're soaked to the bone, and there's no sense in you catching a cold for a fool's errand." Max smiled, Geordie was Geordie.

"Sure," Max said. Both men walked to the hovercar. Geordie entered the driver's compartment, and Max climbed into the passenger's side.

"Wow, she's a beauty, Geordie," Max said, appraising the vehicle.

"You like her?" Geordie asked, "She's brand new. I got tired of the previous car I had. This one is straight off the floor. A *Campbell's Carriage*—why Alasdair Campbell himself fulfilled my order. Not a bad chap, for my liege's liege."

Max grinned. He couldn't tell whether Geordie was being truthful. The dash lit up as Geordie turned the ignition, and the fans whirred to life. The hover blades were as silent as a gentle breeze. Geordie backed the car up, performed a K-turn, and coasted to the village's main roadway. Max wondered what he should say. Should he tell his friend his intentions with Isobel?

Geordie broke the silence and said, "I've been a fool, Max. Isobel has rejected my latest proposal. This makes strike three. I won't ask her again. I have my pride, you know."

"Oh really," was all Max could muster.

"I heard about you and she and the ball, then the gathering..." Geordie said, and Max attempted to cut him off, but Geordie continued, "No, no, you should know the whole story. You are about to put your head into the dragon's mouth, and I hope you shan't have your skull bitten off."

Max kept silent. He wished to do no offense to Geordie, and silence was the safest path.

"We grew up, always together, those many years ago. I can't say I ever loved Isobel, but I can't say I didn't either. Our mothers were close friends. Isobel's mother, Madelyn, was James's—Isobel's father's—second wife. James's first wife was a woman named Annis. Annis and James had his son and heir, also named James. We all called him Jamie. If this all sounds circuitous, but this background will help you understand where I stood with Isobel."

"Go on, Geordie," Max said.

"Madelyn married James after Annis left him. As you are well aware, religiously, divorce isn't allowed. James and Madelyn's marriage was quite scandalous, and Isobel grew up with all this shame in her immediate family. To escape the turbulent great house, she visited my manor quite frequently. My mother was delighted, as she could only see us as a future married couple. Isobel was, and I believe still is, *my friend*. I went away to school and then the Assault. Once in the Assault, I earned my commission rapidly. You know how that works," Geordie said.

"Aye," Max said, "When we were done with our mission on Nakdong, according to my lieutenant, I was headed for the Academy at Stoneglen. You know how those promises go during wartime."

"Understood and good show. To continue, I was an officer, and the war came upon us. Only then, the conflict was just a border skirmish. It was one of the many that the old protector would use to bleed off resentment against the Terrans. Well, the resentment boiled up, and my unit was off to Asimov. I've told you that part, but what I didn't tell you was what happened when I thought I was on my deathbed. I called out for her... for Isobel."

"There is no shame in that, Geordie. I was wounded once, nothing even to make an award for, but as I went under—the medic gave me a nice anesthetic to dull the pain—well, I called out for my mother. At the time, she'd been dead for almost fifteen years," Max said, "The old salts told me that all wounded men cry for the woman who made a difference in their lives."

"I hadn't realized, and thanks for sharing, Max," Geordie said. His demeanor was radically different. Instead of being a rough-and-tumble playboy or cartoonish squire, Geordie was quiet and reflective. Max watched as Geordie drove down the highway and estimated the trip's length. They were taking the road around the mountain. They would be together for a while.

"So Isobel," Max said, urging Geordie to continue.

"I wrote to her when I was in the Union veteran's hospital, begged her to come to me... She never did. When the doctors released me and I was well enough to travel, I returned to the county. Went straight to her door, like today. I bowed down to her, for I was so injured I couldn't kneel, and asked her to marry me.

"She turned me down. I suspected that she considered me damaged. Nevertheless, I healed and vowed to forget her. Perhaps brazenly, I traveled to sow my wild oats across the galaxy. Like a pilgrim, I traveled to all the most extravagant flesh pots known to humanity. I witnessed horrors I cover with jests—stories I've cleaned up. My jests are children's tales compared to what I saw. I came back from Eridani, after a particular atrocity, a changed man," Geordie said. Max felt like a priest in a confessional.

"Wow, I never guessed..." Max began.

"No one knows but you, Max. I ran to her, my friend. I knocked on her door and begged her, again, to marry me. She was older, her brother and father were gone. She was the baroness while I was still my father's heir. She flatly told me, 'No.' I told her I would swear off my inheritance and be her consort. She still told me 'No.' I left again broken-hearted."

"I'm sorry, Geordie," Max said.

"Wait, wait, hold your pity for one moment. I must get this out," Geordie said, tears in his eyes, "I called on her each fortnight, just as friends. I knew I was losing her as if I ever had her heart from the start. I tried one last time at the ball just a few days ago. Unsurprisingly, she rejected me again. Max, my clan wants me to marry. They all tire of the innuendo surrounding my reputation. They want a proper baron, and a proper baron has a wife."

"I see," Max said, "what are you going to do?"

"I have some options. One of my fellows from my Assault days has a sister. A delightful, kind, gracious woman who visited me—often —when I was in hospital. I contacted her to ask her how life was treating her. She responded that her husband had died on Nakdong. She sounded quite alone. With Isobel now in my past, I intend to call on my widow friend and see what might happen," Geordie said. He changed lanes and set the hover car to autopilot. He then turned his chair to face Max, and Max turned his seat to face Geordie.

"I wanted you to know all this because tongues have been wagging about you, Isobel, me, and any other man close to the baroness. I don't know if I should congratulate, warn, or curse you. I suspect that Isobel has set her sights on you. The more I talk about her, the more I feel I've never really known her," Geordie said. The hovercar notified the men there were fifteen minutes left on their travel time.

"I don't know where things are going, to be honest," Max said, "She levied a complaint against me to the Parliament."

Geordie frowned and said, "I don't think so, old chap. I remember Isobel agonizing over the letter when she sent her complaint. She was very angry with Kenneth. He was unkind to her, most unkind. The letter went unanswered, and we all forgot about the complaint. If you hesitate about Isobel because of the complaint, I would tell you that you are being rash. Do yourself and Isobel a favor and let that go. The complaint was intended for Kenneth, not you."

"I suppose I am just not sure what Isobel wants," Max said.

Geordie laughed and said, "Join the club, old chap, but don't fold up shop before the market. Give her at least one chance to reject you. I say this as someone who has given her three."

The car slowed as it neared the destination. Max and Geordie returned their seats to a forward-facing position. Max still wasn't sure what to do, but the words exchanged between him and Geordie had made things better.

"Best of luck with the widow," Max said, hopping out of the hovercar when they reached the Bonnie Dundee.

"I'm making plans to leave in a few weeks for a visit. When I am away, my seneschal will have the reins in Breakin. He is a good, trustworthy man, and, of course, Helen will be near if you're looking for some punishment," Geordie said with a devilish smile.

"Cheers," Max said and closed the hatch. He turned around and entered the Bonnie Dundee. A shower, fresh clothes, and some whisky awaited him. Isobel would be a puzzle for another day.

CHAPTER FIVE

Library and Poachers

Max woke late in the day. He hadn't spent the night nursing a broken heart. Well, that's what he told himself. He sat in the library, working through the books and planning for the future. Love was something that could wait. That's another thing he told himself. He buried himself in work and was startled by a knock on the library doors. Max got up and went to open the door. Behind the door was Isobel.

"Hi, Max," she said. She wore a hiking skirt, boots, and a thick wool sweater with a Douglas tartan kerchief holding her blond hair in place.

"Hello, come in," Max said, opening the door to permit Isobel to enter.

"I am sorry I missed you yesterday," Isobel said, stepping into the library.

"Oh, no worries," Max said coolly.

"Did I do something wrong?" Isobel asked directly.

"Look, I've received your complaint from the auditor. I'm disappointed and hurt. My door is open if you have something to say."

Isobel looked shocked at this statement, like a deer in the headlights.

"Max, I never..." she said, her hands over her face as if to hide from Max, "I was so stupid, that complaint. Oh, me and my rash stupidity! I would never have sent that stupid letter if I knew the

Parliament would act on the complaint against *you*. Now, I've ruined things between us before we could begin."

Max's hurt subsided, but he wasn't sure about Isobel. He stubbornly sat and didn't utter a word.

"Max," Isobel said, tears welling in her eyes, "I made that complaint years ago against your father. I opened a can of worms that was so awful I didn't travel a kilometer outside Douglas Hall. I'm sorry that my past rash and reckless behavior has come back to hurt you. I would never intentionally hurt you."

After a quiet moment, he realized he wasn't angry with Isobel. Her explanation was a balm for Max's sore heart. For all the trouble that had been wrought, Max realized he was smitten with the baroness. He stood and kissed Isobel passionately. He put his hands on her waist, and she put her hands on his shoulders. They continued the deep kiss.

They kissed for a few more moments before Max stopped. They both were breathing heavily. Max said, "Let's let bygones be bygones and start over."

Isobel nodded.

Max stepped away from her and said, "Hi, I'm Max. I'm new to being an earl and am pleased to meet you."

Isobel smiled and said, "Hi Max, I'm Isobel. I can be an impetuous baroness who would rather care too much than too little. I heard my uncle say he was fine with you calling on me, so maybe I can give you a tour of Cairnbahan and buy you a coffee for your troubles?"

"You heard Kensie?" Max said.

"Aye," she said.

"Wait a second, you're buying me a coffee. Shouldn't I be buying you the coffee? You're giving the tour, after all," Max said.

"Sure, why? Can a girl not buy a boy a cup of coffee?" Isobel said, with a look of mischief to Max.

"I'll have to consult the Fraser clan handbook," Max said. Grabbing a random book from a library shelf, he opened the book to a random page. "Yes, except if she's a Douglas, then she has to buy two coffees for the boy!"

Isobel smiled and said, "Sure, that's fair."

"How do I get my tour? Can I take the tour today?" Max asked.

"Let me check my schedule," Isobel said with a wink, "Well, it looks like I am free. Now, let's hold hands. We can walk over to the village."

"That's a long walk. I just took that trail yesterday," Max said.

"No, silly, the long walk is the mountain trail. There's a quicker way around the loch. I'll show you," Isobel said. She and Max left the library, went down the library stairs, and out the cloakroom door. They started down the loch trail, but Isobel turned onto a small track that led back to the village of Cairnbahan. The couple regained their equilibrium as they walked, leaving the past behind.

"Tell me about your family," Max said. Since they had started over, Max was determined to ask all the right questions, doubly so since he was now permitted to get to know Isobel.

"Well, there was my father, James. My mother's name was Madelyn. She was a Ross from Inverkelly. I had an older half-brother, James, from my father's first marriage. He died."

"In service to the Union, yes," Max said respectfully.

Isobel looked at Max, wondering, "How did you know that?"

Max smiled and said, "An earl has to keep an eye on his vassals."

Before Isobel could inquire further, the couple reached the village outskirts. There, Jennie and some other girls appeared. Jennie said, "There he is, the earl! The earl!"

Max gave them a wave made for a parade and said, "Good day, ladies."

"And he is holding hands with the baroness," one of the young girls said.

"Oh!" they all said in unison.

"Are you going to get married?" one of the girls asked.

Isobel smiled at Max, "Your populace demands an answer, your grace."

"I'm only calling on Baroness Douglas," Max said, being honest yet sidestepping that conversation, "We have a long time before we need to decide that."

"Oh!" the girls said.

"Okay, enough fun," Isobel said, "Go on, or I'll tell every one of your mothers that you are all little washerwomen!" The girls giggled and ran off towards the village.

Max turned to Isobel to say something. Before he could speak, she kissed him. Max again wasn't sure if things were moving too fast or too slowly.

"You are a truly gentle man," Isobel said after breaking the lip lock, "You didn't have to humor the girls, but I like your style. Your answer was perfect."

"Listen," Max said as Isobel stared thoughtfully at Max, "I need to know where things are going. I am a little off balance here."

"What do you mean?" Isobel asked, her face showing some apprehension.

"Isobel, you are fantastic..." Max said.

"But..." Isobel said, interrupting.

"Look, you said you didn't want to get married at the games," Max said, "I am torn between being proper and what my heart tells me to do. If I am being proper, kissing doesn't occur before the sixth visit."

"And?" Isobel said, her eyebrow rising in a questioning way.

"My heart just wants to do whatever makes you happy," Max said. Max felt the tension go. He'd put all his chips down for the bet. Now, he needed to see how the cards would play out.

Isobel took Max's hands in hers, gave him a broad smile, and said,

"Oh, Max, you took what I said all wrong! I said I didn't want to be pressured, not that I didn't want to be married."

"I don't know, the village talks about how you are a catch. Geordie and other men have pursued you. I am unsure of what you want, and I feel like I need to know," Max said. Was he just another date? Or was there something genuinely worthwhile in their courting?

Isobel laughed and said, "Many men have turned up at my door, vowing love and undying devotion, but not one of those men ever sent me flowers. Geordie couldn't stay put when he was younger and talks incessantly of his conquests but then grovels at my feet, begging me to marry him. I've known him for years, yet he's never listened to a word I've said. In a few hours together, I have felt more warmth from you than any other man who has talked to me."

"Well, I sent you flowers because I had a good time with you," Max said, his cheeks burning in embarrassment.

"I'm glad, I had a good time with you," Isobel said, "and I find myself wanting more when I am away from you."

Max leaned in for a kiss, which he and Isobel gladly shared. She pushed him away after a moment and said, "Come on, I'll show you all the things I like about Cairnbahan."

Isobel pulled Max along the track. They walked along kilometers of trails, passing in and out of Cairnbahan, talking and being together. When the *Holstensonne* dipped down on the horizon, the couple parted. Max stole one last kiss before Isobel said goodnight and entered Douglas Hall. He walked back along the short track round the loch and quietly slipped into the Bonnie Dundee.

Max made his way to the kitchen, ecstatically happy. He had spent the afternoon with his now sweetheart, Isobel Douglas. He had official permission to call on Isobel, a privilege he would attempt to wear out in the next few days. All was good with the universe! Now, Max only had to wait. Max knew that if he and Isobel could keep the frequency and intensity of their relationship going, they could move from courtship to betrothal. The period of courtship, in the meantime, was supposed to establish whether the couple could handle engagement.

Max remembered there was an "appropriate" amount of time for each stage of their relationship. He could be in the courtship stage for two months to many years.

Max was also obligated to inform the clan that he intended to marry Isobel. And for her part, Isobel would have to let her clan know. The clans could say no, but if Max and Isobel's immediate family said yes, everything was proper, and they could marry. Clans seldom refused. Usually, they were happy for the couple.

The more Max contemplated the situation, the more he realized that only time separated him from Isobel and the altar.

"Where have you been, lad?" Cormac asked as Max entered the formal dining room intending to head through to the kitchen.

"I was in Cairnbahan," Max said.

"I heard as much. It seems Ken the Watcher gave you his permission to see Isobel," Cormac said gruffly. Max could feel the disapproval emanating from the huntsman. May and Hector appeared before Max could ask Cormac why he was so concerned about Isobel.

"Maximilian," May said, "Where have you been? I may only be your aunt, but I was quite concerned about your safety." Max wanted to be irritated with his aunt, but she was right.

"I apologize, Aunt May. I had business in Cairnbahan," Max said.

"I see," was all May said in response. Max attempted to leave to get a quick sandwich from the kitchen. He wasn't in the mood to deal with family or retainers after having such a lovely day with Isobel.

He stood and said, "Excuse me, but I've had a long day. I will see you all in the morning."

"Wait a moment, lad," Cormac said, "there is something we need to discuss."

A knowing glance passed between May and Cormac. Max braced himself. What had happened now?

"Poachers," was all Cormac said.

"I still can't believe that. We've never had poachers," May said, aghast at the thought of someone killing the estate's game without permission.

"What about that one year when I was starting school? You know there was a drought?" Meg asked, entering from the kitchen upon hearing the voices in the dining room.

"Aye, lass," Cormac said, "we did have poachers, but those poor souls needed food. We turned a blind eye back then. From what I saw today, these are dedicated raiders. They laid waste to a herd of deer and didn't even attempt to dress the carcasses." Meg, curiosity satisfied, left the dining room and went back to the drawing room, apple in hand.

Max's blood boiled. As poor as the estate was, he had committed to giving the local parish a generous annual gift. The endowment would run a soup kitchen. The poor would have an opportunity to get a free meal because of the funds Max donated, as was his duty.

As Cormac had said, when things were desperate, the earl would turn a blind eye to an older deer being culled by some poor herdsman or farmer. But raiders, folk who would decimate deer, trample crops, and cause chaos—all to prevent others from the bounty of the land —were not tolerated.

Max recalled the old tales when Stahlburgh lived under tribal law. The Sheeplands were full of raiders whom rival clans commissioned to run down their enemies's food stocks and raise prices. Thankfully, the Union ended the raids.

"What can we do?" Max said. For Max, fighting raiders, pirates, and other human animals was more familiar territory. For an Assaultman, every day's objective was to find the enemy, capture—

but more likely kill—the enemy, and then have a beer. Go to bed, rinse, and repeat the next day.

"We'll set up an ambush and either catch them in the act or put them in the ground," Cormac replied, "I'll take the first watch tonight."

"Go gather some of Donalbaan's folk. They are happy to deal with poachers. When the MacLeods are on patrol, poachers learn they are not welcome," Max said.

Cormac nodded, saying, "If we can contain this raiding, maybe we can stop the foolishness before things get out of hand."

Meg came running into the dining room screaming and in tears, "Oh Max!" she said, "Alasdair Campbell has been assassinated! He was attacked at the spaceport yesterday! The news just reported he is dead!"

The news physically hurt Max. While Max did not know Alasdair personally, he was Max's liege. For Max and others in the peerage, Alasdair wasn't just some far-off lord but a benefactor and a captain of industry, an industry vital for victory in the ongoing war.

"Say that again, please," Max asked. Max desperately wanted to believe he misheard his sister.

"He was at the Midlothian spaceport. Some terrorist group got him," Meg said. "The terrorists claim they are allied to a family in the Sheeplands."

"Blasted MacDonalds!" Hector said, speaking up in the silence.

Max was surprised that his cousin was wise enough to realize that the assassination and the raids had a mutual perpetrator.

"The raiders make sense now," Max said, "looks like things are destabilizing in the Union, and some have decided to revert to the 'old ways.'"

"I'll never get married now," Meg said, tears in her eyes.

"I'm sorry, sis, Loch Urquhart will probably be closed to us now," Max said.

If clans began fighting each other, Max knew that Andrew would have to support his liege and Max, his liege. Meg would be caught in the middle, and their wedding would be suspended at best or canceled at worst.

"Cormac, call the barons. We need to get a handle on this before things go sideways," Max said, "Meg, call Andrew and tell him I will grant him safe passage if he can assure me that he was not involved in the raiding."

"Aye, lad, I'll gather the council," Cormac said leaving.

"Okay, Max, I'll get a hold of Andrew," Meg said, dashing off.

"What can I do, my liege?" Hector asked. Max saw a ferocity and determination he hadn't expected from his cousin.

"Hector, I need you to secure the house, lock all the doors, and gather the rifles. The last thing I need is someone raiding inside the Bonnie Dundee."

"Aye, sir," Hector said, heading towards the manager's office, which held the estate's armory.

"And me, your grace?" May asked. The older woman was visibly shaken and seemed unsure of herself.

"May, I need you to send messages to the Campbells to see who Clan Campbell will support to take over for Alasdair and what they ask of us."

"Aye, be careful, your grace," she said as she left. Max sat down at the head of the table, contemplating his options. He wished that Isobel was with him now.

He also desperately wished his big brother Archibald was here. His elder brother always rode to Max's rescue. As he sat, gentle hands reached around his shoulders to hug him. Max looked up to see Isobel gently holding him.

"I am sure all will be made right. The protector cannot allow civil war," she said as she gripped him from behind. She leaned over the chair, and her chin rested on his shoulder. Max stood and took her in his arms.

"The protector is newly installed. The older families must be testing his resolve. There is an embargo with the Terrans, and many great clans have made significant profits from exports to Earth. Someone must have a grudge against the protector, as his faction pushed for the war," Isobel said.

"I wasn't thinking about that. I was thinking of my brother," Max said sadly, "Archy would have diffused the conflict immediately. They'd all be in the pub having a drink and laughing right now."

"No, Max, not even Archy could solve this one. The families have bottled up with decades of rage. They are ready to fight each other, and we must force the blockheads to fight the Terrans, our real enemies!"

"We are Felgenlanders! Not primitives," Andrew said as he stood at the edge of the formal dining room. The quiet man Max had known was suddenly gone, and his loud voice startled Isobel and Max, who quickly detached. Max turned, ready for anything.

"Andrew..." Max started not knowing what exactly to say.

"Max, you must listen to me," Andrew said, cutting Max short, "the elders of my clan stand in the great hall. We have decided to end this conflict, although these raids seem to have come from our respective lieges. Please follow me."

Max and Isobel glanced at each other before following Andrew into the great hall. There, six gray-haired Urquhart men stood in their Sheepland finery. They wore a black Prince Charlie jacket with full plaid in their clan tartan around their waist. Their ceremonial dirks gleamed in the light. Isobel saw the knives and stood protectively between Max and the men. She worried that, like in the olden days, the men assembled were prepared to ambush Max. As a Douglas, she knew her duty was to aid and protect her liege, even if she must be the sacrifice.

"Well, Andrew," Max said, "what is this all about?"

"Clan Urquhart has heard of MacDonald's heinous act. We do not know whether the MacDonalds will admit guilt for the Campbell's death. However, we clan Urquhart, believe that killing a peer and raiding his lands breaks all bonds of allegiance. Now, our clan stands at the mercy of all, as we are now without a benefactor to offer us a bulwark. Therefore, we look to our future in-laws and neighbors for protection and support," Andrew said. Max gently moved Isobel aside. He moved closer to the men, anticipating what was about to happen.

"To that end, we, the honorable Urquhart clan, have decided to come in supplication to the Fraser, our long-time neighbor with whom we have lived in peace. We come, prepared to bind ourselves in oath to the Fraser, with the Allfather's blessing. With the permission of our protector, the Fraser Earl will lead our clan in war and offer trade and support to Urquhart in peace," Andrew said. When Andrew finished, he and the old men drew their knives in salute and bowed to Max.

"By the Prophet!" Isobel said, in shock, "You've defected! This hasn't been done in decades, you beautiful crazy men!"

Max was silent and startled as Meg came running in, squealing like a banshee. She jumped into Andrew's arms, saying, "You brave man! I love you!"

Max and Isobel smiled, and Max said, "Uh, Meg, I still have yet to accept."

"Oh," Meg said, dismounting from Andrew's arms and standing still, waiting for her brother to say what needed to be said.

Max moved to the assembled men and took Andrew's hands. Max said, "Men of Clan Urquhart by the Allfather, our Union and the protector, I will defend you from all trouble and uphold your rights and privileges as they were in the days of our grandfathers—are now —and will be in the days of our sons."

Max looked past the Urquhart men and saw all his barons, even

Geordie, entering from the far end of the great hall. Meg's eyes welled with tears. The Urquhart men stood solemnly and proudly.

"Good show, old chap," Geordie said as the rest of the Fraser retainers gathered around Max and the Urquhart men.

"We'll see," Max said, "the protector may disapprove of this. However, if the Campbells and MacDonalds engage in all-out war, we will be an island of sanity inside an ocean of madness. Now, my vassals, greet your brothers and sister."

Isobel and the barons offered warm handshakes to the Urquhart men. Most of Max's baronies had land bordering Loch Urquhart. Max knew no one was a stranger, yet all greeted each other warmly. As the men conversed, Cormac entered, holding a youth by his collar. The boy looked to be thirteen or fourteen standard years old.

"Max," Cormac said, "I've got some information for you."

Max moved from the crowd. Isobel noted his movements and followed. They followed Cormac and his prisoner into the grand corridor and then the foyer. After Isobel had cleared the threshold between the foyer and the great hall, she shut the door behind her. Cormac eyed Isobel and then thought better of saying anything about her presence.

"I caught one of the raiders here," Cormac said, jerking the youth by his shirt collar, "he says his name is Finn, and he claims to be a liberator of what, boy?"

"Ha!" the boy said, his youthful voice cracking, "Piss off, jackboot of the taking class! I'm here to free the proletariat from your master's boot on their throat, pig-dog!"

"Great," Max said, "A militant Ultra-Violet."

"When the community takes over after the civil war we bring you, I will be your master, you bourgeoisie pig," the boy said.

"Do you even know what that means, lad?" Cormac said, a scowl on his face.

"Doesn't matter you... rich man's lackey!" the boy said, trying to come up with the right insult.

"Cormac, give the boy a meal, then lock him in one of the spare rooms for the night. In the morning, see him off," Max said.

"He says he is part of a coming revolution, lad," Cormac said, "He may be connected to those who tried to assassinate Heinrich von Machthaber, the protector's son and *Primus.*"

Max had barely remembered the incident as he was on guard duty several dozen light years away.

"Okay," Max said, "This changes things. I'm going to have to go to the *Bundstadt* in the morning. I need an audience with someone in the Parliament or even the protector himself. This Urquhart business needs to be settled quickly. With the entire Sheeplands gearing up for civil war, the last thing we need is militant Ultra-Violets poaching deer and more baronies defecting."

"Aye, you wouldn't want the protector to think you were poaching the Urquhart, then you'd be a poacher too," Cormac said, a wry smile on his face.

"I'm going with you," Isobel said. Cormac scowled, and the would-be terrorist hung his head in silence.

"Isobel, you can't, the propriety," Max said.

Isobel stepped in front of Max and said, "Max, if things get worse, propriety won't matter anyway. I want to come with you. I can help. I know the capital well."

Max debated what to say and settled on brutal honesty, "Isobel, I barely have the money to go, much less get another room for you to stay in. We've been calling on each other for less than eight hours. What would your family say?"

"Who? The village or Kensie?" Isobel asked.

"Well, both," Max said.

"Kensie would not dare to say anything. He knows how headstrong I am. The village, well, they are all gossips anyway, and my 'reputation' for changing paramours is well established now.

Frankly, I don't care what they think anyway. We Douglases have been swimming up the stream since we rode next to Robert the Bruce in old Scotland," she said, a proud smile on her face.

"Well, I guess I can't stop you then," Max said. He and Isobel then looked at Cormac.

"I'm not going to argue," Cormac said.

"Typical of the libertine and wasteful behavior of the bourgeoisie, when the revolution..." the boy said but was cut off by a sharp jerk from Cormac pulling him along.

"Yes... yes... revolution... new order, yes, yes, lad," Cormac said as he dragged his prisoner to the kitchen for food.

"I will see you tomorrow, say nine hundred," Max said to Isobel.

"Nope, I'm staying here. Otherwise, you'll leave without me in the morning," Isobel said as she nodded and crossed her arms in finality.

"Isobel, we are moving at light speed here," Max said.

"Look, I will stay in a separate bedroom. The barons can stay too. Heck, everyone can stay, for form's sake! Although, I like the idea I'm sleeping over a few days after meeting you," Isobel said with her mischievous grin.

"Cormac is right about you..." Max said.

"Look, propriety is nice, but even our beloved first protector abducted his spouse hours after meeting her, and my history may be fuzzy, but I don't even remember a marriage rite involving them in his autobiography," Isobel said in exasperation. Max attempted to get a word in edgewise, but Isobel continued.

"Max, yes, I like you, but I am staying close to my liege in a time of trouble so that Cairnbahan will have a voice in whatever happens next. But, if you shamelessly use my body in your hour of need, I doubt my clan, your vassals, or history will blame you. I am the catch of the Sheeplands," Isobel said, with a small laugh.

"I hope that's a joke," Max said. He wasn't sure if he was

scandalized or flattered.

"Oh, I have a lot more hair-brained schemes. Right now, I'm just warming up. Wait until we're engaged," Isobel said, batting her eyes at Max and trying to look innocent.

"Allfather, please ensure I survive until that happy day," Max said.

"Ha ha, you haven't run away screaming yet," Isobel said.

"I have run away. You keep chasing me," Max said, warming up to the sudden shift with Isobel.

"Of course! I am a Douglas. What would the Cairnbahan washerwomen say if I let you get away? I would never be able to walk through the village with my head held high again," Isobel said. Before the couple could banter further, Meg burst through the doors.

"Andrew's getting the priest. He's marrying me now!" Meg said ecstatically, "Okay, I honestly should be heartbroken as my dress isn't ready, my hair is a mess, and I should paint my nails and wear some makeup. But with all that's happened, Andrew and I need to start on the production of our little Urquhart heirs now. Better breed our army before those bastard MacDonalds come to squish every man, woman, and child who has betrayed them."

"Who is moving fast now?" Isobel said coquettishly at Max.

"Ladies, this isn't a competition," Max said to Isobel and Meg. Then, he shouted, "Clear the hall. We're cementing alliances!"

CHAPTER SIX

On the Train

Max tossed and turned in his bed. All night long, his dreams were filled with armed teenagers screaming, 'Death to the bourgeois!' He gave up on sleep and decided to get up. His mind was awake, but his body needed sleep. His sister had married Andrew, Max's newest vassal. Max hadn't gone to bed until the early morning hours. Max looked out of the window in his bedroom. The oversized silhouette of the *Cruach Mhòr* was just visible through the fog. He would leave today for the capital. Upon arriving, he had hated his inheritance, but now, the Bonnie Dundee was the most precious place in the universe.

Max slowly put his feet on the cold hardwood floor and stood up. He proceeded to shower, shave, pack, and dress for his long day. Max intended to have Cormac drive him to the train station, along with Isobel, who spent all last night hovering a meter away from him until he shooed her away to bed.

Isobel and Max would take a sleeper express from the station to Baldwinstown in Tauber-over-the-Roten. There, the couple would be in the Valley of the First Farmers and out of the Sheeplands. They would change trains and get on a bullet train to the *Bundstadt*. With luck, Max and Isobel would be in the capital by nightfall. If Max had the funds, he could have taken a spacecraft. However, a space trip would have been costly and required four hours of traveling out of the way.

Thankfully, Meg, Andrew, and Cormac could run the estate for the few days Max would be away. Max picked up his duffel and dropped the bag near the downstairs doors for Cormac to collect. He then went to the dining room for a quick breakfast. As he entered the dining room, he saw Isobel sitting at the table. She wore a traveling dress and boots, her golden hair bound by a fancy russet-colored ribbon.

"Good morning, sleepyhead," she said as Max sat down.

"Good morning, Isobel," Max said as he sat down and waited. He noted that Isobel was in the wrong place—she sat beside Max in his old spot, on the left, before he became the earl. She should have been seated in the chair to the right, at the head of the table with Max. Max considered saying something but figured there was nothing to say since they were just dating.

"You'll need to get food from the kitchen. The cook got married, remember?" Isobel said with a mischievous smile. Max made a goofy smile in return. He had forgotten that when he had given his sister away the night before, he had given away his cook and housekeeper. He stood and crossed into the kitchen. Cormac or some other kind soul had put a large pot on the stove. Max peered in to see oatmeal simmering. He took a ladle and spooned some into a bowl. He took a quick bite. The porridge wasn't bacon and eggs, but the food was better than Assault chow. Max then went back into the dining room and sat at his station.

"Are you packed and ready?" Max asked.

"Aye, Matilda brought me some things," Isobel said, still smiling, "She and Jennie send their greetings."

"You've found me out," Max said, his eyes lighting up. He then separated a massive mouthful of oatmeal from the rest in the bowl and shoved the mash into his mouth, effectively gagging himself while he chewed.

"What is your plan when we visit the Parliament? You should have an office in the Parliament. Perhaps we should go there first?" Isobel asked. Max chewed and then cleared his mouth.

"Yes, I should go there first. I am not sure what is happening in the capital and how much they know or care about the Sheeplands," Max said. He then took another oversized bite of oatmeal to finish the bowl as quickly as possible.

"Where are we staying?" Isobel asked.

"I've booked a suite at the Royal Hansaburgh," Max said, clearing the oatmeal from his mouth, "There will be separate beds."

"That's near Kocher Square, right?" Isobel asked, ignoring his statement about the beds.

"Yes," Max said. Looking at the fancy clock in the dining room, he said, "We've got to get going."

Cormac met the couple in front of a hover truck, which had been strategically parked by the manor's main entrance. Max and Isobel hopped into the cab while Cormac stowed their luggage in the bed. The trip to the station was quick and uneventful. Max noticed that there were more parties of hunters out than usual. Now, they hunted game that walked on two legs rather than four.

"Train is waiting," Cormac said, "have a good trip."

The huntsman was unhappy about Max going on the trip, but Max didn't have time to analyze his retainer's mind.

"Thanks, Cormac, we will," Max said.

"Goodbye, Cormac," Isobel said. She and Max left the truck, Max carrying their luggage. They entered the station and presented their ticket before getting on the train. The porter escorted them to the private car. As soon as the door was shut, Isobel kissed Max.

"I was worried the Urquhart men were going to assassinate you," she said, breaking the lip lock. In response, Max kissed her for a few more moments and gently moved her away. He took a seat, and she sat on a bench facing Max.

"I think I can take Andrew and a half dozen gray hairs," Max said with a smile.

"Look, I'm not going to lose you," Isobel said.

"Good, I tend to wander off," Max joked. Max realized that Isobel had infected him with her naughty ways.

"No, Max, I'm serious. I really like you," Isobel said, "I've lost my father, mother, and half-brother. I'm tired of loss. I know what I am saying sounds trite, but you are the first decent man who has called on me."

"I've not met many beautiful baronesses," Max said, "especially ones that are funny and have a good heart."

Isobel smiled. Unlike her usual mischievous smile, this one was genuine. Max saw he had touched Isobel's soul.

"Where do we go from here?" Max asked.

Isobel looked like she was debating with herself.

"So hypothetically, if I had a friend someone like you was calling on, I'd tell her to hang on tight to such a wonderful paramour."

"Well, hypothetically, if I had a friend dating a beautiful baroness, I'd tell him to marry her before she realized what she was getting into."

"Marriage, Max, wow, that's a large step. You think your friend could handle that?"

"Well, with the war coming home, he better make some hard choices. Otherwise, fate will make them for him. What about your friend? If she received a proposal, would she be able to live with such a large pain in the rear as my friend?"

"I don't know. Would they find some willing vicar? Or, would they find a monsignor or bishop and some large cathedral? Would she need to wear a large white dress? My friend isn't made of money, and she's lost her parents too," Isobel said.

"My friend isn't picky. He's got to present your friend before his clan. There'll probably be some caber tossing and hammer throws to go with that and some sore relations who got passed over for a second generation. Still, he'd marry your friend in a cathedral or in a simple ceremony in a small, out-of-the-way church. He tells me he's in love with your friend after all."

"Love, eh? They haven't known each other very long... Can someone love another so quickly, Max?"

"I think it's called 'love at first sight'."

"Okay, what now?" The train had started to depart the station.

Max stood and converted the bench seat into a bed. He flopped on the bed and said, "Now that we're moving, I can relax." Isobel glared at Max.

"What? I'm getting some sleep," he said. Isobel shook her head and lay next to him, snuggling under his arm and next to his chest.

"Mind if I join you?" she asked after moving into position.

"No. Honestly, I find your warmth quite pleasant. I may have to move my arm from under your head, though."

"Are you saying I have a fat head?" Isobel said with mock indignation.

"Something like that..." Max said as he started to fall asleep. Isobel chuckled but quieted after she heard Max's deep, even breathing. Soon, she, too, fell asleep.

The conductor awakened the couple when he rapped on the door. Max rose and fished out the paper tickets he had printed before the journey. The conductor checked the tickets, nodded, and continued to the next compartment. Isobel sat up from the bed as Max shut the door and flipped the lock. Max rifled through his duffel, pulled out his tablet, and checked the time. Hours had passed, and early evening had come.

"Max, I love you," Isobel said. Max looked up from his tablet.

"Wow, where is this coming from?" Max said, sitting back on the bench.

"I was trying out saying the words," Isobel said, "I need to be honest with myself and you."

Max thought momentarily and said, "I love you, too."

Isobel raised an eyebrow and asked, "How did that feel?"

"Pretty good," Max said, "I suppose I should be letting the clan know my intentions."

"On what?" Isobel asked she had a wry smile on her lips.

"Darling, I intend to make you missus earl," Max said, tapping away on the tablet. Isobel put her hand on the tablet and moved the device out of Max's eyesight.

"Let's sleep on that thought first. I haven't accepted," she said.

"Is there a possibility of a 'no,'" Max asked with some apprehension.

"Let's just say right now there is a strong maybe."

"Cormac is right. You're a complete handful!"

"He only says that because my youngest aunt, Margaret, rejected him. I look positively demure in comparison to her."

Max mulled that thought for a few minutes. Cormac had seemed to him like a force of nature or a manifestation of the land. Max remembered that Cormac had mentioned falling in love and that Margaret's rejection was not part of his story.

"Pfennig for your thoughts," Isobel said as Max sat silently.

"I didn't know," was all Max could say.

"I doubt he'd say anything to you. He looks on you as a surrogate son."

"Kenneth gave all of his love to Archy, and my mother died when I was so young that I barely knew her. Meg had me, and I had Cormac. I am still amazed that Meg and I are as well-adjusted as we are. Kenneth was never abusive. That would have required my father to pay attention to us."

Isobel sat next to Max and put her arms around him. After a moment, he put his arms around Isobel. After a few minutes of just sitting with each other, Max stirred.

"I'm getting into pajamas and crawling into bed here," Max said, standing up.

"I'll make up the other bunk and join you in wearing pajamas," Isobel said. Max opened a partition and moved into the changing cubicle. He stripped into his baggy pajama trousers and a loose tunic shirt. When he stepped out from the cubicle, he saw Isobel wearing a long silk nightgown. He closed the partitions, and the room returned to its previous configuration.

Max threw sheets onto the bench and crawled into his bed. Isobel pulled her bench out and put the sheets on the mattress. The benches had a small half-meter gap, and Isobel crawled into her side. The earl and his baroness were exhausted from the events of the past few days.

"Goodnight," Max said before drifting off to sleep.

"Goodnight," Isobel said. The train moved slowly through the evening, inevitably crashing into nightfall like fate, moving Max and Isobel toward the capital and their destiny.

When Max awoke, Isobel was nowhere to be seen. She had packed up her things and returned her bed to a bench. Her bag sat on the bench's edge. Max then noticed the small travel bathroom's fan whirring. The fan was drawing out the moisture from Isobel's morning shower.

Max stretched and went to clean up. He entered the diminutive washroom and closed the door. There was a note on the mirror. Max read the note in Isobel's writing, which said she had gone to breakfast and didn't want to disturb him. Max showered, shaved, and relieved himself. He then put on his best shirt and jacket, pairing the top half with his full plaid kilt, wool socks, and a nice set of dress boots. He checked his hair in the mirror and realized he needed a haircut. Max then decided on a black Tam o'Shanter with a speckled feather; the hat would cover his rough hair. He again checked his appearance in the mirror and decided he could match the description of Sheeplander lord.

The mirror began to move as Isobel entered. She wore a form-fitting black jacket and a tartan full-length skirt, occasionally showing her black boots. Her hair was neatly arranged, and she wore small silver hoop earrings.

"You look lovely," Max said.

"As do you," Isobel said. She looked nervous.

"Something the matter, Isobel?"

"About your question last night, Max."

"Yes?" Max said. Max's heart stopped. He had forgotten that he had, for all purposes, proposed to Isobel.

"I've decided we aren't moving fast enough, so my answer is 'yes'," she said.

Max fell to his knee and said, "I'll do this properly, Isobel. Will you marry me?"

"Let me think a moment," Isobel said with a grin and quickly responded, "Yes!" Max stood up and kissed her.

"I'll get a ring in the city. Best we set a date," he said, pulling out his tablet and tapping away at it.

"I'm glad I came with you. Otherwise, you'd have proposed to another girl," she said, "How does the eleventh of July sound?"

"Good, date—check. Now, you need a ring," Max said. Before Isobel could respond, the couple felt the train decelerate. The first half of the journey was over. The capital was their next destination.

CHAPTER SEVEN
Country to Capital

The bullet train was considerably faster than the sleeper train. Max and Isobel's journey to the capital was a blur. They sat together, holding hands for the entire trip. Max noticed that no one even looked twice at them. Max should have realized that outside of the Sheeplands, no one would even care. Sure, Max had been off-world, but never in the company of a pretty woman. He remembered talk of the burghers who had enlisted about how a city was a giant town where no one cared. Max never realized that people had trained themselves in a metropolis to care only about their own myopic concerns.

The train doors opened when the bullet train arrived at the newly built Douglas Ian MacAlasdair station. The station was brand new and a monument to the Union and the nation's ambitions. Max held Isobel's hand as they departed the train. They queued up at the exit with the rest of the people, some human, some not. Max kept a hand on his bag after he noticed Isobel doing the same. The trip wasn't Max's first time in a big city, but the journey was the first time he'd carried luggage there. After the couple pushed through the turnstiles at the exit, they were in the *Bundstadt,* the capital of the Union. Max looked off to the east, and in the distance, he could see the towering alabaster marble statue of Lena Kocher, humanity's liberator. Lena was important to all the people outside the Kuiper belt. But, to the Felgenlanders, she was essential as she was the current protector's great-great-grandmother.

"The city has changed, and yet the city hasn't," Isobel said, "We should get a taxi to the Parliament."

"I should go to the hotel first, yet I'd rather go to the Silver Road," Max said, referencing the district where the jewelry shops clustered.

"Work first, dear. Off to Parliament, we go," Isobel said, "The ring can wait as much as I yearn for that little precious band."

Isobel tapped her tablet. Moments later, a taxi pulled up to the curb.

"Pick up for the Parliament Building?" the cabbie asked, rolling down his window.

"Yes," Max said.

"I'll get your bags," the cabbie said with his Sud-Stahburghian accent. The man opened the driver's door, climbed out of the hover cab, and waited for the suitcases. He placed Max and Isobel's bags into the small side storage compartments and shut their door after the couple had entered the rear compartment. The cabbie then climbed into the driver's hatch and started his meter. He put the cab into drive and purposefully ignored his passengers.

Isobel sat next to Max, holding his hand. The look on her face was excitement and joy at being back in the *Bundstadt*. Max tried to concentrate on the city, but his eyes were drawn to the baroness. Max finally forced himself to turn and look out of his window.

What Max saw gave him pause. The city was alive with Assaultmen, Navy, and civilians. Posts and placards were everywhere with propaganda about the war and the victory effort. Max's eye was caught by a man wearing a sandwich board that said, "Terra delenda est!" Max smiled. He never underestimated his countrymen's deep appreciation and understanding of history. The cab then accelerated down the street and merged into *Unterhausstrasse* or Commons Street. In front of the cab was the enormous Cathedral of Saint Malcolm. The cathedral towered over the rest of the buildings, and the peak of the central bell tower must have been one hundred meters tall. Karl—the first Protector of the Union, built the structure almost a century ago. To the left and slightly behind the cathedral was the Protector's villa, while to the right and slightly behind the cathedral was the Parliament building. The cab made the right and entered the central circle of the city, the *Bundstrasse*, or Union Street. The cabbie maneuvered smoothly through traffic and halted beside the pedestrian barrier, despite the no parking signs.

"Three griffins, seventy pfennigs," the cabbie said, looking at the fare meter. Max pulled his wallet out of his sporran and paid the man. Upon receipt of payment, the cabbie opened the doors and let the couple out of the cab. Then he hopped out and presented Max with the suitcases. Max and Isobel stepped past the pedestrian barrier, and before a policeman could arrive, the cabbie jumped back into the hover cab and took off. Max watched as the cab merged back into the five lanes of traffic, disappearing in the mass of vehicles. Max and Isobel then went to the large gate guarded by two Assaultmen of the Protector's Line Guard.

"May I help you?" an ensign said as Max approached the foot traffic cut out in the vehicle gate.

"I am Maximilian *Graf* Fraser, here to take my seat in the House of Dynasts in the Parliament," Max said.

"Do you have credentials?" the Assault officer asked.

"No, but I will submit to a thumbprint," Max said. The young officer nodded and produced a tablet. Max pressed his thumb to the tablet, which then glowed green.

"You are granted access, your grace," the officer said. Max proceeded through, but as Isobel tried, she was blocked by the officer.

"Ensign, this is my vassal, Isobel Douglas," Max said.

"She'll need credentials or a thumbprint submission. After the *Campbell* was attacked at Midlothian spaceport, we doubled security in the city," the young officer said. Isobel placed her thumb on the tablet the officer carried. The pad also glowed green.

"Sorry, ma'am, just following orders," the officer said, moving out of Isobel's way.

"I understand, sir," Isobel said. As they started to walk away, the officer motioned for them to stop while he listened to his earpiece.

"Yes, sir, I'll instruct them," the ensign said, looking up at a visible camera. Then, looking at Max and Isobel, he said, "Just got a call. You two will need to go to the main security post and get your badges."

The officer pointed them in the security office's direction, and Max and Isobel took each other's hands and moved toward the building the young officer had pointed out.

When out of earshot, Isobel said, "Off to the ninth circle of hell."

"Come on, the queue won't be bad, and we'll have each other's company," Max said with a smile. The couple moved across the large expanse of concrete and went into a squat building in front of the large Parliament building. Velvet ropes filtered the traffic into a queue, ending in an armored glass booth.

"Malcolm's ashes! You were right, Isobel," Max said, looking at the long line in front of them. Assaultmen, Navy, civilians, and diplomats were in the queue, each waiting for a clerk to process them. In the egalitarian spirit created by the first Protector Karl, there were no unique lines for politicians, nobles, or anyone else. If the protector, himself had needed security credentials, Max figured he too would have had to stand in line.

"Where are we going? After security?" Isobel asked Max.

"I suppose we get our identification, find the office attached to my seat, and head there. Then we'll have to find out how bad the news is about the Sheeplands situation. Maybe we will see what my liege the Campbell, whoever he is now, is planning. If things are horrible, I should try to get an audience with the First Secretary of the House of Dynasts," Max said.

"What good will seeing the First Secretary do?" Isobel said.

"Well, I can try to inform the secretary of what we've seen in the county. I don't know how much anyone here will be willing to help."

"Excuse me, are you a Felgenlander?" a woman said to Max. The woman in line in front of Max and Isobel was a head shorter than Isobel, with coppery red hair, pale skin, and a tight-fitting, yet modest, green silk dress. The woman looked ready for a cocktail party rather than a working day of political tussling.

"Yes, ma'am," Max said to the women. Isobel gripped Max's hand to show through body language that they were together.

"Hello, I'm Yvonne Beornsdottir. I'm an attaché from Protelan. I'm afraid I'm a bit confused and need some help," the woman said.

"Nice to meet you. I am Maximilian *Graf* Fraser, and this is my friend, Isobel *Freifrau* Douglas," Max said, extending his hand to the Protelani.

Yvonne shook Max's hand demurely and said, "*Graf, Freifrau,* I remember this from my Felgenlander orientation. You're nobles, right?"

"Yes, not that our status grants any preference for this queue," Max said with a chuckle. If on cue, he and Isobel took a step forward, and turning around, so did Yvonne. Yvonne then turned to face Max again.

"I apologize, but I overheard you mention the First Secretary of the House of Dynasts, and I'm confused. Isn't the Grand Minister more important?" she asked.

"I can help you. I once was a personal secretary and clerk to a Commons member," Isobel said, "the system is built on a series of checks and balances, much in the mold of the ancient United States or the first Martian Republic of Musk."

Yvonne nodded and said, "Okay, go on."

Isobel shifted her weight to her other side and said, "The First

Secretary of the House of Dynasts is the first government member for the noble families, also called the *Dynasties*. The first secretary also goes by the prime minister, which I know is confusing as ministers are the government members in the Commons. Now, the grand minister is the first government member in the Commons. He or she is like a prime minister elsewhere."

"That makes more sense," Yvonne said, "I am sorry to disturb you two, but I am just here from the spaceport. I read my backgrounders but think I am still a little space-weary. I'm supposed to be briefed by the ambassador, but she has been busy meeting with the Union government due to the war.

Again, thanks for the help."

Yvonne turned around and moved forward in the line. Soon, the light above one of the security cubicles turned green, and Yvonne stepped into the booth. That left Max and Isobel at the front of the queue.

"Here we are," Max said as he waited at the head of the line. Then Max saw a green light flash as a small lizard from Pentothian left the security station. He and Isobel moved to the window.

"State your business at the Parliament," the clerk said dispassionately.

"Maximilian *Graf* Fraser, here with my guest, Isobel *Freifrau* Douglas. I'm taking up my seat in the Parliament," Max said.

"You'll need identity cards and your credentials, yes?" the clerk said.

"Yes, please," Max said.

"Place your thumbs on the small devices on the edge of the desk. I'll snap your photos, and the badges will print out in moments. Your credentials will be logged, and you'll have access to the public areas and the Dynasts's chambers, *Graf* Fraser. Except for the Dynasts chambers, *Freifrau* Douglas must remain in your company, as she is only a visitor."

Max and Isobel followed the procedure and, in moments, wore the appropriate IDs. Max had his so-so mugshot with a large purple 'L' on the front, while Isobel's featured a nice picture of her with a red 'V' overlay.

"Any questions?" the clerk asked.

"No," Max and Isobel said in stereo.

"Have a good day," the clerk said, motioning the couple to exit. Max and Isobel followed the directional signs and soon stepped onto a giant marble floor illustrated with the Union's coat of arms with its giant dragon and griffin supporters. At the far end of the vaulted chamber were two sets of doors leading to the halls: one for the Commons and one for the Dynasts.

"Where to, I wonder?" Max said. As he spoke, an older woman in a business dress approached, clutching a tablet.

She came closer and said, "*Graf* Fraser? I am Martha Clark. I am your personal secretary."

"Good afternoon, *Frau* Clark," Max said, using the title for a woman in the capital, "this is Her Excellency, Baroness Isobel Douglas of Cairnbahan."

"A pleasure," *Frau* Clark said, extending her hand and shaking Isobel's while eschewing Max's, "Now, if you follow me, I'll take you to your office."

Max and Isobel went with the personal secretary, and in moments, they were in the office of the Count of Gilbraith-on-Heather.

CHAPTER EIGHT

Office and Lords

When he entered, Max noticed the sign which read, 'Count of Gilbraith-on-Heather,' and in smaller font, 'Clan Fraser' displayed across the back wall. The office's large, rectangular reception area was approximately five meters by eight meters, with the door on the shorter side. Splashed across the walls were holo projections of the county. Occasionally, the Bonnie Dundee would project, and Max's heart would swell with pride at the sight.

Frau Clark opened the door to a smaller office. Max presumed the office was hers. He peeked in and saw beyond her desk another door with golden letters spelling out Max's father's name, 'Kenneth *Graf* Fraser.'

"Sorry, your grace," Clark said, "I had neglected changing the name on the door. I inquired but thought your cousin Hector would be the next earl. Seeing you, I am glad I hesitated."

Max made a mental note to examine Martha Clark's contract with the earl. He had a sneaking suspicion he would have to fire her. A cautious personal secretary who waited to see who she would work with seemed like a liability, not an asset.

"Quite understandable," Max said, hiding his misgivings, "I expect you'll spell my name right."

The personal secretary laughed and said, "Well, I'll get right on that. Feel free to go in and acquaint yourself with your office. Am I correct in assuming you will quickly survey the office and attend the session? I can get Baroness Douglas a pass for the visitor's gallery, should she wish to attend."

Max looked at Isobel, who nodded.

"Are you former military, *Frau* Clark?" Max asked.

"Yes, sir, Navy. I was the boatswain on the Union Space War Craft *Advantage*." Clark said.

"Oh, I know that ship. You rescued a friend of mine after the disaster at Asimov," Max said.

"Sorry, sir, I barely remember that action. I was always busy on the *Advantage*, and after so many years retired, my time on the ship has blurred together," Clark replied. Something about *Frau* Clark's statement didn't ring true in Max's mind, but he had more significant concerns right at the moment.

"Well, let us know when you have the pass," Max said. Clark nodded and left. Max stood outside as Isobel entered the earl's office.

She looked at him and said, "Well, come on, this is *your* office now, dear."

"I know," Max said, "would you believe I've never even been here? My father spent so much time in this office, and only now, when he is gone, am I seeing the inside." Looking in, Max saw an ornate Steelwood desk dominating the room. There were two comfy leather chairs in front of the desk and an executive-style chair, also made of leather, behind the desk. The desk bore an ornate nameplate with Max's father's name.

"I could auction this desk and make a small fortune off the sale," Max said, looking at the massive desk and leather chairs.

"You'd lose money, dear," Isobel said, pointing at the door, "I don't think the desk can fit through the door without tearing out the wall."

Max sighed, just his luck. Max then noticed the awards and trophies his father had gathered. The awards plastered the walls and dominated the room. Other than a picture of his dead mother, there was nothing personal in the office. The room represented Kenneth's political side. Looking over all the awards, Max realized his father was a competitive man. The office gave Max a negative impression. Max looked over the desk and picked up a tablet that sat on the desktop. The tablet was practically brand new, maybe a year old.

"I'm taking this tablet with me. I can use this back on the estate," Max said, turning on the tablet. The tablet's screen immediately asked for a password or thumbprint. Max thought for a moment and then quickly hacked the password by putting in his dead brother's name. The message service was open. Hundreds of messages appeared, all related to inter-county affairs. Max locked the tablet and placed the device back on the desk. He sat in the executive chair and began to open drawers on the desk. The desk was empty except for an old notebook and a bottle of whisky, *Royal Neep Reserve*.

"You know there is a man in Cairnbahan who does landscapes," Isobel said, "the next time we come up, we should bring a few. They would make this office seem more like home."

"I need to sell these awards," Max said, "I am not even sure I can afford the personal secretary."

At the mention of Clark, there came a knock from outside. Martha Clark opened the door slightly, poked her head in, and said, "Visitor's pass. Can I send your things to the Grand Hotel?"

"Why the Grand?" Max asked.

"Your father always stayed there. The Grand is the closest hotel, after all," Clark said.

"The Grand is also the most expensive. We're at the Royal Hansaburgher," Max said.

"Of course," Martha said, the woman turned a deep shade of red in embarrassment, "Shall I hire a chaperone?"

Max looked to Isobel, who said, "We're engaged. We won't need a chaperone's company."

Max was grateful. Paying for a third room and a professional chaperone would be more than his budget could bear.

"I did not know you had signed the banns, and they were announced," Martha said, scowling.

"I don't see how our engagement is your concern," Max said. The personal secretary was getting on his nerves. *Frau* Clark merely nodded subserviently and left Max and Isobel in the office.

"She's right, Max," Isobel said, "The engagement wouldn't be a concern, except that you are a peer, and we're in the capital. This town is full of intrigue, from within and without. A political rival wouldn't hesitate to drag the Fraser name through the gutter over something even less scandalous than the impropriety of our engagement. I need a moment. I am trying to think what Rosie would say is the best course of action."

Max looked at his beautiful baroness. She sat, arms crossed, arguing with herself.

"The arch cardinal," Isobel said, "Rosie had a friend who was his secretary. I'll send a message immediately."

"What?" Max said. Isobel tapped away on her tablet. After a moment, she looked up and said, "Okay, I'll explain. If we are betrothed officially by the arch cardinal, there can be no higher authority to revoke our engagement except the protector. Since engagement is treated like marriage, we'd have a firm reason for staying in the same suite. The chief cleric's judgment isn't going to be second-guessed, and the protector isn't going to rebuke his nephew publicly."

"What about a ring?" Max asked, "And a date?"

"I know you want to give me a ring so badly, dear, but that needs to wait a little longer. We'll need to tell your clan," Isobel said with a wink, "and don't worry, my Uncle Kensie will back whatever decision I make."

Max opened the door and called for *Frau* Clark, who appeared momentarily.

"*Frau* Clark, if I order from a shop on the Silver Road, can you go and get it?" Max asked.

"Yes, sir, but what, may I ask, are you ordering?"

"A ring—Isobel and I are making our engagement official," Max said.

"Oh, you don't need to get a ring. I have your mother's ring. I was supposed to mail the band to you when Kenneth died. I'm sorry. I've held onto the ring for sentimental reasons. Kenneth and I were… close," *Frau* Clark said, going to her desk and bringing back a small box. She said, "Here is the ring. Kenneth gave it to me when she died. I, unfortunately, disappointed him."

Frau Clark opened the small clamshell box. Inside was a bright silver-colored band with a sizeable rose-cut ruby. The light sparkled through the slightly purplish-red stone.

"What… How?" Max asked, "Father said he lost the ring after Mother died."

"He was drunk in the city. He misplaced the ring… and I found the band," Martha said, "Now take the ring. I have kept it for far too long. By all rights, your mother's ring is yours and not mine."

Max took the ring but said, "The decision is Isobel's."

Isobel looked at the ring and Martha. The older woman felt a connection to the ring. Isobel asked, "Are you sure?"

"Take the ring, your excellency," Martha said, "the ring belongs to the earl's wife."

A knock on the outer office ended the conversation. Martha left to open the door. A middle-aged man in cardinal's vestments stood at the door.

"Your serene eminence, my name is *Frau* Clark. Please follow me this way," Martha said.

"Maximilian *Graf* Fraser and Isobel *Freifrau* Douglass, may I present His Serene Eminence Stephan von Machthaber, Arch Cardinal of the Felgenland Union."

Max and Isobel knelt, kissing the arch cardinal's ring. He

motioned for the couple to stand and said, "Your grace and your excellency, my secretary informed me of your predicament. She noted that I had an opening now, so I came immediately. I shall now ask you the standard questions required for engagement, and then I shall bless your upcoming union, provided there are no impediments. Any questions?"

"No, your serene eminence," the couple said in unison.

The arch cardinal said, "*Frau* Clark, will you be a witness?"

"Yes, your serene eminence," Martha said.

"Your grace, could you please step outside?" the arch cardinal asked Max. Max grabbed his father's tablet off the desk, moved into the personal secretary's office, and opened his father's tablet again. He slowly began reviewing and deleting messages on the tablet. He would have to wipe the account, but he wanted to ensure no vital information remained before he destroyed the data. After a few minutes of combing through the messages, Max saw Isobel coming out of the earl's office.

"Your turn," she said.

"Did he use the thumbscrews on you?" he winked.

She laughed and said, "Only a little."

Max then entered the earl's office, his office, and shut the door.

"Now, my son, state your name, please," the arch cardinal said.

"Maximilian *Graf* Fraser," Max said.

"Are you a member of the state religion?" the arch cardinal said. Martha sat watching.

"Yes, your serene eminence," Max said, "I was baptized in Gilbraith village by the Reverend Roland Fraser."

"Have you ever been previously married?" the arch cardinal said.

"No sir," Max responded. So far, the questions have been reasonably straightforward.

"Is there any impediment that would prevent you from fulfilling your duties as a husband to *Freifrau* Douglas," the arch cardinal asked.

"None, sir," Max said.

The arch cardinal smiled and said, "Bring in *Freifrau* Douglas."

Isobel entered, and the arch cardinal said, "By the Allfather through his anointed, our protector, I now declare your promise of union to be formalized. Note this is not a sacrament of matrimony but rather a promise to wed. You both accept this promise, vow to formalize your marriage, and will do so in full communion with the state religion. As was preached by Jesus the Son of Man, who revealed Himself to the Prophet Malcolm?"

"I do," both Max and Isobel said in unison.

"Then by the Allfather, Jesus the Son of Man, and the Holy Spirit, I declare Isobel *Freifrau* Douglas and Maximilian *Graf* Fraser to be blessed and engaged. Please sign the banns," the arch cardinal said, presenting his tablet. Max used his finger to sign the section bore his name, and Isobel did the same.

"These will be read this Sunday in Saint Malcolm's Cathedral. Do you have the ring?" the arch cardinal asked. Max presented his mother's ring, and the arch cardinal blessed it. Max then put the ring on Isobel's first finger. After they married, she would wear the ring on her ring finger.

"Congratulations," the arch cardinal said, "Now, I must move along. I still have a funeral and a wedding for today."

The supreme prelate left the office, and then Max said, "That's settled. I need to hurry and take my seat in the Parliament. I'll return after that, and we can plan our next moves."

Max left the office and then tore down the corridor towards the large chamber that housed the Dynasts, the marble halls translating his every step into an echo. After a few minutes, he came to the chamber door, and a liveried footman stood in front of the door. Max flashed his identity card, and the footman signaled to wait and placed his ear to the door. After the applause had stopped, the footman signaled the chamber Max was about to enter.

"Maximilian *Graf* Fraser, Count of Gilbraith-on-Heather, will now take his seat in our chamber," the Speaker said. Max entered, and the Campbell retainers clapped while the MacDonald retainers hissed. Max took his seat behind the ornate placard that read "Gilbraith-on-Heather."

"The *Graf* will now have five minutes to speak," the speaker said. Max stood. All eyes were on him. Max had remembered to bring his maiden speech. After Meg's wedding, he scribbled down some thoughts, and Isobel proofed the address, adding her comments and pink hearts over some phrases.

"My peers," Max said, "I come here to take up a mantle I did not desire, but I shall do my solemn duty. I will perform to the same standard that you held my ancestors so that one cannot say the Earl of the Bonnie Dundee has disgraced his dynasty. I have had false accusations levied against my family. My father did his best to maintain the county, and now that it is entrusted into my care, I will bring Gilbraith-on-Heather back to its ancient glory."

The chamber erupted in noise. During a maiden speech, rules permitted no rebuttals. However, booing, hissing, and cheers were within the bounds of decorum.

"I have been put on notice, a notice I accept freely as I endeavor to strengthen the county so we better support the Union and its eventual victory against the Terran directorate and their client states. I have bled and served on the front lines. Not many of you, my peers, can say the same. As a veteran, I seek to make the Dynasts the preeminent leaders that all in the Union can look to for courage in these dark times. Thank you, I yield the rest of my time to the Speaker," Max finished and sat down. The speaker noted a call to speak.

"The speaker recognizes *Graf* Gilmerton-over-Torboultoun."

An older gentleman stood, his face showing indescribable rage,

"Excellency, chamber leadership... Thievery I say, Gilbraith has the nerve to show his face here after stealing my land and retainers!"

The Campbell retainers hissed while the MacDonald retainers cheered.

"What is the matter, *Graf* Gilmerton?" the Speaker asked.

"Less than two days ago, this upstart, this lucky bastard, this thief, stole my Barony of Loch Urquhart. He violated oaths of allegiance without consulting this august body or the protector himself."

"Speaker, I didn't think we tolerated lies in this chamber," a young man's voice said. Max looked down to see a young man standing in Campbell's seat.

"The Campbell will be silent," the Speaker said.

"And see how Gilbraith's liege disrespects this body," Gilmerton said, "the Sheeplands are on the knife edge of the civil war because of this charlatan and his disobedience to the Union's laws and customs!"

Max felt the urge to defend himself. He stood and shouted, "Talk of laws and customs should not come from the mouth of a land pirate! The Urquhart would not have seen fit to come into my protection if my lands had not been raided. More baronies will defect if MacDonald and his retainers do not halt their aggressive behavior."

The chamber erupted. Those allied with the Campbells cheered while the MacDonalds and their retainers booed. Angus MacDonald, patriarch and Great King of the Skye Isles, stood, his nominally pale face red, "My brothers, I may be the leader of the loyal opposition, but I stress that I am loyal. My family, clan, and retainers would never agitate or raid the Campbells or any Dynast's land. The Campbell put the lie—we killed Alasdair—on us. Now, the Campbells compound this insult by reviving their claim to the ownership of the Barony of Glencoe, and you all wondered why the Sheeplands were not in flame as we speak. The only thing that held this in check was my protective hand. The Campbell too, has raided our lands. Farms have been torched, herds shot, and left to rot under the sky. Are we to go back to the olden days of rape and pillage? Back to the days before the protector brought peace to our world? I say, 'No sir,' and here, the Campbell's lackey has the nerve to show his face after stealing a barony. Ask yourselves, how many baronies has the MacDonald stolen—none! Nay, I am the victim as my baronies are stripped from me without a court of law or permission of my liege—our great symbol of the Union, the protector!"

Max attempted to continue to listen, but the new tablet he had absently carried from his father's office kept pinging him. The tablet's short message service received notes from addresses linked to the most prominent political factions. Max looked and saw even some smaller parties trying to recruit him. Max noticed a message proclaiming that Kenneth was a Violet Party member and that Max should make his father proud and join them.

Max saved the message for later. He looked through the tablet, and sure enough, Kenneth was a lukewarm member of the Violet Party. The Violet Party believed in removing the Dynasts and the protector to run the Union under communist principles. Max blocked the messages. He wanted to focus on the debate at hand. Max then noted his new liege, a man about his age named Jason Campbell, was speaking. As the Campbell finished, one of the family heads from Eisenwald suggested a recess, which was seconded by a noble from Hansaburgh. The chamber then recessed, and the room went into a loud buzz as the cacophony of many voices became a loud and constant brown noise. A page raced to Max's position with a note. Max accepted the note, a tiny envelope with a bright, large wax seal on the folds.

Max broke the seal, nodding to the page; the young lady then ran off. Examining the note, he saw the seal of the protector, the triple segreant griffin. He quickly sent a message to Isobel, saying, 'Find my formal plaid. We've got an audience with the protector at eighteen hundred.'

Max then rose from his seat. The Campbell signaled him over.

"Nice to meet you, Gilbraith," the Campbell said.

"The pleasure is mine, sire," Max said.

"I would ask for your oath, Gilbraith, but with the war and my father's cold-blooded murder, I will ask for your allegiance later. However, do not forget that the Campbells will always be your benefactors unless you plan to claim independence. In which case, you will see us before the protector," the Campbell said, both as a promise and a threat.

"Understood, sir, and my condolences on your father's death," Max said.

Jason looked forlorn but then said, "Thank you, now, you have my leave."

Max knew what that meant: get lost. Max was happy to return to his office. He had played the politician today and found the role odious.

Max had little time before meeting the protector. Max's apprehension at meeting the protector grew. Any meeting with the previous protector, Karl, would be terrible and ominous. With Raimond, the consensus was there was no consensus. For some, an audience with the protector was a glorious meeting full of promise. For others, the meeting was a horror show with some loss of honor or face. Max entered the county's office, his office, and proceeded to his personal office, where he noticed the formal suit, complete with plaid, hanging on the front of the door. Max took the suit, entered his office, and shut the door. He changed outfits, putting on the armor of his station to meet the man who, above all, was the personal embodiment of the Union.

CHAPTER NINE

Audience with the Protector

Max finished lacing his shoes. He stood and put on his Tam o' Shanter. He then looked in his office for a mirror and found a full-length one attached to the back of the door.

"I've looked worse," Max said. The door suddenly opened, and *Frau* Clark stood in the doorway.

"You look like your father when I met him," she said, "he was handsome, as are you."

"Thank you, I gather you two..." Max was about to ask when Frau Clark cut him off.

"We were lovers," she said, "I was more than his secretary. I was his mistress. When your mother died, I filled her role in many ways."

Max must have turned three shades of red when he blushed because Frau Clark smiled and continued, "I was slightly younger then, fresh from the service. Your father gave me a job and eventually sent me away to further my education. I think, at first, he saw me as a project. Like the play *Pygmalion*, he wanted to improve my manners and turn me into a lady. In his later years, he relied on me to run this office."

"And my mother's ring?" Max asked. He wanted to know why the ring had disappeared into Clark's possession.

"When we began our relationship, he proposed to me. I said 'no.' I thought I knew better. He told me to keep the ring. I had intended to give the band to Archibald when he assumed the county, but that never happened. I apologize about the door. I couldn't force myself to take down your father's nameplate. Now, please get moving, or you'll be late. The protector does not abide tardiness."

"We'll talk more later," Max said, leaving the office.

"Good luck, and goodbye, Max," Matilda said.

Max's emotional gyro was spinning. His father had always appeared to be inhuman. Max's mother had died when he was a boy, and his father grew even more remote after that. Max stepped out of the building to the private parking lot at the back of Parliament. A hover-limo with his name on a piece of paper waited there. Max approached the hover-limo, sent by the protector, with trepidation. Max wondered what other secrets his father had buried here in the capital.

"Hello, darling," Isobel said as Max entered the limo. She wore a russet gown not too far removed from the one she wore to his masquerade.

"I was looking for Isobel, Abnoba," Max said with a wink.

Isobel's mouth opened in surprise and then said, "How did you guess this was the same dress? I altered the gown so no one could guess the dress was once a costume."

"Just lucky, I suppose," Max said. The driver began to navigate the circle's traffic and, within moments, turned into the protector's underground garage. As the vehicle coasted to a stop, Max watched as Assaultmen, noting by their insignia they were scanning technicians for the Line Guards, began searching outside the limo. Next came Assaultmen leading bomb-sniffing dogs. They, too, gave the vehicle a once-over. He and Isobel exited as the Assault officer motioned them out. The officer waved a wand over the couple and then hand-signed them to proceed.

"I am Otto Weber," an elegantly dressed man said, approaching the couple, "the protector's majordomo. Before you meet the protector of the Union, I must brief you on etiquette. I was expecting you, *Graf* Fraser, but you are *Fräulein*?"

"Isobel *Freifrau* Douglas, I am *Graf* Fraser's fiancée."

"Very good," the Majordomo said without pause. The man was taller than Max and had an imposing frame. His green eyes would jump between Max and Isobel when he talked.

He said, "When you both are presented to the protector, you must wait until he speaks before responding, address him as 'Lord Protector' first and 'sir' afterward. Furthermore, you are not to touch him unless he permits you. Finally, you must at all times give the protector your attention. If you fail to maintain this decorum, I will escort you out. Now follow me."

Max and Isobel followed the Majordomo. Weber led the couple to an elegant elevator. The couple stepped into the lift. Weber came afterward and pressed the floor button. Max noted that the majordomo's smart suit was immaculately tailored with red and gold lacing and embroidery on the black jacket and trousers.

"As the one with standing, I will announce the *Graf* first and then the *Friefrau*," the Majordomo continued. Weber's tone was formal and all business. Max couldn't tell by his demeanor if the majordomo was worried, excited, or concerned.

"First time for an audience?" Weber asked politely.

"Yes, sir," Max said.

"Please, your grace, address me simply as Weber. The honor I covet is only to serve the Union," Weber said firmly.

"Yes, Weber," Max said embarrassed.

"Thank you, sir, I understand you were an Assaultman. I took no umbrage in your promotion of my standing. Yet, in this role, I am a working man," Weber said. He paused as the communications earbud made a subtle noise in the Majordomo's ear. The man said, "Also, if the patroness is with the protector, then the men will greet each other first, as the ladies greet each other. You will switch and greet the other—man to woman—do you understand?"

"Yes, Weber," the couple said in unison.

"I have studied you, *Graf* Fraser. You are new to the peerage, so I am giving you these lessons. Many dynastic leaders do not understand our Union or honor the protector as they should. The protector isn't just our leader. He is the physical representation of the Union. One could argue he is the Union, even. His father, Karl —Allfather, have mercy on his soul—bound all the planets, nations, states, and tribes together in our glorious Union. We all owe the protector the respect his family has earned…" Weber's speech trailed off as the elevator doors opened directly on the protector's quarters.

"His Grace, Maximilian *Graf* Fraser of Gilbraith-on-Heather," the majordomo announced, "and his fiancée, Isobel *Freifrau* Douglas."

Max moved forward at a pace while the majordomo put a gentle hand on Isobel's elbow, holding her in place.

Weber gently nudged the baroness when Max was a meter from the elevator. Max continued forward, returning to his Assault days and marching like he was in a parade with his company.

The protector stood at the end of the ornate room. The floor was a polished oasis marble that was reddish brown, while the furniture was a delicate silver or chrome, depending on how the light reflected from the surface. A chaise lounge and several easy chairs were positioned in a half circle. The chairs all bore crimson cushions with the von Machthaber clan's emblem.

Max continued to the new protector. He was an older man. The protector stood in a perfectly groomed Assault uniform. The protector's uniform bore no award or rank, and the large silver stripe on his deep Prussian blue pants was the only thing Max could find different from his old Assault uniform. Max took a moment to look at the protector. He was bald, with hazel eyes and a short white beard. The protector looked like he had just met with the barber before Max's arrival. The protector looked back at Max like a hawk sizing up prey. Max used his peripheral vision to see if the patroness was also present. If the patroness was in the villa, she was not with her husband.

Max approached and gave a short bow to the protector. Max then stood up, ramrod straight. Max would have preferred to move to a parade rest stance, but his time as an Assaultman had taught him that he could only change positions under orders.

"Do you go by Max or Maximilian, Gilbraith?" the protector asked. The protector's tone was soft, almost cordial.

"Max, Lord Protector," Max said laconically. Within a moment, Max could feel a soft wind and smell the wildflower perfume of Isobel. The smell relaxed Max, and he felt his body soften.

"You must be the lovely *Freifrau* of Cairnbahan," the protector said as Isobel gave a deep curtsy, "I can see why Gilbraith was so eager to call upon my nephew for an engagement."

Isobel responded, "All a part of my diabolical plan, Lord Protector."

The couple waited for a moment in fear of causing some offense or overstepping some boundaries. The protector then let out a deep roar of a laugh.

"Well then, Isobel," the protector said after his laugh subsided, "you are to be congratulated. My Assaultmen have been honed as warriors and taught to avoid all traps."

Spurred on by the comment, Isobel returned to form and said, "The Douglas clan has been ambushing opponents for more than a millennium now, sir."

"Yes, yes, they have. As a man facing an aggressive neighbor who covets his land and title, I feel a kinship with your clan's original patron, Robert the Bruce," the protector said.

Isobel and Max waited for a moment to see if there was more. Isobel said, "The allusion has not been lost on my clan at Cairnbahan, sir."

"No, I know you and your family's sacrifice well. Your brother,

James's, ultimate sacrifice, for one," the protector said, "would you two care to join me in the private gallery?"

"Yes, sir," Max and Isobel said in unison.

"I see you two are already well-practiced at speaking stereophonically. This way," the protector said, leading Max and Isobel to a partially covered gallery with an expansive view of the city. As he did so, the patroness appeared. She was a much smaller person than her husband. She wore a formal gown that matched the Prussian blue of the protector's uniform and white opera gloves. She was the same age as her husband with steel gray hair that was immaculately coiffed and pulled into a side part up-do. She had coppery brown eyes and a cream complexion. The only feature that showed her strength was the conviction in her stare.

"My dear, the lady, Isobel *Freifrau* Douglas of Cairnbahan," the protector said. The patroness reached forward, hand extended in a ladylike fashion.

"A pleasure, Isobel," the patroness said, receiving Isobel's extended hand in a feminine clasp. Isobel then retreated so Max could be presented.

"My dear, the gentleman, Maximilian *Graf* Fraser, Count of Gilbraith-on-Heather and the Earl of the Bonnie Dundee," the protector said, including Max's more colloquial title. Max stepped forward, took the patroness's hand, and kissed the glove gently.

"Oh, my dear, you must bring more of these young peers to our villa more often," the patroness said as Max released her hand and returned to his place.

The protector smiled and said, "Be careful, dear. You could arouse some jealousy from the fierce Baroness Douglas."

Max felt deeply embarrassed at what he assumed was a compliment from the patroness. Isobel smiled and said, "Max is charming, sir and madam, but I know where his heart resides."

"I see. I remember those days of early love," the patroness said, "wait until the children arrive. You will miss these days."

The quartet all smiled. Max and Isobel waited for the next round of questions. Max felt that, so far, the audience was pleasant.

"I suppose you are wondering why a recently installed protector is inviting a hinterland earl and his fiancée to his villa," the protector said.

"Yes, sir," Max said, sticking to being laconic. The audience could make or break a man of high station, especially if he could not follow etiquette or show proper respect.

"You have taken over from your father, Kenneth," Raimond said, "you realize what a surprise this is for me. My council prepared dossiers on your father and your brother, Archibald. My condolences on their losses. I hope not to offend, Max, but the prepared dossiers did not paint your father and brother in the best light."

"I did not know that, sir," Max said. Isobel took his hand, making him worry more about the sweat on his palms than the questions.

"You, on the other hand, have come from nothing. A second son who inherited a title. A position I am familiar with," the protector said, referencing his recent installation where he had been elected protector over his older brother.

"I never wanted to be the earl, sir," Max said honestly.

"That was noted in your dossier," the protector said, "in this time of war, the Union needs their Cincinnati, who will assume their duty when fate calls and return to their farms after they have secured victory. However, your ascension was a surprise and such revelations... Well, they may be good for Gilbraith-on-Heather, but are they good for the Union?" the protector asked.

"Of course, sir," Max said. Max wondered what worried the protector about him. Max suspected Kenneth had skeletons that Max had yet to uncover.

"You may not know this, but your father voted his mind. Even though the Campbell supported me, Kenneth voted for my brother. I understand your father's position. My brother is a man of peace and the arts. The Union needs men of peace, but only after we deal with the Terran Directorate. With my installation, the Union declared war on Terra. Some have said this war is foolhardy or even wicked. What do you think about that, Max?"

"Sir, I watched men under my command die. I was wounded, and I've shed blood on the battlefield for the Union," Max said.

"Yes, Max, but for what?" the protector said.

"For our freedom," Max said hotly, quickly adding, "sir."

"Freedom to do what, Max?" the protector.

"To live how we should choose, sir," Max said. Max wondered why he was being asked these questions.

"The Dynasts claim you are a surprise. They believe you are my curse, and I am paying the price for, as they say—usurping—my brother," the protector said. Max's blood boiled.

"I believe I've paid the price. My brother died, and I've inherited a mess from my father, sir," Max said. He wasn't about to be chastised by the protector for doing the best in a bad situation.

"Quite right, Max," the protector, in a fatherly tone, "Archibald died, your father died, and you became the earl. I requested your presence to get to know you..."

"To know both of you," the patroness said, "dearest, you are grilling Max. When we also know so little of his soon-to-be wife."

"Quite right, dear," the protector said, "I will call Weber and have him fetch us drinks. Shall I have him fetch *Royal Neep* for you, Max, and Isobel? I believe that is popular in the Sheeplands?"

"Water would be preferred, sir," Max said.

"Aye, sir, plain water," Isobel said.

The protector nodded and said, "One moment, I shall return."

The protector left, and the couple stood alone with the patroness. Max suspected that whatever the protector asked him, the patroness would push harder on her questions with Isobel.

"Isobel, I noted that you served your conscription here in the capital. Is that correct?" the patroness asked.

"Yes, madam," Isobel said, "I worked for my cousin, Rosie Douglas-Fairlane, as her clerk."

"I remember her. They called her 'Rosie the Riveting,'" the patroness said, "I believe she holds the record for the longest filibuster in the Parliament. Can you tell me what she was blocking again?"

Max held his breath. If someone had put a pistol to his head, with the threat of pulling the trigger if he couldn't name the issue, Max would beg the assailant to pull the trigger and put him out of his misery!

"Of course, madam, she was unhappy with the salary package for the Navy," Isobel said with a smile, "not to self-congratulate, but I helped her write that speech."

"Oh really," the patroness said, "so you believe the protector should offer a better wage to, as our press calls them, 'the protector's *ship wenches*?'"

Max watched Isobel's face during the question. Whatever jockeying was going on in the conversation, Max was happy that, due to his gender, he was excluded from the fray.

"Yes, madam. My cousin and I believed our service women were more akin to the Amazons or the Valkyries—not the Valkyrie of the Gentlemen's magazine," Isobel said.

"If these Amazons are so valorous, why did you not join their ranks?" the patroness asked. Max wanted to jump in and defend Isobel. He felt her squeeze his hand, reassuring him she could handle the questions.

"My father died, and much like Max, I was duty bound to serve in Cairnbahan, madam," Isobel said, "by your leave, I would like to ask you a question, madam."

"By all means, Isobel," the patroness said.

"What was your rank in our illustrious Navy, madam?" Isobel asked. Her tone was as soft as a dove or lamb.

"Well played, young lady," the patroness said, "You have made a good point. I also did not serve in our Navy. Rather, I serve my husband directly and by him, the Union. Just as you do in Cairnbahan, correct?"

Isobel smiled and said, "Of course, madam."

Max waited for the following questions but was interrupted as the protector and Weber appeared.

"Did I miss anything?" the protector asked.

"No, dear, I was just making friends," the patroness said. Max wondered what the patroness looked like when she was making enemies.

"Bottled water from Lochiel," Weber said, pouring two glasses for Max and Isobel, and then he said, "*Royal Neep,* straight, for you, sir, and ice wine from the Emerald Vineyards for you, madam."

The majordomo efficiently handed out drinks and then disappeared. Glasses in hand, Max, Isobel, and the patroness looked to the protector.

"A toast to the Union and victory," the protector said.

"Indeed," the patroness, Max and Isobel, said, lifting their glasses.

"Now to business, Max. I said I called you here to get to know you," the protector said.

"Yes, sir," Max responded.

"I think we can dispense with formality for now. I am Raimond," the protector said.

"Yes, Raimond," Max replied.

The protector smiled and continued, "Things are... tense... in the Sheeplands. The Union cannot have any distraction drawing away from our singular focus—victory over the tyrants from Earth. As you are well aware, we fight against a regime that has no issue jailing its critics and killing their political rivals. Given an opportunity, the men and women of Earth would do the same here. The only thing that stands against them are our Navy's ships and the Assault's rifles."

"The county of Gilbraith-on-Heather and her people are yours to command, sir," Max said. Isobel squeezed his hand in a silent assent.

"Interesting that you say that," Raimond said, "that's especially enlightening, as you were quick to accept fealty from the Barony of Loch Urquhart. More so, because I learned of this intelligence from Angus MacDonald. The MacDonald is my vassal, directly, by my stature as the living Union. How can I compensate him for the loss of a barony?"

Max felt his stomach drop. The news had reached the protector faster than he had expected. Max looked around for Line Guardsmen or some other authority to swoop down on them and take him off to a speedy trial and hanging.

Raimond smiled at Max's discomfort and said, "Max, I'm not my father, as you aren't yours. I prefer to find out why a young man, new to his county, suddenly annexes—by custom—a hostile neighbor's barony."

"My now brother-in-law came to me and asked for patronage, sir," Max said.

"There are customs and traditions for these actions," Raimond said, "the MacDonald rightly demands remuneration. Shall I levy that on you? A man who barely can afford the trip he is now on?"

Max stood firm. If he was to be indebted, there were worse creditors.

"I accept your judgment, sir," Max said, "I beg forgiveness for overstepping my position..."

"I think you're mistaken here, Max," Raimond said.

"Excuse me, sir, but how?" Max asked.

"What kind of figure would I be if I only accepted one side of an argument?" the protector said, "Angus, dear Angus, would run to me asking for a pension if he stubbed his toe rising from his bed. He wants compensation for the raids on his land, recompense for Glencoe, Urquhart, and a dozen other perceived thefts. Should I levy those costs on your shoulders?"

"If that is your will, sir," Max said, "I will accept that as your decision."

The patroness clapped and said, "Bravo, Saint Max, shall we prepare your canonization now? We can call our nephew and have the arch cardinal make the title official."

Isobel rustled next to Max. As much as he tried to remain focused on Raimond, he glanced at her. She was red-faced, enraged, and said, "Max is not your enemy! he has suffered much and silently! He received the unwelcome appearance of the auditor for dynastic affairs. Many slings and arrows in Parliament this morning from men who have been the cause of this discontent and complaints from the people who should have supported him."

"Interesting," the protector said, "I have read the auditor's report. Although not directly in my lane of government, the Dynasts send me carbon copies in the black boxes, and my staff gathers such reports into a daily brief. I am surprised to see you, *Freifrau* Douglas, a woman adamantly against Kenneth, hanging off his son's arm."

Max lost his grip on his composure. The protector had every right to beat Max with the rod of his authority, but Max felt Isobel was off limits.

"Isobel has withdrawn her complaint," Max said.

"Yes, but only after you had offered marriage to her," the patroness said, "Max, dear boy, adventuresses will lure you away from your duty! Do you think my husband's title is for show? He is your protector as well as your benefactor! I think *Freifrau* Douglas wants to use you and then move on. We have our intelligence, too. We know that *Freifrau* Douglas was rumored to enjoy *Freiherr*

Breakin's company. Am I wrong?"

Max and Isobel looked defeated. Whatever the fate, the patroness and her husband had won. Max spoke up humbly and said, "Geordie is a family friend. I believe Isobel's explanation. If she is an adventuress, so what? If she marries me for a bankrupt house, a worthless title, and an auditor's sword of Damocles, well, she is the Union's most foolish adventuress."

"What do you say, *Freifrau* Douglas," the protector asked, "are you an adventuress?"

"No, sir," Isobel said, "Max does not know, as I suspect you do, that Cairnbahan is dead broke. I have been supplementing the meager salary Kenneth paid the shepherds out of my own money. As a county, his father deeply impoverished Gilbraith-on-Heather. I filed the complaint for that reason, and I endured much. Kenneth made me a pariah. I do not wish to speak for Max, but I know he has suffered from Kenneth's antipathy, if not as a liege, as a father."

"Thank you, Isobel," the patroness said, "for sharing your family and personal skeletons. We, too, must share our skeletons with you."

The patroness nodded and looked to her husband, who nodded. Max watched the interplay. He was still worried, but the underlying dynamics were changing.

"Your cousin, Ewan, also filed several reports. I get reports from the Union Special Intelligence Service, too. What I say now cannot be repeated beyond these walls, but the USIS dossier on you, Max, is highly complimentary. Lieutenant, now Captain Nordlinger, also vouched for your character. In his report, he begged his superiors for a company of 'Weimars' to quote 'bring a swift victory to the war and end the Terran regime,' high praise indeed."

"Why all the theater, sir?"

"Max, being a protector is nothing but theater. The villa's walls have ears. From the MacDonald and the Campbell down to the man who polishes Weber's shoes, they all want something. They all have some game they play. I was waiting to see what your game would be. Would you ask or even demand something from me? Or, would you seek to weasel your way out of all the hardships I had planned for Kenneth?" Max's mind was reeling.

"Isobel," the patroness said, looking at the baroness, "I know you must feel some sting in my words too. In all your time with Rosie, did you ever ask her who provided her the support to enter politics?"

"No, madam," Isobel said, "Rosie was such a force. I always suspected she came from the head of Jove exactly as she was."

The patroness let out a small laugh and said, "I understand how you can feel that way. However, I gave Rosie the funds to start her career. When I was merely the Secundus's wife, I used my influence to advance her with all the right people. In the beginning, she was my project. Later, she was my friend. She would have been one of my lady's maids if our customs had permitted it. Alas, we womenfolk still suffer some of the ancient stigma the Felgenland has for women. I want you to know that I take you into my confidence. My doors, patronage, and influence are yours, should you need them, Isobel."

Again, the patroness nodded to the protector. Both smiled at each other. Max wondered what had happened. Was this audience an interview?

"Now, Max," the protector said, "I don't want you to feel left out. We have some business to discuss, and then I shall reveal my purpose for this audience with you. I'll admit, you took the Barony of Loch Urquhart improperly. But if I were a slave to etiquette, I would not be the protector. Admirably, you've shaken things up after eighty years of the status quo. Now, there is tension in the Sheeplands. What can you tell me about that?"

Max cleared his mind, leaned on his Assault training, and said, "Sir, the nobles appear to be fomenting the raids when one looks outside the Sheeplands."

"Yes, exactly," the protector said, "but go on."

"Well, inside the Sheeplands, I have seen militant Ultra-Violets who attacked my herds, ruined crops, and assaulted the local gentry. We caught one inside my home," Max related.

"I see," the protector said, "the Violets are a political party. They disapprove of the Union. Thankfully, they are a fringe group, but an Ultra-Violet Party is what you said. What is that exactly?"

"I suspect you know, sir," Max said, "but I will tell you what happened. My huntsman captured a teenager with a weapon who spent his interview with me shouting negative political slogans about my station."

"What did you do with this teenager?" the protector asked.

"We disarmed him and let him go," Max answered.

"You fed him too, dear," Isobel said.

The protector laughed and said, "Dear Max, you show more kindness to your enemies than I ever would!"

Max shook his head and said, "Sir, he was just a kid. If I could find the old men who pulled that boy's strings, I would hang them in cages off the Bonnie Dundee as a warning to all who wish to do violence to the Union."

"Indeed?" the protector said, "I see Nordlinger's assessment was spot on about you. You offer me a unique opportunity."

"I am yours to command, sir," Max said. After a moment's pause, he knelt, holding his head low for effect. Isobel joined him in supplication.

The protector's voice changed to his command tone. He said, "Rise, Gilbraith, and know well that from this moment forward, by the Allfather, our Union, and my power as the protector, I will protect you forever from trouble and uphold your rights, by our Constitution now and for long as the Union stands. Stand now in my presence, vassal of the protector, and know the griffin will always be over your shoulder, watching."

Max was flabbergasted. The protector had just made Max a direct vassal. If the Campbell and the MacDonald escalated their conflict to open warfare, his small county would become a bastion of order as Max was now the protector's man, beholden to only the Union.

"I don't know what to say, sir," Max said, tears forming in his eyes. The Fraser had faired well when the Union was established, but not that well. Max always felt his clan was last for recognition and first for trouble. Maybe all that was about to change.

"Don't thank me yet," the protector said, "You are now my sheriff, my constable, in the Sheeplands, the first in almost a century. If the Sheeplands break into open conflict, you have failed me. If you hear or see anything unusual, I expect you to report directly to me. Do we have an understanding?"

"Yes, sir," Max said.

"Now, the fun part," the protector said with a flash in his eye, "Max, you are no longer a mere earl, count, or *graf*. As the Sheeplands have become a frontier or march, I need a peer to defend the march, a Markgraf or Margrave or, as you Sheeplanders would say, a Marquess. From now on, you are the Marquess of the Bonnie Dundee, the *Markgraf* of Gilbraith-on-Heather. As my direct man, I remove the probationary status imposed by the audit. I will inform Markgraf von Huegel of this decision. Furthermore, I offer you a salary of two hundred dragons a year for your service as my sheriff, the sheriff of the Sheeplands. As your patron, I do not wish to see you fail."

"I won't, sir!" Max said. He looked at Isobel, who had unshed tears of pride in her eyes. The patroness gave her husband a small, subtle smile.

"I know you won't, Colonel, as I give you the authority to raise the First Gilbraith Volunteer Rifles. If the Ultra-Violets want a revolution, well, unlike the Soviets and Nazis of the twentieth century, we have guns and a say in that matter. Revolution is not on my dance card. I seek victory with Terra. Fix the Ultra-Violet problem in the Sheeplands so I can focus on winning the war!"

"Yes, sir," Max said. He gave the protector a proper Assaultman salute, and the protector responded crisply.

"Ah yes, now comes the saluting," the patroness said, "we ladies know who really will keep the peace, right, Isobel?" Isobel smiled and nodded, totally caught up in the moment.

"Remember, you have my ear whenever you need me," the patroness said, "guns, rifles, and soldiers are good for a fight, but a woman's sharp rebuke can bring many men low. Perhaps, as Max does his duty, you may need me or another woman to speak with so that we may find the right woman to end a terrible situation with an unkind word."

"Yes, madam," Isobel said, "I won't forget."

"Now, enough business. I give you my leave to enjoy this evening in my fine capital," the protector said, "Max, when you return to the Sheeplands, take this, my sealing ring, as a mark of my good faith, as a benefactor to a beneficiary.," The protector removed a ring from his right hand. Max nodded and accepted the ring.

"Please inspect the ring," the protector said, "I want you to know the band's details. Remember: in the Sheeplands, my word is your word, and your word is my word. If you ever need to make that point, that ring is your punctuation mark."

Max looked at the ring. The face bore the three segreant griffins, the emblem of the Machthabers. In tiny font underneath was scrawled the motto, *"Unio Omnia Obligat,"* or "The Union Binds All."

"Thank you, sir," Max said in gratitude.

The protector took Isobel's hand and chastely kissed the back of it.

The protector said, "Goodnight, soon-to-be Marchioness Fraser. Max has made a wise choice in selecting you as his future wife. If he had not selected you, I would have introduced you to my yet unmarried son, Heinrich, the *Primus*."

As her husband stepped back, the patroness said to Isobel, "Agreed. If I could clone you, I'd have you and my eldest matched any day. Max, be wise and cherish Isobel's counsel. Now, I bid you two a good night."

Max smiled and said, "I do, madam."

The patroness then left the gallery. Weber appeared and signaled to Max and Isobel that they were to follow him. He said, "This way, *Markgraf* Fraser, *Friefrau* Douglas. I'll show you through some of the more public sections of the villa."

The protector waved informally and said, "Good luck to the two of you."

With that, the protector went through a door and disappeared into another section of the expansive villa. The majordomo guided the couple through different doors and down an ornately decorated corridor.

"These are the guest suites for dignitaries and those the protector chooses to invite to the villa," Weber said as he escorted Max and Isobel.

The corridor contained art of all types, giving Max the impression it was a museum rather than a residence. After a few minutes, Weber escorted the couple to a waiting elevator.

"I leave you here. The elevator will take you down to a waiting hover-limo and then to your hotel," Weber said as the lift's doors shut.

Max and Isobel were alone with each other.

"Hi there, marquess, come here often?" Isobel said with a smile.

"You a marquess groupie now?" Max said.

"Only one. He's quite dashing. The patroness even alluded to that."

"What can I say? Patronesses hang off my broad shoulders whenever I'm in the capital," Max said with a cheeky grin. Isobel tittered and would have burst out laughing when the doors opened to a small garage with the promised hover-limo.

Max helped Isobel into the vehicle, closing her door. He then entered on his side of the rear passenger compartment and said to the driver, "Royal Hansaburgher Hotel, please."

The driver nodded, and the limousine floated off the ground into a tunnel leading to the surface. Max and Isobel leaned against each other, completely drained from the evening. Light from the city shone in on the couple as the limo exited the tunnel. The vehicle had traveled several city blocks away from Union Street. Soon, the chauffeur stopped the limo before the hotel's port-cochere. He waited while his two weary passengers entered the hotel before he sped off into the night.

Part Three

Marquess

CHAPTER ONE

Above Stahlburgh and Back

Exhausted, Max and Isobel stumbled into their suite at the hotel. They were in the *Primus* suite. Max had done the calculations, and the suite was more cost-effective than two separate rooms. Max went directly into one of the two bedrooms and promptly flopped face-forward on the bed, fully clothed.

Moments later, Isobel entered, wearing her nightgown. Isobel rolled Max over on his back and began to unbutton his jacket.

"I am too exhausted for you to take advantage of me," Max said.

"Well, you should at least be in your underwear. This outfit is your very best, and there is no need to wrinkle these clothes. Besides, I can't take advantage of you. You are my fiancé," Isobel said, "my marquess."

Max helped her as she undressed him. Minutes later, his clothes were hung, and Max was left wearing underwear and an undershirt. He slid between the sheets in the waiting bed, fully expecting Isobel to go, yet she crawled into the bed beside him.

Max wondered if he should attempt some resistance as Isobel curled into his arms, but he heard her soft breathing next to him before he could utter a sound. He listened to the rhythm of her soft snores.

Max awoke. He felt Isobel's head move on his chest. He looked down to see her blue eyes looking up at him.

"Good morning, brave sheriff of the Sheeplands," Isobel said with a smile.

"Good morning, almost Marchioness Fraser," Max said, smiling.

Isobel kissed him long and passionately. The couple spent several minutes kissing, enjoying the feel of each other's bodies being next to each other.

Isobel broke the lip lock and said, "Marchioness Fraser, not bad for the worst adventuress in the Union. Now, let's get moving before you use me and decide to find a better adventuress to undress you."

"Behave, or I'll put you in the stocks!" Max said, "I can do that now that I am a sheriff."

"What's my crime, officer?" Isobel said, batting her eyes.

"Seducing and then starving the protector's agent," Max said.

"Well, I am guilty on the first count," Isobel said, "but I contest the second charge since I've ordered breakfast for us."

"Well, I will withhold punishment as this is your first infraction of seducing a marquess, but I'm keeping my eyes on you, lady!" Max said.

"I expect nothing less," Isobel said, "that will make things harder for other adventuresses—my competition—to lure you away." Max laughed.

"Well then, the shower is yours if you want to freshen up," Max said.

Max stood up in an undershirt and boxers. Simultaneously, there was a knock on the outermost suite door.

"Your breakfast awaits, your grace," Isobel said, motioning to the door. Max traversed the bedroom, closed the bedroom door, and walked over to open the outer door. Opening the door, Max saw a bellhop with a cart, presumably with the food.

"Breakfast, sir," the bellhop said, wheeling the cart into the suite's common area, bowing, and leaving without raising an eyebrow at Max's attire. Max checked the plate and found a hearty Sheeplands breakfast that would have fed a family of four. Max greedily spooned some eggs and bacon on his plate. He was shoveling a large forkful of eggs into his mouth when his father's old tablet (or Max's new tablet) chirped. Max headed back to his bedroom to find the noisemaker.

Picking up the tablet from the dresser, Max saw he had a message from Martha Clark. The subject said, "Resignation". Max wondered why the personal secretary had chosen this exact moment to resign. He looked for Isobel to mention the odd news to her but heard the shower running, so he returned to eat breakfast in the main room. As he ate, he turned on the holo-set.

The Union News Service logo appeared on the screen, followed by a news announcer. The woman was of Sud-Stahlburghian stock and spoke with the solid Germanic accent of the Southrons.

"Today, we have urgent news. Confidential sources inside the protector's villa tell us that the protector has made Maximilian Fraser the Sheriff of the Sheeplands. Furthermore, our source states that the protector raised the Fraser to the rank of marquess and declared the Sheeplands as a march-frontier. Here at the Union News Service, we are seeking comments from the great houses. We will update this story as more details become available..."

Max's fork and eggs dropped from his hand as he just stared at the screen. How was the news of his elevation reported so quickly? Isobel came out from her shower. She wore a towel around her head and a bathrobe.

"Your turn," she said to Max.

When he didn't respond, she asked, "What's wrong?"

Max pointed to the headlines on the live news service on his tablet. Yaist News – Felgenland read "Sheeplands Militarization?"

"Wow, that's fast for a leak. What is the press saying?" Isobel asked, but she then skimmed the article over Max's shoulder.

"I wonder how the events of last night got leaked?" Max said, looking at Isobel.

"These things happen all the time. Usually, the leaks take a day or two," Isobel said, "You should contact the protector and assure him that we didn't leak the news."

"Good idea, I'll call the villa's switchboard," Max said, punching the comms app on the tablet. The dial tone connected, and the long beep chirp beep of the public exchange sounded.

"Operator, protector's Villa, how may I help you?" a woman said.

"This is *Graf*, err, I mean *Markgraf* Fraser. I need to speak to the protector urgently," Max said, almost forgetting his new title.

"Hold, please," the operator said. Max put the microphone on mute to say something to Isobel.

"Martha up and quit," Max said, "We may need to stay to hire someone."

The tablet hummed with *The Marching Song of the Felgenland*, the Assault's hymn, as Max sat on hold.

Isobel dried her hair, paused momentarily, and said, "What about your aunt?"

"What about May?" Max said.

Isobel was about to respond when a voice on Max's tablet cut her off.

"This is Weber. How may I help?" the majordomo's voice rang out.

Max flipped the mute off, "Hello, Weber, I need to speak with the Lord Protector."

"He is indisposed, your grace. May I convey a message?" Weber asked.

"Yes, please inform him I had nothing to do with the breaking news. Isobel and I returned to our room and went to sleep," Max said.

"I will carry your message," Weber said, "can I help with anything else?"

"No, thank you. Goodbye," Max said.

"Good day, sir," Weber replied and cut the connection.

"May?" Max asked, changing subjects abruptly.

"Oh, May, she is perfect as a personal secretary. She is good with organization, and she's lived here in the capital. "

"Maybe, I'm not sure..." Max said but was cut off by Isobel.

"Consider the possibilities, dear. Give May a trial period, and let her know the position is temporary. She might surprise you. Now, get a shower. It looks like we will have another drama-filled day."

Max nodded and went into the bathroom, and closed the door. Max was still trying to decipher who and why someone had tipped off the news service as he stripped and stepped into the shower. Max also wondered why Martha Clark had quit yesterday and whether it had anything to do with the news. As the shower steamed, Max lathered up reflexively while gathering wool.

Max realized so much had happened, and he hadn't even had his coffee yet. In proposing May to replace *Frau* Clark, Isobel had made a compelling point. Max thought about the trust he would give May as his secretary, and trusting May worried him. Max already had so much on his plate that he didn't know where to start. He had a secret spy camp to build, a civil war to stop, a wedding to plan with Isobel, a personal secretary to hire, a house to rebuild, roads to pave, levies to raise, and finances to balance. The protector had helped him immensely in all these projects, but Max wasn't sure how fast the protector would require results. Max wanted to be proactive and cross off the whole to-do list as soon as possible.

Miraculously, Max had cleaned himself entirely by muscle memory, and he shut off the faucet. He stepped out and wiped a small spot on the mirror to shave the slight stubble on his face, then grabbed a towel, wrapped the towel around him like a kilt, and entered the bedroom.

Max thought about the leak, but for all that his thinking could conjure, he couldn't figure out how the news had discovered his promotion. He saw that Isobel had neatly laid out traveling clothes for him. On one of the easy chairs were a long t-shirt, canvas trousers, hiking socks, a light jacket, and his trail boots. Max heard Isobel moving around in the common area where she had gone to give him privacy. Max dressed and was presentable within a few minutes.

"Max, you ready?" Isobel asked from the other side of the door.

"Yes, you can open the door," Max said as he grabbed his familiar duffel bag. Isobel stood in her usual hiking skirt, sweater, boots, and headscarf. The couple looked like characters from a postcard from the Sheeplands.

"So, about your aunt?"

"I'll give her a go. Now, let's get out here. I doubt I can afford another day in this expensive city," Max said as he looked at the bill for breakfast.

"I was thinking about that. I've got some personal money. How about we take a spaceflight home?"

"They are expensive, and we'd need to land near a railway line to get home. There isn't a spaceport in Gilbraith-on-Heather. Incidentally, I need to talk to you about that."

"Oh really?" Isobel said, "Why so?"

"I've been thinking of clearing some of the forests around Cairnbahan to build a spaceport," Max said.

"Sounds like you have already made your mind up. Were you going to discuss this with me?" Isobel said. She seemed hurt by Max's statement.

"I'm sorry," Max said, looking her in the eyes, "the past few days have been more intense than I ever expected."

Isobel's face softened, "I understand. We've been moving so fast. I want to participate in decision-making, especially with Cairnbahan and everything else! I am sorry I feel so protective of the barony. I keep telling myself we can share responsibility for Cairnbahan, but it is hard to let go."

Max hugged Isobel and said, "We can share all the responsibility down to the dishes. We have to."

The couple remained in each other's arms, drawing comfort from the other for a few minutes, and then Isobel said, "All right, let's get going. I want to hear your ideas. Plus, I need to get back to Cairnbahan. I need to move my things into the Bonnie Dundee, and there is a laundry list of things that must be done. Clans need to be notified, people will have to update our letterhead, and I must practice my marchioness wave—all important stuff!"

Max gave Isobel's hand a tug to signal they needed to leave the suite. They headed to the hotel lobby. Max placed the electronic key in the automated front desk checkout. He and Isobel then went outside to the taxi stand.

Max approached the waiting cabbie. The cabbie leaned against the hover-vehicle's hood, reading a paper titled, "Thursday's News! New Sheriff in Town!" The paper also showed a lousy picture of Max from his Assault days.

Max approached and said "Midlothian Spaceport" to the cabbie.

"Which Spaceline?" the cabbie asked, tossing the paper into the front seat.

"Felgenland Aerospace," Isobel answered as she hopped into the cab. Max handed the bags to the cabbie, who placed them into the storage compartment. Max climbed inside next to Isobel and waited as the cabbie closed the door. Then, the cabbie took his station at the hovercab's controls, and the vehicle lifted from the ground with a whir of fans.

"I have a few plans for the earldom—dang! I mean march! That I want to share with you, Isobel," Max said, stumbling over his new demesne's name. Max wanted to reset the discussion on the spaceport with Isobel, and a reset meant starting over.

"Sure, go ahead, I'm listening," Isobel said with a smile. The cab accelerated and journeyed towards the city's edge and the spaceport beyond.

"Well, I need to raise the levies. The Bonnie Dundee is in a terrible state, and so are the roads..." Max said, placing a calming hand on a visibly irritated Isobel at the mention of the roads.

"Yes, I know they are all bad, but we need to make an effort for the protector."

"Oy! You're that lord!" the cabbie said, looking at Max in the mirror.

"Hi, yes," Max said, trying to dissuade the cabbie from the conversation.

"The paper said you're going to declare martial law. Is that true?" the cabbie asked. Max looked at Isobel, who shrugged.

"Don't believe everything in the paper," Max said.

"I figured," the cabbie replied, "I should have known better. I only bought that rag because of the title. Blasted liars!"

"Let's talk later," Isobel said, tilting her head towards the cabbie. Max nodded and waited as the cab moved towards their destination. Max looked forward as the cabbie stared at the couple through the rearview. Max noticed the spaceport past the driver up ahead. Within minutes, the cab pulled into the spaceport's departure drop-off queue.

Max and Isobel hopped out, and Max threw several silver griffins at the cabbie covering the fair and a bit more and said, "Keep the change!"

The cabbie nodded. The excess was a nice tip. Then the cabbie popped the trunk and said to Max, "Good luck, guv! Give them rebels a taste of the protector's boot!"

Max nodded as he grabbed his luggage and handed Isobel hers. The couple stepped onto the sidewalk and headed through the security scanners at the spaceport's entrance.

Max and Isobel frantically searched the departure boards for their terminal and flight. After a moment, Isobel said, "There is our flight, terminal charlie, number two twenty-seven."

Max nodded and grabbed Isobel's hand, and they were off to the "C" terminal.

"Back to the work on the... march," Max said, hesitating to use the correct term.

"Yes, the levies, you know we don't have the labor needed to do a proper job!" Isobel said.

"Yes, we'll need to supplement what we have with skilled labor. I can't make ends meet otherwise," Max said. Isobel nodded.

"I was thinking the same thing myself. We get a little salary from the protector. Do you think the money can cover the costs?" Isobel asked.

"The funds have to go as far as they can. We're going to spend a small fortune on the spaceport. I'm not sure of the timber in those forests. If the trees were Steelwood, the clearing would pay for the spaceport twice over," Max said.

"Wait, where were you planning on putting the spaceport? There are only a few sites where the land could support all that plasticrete."

"I was thinking on the east side of the White Mountain," Max said, "with your assent, your excellency."

"The east side is a little secluded for a spaceport," Isobel said with a frown.

"Well, I was thinking that the spaceport would be located in an area away from the natural vistas of the mountains, as well as between Gilbraith village and Cairnbahan village. Then we would have two possible labor pools..."

Isobel stopped Max by kissing him. Max eagerly kissed her, stopping momentarily to ask, "What was that for?"

Isobel smiled and said, "Now I see your plan, you beautiful man! The spaceport project is located between Gilbraith and Cairnbahan equally, spreading prosperity to both villages. I thought you would place the spaceport on the south side, which would have been terrible. A south location would destroy the views and make Cairnbahan less central to the March. Did anyone ever tell you that you aren't just a pretty face, mister marquess?"

Max laughed. He said, "Well, I thought with my good looks and your brains, we could go places..."

Isobel's demeanor softened, and she said, "I don't know why I was so irritated about you developing the barony, but now I see that you aren't being selfish with those plans. My clan will be very pleased by them."

"You realize Cairnbahan will fold into the march with our marriage?" Max said, "The Douglases will become my kinsmen, too."

Isobel looked slightly surprised, "I hadn't thought of that. I suppose that will cause some issues with my people. We prefer to lead."

Isobel then stopped walking, hand on her chin, thinking. Max waited for a moment. He envisioned smoke pouring from her ears. She was so deep in thought.

Max poked Isobel and said, "Pfennig for your thoughts?"

"All of these developments seriously complicate the two children we would have."

"Who said I signed on for just two?" Max said.

"Exactly. Our eldest son will get the March, and then we'll need a few spares for the barony and any other territory you confiscate."

"Confiscate what?" Max said quizzically.

"Oh dearest, as the protector's direct vassal and sheriff, any lands or titles that were forfeit become yours as the right of payment. If someone so much as jaywalks, you could seize their assets. Even if Parliament or the protector later revoked your actions, you would still keep any rent paid during possession. These laws have been in place for almost a hundred years," Isobel said, "we often forget, but the Union was not always a peaceful place."

"Sure, but let's focus on current problems, dear," Max said, "I'll worry about counting my seizures another day."

"Speaking of current problems, I have an idea. Let me worry about the Bonnie Dundee, Max dear. I have some ideas on where I'd like to go with the great house, and the old pile will soon be my responsibility anyway."

"Well..." Max said, not entirely ready to let go of the responsibility of his ancestral home.

"If I oversee the house renovations, I have a perfect excuse to stay at the Bonnie Dundee. Would you like to have a permanent sleepover with me, Max?" Isobel batted her eyes at Max.

"Well, if those are the conditions, I suppose," Max replied. He was rewarded with a long, slow kiss from Isobel.

When they broke the lip lock, she said, "Oh! I am so excited. We'll start tearing down walls, and the blue room will get repainted or go!"

Max laughed, "I'm not going fight you to keep the blue room. Now, the red room is another story. Ewan and I used to play Assaultmen and Pirates there!"

"Sure, the red room can stay. You'll need a billiards room too! So you can do boy stuff with your privy council there. My girls and I shall repaint and enlarge that drawing room into a modern one."

Max was about to respond when a voice came over the intercom and said, "Attention, attention, now boarding flight two two seven."

"That's us!" Isobel said, "I'm so excited. This trip will be my first time off the planet."

Isobel grabbed Max's hand and started pulling him along to the gate. Max smiled. He had been off-world many times, and the gate was no big deal. Reaching the gate agent, the couple flashed their tickets on Isobel's tablet. Max dropped his bag on the conveyor that sat nearby. Isobel followed suit, and the conveyor took their luggage into the spacecraft's cargo bay.

Max and Isobel then went through the door and into the skyway. Isobel was like a child as she eagerly popped her head into the small round windows, looking out at the spacecraft that sat refueling for their journey. The flight safety attendant directed them to their seats as they entered the passenger cabin. Max couldn't help but give the attractive attendant a side-eye.

As they walked down the long aisle to their seat, Isobel scowled at Max playfully and pointed two fingers at her eyes, then at Max to signal she was watching him.

"I was just window shopping. Thank the Allfather I have you," Max said, "the attendant is so homely compared to you."

"I love you, you big fat liar," Isobel said, "she was way better looking than I am."

"Not my type," Max said, "Pretty women just get you into trouble."

"Oh, I'm not a pretty woman now, eh?" Isobel said with a mischievous smile.

"You never were. You're a beautiful woman," Max said.

"That was a smooth recovery," Isobel said, pulling Max close for a quick kiss, temporarily blocking traffic. Just as quickly, she broke the lip lock as they turned and found their seats.

Sitting down, Max gave Isobel the window seat. Her blond ringlets bounced up and down as she tried to crane her neck to look out the window to the left and right. After a few minutes of gawking, Isobel stopped and rested her head against Max's shoulder.

"I love you, Isobel," Max said as she relaxed against him.

"I love you too, Max," she replied. The spacecraft jumped as the attendants shut the hatches. The couple was on their way. In a few hours, they would be back where they belonged in the Sheeplands.

CHAPTER TWO
Congratulations and Cautions

After two hours of transit, with Isobel oohing and ah-ing over weightlessness, the stars, and seeing Stahlburgh curving underneath, the spacecraft entered the atmosphere and landed. Max and Isobel departed from the spacecraft and collected their luggage at the terminal. They then went to the ground transport deck and found their train waiting. They boarded and found their private room. Max tossed the bags in a cargo bin and sat on one of the benches.

As Isobel sat beside Max, she coquettishly said, "Is this seat taken, sir?"

"The seat is occupied now. What is a beautiful woman like you doing on a train like this?" Max asked with a smile.

"Oh, I am glad my reputation hasn't proceeded me. I'm an adventuress, you see, Stahlburgh's worst, in fact."

"That's terrible because I am, in fact, Stahlburgh's newest marquess and sadly unmarried. I'd be an easy mark for even the worst adventuress. Especially if she kissed me," Max said.

"Let's find out," Isobel said, drawing close and kissing Max. For several minutes, the couple kissed each other softly and then passionately.

Max broke the lip-lock and said, "Marry me, beautiful... See, I am the easiest mark!"

"Of course, I'll marry you. I hope you're rich, with a flashy car, and I can spend my weekends in some snobby spa in the capital," Isobel said, winking.

"Yeah, about that fortune..." Max said.

"Oh, drat! This always happens to me: I meet a cute marquess, and he has no flashy car or fortune! Wah, woe unto me!" Isobel said, "Quick, kiss me again before I melt down some more."

"Okay," Max said eagerly, leaning in towards Isobel. The couple spent several hours kissing and holding each other. Neither Max nor Isobel were brave enough to do anymore, just yet. But the long, passionate kissing was a pleasant speed for Max, and he stopped a kiss with Isobel long enough to realize they had reached the station outside of Gilbraith-on-Heather. For Max, the previous arrival, when he claimed his inheritance, seemed like another lifetime. Isobel stood and checked herself in the full-length mirror mounted on the door to their private compartment.

Max peered at his reflection over Isobel's shoulder. Max noticed that when Isobel was in flats, he stood half a head taller than she. Then, he focused on the business at hand: checking for lipstick. He'd be damned if May insinuated he was a playboy again.

Both Isobel and Max, looking less like two randy teenagers and more like stately nobles, left their compartment, bags in hand, and exited the train.

Crossing the station, Max saw Cormac in the parking lot. The huntsman waited in the estate's beat-up hover truck. Max's step stuttered when he noticed Cormac wore a sling.

"Cormac, what happened to your arm," Max asked as he and Isobel reached the truck.

"Oh, nothing," Cormac said, "We've had a few more raids."

"That's about to stop," Max said. He threw the luggage into the truck bed and showed Cormac the protector's ring.

"Well done, lad," Cormac said, looking at the ring and flashing Max a smile.

"He's a marquess now, and we got engaged," Isobel said. Max wasn't sure what Isobel was trying to do, but to his untrained eye,

Max suspected Isobel was baiting Cormac.

Cormac smiled and said, "I'm glad to see a Fraser finally tamed one of the Douglas women."

"I tamed him," Isobel said with a giggle, "and he's finally housebroken too."

"That remains to be seen, lass. I've never met a woman who can take the wildness out of our Max. Still, congratulations are in order," Cormac said dryly, "we'll head back to the Bonnie Dundee immediately." Max nodded.

He helped Isobel into the hover truck before climbing in after her and closing the passenger door. The vehicle moved a bit slower with a one-armed Cormac at the controls. Max watched as Cormac tried to control the truck. The huntsman would grimace every time he needed to make a turn due to the pain in his slung right arm.

"Cormac, I should have driven," Max said, "Or you could just use the driving app."

"That app is older than I am. No, thank you," Cormac said as he continued to work the controls. The truck wound along the track of the main road between the station and the village. When the truck reached the outskirts of Gilbraith village, a large group of people blocked the way.

"What's this?" Max asked.

"Best to get out and investigate," Cormac said. Max stepped out of the truck. Meg and Andrew were at the head of the assembled folk.

"Hip, hip," Meg and Andrew cheered.

"Hooray!" the crowd roared. Max noted his barons, even Geordie, were present.

"What's this all about?" Max asked.

"Your vassals are here to greet you, your grace," Andrew said, "We congratulate you on your engagement and elevation and offer support in your duty as sheriff of the Sheeplands."

Isobel stepped out of the truck, joined Max, and asked, "What was the cheering for?"

Meg approached Isobel and said, "Congratulations, soon-to-be sister."

"Megan…" Isobel said but was cut off by Meg.

"Call me Meg, we're family," she said.

"Okay, Meg," Isobel said, "there is no need for all this. People should be working."

"Isobel, hush," Meg said, "The county hasn't had a lady in decades. Enjoy your moment."

"We're a march now, love," Andrew said.

Meg rolled her eyes at her husband and said, "Whatever, dear."

Max stood watching everyone. He didn't know what to think. The rest of the Sheeplands was on the knife edge of civil war, and his county, or now his march, had a festival atmosphere. Max remembered the plans he and Isobel had made and decided to act. If the people were happy, he had a better chance of harnessing that energy for what needed to be done.

"I'm glad you are all here," Max said as the commotion in the crowd died down at his words, "After our trip to the capital, we have come back with news and many plans for the future. We need your support in morale, effort, and money."

The crowd grew somber, but Max continued, "First, the good news is we will build a spaceport in the march."

The crowd went wild with cheering. A spaceport meant more tourism, trade, and money. A province with a spaceport, even a small one, was a destination the galaxy could visit.

"Next, we will need to raise the levies," Max said, and the crowd's enthusiasm died. No one wanted to work their conscription even though the law mandated service.

"The soon-to-be Marchioness Fraser, our beloved Isobel, and I have identified several projects all of us must complete. Upon completion, these projects will bring jobs and much-needed money into March. One of our first projects is to convert the Bonnie Dundee into a destination hotel destination for tourists. To that end, we will also start improving the camping areas; hunting and fishing spots; and hiking trails to increase tourism in our march."

The crowd cheered as what Max said sounded like more money to the assembled folks.

Max ended his speech and said, "However, I recognize we should celebrate all our good fortune. Therefore, I declare a celebration of our engagement and the county becoming a march. We will have a fair eleven weeks hence. The first full week of July will be a public holiday."

The crowd cheered and immediately began to disperse. Max felt a little cynicism about the quick exit. He knew the people rushed to return to their kitchens and workshops. Each village family would start working day and night, preparing goods for the fair. The townsfolk left, and Geordie and the other barons approached.

"Congratulations, old chap," he said to Max. The genuine pleasure on his face made Max feel better about their last parting.

Max took his extended hand and said, "Thank you, Geordie, this means a lot to me."

"I'm glad to see Isobel chose you, Max. I was concerned that she would end up a spinster," Geordie said with a wink, "Now, if you'll permit me, I would like to kiss your fiancée."

"If she has no objections," Max said.

"Spinster, really Geordie," Isobel said, in mock anger, and then softly she said, "Thank you, my friend."

Geordie gave Isobel a quick peck on the cheek and said, "I am happy to see you happy, and I wish you both long life and joy."

Geordie stepped back and said quietly to Max, "And I have news, my widow friend is closing up her affairs on Lochiel and relocating here to Gilbraith. She seemed very keen to attempt a more conventional relationship. Wish me luck."

Max smiled wide at Geordie's statement and clapped him on the shoulder, "I wish you the best of all luck!"

Geordie nodded and stepped aside as the other barons jostled into a queue to wish the couple well. At the end of the queue, after many handshakes, congratulations, and, for Max, pats on the back, Andrew, Meg, May, and Hector approached.

"We wish you a long life and joy," Andrew said.

"And welcome to the family," said Meg.

Hector then stepped forward. He looked flush as if he had run to the gathering. Max noted dirt on Hector's trousers as if the man had been doing honest work.

Hector rushed forward and said, "Best wishes, cousin, and you too, baroness."

"Hector," Max said, "I have a proposal for you when we return to the Bonnie Dundee, as well as for your mother."

At the mention of her name, May stepped forward. Unlike her everyday restraint, she was tearful. She composed herself momentarily and said, "I love a good wedding. Congratulations, nephew and soon-to-be niece."

"May," Isobel said, "Kenneth's personal secretary has resigned. We thought you might be willing to become the marquess' personal secretary in the capital."

Had Isobel offered to make May the patroness, she couldn't have made a better impression on the woman. May's normally biddy face lit up like fireworks. May seemed to lose years, almost becoming younger before Max and Isobel's eyes.

"I'd be honored with such an intelligent woman as you, the first Baroness of Cairnbahan and the soon-to-be Marchioness Fraser. I can see my abilities are no longer needed here. Alas, I know you both fear that the estate will never be the same without my presence, but you will manage. If I must sacrifice my life here in the country for the bright lights of the capital to assist my liege, I will do so."

Max struggled not to laugh. He was sure May would pack and be on a train first thing in the morning. Isobel had won May's undying loyalty, and Max's concerns about his aunt's potential mischief evaporated. Isobel had turned a potential foe into her staunchest ally in one request. Max looked at Isobel. She was beautiful, and thankfully, she was on his side.

As Meg and Andrew left for Loch Urquhart, stragglers from the outlying shires came forward. The stragglers comprised the elders of the various surrounding villages, who came and praised Max and Isobel, declaring the match to be the best since Adam and Eve.

As the *Holstensonne* dipped below the horizon, the remaining well-wishers started to disperse. Max stretched, glad to have a moment of peace and space. He moved to the truck and reached the driver's seat before Cormac.

"I should drive you, lad," Cormac said, "my duty demands as much."

"Cormac, I request that you guard my intended," Max said. He had an edge of sternness in his voice for good measure.

"As you wish, lad," Cormac said, resigning himself to sitting next to Isobel. Max smiled inwardly. He either had sounded stern enough, or Cormac hurt sufficiently to comply.

Isobel appeared shortly and sat in the truck's middle seat. Cormac sat next to the door. Max started up the hover-truck and put the vehicle into drive. As the fans spun up, Max asked, "Where to first?"

"Cairnbahan, I'd like to see my family and pack up," Isobel said.

"Pack? Where are you going, Isobel?" Max asked, completely forgetting the plans Isobel had made hours before.

"Home with you, love," she said, "I need to be at ground zero for wedding planning, house reconstruction, and spaceport building."

Max smiled, chagrined, "Oh yeah, that's right..."

Cormac grunted in disapproval but moments later asked, "Shall I prepare your mother's rooms for her excellency?"

Isobel looked to Max, unsure of how this would affect him. The rooms were dust- and cobweb-ridden, and they had been closed for almost two decades. Max supposed that room renovation of the rooms had been too emotionally difficult for Kenneth.

Max pondered how he felt about Isobel in his mother's apartments. Max expected to feel sadness or remorse, but the more he thought about the circumstance, the happier he felt. Max envisioned his mother today and imagined she would be ecstatic with happiness for her son.

"Yes, Cormac," Max said, then he said to Isobel, "The rooms are dusty and full of cobwebs. I don't think anyone has been in them in a score of years."

"Will I be close to your room," asked Isobel.

"Of course, my mother's rooms are attached to the state apartments across from my father's rooms. I'm not a huge fan of the design, so perhaps we can discuss renovations later," Max said.

"Well then, some dust and spiders don't bother me," Isobel said.

"I will get rid of critters," Cormac said, "part of my job, after all."

"Thank you, Cormac," Isobel said, even though her thanks made the old huntsman even more uncomfortable. Max started driving towards Cairnbahan.

Max said, "I think the Bonnie Dundee needs a renovation to modernize the space and make the house more livable."

"The Bonnie Dundee has functioned well for over two hundred years. Why change now, lad," Cormac asked.

"Cormac, let's be realistic here. The house is falling apart," Max said as he guided the truck through the village and down the track to Douglas Hall. Cormac sat and remained silent. Max figured he had upset the man, violating some sacred tradition about the house.

"Besides, I am a marquess now. The protector may decide to visit his direct vassal. We need to make sure the Bonnie Dundee doesn't collapse on him," Max said.

If Cormac heard Max's statement, he refused further comment. Max felt every minute of the awkward silence until the vehicle popped over the hill on the track, revealing the back side of Douglas Hall.

Like an old hound waiting for his master, Kensie stood at the house's back entrance. Max wondered if Kensie was some space wizard since he always seemed to know Isobel's whereabouts and be there. Max coasted the truck into a spot near the entrance, and Isobel immediately crawled over Max and out of the vehicle.

"Kensie," Isobel said as she ran up and hugged her uncle. He hugged her back with a paternal smile on his face.

"Niece, you've come back in one piece, and from what the village is saying, with a soon-to-be husband as well," Kensie said as Isobel released her grip.

"You remember Max, right, Kensie?" Isobel said.

"Of course, my confused wanderer, confused no more, I hope?" Kensie said to Max. Max shut down the hover truck, exited, and stood beside the driver's door.

"No, sir, I know what I want now is... Your blessing on our impending nuptials," Max said.

"Who am I to stand in the way of love or Isobel?" Kensie said, "Go forth and be happy with my blessing."

"Thank you, Kensie," Isobel said, detaching from the man.

"Would you have decided not to marry Max if I said no?" Kensie asked.

"Um, no," Isobel said.

"Then I shall bend like a reed in the wind," Kensie said, "That's good advice for you too, young Max."

Max smiled, and the old man gave him a knowing wink.

"Kensie, will you entertain Max and Cormac while I get my things?" Isobel said.

"I am a reed, my dear young wind," he said. Isobel smiled and ran off into the house.

"Max," Kensie said in a more serious tone than usual, "be careful. Being an agent of the Protector is dangerous business."

"You've seen the news?" Max said. Kensie nodded.

"I'll be careful. The stakes are much higher now," Max said.

"Aye. Remember that the Sheeplanders have always believed themselves to be the last bastion of independence in the Union. They will see you as the protector's ambitious lackey. Being sheriff will not endear you to anyone outside our new march," Kensie said, "I know you are a brave man, but you will now learn if you are a wise man. If you let her, Isobel will help you. I do worry, though, that the both of you will charge blindly off a cliff at the bidding of a very fickle master."

"Why are you worried, Kensie?" Max asked, "Has anything happened?"

"No, maybe I worry needlessly. I am old enough to remember the earlier years of the last protector, Karl. The old protector was more about order, even if he had to destroy families to achieve his goals. Stahlburgh has been settled for a long time compared to other worlds in the rim of human expansion. However, the protectors are new, and they've only been here for one hundred years. We Sheeplanders like old things, maybe overmuch. All I am saying is be careful, trust Isobel, your clan, the Douglas—your new kinsmen, and your retainers, but give everyone else little consideration. I offer some friendly advice from an old man who has seen great lords cut down while not-so-great lords, with bloody hands, usurp their places."

Kensie finished just as Isobel returned from the house, rolling three suitcases behind her.

"Is that all you're taking?" Kensie asked, again winking to Max, "I doubt that would even empty your main closet, and poor Cormac only has one hand after the ambush..."

Max looked at the truck. Cormac hadn't moved nor spoken the entire time.

"Oh, I'll send for the rest. This will get me through the next twenty-five hours," Isobel said at Kensie's teasing. She hefted a suitcase while Max quickly claimed the other two. Max was about to throw the cases into the truck bed, but as he picked them up, he groaned at their weight.

"You didn't have to bring the radiation-shielded space suits, dear," Max said as he threw the cases one by one into the bed.

"Have spacesuit, will travel is what I always say," Isobel said with a wink, "besides, a big strong marquess like you should be able to manhandle my suitcases considering how you've dragged me these past two days, right caveman?"

"Ugha boogah!" Max said, beating his chest and heading over to the driver's side hatch. Isobel had already climbed into the truck and was sitting beside the silent Cormac.

Kensie stepped off the patio, approached the passenger side window, and said to Cormac, "Hello, old friend, you've been uncharacteristically quiet. I've missed you around the house here. You are always welcome on the stoop with me."

Cormac turned bright red. Whether in anger or embarrassment, Max wasn't quite sure.

"I wish I could," Cormac said, "but with the poachers about, I've got enough work left for a lifetime, old friend. Besides, I can't tolerate your whisky. I always wake up with a hangover," Cormac said with a smile.

"Well, you'll get used to the whisky if you drink enough of the stuff," Kensie said with a smile, "Maybe next time?"

"Aye," was all Cormac said. Max wasn't sure what was going on with the huntsman, but whatever bothered Cormac fiercely irritated the man.

Kensie told the three, "Don't be strangers."

"I'll be back. Goodbye, Kensie," Isobel said, waving as Max sat and started the fans. Over the roar of the fans, Cormac said to Kensie, "Next time, for sure."

Max put the vehicle into drive, made a K-turn, and headed towards the estate. After a long day, the trio was bound for the Bonnie Dundee.

CHAPTER THREE

Tearing Up the House

Max banged on the nail again with his hammer. Finally, the stubborn bit of metal started sinking into the frame. Max cursed his current poverty. Sure, the protector promised Max a salary, but Max wasn't sure if or when he'd receive the funds. Max wondered if the news leak had foiled some plan. Max hefted the hammer and struck the nail. Both the hammer and the nail were rusty. Max had found them in an outbuilding barely sealed against the elements. Despite the rust, Max noted they still worked.

Max wished he had a discretionary fund. Then, he could have bought power tools to speed up the work. Instead, he and Isobel rolled up their sleeves and vowed to do the work themselves with materials at hand. Max had been working on the renovations for almost two months. Max would soon have a small bump in his finances as the fair would begin. The nascent hotel that was the Bonnie Dundee had started receiving booking requests, and there were rents Max would collect from the village for the fair. The village folk were frantically decorating and preparing for the festivities. Max's father, Kenneth, hadn't had a fair or celebration in decades, and the people of the new march had received a lot of good fortune that they wished to celebrate.

"Just two more weeks and the house will be in a better state, and Isobel and I will be married," Max said.

"Sounds too easy," Isobel said, startling Max and causing him to hit his thumb.

"Ouch!" Max said as the hammer made contact with his thumb.

"Oh, I'm sorry, dear," Isobel said, suppressing a laugh, "I just came to see if you were finished yet?"

Max sucked on the dirty thumb to quell the pain. Removing the digit, Max said, "No, in fact, I feel like I am moving in reverse!"

Isobel nodded. She wore her work overalls, her hair tied back with an old strip of Fraser tartan from Max's mother's rooms.

"Well, we need to be done with the framing by evening. If we aren't ready, the drywall installers won't be able to start work tomorrow," Isobel said, a hint of frustration in her voice.

"Yeah," Max said, getting frustrated, "I need help. I'm, apparently, terrible at this sort of work." Isobel looked even more frustrated at Max's retort but closed her eyes and took a deep breath.

"Okay, I'll help, but I can only spare a half hour," Isobel said, picking up another hammer. She then grabbed a handful of nails and began pounding nails on the wooden frame in front of Max. Max checked the hurt thumb. The digit was serviceable. Max returned to the task.

The couple banged in nails and stood the frame against the wall. Isobel and Max checked the frame was square and then tacked down their work. Isobel tossed her hammer to the floor as the front door chimes echoed throughout the house.

"That's the paint delivery," Isobel said, "I'm going to see what's been delivered. Now, be a sweetie. Continue working on the walls marked for demolition in my rooms."

"This would be easier with the conscripts," Max said.

"Yes, Max, my love, but we need to prep the house so that the conscripts have a straightforward task. I doubt our conscripts will include a crew of master-finishing carpenters. With our luck, the conscripts will be more dangerous than you are at swinging a hammer. Now I'm off to supervise the paint delivery. Go up and finish the demolition, please. Just knock down the marked walls."

Max nodded and said, "Aye, I remember. 'X' means non-load bearing, according to the architect. Those are the ones safe to demolish."

"Yup, well, go on before I rip your clothes off," Isobel said, "there is something about a Union peer doing manual labor that gives me butterflies in my stomach."

Max pulled Isobel closer, kissed her, and said, "Maybe I should calm those butterflies."

"Later," Isobel said, pushing him away, "I need to check that the paint delivery is accurate after all the money we spent. I'd hate to see the five paint pallets contain the wrong shade or color."

"Aye," Max said, winking, "I'll knock down some walls with all this pent-up energy."

"Have fun," Isobel said, cocking her head alluringly, and then she turned and ran off. Max eyed the curves of her body as he watched her go. He wondered how he had managed without her.

Max could have planned and done the renovation by himself, but working together with Isobel, he felt more relaxed. Isobel would appear when the work began to pile up, making the load seem conquerable. She was a dynamo of planning, creativity, and energy.

Max then picked up and hefted the giant sledgehammer. He walked to the staircase that led down from the state apartments. Looking down the stairs, he was distracted by the nearby framing for the lock-out door.

Moving down the stairs to check the door, he felt satisfied with his and Isobel's work. The framing looked sturdy, and once roughed in, the door would separate the sixteen rooms of the Bonnie Dundee's family chambers.

Ewan and Molly resided in an ancient cabin between Gilbraith and Cairnbahan. The cabin was the epicenter of a new camping area by *Cruach Mhòr*. Their guests were in the developing hotel inside the Bonnie Dundee. USIS would complete the cabins in a few days, and Ewan's guests would move out of the Bonnie Dundee and into the camp. Then, Max would use Ewan's guests' rooms as a hotel. A hotel that was almost ready for its grand opening and the fair.

Max climbed back up the stairs. The stairs opened on the second floor near Max's bedroom and the state apartments. The state apartments were musty and full of dust. Max knew the rooms weren't dirty from the current work alone. Cleaning the rooms was yet another task on his to-do list. Max looked down the grand corridor leading to the state apartments. An expansive oil painting hung in the corridor. The canvas depicted MacLeod's first landing on Stahlburgh almost two hundred years ago. Max moved closer to the painting to examine the details. Max couldn't recall when he had last really looked at the composition. Taking in the painting as light poured in from the noonday sun, Max marveled at how the artist had painted the old MacLeod—the pirate looked determined. The artist's depiction showed the landing as monumental, but Max chuckled, remembering that MacLeod probably felt like Stahlburgh was just another pit stop on the way to more booty.

Max decided he had procrastinated enough and turned to his task. He needed to remove the walls that separated his mother's old rooms from the main section of state apartments. Max readied the sledgehammer and started knocking down the first wall with a large "X."

Max and Isobel had decided to reconstruct his bedroom, the state apartments, and the apartments Isobel currently occupied. A waft of Isobel's perfume reached Max's nose as he struck another hole in the wall. She had dowsed the dank rooms where she now lived with her scent to mask the stinky smell. Max assumed that since he smelled her perfume, he was in the right place and doing the right thing.

He struck another hole again. Soon, Isobel's rooms would be one grand suite that the plans called "the Marchioness's Suite." The name delighted Isobel, and Max did not contest the title, even though he'd live there too. As he continued to strike the wall, the drywall shattered and fell. Soon, the underlying studs were visible. After these rooms were demolished, Max would perform a similar deconstruction on his bedroom's side of the house.

Max's bedroom would be a part of grand apartments fit for the protector and his entourage. The work was all in preparation in case Max's liege should visit. Hector appeared as he made another strike, saying, "Max, I believe we needed to have a chat?"

Max put down the hammer, happy to have a moment to catch his breath, "Yes, Hector, I have been thinking..."

"Hopefully, good thoughts," Hector said, cutting Max off. Max realized the man was nervous and that Hector felt this conversation was a prelude to punishment.

"Hector," Max said in a cordial tone, "how would you like to be in charge of the spaceport construction?" Max and Isobel had repeatedly considered the spaceport and discussed Hector's role in the spaceport construction. They finally decided that the project manager was the best fit for Hector. He would need to supervise the project and report back to Max on the progress. The biggest challenge was ensuring the contractors stayed on schedule. The architects and engineers would own the technical details, while the construction crews and associated laborers would build the spaceport. As project manager, Hector would have a high visibility title that didn't require Max to micro-manage his cousin. Max had lined up an assistant project manager from a firm based in the capital, and the assistant would help keep the project on track should Hector find himself in over his head.

"Project Manager for the spaceport? Are you sure, cousin?" Hector asked.

"Yes, provided you feel you are up for the job," Max asked.

"I'll do my best, Max," Hector said. Max noted his cousin's sober attitude. Hector had changed from a man-child into a solemn gentleman in the past few weeks. May's departure had accelerated Hector's evolution. Max wasn't sure if Hector was pining for his mother's company or glad to be free of her.

"I expect nothing less," Max said, "being project manager will mean a lot of time bouncing between Cairnbahan and Gilbraith. I know you wanted to lead hunting and fishing expeditions, but your new responsibilities won't give you the time to do both. Are you all right with this change of duties?"

Hector smiled, nodded, and said, "Absolutely, I won't let you down."

"Good. The first meeting between the architects and engineers is tomorrow in Cairnbahan. When I finish here, I will forward you the pertinent documents. In the meantime, you might want to go down to the village and find a new suit," Max said, "have the tailor charge the estate accounts and consider the suit a signing bonus."

"I shall, and thank you again, cousin," Hector said. Hector bowed in thanks to Max and quickly left where Max was working. Max lifted the sledgehammer for another blow when Cormac's voice interrupted his work.

"A wise move, lad. Was that your thinking or Isobel's?"

Max sensed his anger rising. Max wasn't sure what had transpired between Cormac, Isobel, and her clan, but he wouldn't let this rift continue.

"I've never known you to hold such a fierce grudge," Max told his retainer, "Why don't you cut her a break."

"I am sorry, lad. I suppose I need to explain myself," Cormac said.

Max dropped the sledgehammer, stood facing Cormac, and said, "I know about Isobel's aunt Margaret."

"Isobel looks and acts like her so much, at times I forget they are different people," Cormac said.

"What happened?" Max asked. Max rested the sledgehammer on the floor, leaving the handle leaning against his leg.

"Back before you and even Archy, I was a young lad who had just become the chief huntsman here. The Bonnie Dundee was lively in those ancient days, and all the vassals would visit often. We all were younger then, and there were frequent hunts and fishing trips. One day, the Douglases show up at the house in all their finery, and Kenneth tells me to gear up for a stalking party off the range not far from where I found Archy..." Cormac paused and said, "Well, I gear up and all assemble, and I saw her, James's sister. She was decked out in Douglas tartan and looked like a right goddess coming to life in the Sheeplands. Well, I go out, leading all involved, and along the way, Margaret, or as she liked to be called Peg, comes next to me. We get to talking and strike up a little banter."

"And something deeper developed?" Max asked, suspicious of where the story was going.

"Aye," Cormac said nodding, "I began calling on her, even got James's permission to court Peg. Those were some of the happiest days of my life..."

"What happened?" Max asked.

"John Mercy happened," Cormac said the man's name like a curse, "Mercy shows up, in his best Assault uniform, to Douglas Hall one day. He was some distaff relation or perhaps a friend of the family. I never did find out."

"And she fell in love with him?" Max asked.

"Worse, they ran off—eloped," Cormac said, "you see, James favored our match. Kensie and I had become good friends as well. The menfolk would have seen Peg in a white dress with me as the groom."

"But Margaret didn't feel the same way?" Max asked.

"Mercy was gentry. He had lands, money, and was a dashing soldier. I guess Peg felt he was just a better choice," Cormac said, a tear rolling down his cheek, "I never found out. She left, and that was the last we heard from her."

"I'm sorry, Cormac," Max said. He wanted to hug Cormac, punch him on the shoulder, or do something to cheer the man up.

"There's more, lad," Cormac said, "A while ago, I decided to do some tracking of my own and find out where Peg went to. She and Mercy had a boy named John Junior, a fellow around your age."

"Maybe you could write her, Cormac?"

"Not possible, lad. Peg died giving birth to the boy, so she's gone now," Cormac said, another tear track rolling down his cheek, "I just find looking at Isobel so hard. They are so much alike. You are like a son to me..."

"But you also feel jealous, too," Max said.

Cormac straightened as if insulted but quickly deflated, saying, "Yes, lad. I am a wreck, and I think things would be best for all if I leave the Bonnie Dundee for a while."

"But, Cormac, I can't run this place without you," Max said.

"I can't stay right now. I need time to sort all this out," Cormac said, "Don't look so sad, laddie. Call my trip an overdue vacation. I'll return once I straighten myself out."

Max quickly released the sledgehammer's handle and hugged Cormac. Max worried the embrace would be awkward for the huntsman, but he felt Cormac's free arm gently clasp his back. The embrace was the closest thing Max had ever come to a paternal embrace.

"Take your time, old friend," Max said as the two broke the hug, "The Bonnie Dundee needs you."

"Not a moment longer than needed," Cormac said.

"Where will you go?" Max said.

"I've always fancied a vacation to Eisenwald, with its sun, sand, and beaches. All that would be a welcome change from cold, rain, cold, and clouds."

"Be careful you don't burn," Max said with a smile.

"I'm sure there will be ladies there that will rub lotion on any red that shows up," Cormac said with a slight grin, "Now that I've said my piece, I'm leaving."

"I see," Max said, "sounds like you have been planning this for a while."

"Aye, Max."

"Well, goodbye, old friend," Max said.

Cormac smiled wryly and said, "No, I'll see you later."

Max watched as his chief retainer and substitute father figure walked down the stairs and out of sight. He picked up the sledgehammer and smashed it against the wall with all his might. Max felt his eyes water. All because of the dust, Max reassured himself. After an hour of taking out his feelings on the walls, all that remained was the bare framing as a large partition between chambers. Max could see into the corridor connecting the state apartments from Isobel's room.

Isobel appeared and said, "Not too shabby, you've done a good job with the demolition."

Max smiled through his sweat, grime, and tears. He said, "Of course, I can break things. I was an Assaultman. We were paid to destroy stuff."

"Good, there will be more to do tomorrow. Now you need to go and clean up," Isobel said.

"What for?" Max asked.

"We've got a dinner with the Reverend James Fraser and his wife," Isobel said, "it part of our nuptial preparation classes remember?"

"That is today?" Max asked.

"Yes, dearest," Isobel replied, "The reverend has invited you and me to the Gilbraith parish hall to discuss our wedding."

"Drat, I thought that was tomorrow," Max said, "I had plans to knock down all of these walls today."

"One day at a time, Max. Go, get cleaned up. We need to get moving soon, especially if Cormac is driving."

"He won't be. He's left on an extended holiday on Eisenwald."

"Oh," Isobel said, unsure of what to say next, "Well, let's get going. The reverend and his wife await the pleasure of our company."

Max leaned the sledgehammer against a wall and returned to his room with its private bath. He noticed Isobel had laid out his formal jacket and his kilt. Max marveled at how much Isobel had integrated into his life in the weeks since the engagement. She was aided by the fact that both Meg and May had moved out. Isobel quickly became the woman of the house. There were no other contenders.

Max stepped into the shower after he stripped off the dirty work clothes. Max reviewed the list of what needed to be completed as he showered. Tasks would need to be changed in order of priority, all because of Cormac's sudden departure. Now, Max would need someone to manage the hunting and fishing.

Isobel had been complaining about the lack of help, specifically with the estate, and Max was determined to make screening candidates for a cook and butler his top priority. Max thought about how hard he and his soon-to-be wife worked as the dirt came off his body and swirled down the drain.

Toweling off, Max remembered that he needed to talk to Eoin about the conscripts. Eoin's clan had the duty of managing the conscript crews. Thankfully, Eoin and his clan would house and feed the conscripts as part of those duties, so Max only need provide the crews with directions.

Max quickly squeezed paste on a brush and began cleaning his teeth. Max looked at his reflection in the mirror and remembered he needed to check with Hector tomorrow on how the spaceport planning meeting went. Max then styled his hair. Isobel was a passable barber, and she had cut his mane into a high and tight comb over. Max then checked his chin to see if the stubble had gotten worse. His beard's shadow was still thin, and Max decided he did not need a shave. Max then exited the washroom and went into his bedroom to dress. The room would be enlarged in a day or two after the walls came down.

Max set about clothing himself, and in ten minutes, he was ready. He stood in the mirror and watched as his reflection completed belting the kilt. He exited his room and crossed the corridor before the state apartments to await Isobel's appearance. As he was halfway across the corridor, he heard a series of loud shouts coming from somewhere downstairs. Forgetting Isobel, Max ran to where he assumed the noise was coming from.

He proceeded down the stairs from the state apartments. Turning the corner, he saw the paint delivery men herded by gun-toting Ultra-Violets inside the house by the chapel. Max noted the terrorists wore purple bands that bore a silkscreen of the hammer and sickle. His Assault training took over. He turned away from the corridor and cautiously waited a few moments as the Ultra-Violets shoved their prisoners into the torn-up drawing room. Max needed a rifle.

Max decided to double back up the stairs. He moved down the corridor away from the state apartments and into the second floor of the grand corridor. He headed east, down the grand corridor, and to the grand staircase. He then descended the stairs and moved through the foyer, crossed the first floor of the grand corridor, and then the exit. Once outside, he proceeded to the estate manager's office. Max slipped inside, closed, and locked the door. Then, he crossed the room and unlocked the gun vault.

As a new colonel of volunteers in the Assault, he had been given five pallets of brand-new rifles. Most of the rifles sat in boxes coated in protective oil in one of the sheds, waiting for Max to build an armory. Max pulled the door open to the vault at the gun safe's open tone. Reaching in, Max pulled out an Anderson and Campbell 2350 pin rifle, which he'd claimed when the pallets arrived. He had already broken the gun apart, cleaned out the manufacturing medium, and re-oiled and lubricated all the parts as he had done in the service. Holding the rifle, Max felt like an avenging angel. He was most familiar with the gun's make, and in his hands, he felt fully a colonel and commander of men.

Max tried the digital phone inside the office but didn't hear a dial tone. Max suspected the Ultra-Violets had cut the line or had assistance with their current mayhem. Ridding the Bonnie Dundee of terrorists would be up to Max.

Moving quietly but purposefully, Max returned to the grand staircase and into the second-floor grand corridor. He retraced his steps, creeping down the stairs next to the state apartments. Pausing at the bottom, he heard the terrorists berating the deliverymen. They screamed about working for the taking class and how the top ten percent of the Union held all the wealth. Max tuned out their rhetoric, focusing on how to get the Ultra-Violets to lay down their arms and leave his house.

Max ran through all the strategies he could adopt, discarding one or the other as impractical. Finally, he settled on slowly ambushing the half-dozen figures and taking the group apart piece by piece.

Max turned left around the corner after stepping down from the stairs. Checking for the enemy, Max tossed a shard of plaster down the hall. He heard the Ultra-Violets go silent and the stomp of boots as some of the terrorists moved to check out the noise the plaster created.

A figure moved down and back through the corridor. As the terrorist turned away, Max strode forward quickly and knocked out the figure with the butt of his rifle. The figure's black cap fell off as the terrorist's body dropped to the ground. Max realized the terrorist was a teenage girl. The girl was out, and Max mentally ticked off one terrorist from his list—five remained.

Max grabbed an ankle and dumped the Ultra-Violet into the music room and out of the way. Max turned and returned to the corridor with the chapel and drawing room. He didn't want to shoot the Ultra-Violets, especially if they were just dumb kids. While the rifle was almost whisper-quiet, the hollow chambers in this part of the house would amplify the sound. If the Ultra-Violets guessed the shot's source, they'd come for Max in force or kill the delivery men—that would make things escalate quickly.

Max slowed his steps and moved forward in a crouch. He turned the corner and saw yet another Ultra-Violet. Max raced at the terrorist and, again, used his rifle as a club to knock out the terrorist. Max looked at the incapacitated terrorist. The Ultra-Violet was a young man who barely had enough whiskers to call a beard covering his face. Max again dragged the terrorist into the music room.

Max returned to the area outside of the drawing room. He knew the violets were standing guard over the workers in there. He had decided to take his chances, four terrorists to his one rifle. He was about to cross the distance between the corridor and the drawing room when he felt a cold ceramic-metal rifle barrel placed against the back of his head.

"If you make another move, I'll pull the trigger," a young female voice said. Max froze. He cursed mentally, remembering his von Moltke and how the general had proclaimed a plan of operations had no certainty beyond the first contact with the enemy. Max's plan had failed, and now he had been captured.

CHAPTER FOUR
Counter Ambush

Max felt the rifle press against the back of his head, pushing him forward.

"Move," the terrorist said, prodding him again. Max debated on his next move. All his options were terrible. Max decided to act. He would rather die with courage than surrender to an uncertain future.

Max quickly whipped around to face his captor. As he did so, he saw the Terran rifle pointed at him. The magazine had a small LED indicator that glowed a cherry hue. Max seized his opportunity, kicking the girl in the belly and smashing his rifle into hers. The girl pulled her trigger, but nothing happened. Max smashed down again, rifle to rifle. The girl fell backward, losing her grip on the gun, which skittered down the hall.

"Blue is true, while red is dead. That's Assault poetry and the first thing they teach you in basic," Max said, pointing his pin rifle in the girl's face. The girl shrieked. Max had to hurry as her comrades would be on him at any moment.

"Stupid girl, you should have checked the ammo in your magazine. You can't win a gunfight with an unloaded weapon!" Max said, his voice a deadly hiss.

The Ultra-Violet raised her hands. She was sixteen or seventeen standard years old. Max hauled the girl up using her hair. She mewed in pain and clung to Max's iron grip but didn't cry out. Max thrust the girl in front of him as he checked his six o'clock. No one was behind him. Max had let his awareness drop once. He wouldn't repeat that mistake.

"Why are you here?" Max said, pushing the girl forward toward his original objective.

"I won't answer your questions, taker!" she said. Max yanked her hair, and the girl bit her lip to stifle her cry of pain.

"Look, I don't want to shoot you, but I will if you don't start talking," Max said. Max didn't want to harm the child, but he had a limited window if he wanted to maintain surprise. Max was fine with bluffing about killing the girl to get information.

"Liar," she said. Her voice was full of bitterness, and her reply came with an air of defiance. Max checked the angles. The girl would be between him and the remaining Ultra-Violets when he entered the next room. If the terrorists fired on him, they would hurt their own. Max didn't care for his options. Potentially, he'd have to trade the girl's life for his. He reassured himself that he hadn't started the current chain of events. He needed to end them.

"Fine," Max said, his bluff failing, "move!"

Max pushed her with his left hand. His rifle was ready to fire, and Max held the muzzle over the girl's right shoulder. He checked the light on his magazine, and the small LED glowed bright blue. The magazine held fifty small bohrium rounds in a chemical stasis. Once Max pulled the trigger, the round cycled into the barrel and would be magnetically propelled out the muzzle at two kilometers per second. Once fired, the pin would begin to degrade, and upon contact with an object, the bohrium would start a slight fission reaction. The target would absorb the energy as heat and radiation. That was if the target was wearing a modern battle suit. If the target were unarmored, the bohrium would pass through their bodies, creating a larger hole on exit.

Max and the girl started moving towards the door where her comrades were. He forced her to the side and kicked the door open. He pushed her through and charged in after her.

"Help!" she screamed as she toppled forward, falling over her legs and into a heap two meters from the threshold.

Max quickly assessed the situation. The two deliverymen sat in the room's center. Two Ultra-Violets covered the prisoners while the Ultra-Violet leader stood near the back with a radio. The two guards looked fifteen on a good day while their leader was in his twenties.

"Finn, Hamish, kill the pig," the leader said.

"Move, and I'll kill the girl," Max said cocking his weapon for effect. His hands triple-checked the safety instinctively. Max heard his rifle instructor's voice in his head, "Breathe, squeeze, don't slap the trigger." Max waited for the next move. His weapon was ready to fire.

"You're bluffing," the Ultra-Violet leader said, "You're outnumbered, three to one."

"Three to two," Isobel said. Max could see her plainly in his peripheral vision, she had Cormac's hunting rifle in her hands, and she looked down at the scope while resting the butt squarely on her shoulder. Max's heart swelled up in admiration for his beautiful Amazon, standing by his side while the specter of death hovered over the room.

"A pretty little tool of the fascists!" the leader said, sneering at Isobel's appearance.

Isobel squeezed her finger, and a round whizzed by one of the younger boys, who dropped his rifle and ran in panic. She released a gleeful cackle and said, "I'm a woman of the Sheeplands. Unlike you lads, I know how to use a rifle."

"Sure, I'm bluffing," Max said, moving forward, his rifle now pointed at the leader, "Last chance, drop your weapons, or I'll start firing."

"I'm sorry, Brody, I am not cut out to be a revolutionary!" said the other young guard as he dropped his rifle and raised his hands.

"You too now, Brody," Isobel said. Brody reached for something at his waistband. Max didn't hesitate. He took a quick half breath and gently squeezed the trigger. The discharge was a whisper as the round raced between Max's rifle and the terrorist. Brody dropped as the kinetic impact of the round carried the bohrium through his body. The round continued through the drywall behind Brody and then out the house's exterior wall. Max sighed. Now, he had another task on his to-do list: patch the bullet hole.

The girl stood up and screamed, "You killed Brody!"

Isobel nodded to the deliverymen, who had stood up as soon as the leader fell. They grabbed hold of the remaining guard. Max dropped the rifle from his cheek. He could relax now that the adults had control of the situation. He slung his rifle across his back, grabbed a painter's tarp, the only bit of cloth available, and tore a large wad off. Max walked over to where the leader was bleeding all over his floor.

The youth's face was a terrible sight. The young man was ashen gray and in shock. The front hole of the pin shot was clean. The bohrium's energy had cauterized the wound as the round passed through. However, Max rolled the youth over to see that Brody's back was a mess of bloody hamburger. Max noted that Brody's scapula had been wrenched from the clavicle, well, what remained of the scapula. Max placed the tarp on the large fist-sized wound, getting on his knees to apply pressure.

"Isobel, call an ambulance," Max said. Isobel nodded and stepped outside to make the call.

"You killed Brody!" the girl screamed again, tears running down her cheeks.

"He's not dead," Max said to the girl, "He's in shock from the shot. I think he'll live. Maybe not much longer after the hospital puts him back together. The protector will string him up on the gallows for the stunt he pulled today."

"What do you want us to do with this one, your grace?" one of the deliverymen asked.

"Hold him here for the constable, and we'll let the police take care of the next steps," Max said. He continued to apply pressure to the leader's wound even though the terrorist's blood was covering the floor and slowly drenching Max's shoes, socks, and kilt.

"Ambulance is on the way," Isobel said, returning, "I see you found a way to get out of our meeting with the reverend. Next time, promise me, love, you'll go to dinner and not shoot stupid children playing terrorists."

"Yes, I promise, dear," Max said, "However, they aren't all children. Based on this one's age and the fact he has a radio, I'd say I have a militant Ultra-Violet here. This one gathered up some idiot kids with the intent of causing trouble in the Bonnie Dundee." Max couldn't honestly condemn the children as terrorists. They were all minors. The constabulary would drag the children to the station and hold them until a parent showed up.

"I'll let the reverend know we'll have to cancel tonight. I'll wait to escort the EMTs since the house is all torn up," said Isobel, leaving the room again.

The older delivery man said, "Thank you kindly, sir. They were going to kill us."

"Part of being a marquess. I'd appreciate it if you only pressed charges against the leader. These youngsters here don't seem to have the same zeal as this refuse pile," Max said.

"Why did you kill Brody?" the young lady who had attempted to capture Max asked. Max realized the young girl had never seen anyone shot before. Max continued to apply pressure, hopeful that Brody would live. Max wasn't a surgeon, and turning the hamburger back into a body part was beyond his ken. Max had seen people shot with much worse wounds. He suspected Brody might be able to hang on. However, the shoulder was lost.

"He's not dead yet," Max said, "what is your name?"

"Kate..." she said, "You are the boss, man, aren't you?"

"Yes, Kate, I am the Marquess of the Bonnie Dundee."

"You don't look rich," Kate said, "your house is torn up, and the part that ain't is falling apart."

"Who told you I was rich?"

"Finn did. He returned to our camp and told Brody you were a rich man who oppressed the village. Brody said we had orders to find you and kill you. We've been planning for weeks to take you down, you being an oppressor and all..."

"What do you think Kate?" Max asked. The young woman looked confused.

"I don't know. Brody came from an island in the south. He said the nobles oppress the people, and we should rise and throw off the yoke of oppression. Other than shooting Brody, you don't seem too bad."

"I shot him so he wouldn't kill that woman who left. She's..." Max said, fumbling for a moment and then deciding. He said, "She's my wife. Hurting her would have escalated the violence and would have led to your friends' deaths. Now help me here as I working to hold Brody's wound together before he bleeds out."

"Why?" Kate asked, dropping to her knees and taking over, "Don't you hate us?"

"No," Max said, "up until a few minutes ago, I had no idea you existed."

"But aren't the Violets in an existential struggle against the landowner class?" Kate asked.

Max laughed and said, "Who told you that? The Violets are a minority party in the Parliament, where they are treated like a circus freak show."

"Brody," Kate said, "He was trying to impress my sister Susan."

"Let me guess, Susan is your older sister?" Max asked.

"Yes, how did you know?"

"Just speculation. Do you want to go to jail?" Max asked, "Or would you rather have your parents come collect you?"

Max could waive any charges against Kate if he chose. The girl was a deluded youth, as Max had initially suspected.

"My parents died, well... I should say my mum died. My dad was in the Assault and died a while ago in the battle over Asimov. My mum died recently. She was in the Navy, a petty officer onboard the *USWC Chance*. She was killed in action when the Terrans attacked the *Chance* over Nakdong."

"Why are you here, Kate? Where are your kinfolk?" Max asked. Max was concerned with the social fabric of the Sheeplands. If kin and clan weren't caring for their own, then he had even more significant problems.

"Susan was seventeen when Mum died, so she got the house and Mum's pension. We let the Ultra-Violets live in the house," Kate said. She tried to look brave but looked more like a scared little girl.

"Where is your home and your sister?" Max said. Max would make sure to visit with some armed backup. If the Ultra-Violets used the house as a base, then Max needed to neutralize their headquarters. Max was concerned. Why did the Ultra-Violets decide to attack the Bonnie Dundee? The house was a private residence. If the Ultra-Violets wanted to cause trouble, the Gilbraith town hall was a better target. Max suspected the recent renovation had confused their leader. Otherwise, the terrorists would have achieved their objectives before Max knew they were in the manor. Max would have to raise his volunteer unit now. All the tasks Max wanted to avoid, mostly surrounding the force of arms, were now becoming the most important.

"Um," Kate said, unsure if she should tell Max where she lived.

"Kate, I only want to help. If you live in this region, I must help you," Max said. Isobel came in leading two Assaultmen, police constables by their uniform insignia. The Assaultmen came, weapons drawn, with emergency medical technicians following with a litter.

"Over here," Max said, waving a hand. The techs rushed over and took over for Kate, attempting to stabilize Brody.

"Will Brody be all right?" Kate asked.

"We'll take the best care of him, miss," one EMT said. The EMTs carried Brody and put him on the litter. The other inserted an I.V. and started giving him meds via the I.V. Having stabilized Brody, the EMTs raised the gurney and left the room. Meanwhile, the constables were rounding up the other terrorists.

Max down at himself. Blood soaked his kilt's hem and his wool socks, but Max thought he could salvage his dress shoes. Brody's blood had dried to a tacky consistency on the floor.

"Kate, you can go home, but only if you show me where you live, or you can go to jail. Just decide," Max said. He had started to worry that the bohrium round had caught something on fire on its way out of the manor.

Kate looked conflicted but eventually said, "I'll show you where I live."

Isobel approached Max and said, "I've contacted the reverend. He was very understanding."

"Good, we're going to head over to Kate's place," Max said, "Get a hold of Hector and anyone else you can."

"Who is Kate?" Isobel asked. Max motioned to the young woman.

"Any particular reason?" Isobel asked.

"Duty calls," Max said. Isobel kissed his cheek. Max needed to change, and then he'd clean out the Ultra-Violet headquarters. Their insanity had to end.

CHAPTER FIVE

A Bug Not an Insect

Max took Kate with him to the Manager's office. Max realized that he had never shut the armory door as he entered. This time, the mistake had worked in his favor since Isobel had been able to seize Cormac's rifle and provide backup. He closed the armory door and spun the three-dimensional combination, making a note to share the code with Isobel. Max looked up as he turned the dials to see Hector entering.

"Are you all right, your grace?" his cousin asked. Hector's face showed the man's horror at all the blood on Max.

"I'm fine, cousin," Max said, "this isn't my blood."

Hector visibly relaxed, "Good show. As much as I wanted to be the earl, these past few weeks have made me happy that you are here. I am not capable of being the chieftain."

Max was surprised at the admission. Hector had always seemed to be waiting for the title to come to him. Max said, "What made you change your mind?"

"I thought being a peer would be like what you see in the movies," Hector said, "I'd order around a dozen lackeys, always get my supper on silver plates and such. Now I see that being a peer is a lot of hard work—far more work than I expected."

"Work? What does he mean you work," Kate asked.

"Oh yes, Hector, meet Kate. Kate, this is my cousin, Hector," Max said.

"Hi," the girl said.

"Pleasure," Hector said dismissively.

"And yes, I work. Recently, I have worked all day from dawn to dusk," Max said.

"Like ordering people around, right?" Kate asked.

Max laughed, "Um, no."

"What about the stiff?" Kate said, pointing to Hector.

"Hector and I have an arrangement. He is helping me, and I am helping him," Max said.

"Quite right," Hector said to strengthen Max's point.

"Now, Hector," Max said, "Can you keep an eye on Kate? I have to change, and then we'll all visit her house. In the meantime, keep her here in the office."

"Aye, Max," Hector said.

"Wait, you can't leave me with him," Kate said.

"Why not?" Max asked.

"He's a turd!" Kate said.

"You'll warm up to him," Max said with a smile, "give him a chance."

Kate folded her arms across her chest in a sign of teenage irritation.

"Don't tarry, Max," Hector said, "I'll keep both eyes on this one."

Absolved of Kate-watching duty, Max returned to the house. As he entered the Bonnie Dundee, the halls buzzed with people. Some were from the village, and others were of the Douglas clan. Donalbaan and his MacLeods were armed with rifles and patrolled the corridors. Ewan materialized from the mass of people in the crowd.

"Max," Ewan said, "a word if you can spare a moment?"

Max wasn't sure what his distaff cousin wanted, but Max needed a channel to the protector. USIS would be the perfect way to send a message. The protector had demanded Max let him know about anything unusual. Being attacked by terrorists in his home was pretty unusual, at least for Max. Besides, Max was expecting more than some small sum of money and promises of support from his liege. Max would call in his markers. He needed help and fast.

"Sure, Ewan, let's head up to the library. We should have more privacy there," Max said. Ewan nodded and followed Max as he traversed the crowded house. Max realized he was used to zipping down the corridors, headless of anyone else. He had grown used to the empty house. With all the folk here, Max realized that the Bonnie Dundee had become an ancient ruin rather than the stately home his ancestors originally envisioned. After climbing the grand staircase and heading west down the second floor of the grand corridor, Max stood in front of the reproduction of the first Viscount Dundee.

He and Ewan entered the library and sat at his desk. Max saw that Ewan looked tired, a man with too much work and little sleep. Around Ewan's waist was a tool belt with an assortment of tools, many of which Max had never seen before. Leaning back and pinching the bridge of his nose, Ewan looked like he was about to topple over. The movement dislodged a tool from Ewan's belt. The tool clattered onto the floor. Ewan looked down at where the tool had fallen. He bent over to retrieve the device. At the same time, Max noticed a message on the tablet he brought back from the capital. He opened the message and turned to say something to Ewan with the tablet in his hand. The tablet and Ewan's tool touched, and a loud, scratchy whine sounded from Ewan's device.

"What, what," Ewan said, startled by the sound.

"Looks like your device is broken, Ewan," Max suggested.

"No, Max, that's not what you think that sound means," Ewan said, his voice grave, "Can you place that on the desk?"

"What, the tablet?" Max asked as Ewan pointed at the tablet. Ewan nodded his head vigorously but didn't make a sound. Ewan stared as Max put the tablet down. Max was concerned as Ewan looked like he expected a monster to pop out from the tablet. Max dropped the device on his ornate computer desk desktop. Like a medieval wizard casting a spell, Ewan stood and assumed a stance over the tablet. Ewan circled the device he had dropped over the tablet. The small wand-like tool made squeaks and whirs as Ewan passed the device across Max's tablet.

Max was about to say something when Ewan touched his lips, motioning for quiet. Max nodded and watched as his cousin started putting other devices from his belt on the table. LED lights flashed, and the device's signals began to synchronize. Ewan motioned for Max to stand up and spread his arms. Max wasn't sure what was happening, but Ewan seemed very concerned about what had occurred. Max stood and raised his arms. Ewan swept the original device that had started the exercise across Max's body. He then began swinging the device across the entire library, returning in a moment or two.

"Sloppy, very sloppy," Ewan said, "you can talk now, Max."

"Huh," Max asked, "what is sloppy?"

"They should have at least dropped two bugs on you," Ewan said, "I'm dealing with amateurs here. That's a small relief."

"Huh? Bugs, what are you talking about?" Max said, "Cormac fumigated the place for insects not long after I took over. We're good for a few more months at least, Ewan."

Ewan let out a belly laugh and said, "Max, dear Max, you always were my favorite... Oh, where to begin."

Max was tired, and he had given up trying to understand what the matter was. Whatever Ewan was about to reveal, Max would have to absorb the information passively. He was exhausted from the day's events.

"Max, do you remember the saying, 'Loose lips, destroy star ships'?" Ewan asked.

A lazy, tired corner of Max's brain suddenly fired in alarm, and Max said, "A bug! Oh no! I've been bugged!"

Max suddenly realized where the leaks had come from. Max was the leaker! He immediately thought about the night with the protector and said out loud, "Wait! I didn't have the tablet when we met the protector!"

Max looked questioningly to Ewan, who looked back, studying Max. Both men put their hands on their chins. After a moment, Ewan said, "Think, Max, this is important. We have to get to the bottom of who gave you this device before we can get anyone else involved. Now, where did you get that tablet?"

Max thought back. The tablet had become almost a part of him. Max had a flash of a memory and said, "The tablet was my father's. After my whirlwind trip to the capital, I brought the stupid thing back with me from my office in the House of Dynasties."

Ewan shook his head enthusiastically and said, "Good, good. Now we're getting somewhere, Max. You mentioned that you didn't have the tablet at your meeting. Was there something else you acquired from the office that you may have brought to meet the protector? An article of clothing, a writing implement, or perhaps a souvenir?"

Max was wracking his tired brain when Isobel appeared.

"Max, there you are. I was getting worried," she said. Upon seeing his beloved, Max realized Martha Clark had also given Isobel his mother's ring. Max snatched the wand device from Ewan without warning and pressed the tool against Isobel's left hand. The device again made squeaks and whirs as the tip of the tool touched the ring that sat on Isobel's index finger.

"Max, what..." Isobel was about to say, but Max clamped his hand over her mouth. He then motioned to her to be quiet and removed his hand. Isobel nodded. Ewan signaled to Isobel to remove the band and place the ring next to Max's tablet on the desktop.

As she did so, Ewan said, "Right, that's two. Whoever planted these bugs was trying to follow best trade practices. I still find the bugging to be sloppy. I would have given you *each* two bugs."

"That's fine, Ewan, but how do we dispose of the bugs," Max asked.

"Oh, that's simple," Ewan said, "we don't. We now have a slight advantage over whoever was trying to plant these devices."

Ewan was about to say more when Meg appeared, "Max, is everything all right? Andrew and some of his kin wondered if you still needed their help?"

"Yes, Meg, we've just discovered where the leak to the news has been coming from," Max said, pointing to the table.

"Your new tablet and the ring you bought for Isobel?" Meg said more as a question than a statement.

"He didn't buy the ring," Isobel said, "the band belonged to your mother."

"No, that's not Mum's ring. I have that in my jewelry box, back at my house in Loch Urquhart," Meg said, "I thought Max bought you the ring in the capital like he said he was going to do?"

"Martha Clark said the ring belonged to Mum," Max said, "she said father gave the band to her a while ago."

"Who is Martha Clark?" Meg asked.

"Father's secretary," Max said, "we met her in the capital."

"No, I remember, his secretary was a man called Simmons," Meg said, "I've never heard of anyone named Clark."

Max thought back to the discussion he had with the shady woman. Max had tried to gather more details on her service, and all he was told was a vague story of her serving on the *Advantage*. Max should have realized something was missing from her story. Max started kicking himself. Of course, his liege had suddenly gone cold with his support. The protector probably believed Max to be untrustworthy or duplicitous! Max would have to fix the situation somehow, but for now, Max was in Ewan's hands. The espionage work was what USIS was handling.

"Max, could you give me a description of the woman?" Ewan asked.

"Sure, Ewan," Max replied.

"I'll work with some colleagues, and we'll come up with some leads. Having a name will help, and I am sure our *Frau* Clark will come up on the security cameras in the Parliament building. That will give us a face," Ewan said, "For now..."

Ewan was about to continue when a petite woman entered. She was a plain-looking lady with the air of a woman whose most significant concern was bringing her children to football practice.

"Ewan, were you able to get Max's permission to move the cabins?" the woman asked.

"Max, you remember Molly, right?" Ewan said, introducing his wife.

"Yes, but I haven't seen you in some time, Molly," Max said, "you look different." Molly laughed.

"Well, why thank you, Max. If you are referring to my current appearance, I gave up the honey-pot lifestyle a while back when I entered the Tech branch. I got tired of the constant dieting and decided..." Molly said, but her eyes went wide at the collection of devices on the desktop, "Oh! Someone is *interested* in you, Max. Let's see what we have here!" Ewan chuckled as his wife forgot her reason for being in the library. She ran to the desktop with childlike fascination.

"You've got the devices in a good screening loop," she said, appraising her husband's work, "have you started the forensics? If they are listening now, the monitors will get suspicious if we don't provide them some of Max's or Isobel's voice."

"Yes, dear," Ewan said sourly, "I've only had the bugs in the loop for a few minutes, and by my watch, we're coming on twenty-one hundred hours, with four hours to midnight. I am gambling on the monitors, believing Max and Isobel are in bed."

"Hand me the emission scope. I will get a signature on the tablet. I can probably diagnose the bug's origin and other details here in the field," Molly said. Ewan handed her a small square device. Molly pulled out a set of glasses and briefly pointed the device's laser. Molly tapped the square device, and it gave a slight hum.

"Got you, you ornery little devil," she said after a few minutes. Everyone had watched the little woman work with bated breath.

"Ewan, I'm sending you the data, but these are Terran make," Molly said.

"Terrans, why would they be bugging me?" Max asked. He had suspicions but wanted the spies to confirm his thoughts.

"Not Terrans *per se*," Ewan said, looking at the data on a tablet, "but the bug is from Earth, or rather, made there. Aha, did you see..."

"The telltale unsigned cert and cryptographic back door are still present," Molly said, cutting her husband off, "Sloppy work, we're not dealing with..."

"The Directorate's intelligence services, yes," Ewan said, taking control of the conversation again, "Max, we need to send this data back to headquarters. USIS will need time to place these signatures to the appropriate group."

"Aye," Molly said, "I'd expect that we're dealing with a Terran-provisioned group operating inside the Union."

"So, what does all that mean?" Max said.

"Well, as I was about to say before, I was rudely interrupted by my nerd wife," Ewan said in mock anger, "For now, we're going to have to leave you bugged. But let's use this to our advantage. What were you up to before we discovered our little uninvited guests?"

Max said, "I was off to change. I planned to take some men over to perform a safety check on the house. One of the girls involved in the raid said the Ultra-Violets live in her house."

Ewan rubbed his chin with his hand, thinking. Molly began to dissect the ring's bug, removing small wires from the band. Max stood and watched, and Isobel came over and placed her hand in his. Meg stared on, chewing her lip, a sign Max recognized as her worrying.

"Aha, we'll use a Lacheln Reversal," Ewan declared. Molly nodded vigorously and said, "I agree, we'll need to coordinate with another USIS team on this. You and I aren't supposed to be working on domestic issues."

Max watched as the spies, err, intelligence officers debated for a moment. He tried to follow, but Ewan and Molly's arguments quickly devolved into jargon and trade terms that flew over Max's head. Max looked at Isobel as he suddenly felt her stare at him. She smiled and said, "Old married couples are so cute."

Max laughed. The joke had landed squarely on his funny bone, and he continued to laugh, interrupting Ewan and Molly.

"Go on, Max," Ewan said, "Molly and I will refine the details here and get back to you. For now, act normally. We don't want to give away that we know we are being watched."

"What about my trip over to Kate's house?" Max asked.

"Undoubtedly a trap," Ewan said, "Let that chore rest. We can prepare our reversal and enact what needs to be done in the morning."

Max nodded. He was tired. Max turned to Meg and said, "Tell Andrew he can stand down but be ready for something in the morning. Why didn't you tell me you had Mum's ring?"

Meg nodded and said, "I'll let him know. Dad gave me that ring just after you ran off. You said you would *buy* a ring. I naturally assumed the ring was from a shop on the Silver Road."

Max shrugged, "Sorry, I've been busy planning a fair, spaceport, stately home remodel, raising a unit of volunteer Assaultmen, and being scheduled for dinners across the march. The ring slipped my mind."

"See what you'll have to deal with, Isobel," Meg said, turning to Max's love, "Menfolk, always concerned about the trivial things!"

Isobel leaned over and kissed Max on the cheek. "I think he's adorable when doing his job as a peer. He does a good job, too! I wish he were as good at swinging a hammer as he is at being a peer and controlling our destiny."

With the kiss, Max wanted nothing more than to run to his bedroom, strip off the bloody clothes, shower, and run to Isobel's chamber. But, he knew that more matters would need his attention in the morning. As much as he yearned for a night with Isobel, he reasoned that a good sleep would better prepare him for tomorrow.

"Well, I'm done," Max said, "I need to get the terrorist's blood off my body, and I am crawling into bed after that. Meg, can you take charge of Kate? I am sure Hector is at his wits end with her by now. Isobel, tell Donal, the other barons, and the Douglases that I will have an operations briefing at nine hundred tomorrow."

Meg nodded and skipped out. Ewan and Molly were still deep in their conversations and didn't notice Max and Isobel. Isobel took Max's hand and led him towards his chambers. As Max and Isobel began heading across the manor towards their bedrooms, Isobel asked quietly, "Of course, after your shower, would you like to visit my room for a sleepover?"

Max smiled. "I'd love to, but I am afraid tonight is all business and no pleasure."

"Fair enough, I'm also happy to be your teddy bear. You can cuddle me if you have any nightmares," she said, batting her eyes at Max.

"Tempting, but I need rest. I feel like I'm way past empty and haven't figured out how to sleep with your snoring yet."

"I do not snore," Isobel said, acting hurt, "that's all in your imagination!"

She and Max then laughed for a moment.

"I'll hop in the shower and wash your back. I am sure you need a good scrub there," Isobel said, "what happens if you get wounded tomorrow? I'd be ashamed if my soon-to-be husband were carted off to the hospital with a dirty back. How would that look to the populace? They'll gossip all day about how I can't even keep you clean."

Max smiled, mentally accepted the proposal, and responded to Isobel, "I suppose you are right. If a man can't get a good scrub before combat, I don't know what this galaxy is coming to."

The couple finally entered Max's private bathroom. Max and Isobel stripped and entered the shower. Between the steam, the scrub, and Isobel's tender help, Max felt ready for the day rushing towards him, his bond with Isobel reinforcing his strength to face whatever fate would give him.

CHAPTER SIX

The Lacheln Reversal - Part One

Max awoke at the alarm. He prepared to leave his bed, but a feminine hand grabbed him, and a mouth came down over his in a passionate kiss.

"Curly bear never kissed me like that when I was growing up," Max said after breaking the lip lock. Max smiled as he remembered the name of his childhood stuffed animal.

"A big boy like you needs a more mature stuffy," Isobel said, a mischievous smile on her face, "you need that kiss for luck."

"Well, if one makes me lucky, what would two make me?" Max said.

"Late for your big briefing, and you still have no idea what Ewan and Molly have planned, so get going."

"Aye," Max replied, "duty calls. Are you planning to join me?"

"No, I'm having a late morning after all the hard labor I put into scrubbing your back last night, and you made me run around like a page boy. I'll let you know that I scandalized the entire march, running around in my nightgown and delivering your messages. As a result, Max, I am sleeping in like a married lady can."

"Well, for one, you aren't a married woman just yet," Max said but was cut off.

"Today, I'm declaring us close enough," Isobel said.

"Okay, I'm not going to argue as you are shamelessly snuggled next to me in my bed," Max said, "and as to your scandalizing the populace with your night clothes, I highly doubt any of my soon-to-be Douglas kinsmen even batted an eye, as you probably have spent many a night floating around Cairnbahan in your nightgown or perhaps even less!"

"Keep that thought in your head for tonight, and now go," Isobel said with a gentle shove, "I want a little more sleep before the world comes knocking on my door, and you need to go be the super sexy peer I'm going to marry, before I forget our lack of a wedding and wantonly keep you here all day."

Max laughed and stood. Whatever would come, Max promised himself he'd ensure he would come back to Isobel. After all, she had promised tantalizing rewards for his success and survival. Max stood naked and went to his armoire to look at his clothing options. As he opened the door, he saw Isobel staring at him.

"You know, propriety demands one does not stare as a gentleman dresses," Max said jokingly. Max had been in the Assault and could walk naked across his march without much thought. Hans Christian Andersen's story "The Emperor's New Clothes" suddenly came to mind. Max laughed inwardly at the idea of him walking around naked. Only Cormac would have the nerve to say anything to Max. The thought of the huntsman made him suddenly feel melancholy.

"When a gentleman arrives, I'll stop looking at you, sexy," Isobel said with a yawn, "Okay, enough fun, I'm rolling over now."

Max grabbed his old battle dress uniform and some underwear from the armoire. He was about to respond to Isobel when he heard her soft snore. He threw the uniform on a dressing chair and put on the undershirt and underpants. Quickly, he pulled on the uniform trousers and threw on the battle dress jacket. He noted, with some irritation, that he had yet to cut the Sergeant's stripes from the uniform, well, no matter. Today, he could slum as an enlisted man. After all, the protector had promoted Max to the mighty rank of colonel, even if the position was only as a commander of volunteers rather than the professional military. Max grabbed socks and looked for his combat boots. After digging through his armoire, he found both and put them on.

Standing and looking in the mirror, Max felt ready. He had a knock at the door and a voice that said, "Max, are you awake?"

Max opened the suite door slightly to reveal Ewan standing in the corridor. Max pushed through the door and into the corridor, closing the door gently on the sleeping Isobel.

"Sorry to disturb you, cousin," Ewan said, "but I wanted a few minutes to review our plans."

"Aye, I was up and moving, so there was no disruption," Max said, motioning Ewan toward the kitchen. Ewan nodded and said, "I'm glad Isobel is sleeping in. She was so animated last night, organizing the troops, so to speak."

Max blushed and said, "You noticed her in my room?"

"Of course, Max," Ewan said, "noticing things is my job after all! But don't fear. I, too, had plenty of sleepovers with Molly after we were engaged. I rather miss those these days... Well, to the matter at hand, we will perform a Lacheln Reversal on the Ultras. "

"What's that? And why do you call them Ultras?" Max asked.

As the two reached the kitchen, they passed many people. Max felt the Bonnie Dundee had gotten smaller after the terrorist attack... Smaller or just more crowded.

"Ultras is the domestic branch's slang for the Ultra-Violets. The Ultras are a terrorist cell that is run by a man called Gunter Helmut. The domestic branch has given him the codename "Mammon." So Max, let's stick to that term, as we don't know who may be listening in, okay?"

"Aye, Mammon, understood," Max replied.

"Mammon has been incredibly elusive. The domestic branch has been after him since they learned of his activities three years ago. The domestic branch believes that Mammon is responsible for the attack on the *Primus,* and they have made his capture a top priority. After I got the brief on Mammon, I also received some dossiers. One caught my eye. No name is attached to the dossier, just the codename "Lamia." Lamia is a subordinate to Mammon and is good at gathering intelligence. The domestic branch thinks you were quite unlucky and discovered Lamia while she was doing some level of intelligence gathering. We're still analyzing how she entered the Parliament building, but for now, I'm guessing she bluffed her way in as your secretary. Due to your encounter, the domestic branch has issued an alert, and security will redouble their efforts to verify all identities."

Max said, "Great, let's pause as we enter the kitchen. I'll grab some breakfast, and we can head to the library."

"Splendid idea, I'm famished," Ewan said, dropping the conversation.

The MacLeods' womenfolk had set up the kitchen to distribute breakfast buffet style. Both men grabbed plates and scooped some of the hardy Sheepland's breakfast onto their plates. After grabbing silverware and coffee, Max and Ewan headed to the library. Upon entering, they once again gathered at Max's desk. Consolidated

"Lamia," Max said.

"I don't want to alarm you, but you were fortunate, Max," Ewan said, "The domestic branch's dossier on Lamia says that not many who have met with her lived to tell the tale. I suspect that being with Isobel made Lamia hesitant to move too aggressively. Then again, Kenneth seemed to be a Violet ally, so perhaps Lamia felt you were an 'ally to the cause,' as the Ultras say."

"Wow, my luck wasn't as bad as I thought," Max said. "What does Lamia want, and what is the Lacheln Reversal?"

"The domestic branch is still analyzing Lamia's objectives. After I informed them of the bugs we found, they did a full sweep of your Parliament office and then the entire building. Your office was a virtual hive of bugs. USIS has taken care of them, and the Parliament building has tightened counter-electronic intelligence gathering protocols, so in a way, you and Isobel have provided a valuable service to the Union."

"Max and Isobel, minefield dancers," Max said with a laugh. Max took a moment to gobble down his breakfast.

"Heroes sometimes wear tap shoes, Max," Ewan said with a smile, stopping for a moment to eat. After finishing his plate, Ewan continued, "Now, about the Lacheln reversal, the operation is named after one of our idols, Georg Lacheln. When Lacheln was a young intelligence officer on a mission, he, through a series of events —always changed by the person telling the tale—ended up covered in bugs. Most officers at that early stage in their career would have panicked, called for extraction, and scrubbed the operation. Not Georg. He spends weeks wearing the wires, transmitting grander and grander plans for his monitors to record. All the while, Georg is slowly making progress on his mission parameters. Finally, as he grew close to mission success, Georg decided to lure out the monitors. He set up a decoy, and when they pounced, Georg puzzled out their base of operations and invited himself in. His monitors found the decoy but were left scratching their heads. All the while, Lacheln was rifling through their records and data. As a capstone, he dropped bugs throughout his monitors' headquarters and then crept out of their base like a tomcat running off with the cook's fish. Lacheln was extracted, and USIS spent months collecting on the collectors. Sadly, Georg's success was such that he was quickly promoted out of fieldwork."

"Sounds like quite the field agent," Max said, "How are we going to apply his methods?"

"I was getting to that. I don't often get to relate USIS tales to the masses," Ewan said, "I suppose Molly is right, and we should retire and write our memoirs. Now, I digress... To your question, well, we're going to lure out whoever decided you were such a brilliant boy, and Molly and I will see if, as mid-careerists, we have the same level of tradecraft Lacheln had as a junior officer."

"Perfect, how do I help?" Max asked.

"You, my dear cousin, will be the decoy."

"Oh lovely," Max said.

"Cheer up, Max, this will be fun. We're going to orchestrate your movements. Hopefully, we can locate the baddies and their headquarters while they are focused on you. Then, USIS can pinpoint the location and take it out. The domestic branch set up a crisis team after I sent my report. You won't be going at this alone. The protector's line guards have a detachment of Assaultmen arriving briefly to back you up. We will set the stage that you'll be taking Kate back to her house. USIS suspects that the main body of Ultras is centered somewhere close to her family's cottage, so their leadership should be somewhere else nearby."

"I prefer a stand-up fight to all this sneaking around," Max said.

Ewan only chuckled. Then, he stood up and said, "Well, now you know what my USIS team will be doing. Go on and formulate what you need from your retainers to pull off your end of the operation."

"Aye," Max said, "good luck."

"You as well," Ewan said, leaving the library. Max stood and grabbed the breakfast dishes and dropped them in the kitchen sink for a retainer to deal with. Max then headed for the great hall where folk would be assembling.

Max walked down the grand corridor and entered through the large eastern doors. Looking across the great hall, Max felt the scene was more like a market before a cattle auction than a military briefing. Before he could move forward, an Assaultmen in a battle suit strode up to Max and saluted.

"*Feldfähnrich* Jurgen Wulfjaeger, reporting, *Oberst*," the Assaultman said, using the official rank designation for subaltern and colonel. Wulfjaeger snapped a salute to Max. Max returned the salute, remembering his Assault days and the many times Max had saluted or been given a salute.

"Parade rest, Subaltern," Max said. Wulfjaeger went to the position, opening his legs and crossing his hands behind his back.

"We're ready for the Sit Rep, sir," Wulfjaeger said.

"I'll be briefing everyone in a moment," Max said, "how many men did you bring?"

"Two fire teams, sir," Wulfjaeger replied, "best we could do on such short notice."

"Two fire teams, and you?" Max asked, trying to determine whether Wulfjaeger was a plus one.

"No, sir," Wulfjaeger said, "One full team and a second team led by me."

Max cursed inwardly; six Assaultmen. That was the extent of the help. Max looked at Wulfjaeger with a sudden realization, "Wait! I know you, you're the Lion of Llande!"

Wulfjaeger turned a deep crimson and said, "I just did my duty, sir. Or should I call you *Maximum Carnage?*"

Max jovially patted Wulfjaeger on the shoulder. "Point taken, subaltern. Let me get the rest of the folk here ready to move out."

Wulfjaeger nodded and strode over to a corner with five other battlesuit-protected Assaultmen. Max went to the center of the great hall. He looked out over the gathering. Douglases, MacLeods, Frasers, and a score of village folk were there. Most were men, but a few womenfolk were also in attendance. As he walked into the center of the gathering, he saw his barons, Andrew and the Urquhart men standing together. All wore clothes appropriate for a day out in the mountains, and their mood was anxious.

Max cleared his throat, all eyes went to him, and he said, "The past few hours have revealed the source of the troubles in the Sheeplands. Many, myself included, have erred in our judgment. We blamed old grievances and tribal grudges for the troubles rather than searching for the true source. A group of terrorists has become a nest of vipers within our own Union!"

"Here, here!" a few of the gathering shouted.

"The terrorists seek to sow division among us all. Therefore, today in the March of Gilbraith-on-Heather, those gathered here are all Saint Patrick, and we will drive these snakes from the Sheeplands, Allfather willing—Stahlburgh, and the Union!"

The crowd gathered and cheered wildly. Max waited momentarily, letting the assembled channel their nervousness.

"Now, I need you to find a baron and group with him. For their part, the barons will be their group's leader. We'll leave here, mount up, and head off to a small village called *Roumielet* in the southern part of the march. I'll head into the village. Each baron will position their group along a point of the compass. I don't need anyone to do anything but watch. I will enter the small hamlet along with the Assaultmen who are present. If rifle fire occurs, the barons and their groups will *contain the enemies to the hamlet*," Max said, emphasizing the end. "Like always, I rely on you to keep cool heads and pay attention. This is another day of stalking. We're hunting two-legged game today. Now, any questions?"

The room became so quiet that Max could have heard a pin drop. Max looked out at the crowd. He wanted to memorize every face, young, old, veteran, non-veteran, noble, and commoner. These folk had come at the call and willingly followed Max, potentially to their deaths. When Max began, he never wanted his inheritance and was unsure what he wanted. Staring at all the faces looking at him, he knew what he wanted: to be their hope and leader. For good or ill, today, Max would give them the future they wanted—peace and prosperity in their corner of the universe. Max couldn't control what happened beyond the march's borders but vowed inside Gilbraith-on-Heather that his people would live in peace.

"Okay then, mount up!" Max said. The folk dispersed, each

following a baron of their choosing. As the room cleared, the Assaultmen remained.

"What's the play, Colonel?" Wulfjaeger said, switching to the informal for Max's rank.

"I remember hearing some rumor about how the line guards have a personal cloak on their battlesuits. That wouldn't be part of the kit you're wearing by chance?"

"Colonel, that is on a need-to-know basis," Wulfjaeger replied.

"Awesome, you came with all the cool toys," Max said, "remember, I served and was taught all the right things to say or not say."

"Again, what's the play?" Wulfjaeger asked.

"Well, subaltern," Max said, "you and your men will stroll with me across a hamlet. If we get shot at, we shoot back."

"Affirmative," Wulfjaeger said, "You want to suit up? We've brought spare erm—toys."

"Nope, I'm an all-or-nothing guy. Either everyone gets a suit or no one does, present company excluded. Besides, I might tip someone off if I show up in a battlesuit. I'm expecting all of you to be my friendly ghosts. Dismissed."

Wulfjaeger snapped to attention and saluted Max; the other Assaultmen did the same. Max returned the salute and the respect they gave him. All dropped their salutes nearly simultaneously, and Wulfjaeger turned to the men and said, "All right, Bitner, you take Munster and Pertti on my left. Ackbar, you and Keller are on my right. We will surround the *Markgraf* like the flaming sword-wielding angels we are, and Keller..."

"Yes, sir," Keller said.

"Wake up the mutt. He's our ace in the hole!"

"His name is *Moray*, sir, and yes, sir," Keller responded.

"Well, today, his name better be Mongoose. We're killing snakes," Wulfjaeger said, "Now, Colonel, we're going to mount up and follow. We'll have your six when you head in."

The Assaultmen left, and the only other person in the hall was a Cairnbahan shepherdess.

"Hello," Max said, "will I see Isobel and Abnoba today, too, shepherdess?"

"Hey, this is the most rugged outfit I have," Isobel responded, kissing Max.

She stopped and said, "Besides, all hands are on deck today! Ewan and Molly left a few minutes ago. Meg and I are on the radio to provide backup in case things don't go according to plan."

"I love you," Max said, "be careful. You are the most important woman in the universe to me."

Isobel held Max tight and said, "You too, I am not planning on walking up to the door of a terrorist hideout and knocking."

"I've got backup, *snake eater* backup," Max said, referencing the ancient nickname for military special forces.

"Good, plenty of snakes need to be driven off or killed today," Isobel said, "I love you! Come back to me!"

Max and Isobel shared a final kiss, interrupted by a truck horn.

"Duty calls," Max said, leaving his love in the great hall.

"Kill them all and let the Allfather sort them out!" Max could hear Isobel shout as he exited the Bonnie Dundee. He looked back at the stately home. All the chips were on the poker table. Now, Max waited to see the cards that were dealt. Max turned, unsure if he'd see the stately home again.

Max trotted down to where the assembled groups waited. He hopped into the passenger side of the hover truck. In the driver's seat, Hector played a game with Kate.

"Lance breaks shield," the girl said.

"Another round," Hector said. He and Kate each made a fist, and they said, "One two three shoot!"

While Hector held up two fingers, Kate made a flat hand. "Aha!

Man-Catcher dismounts Lance-man, Kate!"

"Aww! Best three out of five?" Kate said.

"Okay, you two, are you ready?" Max asked.

"Yes," they both said. Max smiled. Kate and Hector had found their equilibrium. Hector pressed the ignition button, and the fans whirred. Hector engaged the drive, and the truck moved forward, picking up speed.

"Cousin, I intend to go with you to Kate's house," Hector said as Max turned to watch the other vehicles in the convoy depart.

"Hector, that's not in the plan," Max said.

"I know, I don't feel..." Hector said, searching for the right word, "Honorable, letting you and Miss Kate go up alone."

"You know that isn't entirely true," Max said.

"Cousin, I can't stomach you and Miss Kate risking your lives while I sit like a heel in the truck. If you are worried, I'll go unarmed," Hector said.

"Well..." Max said.

"Cousin, I insist," Hector said. Max wasn't sure what had gotten into Hector. His cousin wasn't this brave usually. Max wanted desperately to say no but instead said, "Fine, but if things go sideways, you two need to clear out."

"Absolutely," Hector said, pushing down on the accelerator pedal. The truck picked up speed and soon was violating the posted limit. Max let the infraction slide. Hector was unlikely to be fined for the violation on this mission, as Max would immediately dragoon any constable who dared stop them. Max feared his motley band would need all available manpower today. Whether the manpower was voluntary or not was another matter. The truck slalomed onto the highway and, in a short half hour, was making its way into the hamlet. Max hated the time before action. When he was an Assaultman, he'd try to devise a tongue twister that he couldn't repeat to occupy his mind. During this trip, Max constantly looked back and forth along the road, fraught with worry that something would look out of the ordinary and alert any potential foe to Max's intentions.

Max took a deep breath as the truck coasted into the hamlet. Five identical cottages stood in a semi-circle around a traffic roundabout. The cottages were in poor shape. The roofs of all the houses were in horrible condition. The cottages were missing significant amounts of shingles. Heavy rain would allow water into the dwellings. Max wondered if the homes were even livable inside. Hector killed the ignition.

"Not too late to back out," Max said. Hector looked pale but grim. Max had seen that look on scores of young Assaultmen's faces. The first action was always the worst, Max remembered.

"Not today," Hector replied. Kate looked at the men and sensed their nervousness. She put her hand into Hector's, squeezing his hand. Max opened the door. He felt the small central glove compartment for the service pistol. Max felt the grip and pulled out the weapon. He did a quick check of the pistol to ensure a bohrium round was prepped for shooting. Max placed the gun into its holster at his waist. The sheriff was ready for the showdown.

Max, Hector, and Kate all moved towards the cottage Kate had identified as hers. A wrinkled old man came out from a house to stare at the trio. Max wanted to yell at him to go inside.

"Ignore him," Kate said, "He's an odd wanker. He's always staring at Susan and me."

The trio went to the porch of Kate's cottage. Max felt an ominous silence and stillness as he reached to knock on the door. Max pounded on the door's wood, and the door boomed with every strike Max made. A woman of around nineteen or twenty years opened the door.

"Susan, wait!" Kate screamed. Susan pointed a shotgun's muzzle at the trio. She intended to squeeze the trigger. Max leaped forward and pushed the muzzle away from Hector, Kate, and himself. The slug-thrower barked as Susan depressed the trigger, and the hamlet erupted in violence. Max was far enough inside the shot to avoid getting hit. Hector and Kate weren't so fortunate. Hector's instinct was to roll to shield Kate, and he caught the brunt of the blast on his side and back. He fell, dragging the young woman to the ground with him and landing on top of her.

Max savagely struck Susan with his left elbow and knocked her out. The unconscious woman dropped before the threshold of the inner door of the cottage's foyer, effectively blocking the internal entrance to the house. The Sheeplands design of an exterior door that opened inward and an inner door that opened outward was a feature of the cold weather, where warmth could be trapped to preserve a home's heat. The senseless woman's body saved Max's life, as the internal door tried to open but couldn't.

Max watched as a rifle and an arm tried to clear the door and aim at him. Max braced himself and slammed the inner door. He intended to shut the door on whatever poked out arm, leg, or weapon. Max pushed, vainly trying to close the door as more guns started poking out. Max jumped from the door as a slug ripped through one side, putting time and distance from the enemy.

Exiting the cottage, Max nearly tripped over the twin forms of Hector and Kate, who lay on the ground. Max didn't have time to assess whether they were alive. He ran towards the truck. As he ran, Max heard the soft report of pin rifles and the loud bangs of slug throwers. The half-circle of houses was filled with weapons fire. With a terrible blow, the inner door of the cottage swung outward. The door shoved the unconscious Susan out of the way and revealed young men and women toting weapons.

Max dove into the truck's bed. The bed wasn't great cover, but it provided good concealment. Max looked up over the side of the bed, pulling the pistol from his holster. The fight was now between the terrorists and the Assaultmen.

Max watched as Wulfjaeger and his men uncloaked with their weapons blazing. More terrorists had exited from the other cottages in the village. The whole hamlet was one big trap. Max cursed his lack of an artillery strike, an interceptor bombing run, or even a hand grenade.

Max watched the action, ducking up and down as rounds pinged against the truck, more collateral than intentional. Wulfjaeger's men spread out, and one of the Assaultmen on the left was hit with slug fire. The Assaultman was knocked back and fell to the ground. As soon as he hit the ground, the Assaultman popped up again, aiming his rifle and shooting at the enemy that dared snipe at him. Max watched as the Assaultmen moved forward. Now, Wulfjaeger and his men would kill the terrorists and capture any that chose to surrender.

The sight that perplexed him the most was the almost robotic form of the armored dog moving along with the Assaultmen. In all his days in the Assault, he hadn't seen anything like Moray. All of the men appeared to be bullet sponges, occasionally being thrown back but then standing up and moving forward, killing the enemies who shot at them in return. All that was good, but the dog was wracking up the highest kill count!

The dog had a scaled-down sniper rifle attached to his back. He would fire as he moved forward and then leap right or left before return fire could target him. Max watched as the dog dropped three terrorists in a matter of seconds, the last with a headshot.

"I've got to get a dog like that," Max said to himself. He watched as two cottages were in flames, and the other three stood doors open with terrorists' bodies piled up at their entrances. Wulfjaeger signaled two Assaultmen to check the leftmost cottage and then repeated the signal, pointing to the rightmost one. The group split up. The two Assaultmen on the left, battle suits riddled with score marks, charged into the leftmost cottage.

Max watched as the right two Assaultmen crossed the space and pushed into the rightmost cottage. Max was rising to hop out of the truck bed. As his waist crested the side of the truck bed, he was given the signal to stay put by Wulfjaeger. He dropped down and watched the scene as the dog raced into the center house, ran through the entire building, and out the back, returning to an Assaultman, whom Max assumed was Keller, the handler. The dog sat and waited, as did Max. In a few moments, Wulfjaeger's microphone blasted out his voice, "All clear, sir! Negative on hostile activity. We've got multiple ambulances on the way. The barons report zero squirter activity. We're hermetically sealed."

Max stood up from the truck bed and hopped off the back. He ran to Hector and Kate, who lay together in a pool of blood.

Max dropped down and checked Kate's pulse. The beat was strong and regular. He then checked Hector's pulse. The beat was faint but steady. Max recalled his battlefield first aid and ran his hands across Hector's back, looking to see if he'd been wounded. Max's hands came back a bloody mess.

"Someone, get over here!" Max said, "We've got wounded."

An Assaultman came over. Max realized it was Ackbar, who was the team's medic. Ackbar took a knee and nudged Max out of the way, unraveling a pouch of medical tools from his suit's waist. Max stood up as the dog and Keller came over.

"Moray and I are on over-watch, sir," Keller reported to Wulfjaeger.

"Good," Wulfjaeger said, "Colonel, you want to have the honor of inspecting the ambush site with me? I hope you can help me identify anything of value from this spot."

"Aye," Max said, watching Ackbar work on his cousin. Under Ackbar's direction, Munster and Pertti came over and lifted Hector off of Kate. Max watched and realized that Hector's quick action had absorbed the blast that would have sprayed Kate. Ackbar gave Kate a quick check and then gave Max a thumbs up. He then returned to working on Hector.

"Colonel, sir," Wulfjaeger said as if to bring Max back from his thoughts. Max looked at the officer and nodded. Wulfjaeger strode towards the cottage's entryway. Max followed a meter and a half behind as Wulfjaeger approached the door to position himself to breach the cottage. Max stacked behind the subaltern and tapped his shoulder, signaling he was ready to enter.

Max knew that Wulfjaeger was taking no chances. Just because the violence seemed over didn't always mean that was the case. Max and Wulfjaeger needed to exercise caution. Enemies could be hiding or have booby-trapped the cottage.

Wulfjaeger entered the small foyer. The foyer design had given Max enough of a barrier that he wasn't cut down on the outer patio. As Wulfjaeger passed through, Max saw a mess of blood and bodies. Susan stirred and moaned, apparently alive, even though the inner door was repeatedly smashed into her. The other side of the door had three bodies piled on top of each other. None of the stacked bodies moved, and Max had to pay attention to ensure he wouldn't trip over the carnage as he passed through the inner door.

Inside the cottage was a four square meter combination kitchen and dining room. Paper maps, several electronic one-time pads, and tablets were on the table. Blast holes riddled the drywall. Some of them smoked and looked ready to ignite fully. Wulfjaeger grabbed a small fire extinguisher next to the stove and said, "Hold your breath, sir," as he pulled the pin and squeezed the handle. The extinguisher belched out a gas that calmed the ambitious sparks as Wulfjaeger sprayed the walls.

"We'll need a clean-up crew from Assault Signals Intelligence to analyze these. I'll get my men to come in here and do a full sweep with a bag and tag, sir."

"Sure, give me a second to poke around," Max said. He looked at the tablets and the maps. The tablet had a short message service active. Max picked up the pad and read the last message, "Under attack, be prepared!"

Underscoring the message, Wulfjaeger said, "Sir, trouble over the comms, Ewan is wounded, and the USIS team is under fire."

Max cursed and wished for a pair of angel wings to fly to where his cousin Ewan was. He then looked at Wulfjaeger, and both men ran out of the cottage to get in their vehicles. Reaching the armored personnel carrier, Wulfjaeger gave the team the signal to load up. The USIS team needed their help!

CHAPTER SEVEN

The Lacheln Reversal - Part Two

Isobel watched as Max left the great hall.

"Kill them all and let the Allfather sort them out!" she yelled after her man as she then headed back to the house. She pulled the small USIS radio from a skirt pocket. She clutched the handset like a talisman and whispered a small prayer to the Allfather for success.

She moved into the manor. Soon, the house would be hers. She paused, caressing the handle on the door. She was eager to bring the Bonnie Dundee back to life like a phoenix. Stepping into the kitchen, she checked the food on the buffet. The buffet was almost gone, showing small remnants of food. The remaining food would be collected for the soup kitchen. She would deal with the mess later after she knew Max was safe and the terrorists stopped.

Isobel climbed the stairs and made her way into the library. Ewan's USIS team members had converted part of the library into a makeshift command center, and three techs sat watching monitors as drones floated over the countryside and other monitors were feeds from the Assault team's armored personnel carrier. The techs worked the controls for the drones, and every few seconds, the screens would change as the drones scanned for details in different light spectrums. The drones scoured the southern area of the march. They seemed to converge on a cave nearby.

"There, the cave," one of the techs said, "Ewan, the cave is showing abnormal RF emissions. That's got to be the place."

Isobel knew the cave the tech had flagged. The locals called the hole *MacLeod's Rest*. Whether the pirate had even set foot in that area of the Sheeplands was debatable, but the name hung on. As a girl, she went spelunking in the tunnels there, often dragging Geordie with her.

After a moment, a hover van appeared on the drone feed by the cave. Ewan had called in a drop team, USIS' combat and rescue forces, to help in locating and capturing Lamia.

"The drop team, Molly, and I are going in," Ewan said. Isobel could see one of the Assaultmen's helmet cams in another monitor. The helmet cam showed Max approaching the cottage that belonged to the girl, Kate.

Isobel watched in horror as a girl opened the cottage's door and pointed a slug thrower at Max. The camera at Max's location bounced and lost focus. The USIS techs at the console started getting jumpy, "Ewan, shots fired, shots fired," the techs said over the radio. The message echoed in the radio in Isobel's hands.

Isobel looked at the Assaultmen's cameras but couldn't determine what was happening or where Max was. Fear gripped her as she saw crumpled bodies lying next to the cottage where Max had been moments before. What happened next made her feel sick to her stomach.

"Drop team down, repeat, drop team down!" the radio in her hands called out. Molly's voice was calm, but Isobel knew she was in trouble.

"On our way," the techs said, standing from their monitors. The three men grabbed their submachine guns and began to move.

"I'm coming too!" Isobel said. She wanted to do something. The techs looked Isobel over, and finally, one said, "Do you know where the cave is?"

"Yes, been there plenty of times," Isobel said.

"Good, you can drive us. That'd be fastest," the tech said. Isobel just nodded as she and the techs raced towards the parking area.

Along the way, Isobel saw Meg approaching. Meg jumped in Isobel's way and said, "I'm going too, and don't even try to argue with me, Isobel. I can tell by the look on your face that something's happened. I will not sit around and wait to see if Ewan, Max, or Andrew are alive or dead."

"Fine, follow me," Isobel said. The techs didn't say a word. Time spent arguing was time wasted. Meg followed along as Isobel continued her run through the Manor. Isobel charged down the main stairs and threw open the main doors. Isobel was about to leave the manor when she collided with someone trying to get in. Isobel fell, seeing stars. After a moment, her vision cleared, and at the main entrance stood Cormac.

"Cormac! Bless the Allfather and the Prophet," Isobel said, jumping up and hugging the huntsman, who sported a deep tan and carried a pair of suitcases. To the huntsman's side was an older woman who was taken aback by Isobel's head-on collision.

"Cormac! You're back!" Meg said, "And in the nick of time! We've got to help Max!"

"What's wrong, lass?" Cormac asked, "Where is Max?"

"There's no time," Isobel said, "Everyone is in trouble! We've got to go!"

Cormac turned to the woman and said, "Sorry, love, wait here. I'll return."

The woman, still in shock, nodded. Isobel turned and ran to the parking area as she heard Meg's banshee wail.

Isobel had never seen Cormac run so fast in her life. He sprinted up next to Isobel like the devil was chasing him. "What's happened? What's happening? Where is Max? Why are all these folks here?"

"No time," Isobel said as she reached the edge of the parking area. Her uncle stood nearby chatting with another older gentleman.

"Uncle Kensie," Isobel shouted, "give me the keys to your truck!"

"No, dear! I know how you drive," Kensie said in return. "I've got only three more payments, and then I'll own the truck. I'll go with you... only I'll drive!"

If Isobel hadn't been so worried, she would have fallen laughing. Instead, she, Kensie, and the others ran to the truck. Isobel jumped into the back with the techs while Meg, Cormac, and Kensie slid into the cab. Isobel watched as the techs hung on to the outside of the bed. Kensie shut the door and hit the ignition button. The fans whirred, and then Kensie slammed his foot on the accelerator. The truck lunged forward, making Isobel and the techs rock back and forth. Everyone clung tight as the vehicle gained speed.

"Where to?" Kensie asked as he opened the slider window.

"*MacLeod's Rest*," Isobel said.

"On our way," Kensie said. Isobel felt the engine's rumble and heard the loud whine of the torque on the fans as Kensie again slammed the acceleration pedal down. Up to speed, Isobel watched as the techs unslung submachine guns from their backs. They were checking their ammo and readying their weapons. Isobel assessed the techs. The USIS techs looked pretty tough for geeks, but would that be enough to save Ewan and Molly? The truck sped along the track, and Isobel could see through the window that Kensie was significantly over the speed limit. Isobel had a crazy thought that if a traffic cop stopped Kensie for speeding, they could guilt the officer into their war band—anything to help USIS and Ewan.

The truck came to a crossroad, and Kensie swung onto the left branch, causing the truck to fishtail and slide onto the shoulder. Isobel and the techs braced themselves again as Kensie corrected the slide. Straightened out, the truck rocketed forward. A roadside information marker proudly displayed that *MacLeod's Rest* was only two kilometers away on the right.

Noting the sign, Kensie poured the gas on again, and soon, the truck wheeled to the right, floating onto a dirt track. The road led to a parking area with a barricade in front of the cave's mouth to prevent people from driving right up to the cave. Isobel could see a stream of dark smoke pouring from the cave's mouth.

Isobel felt the truck thrust fans cut off. The vehicle started to coast one hundred meters from the entrance. Just when she thought the hover-truck would hit the barricade at the end of the road, Kensie applied reverse thrust. The truck stopped two meters before the barrier. Before the vehicle had begun breaking, the techs hopped off. The three ran into the tunnel as Isobel hopped out of the bed. She ran to Kensie's open window. Quickly, she whipped out her hunting rifle from the gun rack in the truck's back window and pulled out her flashlight. She closed the bolt on the rifle and eyed the scope. Satisfied, she cycled the bolt again to chamber a round of the 7.62-millimeter ammo. While not nearly as deadly as an Anderson-Campbell bohrium round, the ancient technology of the hunting rife would still be lethal in the cave's confines.

She prepared to charge ahead when Cormac ran up and stopped her. He was carrying Kensie's rifle in one hand and grabbed her waist in the other.

"Oh no, lass," Cormac said, "I'm not letting you go in that cave."

Isobel thought about trying to wriggle out of his grasp when an explosion shook the ground, knocking the pair down.

Isobel bounced up and charged towards the cave. She ran into the mouth, which was continuing to billow black smoke. The initial smoke and heat of the black plume nearly stopped Isobel. A few meters inside the cave's mouth, she nearly toppled over a form on the ground. Isobel's eyes stung, and her lungs burned. She dropped down on her hands and knees, clearing the fumes hanging from the cave's ceiling. Out of the smoke and regaining her vision, Isobel saw Molly lying on the ground next to her. Cormac charged in through the dark cloud and almost collided with Isobel.

Isobel turned to look at the entrance to see where Meg was. She could make out Meg's shape from the brightly lit exterior.

"Molly is right here," Isobel said, "I can't see how badly she's wounded! Meg, can you reach her?"

"Sure, Isobel, give me a second," Meg said. Meg pulled a scarf, wrapped it around her mouth, and charged into the cave. Cormac crouched below the smoke and coughed. Isobel watched as Meg entered, coming over to Molly. Meg held Molly's arms and pulled the unconscious woman outside. Isobel watched for a moment, debating what to do next.

"We stay together, lass. Let's go find out what happened to the other," Cormac said, finally clearing his lungs. He was hunched over, holding Kensie's hunting rifle at the ready beneath the smoke.

"Aye, together," Isobel said, her voice a croak. She stood into a half crouch, rifle at the ready. Together, Isobel and Cormac moved forward. The floor underneath changed from sand and rock to pavement as they traveled. Isobel turned on her flashlight and attached it to the underside of her rifle. Cormac did the same, and Isobel saw the huntsman moving as if stalking his prey. Isobel mimicked his actions.

"Aye, I remember this place. We are where the paved trails lead into the network," Cormac said. Isobel recalled the caves were a vast labyrinth. The main passages were paved, but the unexplored passages were rough. The terrorists could be anywhere in the extensive network of tunnels. The smoke was high above Cormac and Isobel, and they traveled quickly down the main paved keyhole tunnel.

They continued forward until they reached a fork in the tunnel. They found several forms at the edge of their flashlight's beam. Cormac raced to one of the forms to feel for a pulse on the body lying on the ground. Isobel shifted, and her boot tapped something.

Looking through her scope and illuminated by the flashlight, Isobel could see a USIS member's body. Isobel recognized the man as one of the techs from the library. She said a small prayer for the man's soul. Then, she pointed her rifle toward what her boot had tapped. She picked up a submachine gun, complete with a sling. The USIS team member had dropped the weapon. She slung the submachine gun around her neck. Cormac interrupted her before she could continue to examine the bodies.

"Close your eyes," the huntsman said as a bright light flared. Cormac had found a flare. He dropped the light, and after a moment to adjust, Cormac and Isobel checked the bodies. In the bright red light, they could see that Ewan wasn't among the bodies. Cormac pointed towards the split in the tunnel.

"Well, lass," Cormac said, "do we go right or left?"

"We don't have much time! We should split up!"

"Oh no," Cormac said, "that's a recipe for disaster!"

Isobel didn't want to argue with the huntsman, but she was unsure. There was no way to determine the correct tunnel. She and Cormac stood puzzling over which fork to take. They were roused by a crack-crack of weapons fire echoing from the right tunnel.

"Right!" they both shouted and raced down the right tunnel.

The smell of cordite and metallic weapons filled Isobel's nose as she and Cormac ran along the trail. They ran forward into a large open antechamber. Ten meters on, the antechamber opened into a magnificent chamber. Coming out of the shadows, Isobel was blinded by the lights in the main chamber, which was as bright as day.

Slowing their speed as they entered the main chamber, Isobel noticed lamps across the ceiling, walls, and floor. Another dozen meters farther in, someone had pitched camping tents. The tents formed a rough ring in the center of the large chamber. A makeshift command table sat between the canvas structures. Terrorist's bodies lay all around the tents. The USIS team must have gotten the drop on some of the terrorists as they were in states of undress. Some had died in their cots, while others looked like they had attempted to counterattack. There were bullet holes in the canvas, and the holes still smoked. Isobel wondered where the USIS team was, specifically where Ewan was. She moved a few paces forward and saw the USIS team's bodies lying motionless behind cover. Isobel realized the USIS officers had died where they stood, giving as good as they got. The scene indicated the Ultra-Violets had, based on the number of corpses, the advantage. Scanning over the camp, Isobel saw Ewan lying prone near the makeshift command center. Isobel couldn't tell if he was alive or dead from the dozen or so meters between them.

"Cormac, look, Ewan!" Isobel said. She darted forward, and Cormac ran after her. As they approached the camp, Cormac shoved Isobel to the side of the trail. As he pushed her away, he shouted, "Look out!"

Isobel stumbled to the side, tripped over some stalagmites, and then she heard a loud pop. The next thing she knew, she was tumbling down a sharp grade. As she rolled down, she dropped her rifle. Isobel then felt heat on the back of her neck. She was peppered with tiny bits of shrapnel. The heat only lasted until she rolled into the water. She quickly put her feet under her body and stood. She looked around and discovered she was standing waist-deep in a dark cave pool. The water had soaked her from head to toe. She put the discomfort of being wet from her mind and looked around to see where she had tumbled from.

Isobel decided that Cormac must have pushed her off the trail after she had triggered a trap. The push, trip, and roll had saved her from the blast. Isobel couldn't see Cormac and wasn't sure if he was alive or dead. The ravine was steep, but Isobel was sure she could climb back up to the terrorist's camp. Isobel scanned the rock face, looking for the most straightforward climb. She realized she didn't have her hunting rifle and stopped to search for the weapon. Isobel didn't see it on the ravine, so she felt around in the black water where she stood but had no luck.

Plotting her potential way up, Isobel felt the submachine gun bounce against her back. She moved the sling forward and the shouldered the weapon. She then prepared to ascend the grade. Moving up the slope, she paused momentarily to catch her breath. Then she pushed the last few meters to the place on the trail from which she had tumbled.

Isobel looked around for Cormac. The huntsman's prone form was about ten meters away. He lay face down with his feet towards her. Isobel longed to run and see if Cormac was all right but checked her impulse. She didn't want to trigger another trap.

Isobel stepped gingerly towards where Cormac lay, taking her time and examining the trail. She passed over the downed tripwire that she must have triggered and which had set off the explosion. Finally, she arrived at where the huntsman had fallen. From the waist up, he looked fine, except for an angry-looking bruise where he had hit his head. She checked his legs. The left leg was fine. The blast had shredded his trouser leg, but the limb itself only had minor abrasions. The right leg was a dreadful mess, with a part of the huntsman's calf missing and the rest badly burned. The wound still leaked blood. Based on the wounds and how Cormac lay, Isobel imagined that he had tried to avoid the blast, but the explosion had thrown him forward into the cave wall, where he likely hit his head. She checked his pulse. His heart was still beating.

Isobel quickly used the submachine gun's sling to create a makeshift tourniquet and tied the band as tightly as she could below the huntsman's knee. She figured Kensie or Meg would send help after them. For now, this was the best first aid she could give Cormac.

She stood up and scanned for anything else to give her a sense of what had happened in the cave. She brought the submachine gun up to her cheek and looked down at the iron sights. She didn't want the Ultra-Violets to catch her unaware.

Putting the submachine up to her cheek, she remembered her youth when she and her half-brother had gone out with the dogs on a boar hunt. James, or as she called him, Jamie, had always told her to keep her weapon ready in case a wild pig jumped out of the brush at her. Isobel stepped forward. Pigs wouldn't be rushing at her today, but vipers were possible in the cave—the humankind.

"Jamie, if only you were here..." Isobel whispered.

"Well, well," a woman said, "welcome to my parlor, said the spider to the fly."

Isobel froze. The voice was that of *Frau* Clark. Isobel wondered where the woman was. Isobel swept right and then left. Crossing her sweep, Isobel spotted the woman concealed by the door of one of the tents near the command table. She held a rifle to her eye and trained on Isobel. Lamia was about four meters from where Ewan lay.

"Give up!" Isobel said, trying to bluff the woman into surrender. Scanning the scene, Isobel realized that Lamia must have booby-trapped the entire area. By pure luck, she and Cormac had made it this far.

"Why?" the woman responded, "we're winning. Soon, Gunter will bring the whole edifice down."

"What are you talking about?" Isobel demanded.

"We are moments away from the end of the Parliament Building. With luck, the nuclear weapon will irradiate the tyrant's villa, too. We'll kill or fry all the pigs, and the Union will dissolve. The bourgeois will turn on each other, and our glorious revolution will come to fruition. Gunter will lead us to our new worker's utopia," the woman said.

"You're insane..." Isobel said. She was going to continue, but the woman shot at her. Isobel felt the projectile pass through her hair, and she ducked down, scurrying to find some cover while keeping an eye on the woman.

"Next shot, I will kill you," the woman said, "little empty-headed fool. What was your plan? Seduce Maximilian and raise your status by being his woman?"

"Screw you," Isobel said in defiance, "If I get a good bead on you, I'll kill you and put your head on a spike!"

The terrorist laughed and said, "Adventuress fool, I corrupted Kenneth. He was my willing follower! In time, I would have done the same to Maximilian. I knew I should have killed you in the capital!"

Isobel saw the terrorist shift. Isobel aimed at the terrorist with her iron sight, and she squeezed the submachinegun trigger. Isobel's shot went wide, but at least the terrorist was quiet for a moment.

"We're at a standoff. Put your weapon down, and I'll let you live," the woman said after a moment's recovery.

"Not going to happen," Isobel said, "you're not going anywhere..."

Isobel was interrupted by a muffled call from her skirt. Inside her pocket, the USIS radio was transmitting.

"USIS team," Max's voice said on the radio, "Can you hear me?"

CHAPTER EIGHT

Lair of the Serpent Queen

"USIS team," Max said into the radio, "Can you hear me?"

He waited for a few moments, but no one responded. He was in an Armored Personnel Carrier surrounded by the two Assault fire teams Wulfjaeger commanded. The APC was moving at breakneck speeds towards the cave. Max shook his head at Ewan's plan. The whole operation seemed so simple on paper. Now, Ewan was hurt, the USIS agents were dead or captured, and the terrorist leaders were escaping.

"Almost there, Colonel," the driver said. Max scanned the interior. The Assaultmen were reloading their weapons and checking their gear. After spending most of the last fight hiding in the truck bed, Max decided he would take the offered battlesuit. He moved back to the extra suit's storage compartment. The dog was curled up in front of the locker.

"Sorry, boy, I've got to get in that locker," Max said, opening the door.

"Moray understands," Keller said, "He says he will go with you in the cave. He insists, sir."

Max wanted to ask Keller what he was going on about, but he decided to focus on putting on the suit. Max untied and pulled off his boots and stepped into the battlesuit's bottom half, pulling each of the battlesuit's boots on. Then he worked the connected leg to his knees and wriggled the rest up to his waist. He secured the lower section by threading his arms into the underlayer's suspenders. Max grabbed the top half of the suit from the locker. Max began to pull the armor over his head, and Keller came over to assist. As Max pulled his arms into the top half, he felt Keller give a good tug. Max's head then popped through the collar. Max quickly fed the top's front hooks into the bottom's locks while Keller fed the back hooks.

"Back's good, sir," Keller said. Max nodded and slapped the seal button on the suit's chest. The top and bottom cinched up, becoming one unbroken garment. Keller handed Max the helmet from its cradle in the locker. Max nodded, turned the helmet a little off center from his face, pulled the headgear down onto the bayonet-fitting neck collar, and snapped the helmet to center. The fit wasn't as good as Max's old battlesuit, which had been custom-fitted to his body's dimensions. Max decided he could overlook the current fit as the HUD booted up and greeted him with the text 'Welcome *Oberst* Maximilian Fraser, First Gilbraith Volunteer Rifles.'

"Feels good to be back in a suit, right sir," Keller asked.

"Aye," Max said. He was about to continue, but all the Assaultmen rocked forward as the APC stopped suddenly.

"We're here!" the driver said over the detachment's channel. Max looked at the HUD. His allowed channels showed in the corner of his helmet. The fire teams' channels were available, plus Max had access to the O-channel, the officer's commlink. Max smiled at the thought of broadcasting on the—once forbidden—O-channel but quickly returned to the present. The USIS team needed help. Max watched as Keller and Moray strode out of the back hatch of the APC. Max had missed the door opening as he familiarized himself with his helmet's HUD. Max was about to head out when he checked for a rifle. He grabbed an Anderson-Campbell from the weapons rack. The suit immediately synced to the weapon's electronics. Max noted the rifle's magazine was fully loaded, and the weapon's scope was synced up with his helmet. His HUD indicated that he was missing the two extra magazines and pistol in his waist pouch.

"Coming, sir," the subaltern asked. Wulfjaeger's voice intruded over the O-channel to Max.

"Been a hot minute since I've been in a suit. I'm ready now," Max said. Max walked down the ramp to see Ackbar hovering over Molly while Meg and Kensie stood nearby watching. Max raced over to his sister, flipping his face plate up to be able to talk.

"Meg, what is going on?" Max said.

"Isobel! She and Cormac raced into the cave after Ewan. Max, there is more smoke coming out!" Meg said, the words tumbling.

"Isobel, oh no," Max said. Max flipped his face plate down without hesitation and ran into the cave. Calls flooded his comm channels, but Max ignored them. He noted that a marker on his HUD hovered right on his heels. The marker said 'K9-Desig: Moray'. Max ran into the smoke several meters until he came to a fork in the tunnel.

"Bark!" Max heard from his external microphone while a message in his HUD said, 'Moray:> This way!'

Max watched as the dog ran down the right tunnel. Max ran after the dog, trotting along. Max moved forward to the spot where he saw the prone shape of his friend, Cormac. Max hesitated when another message pinged on his HUD, 'Moray:> Danger! Enemies near!'

Max would have to ignore the downed huntsman for the time being. He looked up, not noticing that his helmet had compensated for the rapid change from the tunnel's low light to the brightly lit cavern. He saw the trails and the terrorist encampment in the center of the large chamber. He also saw Ewan's prone form. Max grew worried when he didn't see Isobel.

Max trotted forward, rifle at the ready. Moving about three meters closer, he felt a white-hot flash of pain in his left shoulder. Max dropped prone. He instantly recognized he'd been shot. The suit registered the damage, and Max wasn't sure if the round had penetrated his armor. He crawled forward and saw Isobel hunkered to his right behind several giant stalagmites.

"Maximilian," a woman said, "how good of you to join us."

"Hello, *Frau* Clark," Max said over his external speakers, "although I doubt that is your real name."

"Max," Isobel said, looking towards him. He knew she had seen him get shot and wanted to come to him.

"For a time, that was my name," the woman said, "but I am sure you are wondering how I knew you were in that suit... You hesitated over the fool who triggered one of my traps. Only someone who cared for him would have paused. I am sure he is bleeding out as we speak. You don't have much time. I am glad you showed up. You've made my escape easier now."

"You're not going anywhere, Lamia," Max said, his voice echoing from his helmet speakers.

"Lamia, is that what they call me," the terrorist asked. She paused momentarily and said, "The Serpent Queen, well, I suppose that works. I am afraid I hold all the cards, Maximilian, just like I did with your father."

"I don't think so, Lamia," Max said, "you'll not be able to take one step outside this cave, as Assaultmen are waiting for you."

"Silly fool," Lamia replied, "I have other means to leave from here. Your Assaultmen will let me leave willingly. I have rigged this entire cave complex to explode on a dead man's switch. Now, I'm willing to talk all day. However, that fool you paused by doesn't have the same luxury of time."

Max cursed inwardly. Lamia was right. He'd need a better plan or be forced to consent to her demands if he wanted Cormac to live. Max weighed his options. His HUD flashed with a message, 'Wulfjaeger:> On our way in.'

Max shut down his externals and said on the O-channel, "Subaltern, wait! The entire complex is booby-trapped. Lamia has a dead man's switch!"

"Roger, holding fast. I'm prioritizing Explosives Ordinance Disposal. Don't worry, sir, we're going to get this witch," Wulfjaeger said.

"Cat got your tongue, Maximilian," Lamia said, "or are you talking with your minions outside? They can't help you. Your only chance is to let me go. Otherwise, you, the fool and the adventuress, will die!"

Max turned on his externals and said, "I'm working out the details, but one thing has me curious: what went on between my father and you?"

"Oh sure, we can chat," Lamia said casually, "I already answered your question. I was his lover. He never did give me a ring, but he gave me everything else. I ruled his life when he was in the capital. I owned his body, and he gave me everything! I got him to support the Violets, even though they are pathetic cowards. He was easy to dominate. The poor man became my willing slave. The fool didn't even know I had poisoned him. You ignoramuses thought he died of pneumonia, no! He died from the slow-acting poison I gave to him. He only lived as long as I wanted him, and whenever he returned to the country, the timer to his death activated. I would slip him the antidote while he was with me in the capital."

Max became furious. Lamia had caused the fall of his family and his father's death! No wonder why his loyalty was always in question! No wonder why things on the estate were so wrong! But now, Cormac, Isobel, and he were in the woman's clutches.

"Well, the one thing you haven't said is why? Why did you need my father," Max asked.

Lamia laughed. "Fool!" she said, "Power, of course! Your father and your family have a reputation that carries power. The fools in the Sheeplands fall over themselves to curry favor with your family, a 'first family.' The human sheep here are so quick to give a Fraser their loyalty that they don't think to ask why they do the things I demanded through your pathetic father."

Max looked down at the scope from his HUD. He moved the rifle slightly. Max wanted to keep Lamia talking. He had to. If he could figure out where the dead man's trigger was, he might have a chance. He sighted in on the terrorist, noting the shape of her rifle, and then changed the visible spectrum on his HUD. He saw the switch. Lamia had taped the device to her gun. Lamia had both hands on her rifle, so the terrorist couldn't easily manipulate the switch. Max sought a firing angle on the woman. If Max could get Lamia in his crosshairs, he and his friends could leave this cave.

"Why? What do you think you can do here?" Max again asked.

"Gunter will do his part in the capital," Lamia said, "I'm here to bring all you Sheeplanders to war. Your silly tribal alliances will activate, and you all will start destroying each other. Internally divided, the Terrans will crush your military, and the Union will fall! Then Gunter will take over, and I will rule at his side. I will..."

Lamia's voice stopped as the bohrium dart went through her forehead. Max jerked as he saw the bloody impact. His HUD registered a message, 'Moray:> Terrorist dead. Am I a good boy? Treat time?'

Isobel shrieked as Lamia slumped forward, dead. She stood and raced to Max, "Max! Are you alright?" she said. Reaching him, she began hugging him around the waist. Max stood and looked at where he was shot. The suit had protected him, but the plating was wrecked.

"I'm fine, love," Max said, flipping up his face plate, then to the O-channel, he said, "Target neutralized, Subaltern, bring your folks in, and have Ackbar ready. We've got multiple wounded."

"Roger, sir," Wulfjaeger said.

"Max, she said they were going to nuke the Parliament! We've got to warn the capital!" Isobel said, "I don't know if Ewan is alive and Cormac is hurt!"

"Hang on, love, one thing at a time," Max said. He slammed the face plate down and switched to the O-channel. He said, "Subaltern, can you get a sat link? This is a priority alpha!"

"One minute, sir, gotta step outside," Wulfjaeger said calmly, then a moment later, he said, "We're a go for sat link."

Max cleared his throat and said, "Flash traffic, flash traffic. Priority alpha! This is *Oberst* Fraser of the First Gilbraith Volunteer Rifles. We've discovered a plot by the Ultra-Violet terrorist group to detonate a nuke in the Parliament Building. All personnel be advised and take action! Flash traffic, flash traffic. Priority alpha!"

Max repeated the statement several times until a voice came over his headset and said, "Roger, Colonel. Thanks for the info. We'll deal with the threat."

Max recognized the voice but couldn't put a name to the speaker. He sighed. Someone in the capital was on the bounce. He'd informed them of the threat. That would be enough for now. Max opened his faceplate as he walked over to Cormac. Isobel followed. Max said, "We've alerted the Assault to the threat in the capital, and they're responding."

Max started to kneel to check Cormac when Moray appeared in his face. Max's HUD became a wall of green text: "TREAT NOW? TREAT NOW? TREAT NOW?" Max moved around Moray and looked at his friend and surrogate father, the huntsman. Cormac's skin was turning gray, and even unconscious, the man looked like he was in tremendous pain. Max was about to touch the huntsman when he heard, "I've got this, sir," over his helmet. Max looked up to see Ackbar, med-pack in hand, preparing to field treat Cormac.

Max turned and carefully picked his way closer to Ewan. His cousin had been thrown by a blast, presumably from one of Lamia's many traps in the cave. Max placed his gloved hand on Ewan's throat to feel for a pulse and looked his cousin over for injuries. Ewan's pulse was steady, and his head sported some nasty bruising, but otherwise, the USIS officer looked unscathed.

"Got Ewan over here, Ackbar," Max said over the squad channel.

"Aye, sir," Ackbar said, "I'll be over to check him in a second."

Max stood up. Isobel walked over and faced him.

"Come here often?" Max said, raising his face plate.

"Oh Max, I thought..." Isobel said, but Max put a finger to her lips.

"You aren't going to lose me," Max said, "I plan on spending the next ninety years with you, my love, Allfather willing."

Isobel had tears forming in her eyes, "I'd kiss you, but I'm not sure how I can reach you in that suit."

"I think that's a feature, my darling," Max said. He then heard Wulfjaeger over the O-channel, "From what we can tell, the site is clear. There are no more enemies, sir."

"Roger, we're coming out," Max said, then to Isobel, he said, "Let's get out of here."

He and Isobel turned to go. As they did, they saw Keller kneeling next to Moray, who was happily crunching a treat.

"Anytime he wants a promotion, I'll gladly make Moray an officer in the First Gilbraith Volunteer Rifles," Max said to Keller.

"Sorry, sir," Keller said, "He's a working dog. I don't think he's officer material."

"He's a damn fine animal, Keller," Max said, "give him a treat for me."

Keller nodded and replied, "Yes, sir. I'll let special projects know this was a successful field test."

Max took Isobel's hand, and they moved forward through the tunnel. Upon exiting the cave, Max hit the quick release and removed his helmet. He saw that his barons and their people had surrounded the area. Policemen and emergency medical technicians worked on the casualties. Max went to where Molly sat. EMTs lined up body bags behind her.

"Looks like your team took the brunt of the terrorist's fight," Max said, "Ewan is alive..."

"Good," Molly said dryly, obviously in shock, "I'm glad he's all right. We went in, and between our team and the terrorists, well, there were a lot of traps and explosions. Smoke started pouring out, and I breathed in a lungful. The whole scene was a nightmare. I thought we weren't..."

"The others weren't so fortunate. I shouldn't be so relieved since only you and Ewan made it from the USIS team. I'm sorry about your team, Molly."

"So am I, Max," Molly said numbly, "I feel guilty that my husband and I survived while the rest died. They were my friends. We'd worked together for almost two years."

"They didn't die for nothing," Isobel said, "we killed that woman and potentially helped stop something in the capital. Their sacrifice made that happen."

"We'll see," Molly said, "Now, I've got work to do. As the ranking and least injured USIS officer, I need to get back into that cave and assess whatever intelligence we might have uncovered. Your Assaultmen won't know what they need to look for."

"Are you sure," Max asked, "no need for you to return inside..."

"Sorry, Max, I need to go in there. My team's memory requires it," Molly said, "I'll also check on Ewan. I will see you two later."

Max and Isobel nodded. Molly stood up, turning to the body bags piling up behind her. She silently crossed herself and then headed resolutely into the cave. Max was about to say something else when he was nearly bowled over by someone grappling him.

"You're safe, you're okay!" Meg said, hugging Max tightly. Max mused that this was the second time the suit had saved his life. Meg's ferocious hug might have broken him in two without the battlesuit.

"Yes," Max said, seeing the two EMTs with a stretcher bearing Cormac. They lowered the stretcher, staging it for the ambulance. The EMTs went back into the cave. Max noted that others came out from the cave and were carrying the bodies of USIS and terrorists. Ackbar had stabilized Cormac in the cave. Max, Meg, and Isobel ran over.

"I knew I should have come back yesterday," Cormac said weakly as the trio approached.

"Cormac," Max said, "what are you doing here?"

"Oh, laddie," Cormac said, "such a long story, and I'm so tired."

Max was going to continue when Ackbar approached, "He'll be fine, sir. I gave him a fair bit of morphine for the pain. He's feeling the effects. The EMTs will take him to the hospital in the village. They said with hospital care, he'll make a full recovery."

"Thanks," Max said as the EMTs carried the huntsman to a waiting ambulance. Andrew noticed the group and came over.

"Lovely day for hunting, eh, your grace," Andrew said to Max.

"For some, yes. In the end, we did bag our prey," Max said.

"Well, for my group, we didn't bag anything. At one point, I had a doe in my scope. She pranced off, as we needed to hold our fire for the bad guys."

Max was about to say something but was stopped as Meg slipped her arms around Andrew and kissed him. Stopping, she said, "My brave hunter!"

Max looked at Isobel, who smiled. He then went over to a picnic table that someone had put there for cave visitors. In the interim between the hamlet and cave, Max's barons must have determined his position, and they were converging on the cave.

Max stood on the table and said to the crowd, "The threat has been neutralized!" The crowd cheered. "I invite you all to the Bonnie Dundee for some light refreshments to thank you all for your aid."

The crowd cheered again. As they left, Max realized that he didn't know the fate of Hector or Kate. He climbed down from the table, a serious look on his face.

"What's the matter," Isobel asked.

"I just remembered, Hector was shot," Max said.

"Well, the hospital is only a short detour from the house. Let's get Kensie to take us."

Max nodded, sat on the picnic bench, and took off the battle suit. Isobel went off to find Kensie. Max had the top half off when Wulfjaeger appeared.

"We've surveyed the caves and marked where the explosives were placed for the inbound EOD unit. I have the fire teams guarding the site, and that USIS lady is going over the site and gathering intelligence, sir," the subaltern said, "I've got this command, provided you don't have any more need to be here."

Max pulled the bottom half of the suit off and stood up. He was barefoot, as his boots were in the back of the APC, but he'd collect those in a moment.

"Thanks, Wulfjaeger," Max said, "you guys have been a huge help."

"Just all in a day's duty, sir," Wulfjaeger said, "I'm sad they kicked you out. I've enjoyed serving with you, Colonel Fraser."

"Thanks, I appreciate that," Max said, "What's next for you, Wulfjaeger?"

"Off to the Academy," Wulfjaeger said, "We could use you back on the front lines, sir."

"Not on my dance card anymore," Max said, "I've got my duty here, but I wish you success and victory."

Wulfjaeger stood to attention and snapped a salute. Max went to attention and returned the salute. Max relaxed his salute, and Wulfjaeger followed.

"Aye, success and victory to you too, sir," Wulfjaeger said, "farewell."

"Aye, farewell," Max said. He watched the subaltern turn and go back to his duty. A part of Max wanted to march on his shoulder and return to the Assault. Max unconsciously took a step to do so and was rewarded with a sharp rock stabbing into his foot. He silently cursed himself and carefully went to the open APC. There, he sat on the hatch and put on his boots. By the time he had finished lacing the combat boots, Isobel and Kensie had appeared.

"We're ready to go," Isobel said.

"You can even ride in the cab this time, dear niece," Kensie said.

"I'm driving this time then?" Isobel said with a devilish smile.

"Ah, no," Kensie said, "but we can tell young Max all about your attempt to drive my truck and your reckless desire to meet your maker today."

"Are you sure I can't drive," Isobel said with a giggle. Kensie just shook his head and started towards the truck.

Max took Isobel's hand and looked her in the eye, "I love you."

She took his other hand and said, "I love you too."

Max put his arms around her waist and kissed Isobel passionately. She responded, and they stood there kissing until the blast of a truck horn interrupted them.

"Come on, you two," Kensie said, "time and tide wait for no one!"

Isobel and Max strode over to the truck and climbed in. Kensie reversed the hover vehicle and then drove towards Gilbraith village. Along the way, Max and Isobel exchanged stories about the day. By the time the couple arrived at the hospital, they were worn down from all the excitement. By contrast, the hospital was a hive of activity. The minor flood of wounded had overwhelmed the medical center. Folks waited in a queue outside the emergency room registration. Max and Isobel entered the hospital doors—Kensie had said he'd stay in the truck.

Max led Isobel, walked around the ER queue to the main reception, and asked the woman at the desk, "I'm here to see Hector Fleming-Fraser."

"Are you family?" the nurse asked.

"Yes," Max said, "he's my cousin."

"Room 24 C. Once you turn around, the entrance to the wing is on my left. Follow that corridor to the end of the hallway."

"Thank you," Max said, turning around and following her directions. As he approached the end of the hall, he saw Hector through the glass in his room. Hector lay in bed, an oxygen tube in his nose and an I.V. in his arm. Sitting in a chair next to the bed was a very bandaged Kate. She held Hector's hand. She stood when Max entered.

"How is he?" Max asked.

"He'll pull through," Kate said, "well, that is what the doctors say."

"Good," Max said. He was about to turn and leave when Kate stopped him.

"He saved my life. He's the bravest, nicest man I've ever met."

Max nodded. Whatever wrong he could say about Hector had been washed away during their encounter at the cottage.

"How is your sister?" Max asked.

"I don't know, she's not my sister any longer," Kate said, "I disown her and all of those terrorists."

Isobel stepped forward, "Don't be hasty..."

Kate cut her off, "No, no, I'll be seventeen in a few days. I have decided to make my way..."

Kate was going to continue when Hector opened his eyes, "Max, did I do a good job?" he asked.

"Spectacularly good, you saved Kate and me, Hector," Max said.

"Good," Hector said, "Now if the ladies would step outside,

there is something I wish to discuss with Max."

Kate and Isobel nodded and moved into the corridor to wait. Max moved in closer to Hector.

"I am sorry, dear Max, for all the pain I have caused you," Hector began. Max shook his head, but Hector continued, "I am sorry for my wrongdoings. I intend to make things right. I wish to release you from any promise of matching me, and I want your permission for something. But first, what will happen to Susan and Kate?"

"I don't know. Susan will be tried for attempted murder, provided the Union Procurators don't decide to drag her to the capital to face terrorism charges. She harbored violent terrorists. The whole hamlet will be mine in compensation for the damages done, if I don't already own the plots. Unfortunately, I expect we'll be forced to destroy the hamlet." Max said.

"And Kate," Hector asked.

"Not sure. Based on her cooperation, I planned to shield her from the worst. Why?"

"I release you from your promise to match me and want your permission..." Hector said, stopping.

"Permission for what?" Max said. He wasn't sure what his cousin was so focused on. Max wasn't even sure he had committed to a match, but Hector was asking something important of Max. So, Max listened carefully.

"Permission to marry Miss Kate," Hector said. He was floating in and out of the medicine.

"She's very young, don't you think?" Max asked. Hector shook his head.

"I'm twenty-five, and she's just seventeen. Mom was ten years younger than Dad. Plus, I've become... quite fond of her."

Max paused. He wasn't sure what to say, and Hector didn't look like he was in the best state for the conversation.

"Let's talk after you get out of here," Max said.

"Aye, I'm tired now," Hector said, and he closed his eyes and started snoring softly. Max strode out to the hall, joining the ladies.

"Hector's sleeping," Max said.

"That's good," Kate said, "I was planning to say goodbye and leave tomorrow. I'm off to the capital to start anew."

Max suddenly felt a duty to his cousin to keep Kate nearby. Max said, "Kate, if you'd reconsider leaving, Isobel and I could use your help. We're woefully behind on what needs to be done to renovate the manor. Even if you can cook the occasional meal, we'd find that help invaluable. You could stay with us rent-free while you helped out."

Isobel lifted an eyebrow in a subtle question. Max squeezed her hand, and she played along, saying, "Yes, even if you'd help by swinging a paintbrush, that would be one less room for us to do."

Kate said, "I see. I'll think about the offer. Now, I'd like to go back to sit with Hector. He saved my life, after all."

"Goodbye, Kate," Isobel said.

"Goodbye, Kate. Please let me know if you are interested in that room," Max said. Kate nodded and left them. Max took Isobel's hand and threaded their way back towards the entrance. They had only walked a few steps when they heard a familiar voice.

"Max," Ewan said, "in here, cousin!"

Max stepped into the room. Ewan looked downright healthy compared to Hector. He sat in bed with a bandage across his head and face and sling around an arm. Max could see several bruises along Ewan's exposed arm and face.

"Ewan, I'm glad to see you are still in the land of the living," Max said. "How do you feel?"

"Where's Molly? Did you get Lamia?" Ewan asked, sidestepping the question.

"Molly is fine, and Lamia is dead," Max said, "What happened?"

"We all went in so cavalier," Ewan said, "I should have known better. We ran forward, and the Ultras started shooting at us. The drop team was pushing them back when I hit a trap. All I can remember was flying through the air before waking up in the ambulance with a splitting headache. I wonder what they were after," Ewan said.

"They were going to plant a nuke under the Parliament. Lamia and her team were here to start a civil war," Isobel said.

Ewan's eyes grew wide, but Max calmed him down. "We reported the intelligence. The capital is on high alert now. There is nothing more for us to do on this end."

"Good," Ewan said, visibly relaxing, "good to see my team didn't die in vain."

"They are heroes," Isobel said, "they cleared the cave and enabled us to go after Lamia."

"Where is Molly?" Ewan asked.

"She stayed behind. She said she needed to go through the scene. She wasn't in a good spot," Max said.

"Yes, that's my wife," Ewan said, "I can see why she wanted to stay. She'd worked with the techs the longest. She probably feels like her staying and working is some penance. She's going to need some time. I'll be there for her. We need to reconnect with each other, and this is our opportunity."

"I understand," Max said. Isobel nodded.

"Now, I shan't keep you. I expect you two have much to do," Ewan said.

"Aye, farewell, Ewan, and for all that matters, thanks," Max said.

"Best of luck. I should be up and moving soon. I'll see you two in a few weeks. Until then, cheers," Ewan said. Max and Isobel moved from Ewan's bedside to the corridor and glimpsed a stretcher bearing Cormac's form being wheeled into another room. Max and Isobel ran to the room and tried to enter but were blocked by a middle-aged woman with dark hair and olive skin.

"Who are you?" she demanded.

"Who are you?" Max and Isobel asked in unison.

"I'm Devanna, Cormac's wife. Who are you?" the woman said. Max stopped cold. Married, Cormac was married? Max sat there dumbfounded.

"Max," Cormac said weakly, "is that you laddie?"

Devanna moved to the side and allowed Max to enter.

"I'm here, old friend," Max said, reaching out and taking the huntsman's rough hand.

"Isobel," Cormac said weakly.

"She's here. She is safe," Max said. Cormac nodded. He looked tired and drugged.

"Cormac, who is..." Max said but was cut off.

"Devanna, my wife," Cormac said, "I got married, laddie, was going to bring her back home. When I arrived, all hell had broken loose. Should have never left."

"Rest now, old friend," Max said. Cormac nodded his head, and Devanna came to his side.

"I'm sorry, Max," Devanna said, "I didn't realize who you were. Ever since we came together, Cormac has spoken of you incessantly. I almost feel like I know you."

Max nodded, "How did you and Cormac meet?"

"Oh, decades ago," Devanna said, "I was a maid at the Bonnie Dundee, then. We knew each other in service. I suppose I was taken with him then, but he only had eyes for Margaret Douglas in those days. Well, to the present, I was off to Eisenwald to see my daughter and her family there, and I got on the space transport and sat down. The rest of the passengers boarded, and lo and behold, who sits down next to me but Cormac Munro himself."

Max nodded and said, "And then what happened?"

"He just nodded politely at me," Devanna said, "and I said, don't you recognize me, Cormac? His expression was priceless. He stared back and said, 'Vanna Gordon, is that you?' At that moment, I vowed that I wouldn't let him get away again without a fight—this time. I put a guilt trip on my poor man here and made him come with me to meet my daughter and her family. One thing led to another, and the next thing we knew, we were on the altar of my daughter's parish, saying vows. We've only been married for a week, but we both feel like we're an old married couple."

Max didn't know what to say. Fortunately, Isobel picked up the conversation, "Congratulations! Welcome to the family," she said.

"Thank you, and you must be Isobel. Cormac talked about you also," Devanna said, "and kept saying how much you were like your aunt Margaret. But, seeing you in the flesh, I'm afraid I have to disagree. You're nothing like your aunt."

Isobel froze, and Max felt his stomach drop. After a moment's pause, Devanna smiled and said, "You're much nicer and much better looking than poor Peg ever was."

Max smiled inwardly. Whatever Cormac had said to Devanna, she had taken to her core, and the compliment had warmed Isobel's heart.

"Oh, why thank you," Isobel said in surprise, "My uncle and I have always regarded Cormac warmly. Max and I are happy he is back and has an enchanting lady at his side to boot."

Max interjected, "Devanna, please let us know if anything changes with Cormac. Isobel and I must return to the estate. As you can imagine, we've had a long day."

"I shall, Max," Devanna said, "I'll let you know immediately if anything changes."

"Thank you," Max said, "goodbye."

Isobel, too, said her goodbyes, and the couple swiftly retraced their steps through the hospital. Within minutes, they were back with Kensie and on their way to the Bonnie Dundee. Max was ecstatically happy when Kensie rolled up the driveway. He was home!

CHAPTER NINE

Games and a Wedding

Max stood and watched from the front of the box as the games began, and then he turned and returned to his seat. As he sat next to Isobel on this pleasantly warm July Friday, he had a smile of satisfaction on his face. The weeks between the death of Lamia and the fair's start passed quickly.

The fair had been going on since Monday, the sixth, but the significant festivities would start tomorrow, Saturday, the eleventh—Max and Isobel's wedding day. Cormac hovered nearby, with the assistance of a cane, as his leg was still healing. The huntsman marshaled the well-wishers into a queue. They had come to see Max's intended, Isobel, presented to the clan.

"Alexander Fraser, Squire of the Isle of Saltoun on Lochiel, and his daughter Muriel," Cormac said. Alex stood on the platform, and he approached along with his daughter, who was nine months pregnant.

"Marquess, the Saltoun-Frasers wish you joy and long life on this your betrothed's day of presentation as our chieftainess," Alexander said, "and may I present my daughter, Muriel. She and her husband, a distaff Fraser relation, are expecting my first granddaughter. Since we are kinsmen separated by at least six generations of our blood, may I suggest my granddaughter be a potential match, as you and your fair lady will undoubtedly have a strong son as heir." Max put his hand to his mouth as if he was thinking. He was trying to contain his laughter at the thought that the old goat wouldn't be denied. He would somehow get his match with Max's family.

"Cousin, many thanks," Max said, "my betrothed and I will consider your very generous and perhaps—a bit premature—offer when the time arises. We thank you for your attendance and beg you to enjoy the games."

Alexander bowed, and his daughter curtsied. Max noticed the smile of triumph on Alexander's face, as finally, after three generations, his family hadn't received a 'no.' As Alexander and his daughter left, Hector and Kate entered. Both were formally dressed, Hector in a black suit while Kate wore a gown of pale blue.

"Cousin," Hector said.

Max rose and embraced Hector, "Cousin, welcome."

The ladies exchanged their pleasantries, and Max returned to his seat.

"As is proper on a presentation day," Hector said, "I, as your heir, ask for your permission to marry Miss Kate Grenville in front of our assembled clan."

Max was ready for this turn of events and said, "As chieftain, I give you my consent and blessing. I wish you both many long years of happiness."

Kate smiled, tears in her eyes, and looked at Hector with admiration and love. Hector had tears forming in the corners of his eyes, and he said, "Max, thank you."

Kate stood and curtsied as Hector bowed low. Max and Isobel smiled and nodded. Hector and Kate then left. Meanwhile, Geordie Stewart, the Baron Breakin, appeared. Geordie wore a Tam o'shanter, with Prince Charlie jacket, full plaid over his shoulder and around his waist, wool socks, and dress shoes complete with spats. A stately woman with jet-black hair and a fair complexion was on his arm. She wore an elegant dress and fascinator, the formal headpiece a touch dressy for the games.

"Geordie, welcome," Max said.

"Hello, Geordie," Isobel said as well.

"Good day to you both. I've come to present Gisela von Berg. She and I are courting, and I decided to introduce her to my liege and his intended—both my good friends," Geordie said.

If Gisela had known the history between Geordie and Isobel, she didn't display the knowledge. Instead, she took Isobel's hand and said, "A pleasure," in her Eisenwaldian accent.

"Delighted," Isobel said, clasping her hand.

Max stood, gave her a gentlemanly kiss on the back of her hand, and said, "Welcome."

Gisela nodded her head and gave a half-curtsy. Max motioned the two to sit, Geordie taking a spot to Max's left and Gisela to Isobel's right. The ladies began a quiet conversation while Max leaned to speak with Geordie.

"Well, how do you fare, Breakin," Max asked.

The allusion wasn't lost on Geordie, who said, "My days of spilling the beans are over, your grace, but as friends, I will say things are promising. My friends getting married also have me in a mood to marry."

Max smiled, "Happy hunting."

"Always, old chap," Geordie said quietly with a wink, "no shepherdesses for me, though. I'm a man of simple tastes, only looking for widows with kind hearts."

"I wish you well," Max said, "Will you join us for a moment?"

Geordie stood, and Gisela followed, "I'm afraid not your grace. We're off to the old pile. Some of my cousins are there. Apparently, they expect something special to happen."

Max stood, catching the subtlety, "a pleasure to meet you, *Frau* von Berg," he said, switching to the German title to avoid embarrassment on whether Gisela, being a widow, had reverted to her maiden name. Both Geordie and Gisela gave a polite bow and left.

The line continued. Max and Isobel were gracious with cousins, vassals, and well-wishers. Near the end of the line came Ewan and a beautiful woman who was his escort.

"Max, Isobel," Ewan said, informal in his greeting.

"Hello, Ewan," Max said, still seated, "where's Molly? And who is this enchanting lady?"

Isobel wrapped Max on the shoulder as Molly said, "I'm right here, Max."

Molly then moved over to Isobel and said, "Pro tip for the future: a new cut and color, some makeup, and a nice corset can go a long way, dear."

Max, now three shades of red, attempted to recover, saying, "Are you two staying through the fair and tomorrow for the wedding?"

"Sadly, we're here only for a short while and on official business," Ewan said, "I have heard a rumor you will be receiving an important guest tomorrow."

"Tomorrow? But that's our wedding day," Max said. Ewan merely nodded.

"Also, I have a gift for you both," Molly said, presenting two small boxes, "these are given confidentially, and sadly you won't be able to talk about them."

Max was intrigued. He opened the clamshell box. Inside was a purple ribbon with black edges, and dangling from the ribbon was a silver and gold möbius strip arranged as an infinity sign. Isobel's clamshell contained one as well.

"What's this?" Max asked.

"The infinity," Molly said, "these are awarded to those whose contributions furthered intelligence collection significantly. The award states that the recipients' actions were in some way an infinitely valuable help. Based on what happened with Lamia, USIS delivered a report to the protector calling out your actions to end her activities. Due to the nature of USIS business, these awards are never presented publicly, and we're on the edge of that here..."

"Molly and I are here as a social visit. Well, that's our cover," Ewan said, "We're being reassigned and given a long holiday in between. All the details are top secret. I argued passionately to stay and see your wedding, but that wasn't in the plans for the big bosses, who want us on mandatory holiday. I may not see you again, cousin, for a while."

Max stood and reached out to Ewan, who clasped Max's hand. Both men shook hands, and Max said, "Thanks for everything, both of you."

Ewan and Molly bowed, said their goodbyes, and left. Behind them, the games were winding down. Soon, the *Holstensonne* would be low in the summer sky. After Ewan and Molly left, Max stood and stretched.

"Shall we make our way to the manor?" Max said.

"Yes," Isobel said with a smile, "and then you are forbidden to see me."

"Right, bad luck," Max said, referencing the old tradition. He and Isobel left the box, climbing down the bleachers and to the field. The games grew to a close, with only a few remaining events wrapping up. Max and Isobel paused on the field to ensure they were not leaving prematurely. The remaining spectators packed their things, and folks tore down the sporting fields.

Max and Isobel wandered up to the Bonnie Dundee. Max could see the enormous Ferris wheel erected in the village as they climbed a slight rise. They could smell the fried fare and sweets when the wind blew in the right direction. The march was deliriously happy and, most of all, quiet. Max thought about how the raiding had collapsed after Lamia's death. Occasionally, there were Ultra-Violets intent on mischief, but the constabulary quickly apprehended the troublemakers. Mostly, the only concern folks had in the Sheeplands was the war with Terra. On this lovely summer day, Max resolved not to worry about anything as he and his soon-to-be wife made their way to the house.

Approaching the manor, Max looked at the stately home. In the past few weeks, Max and Isobel, along with the conscripts, carpenters, masons, and other tradesmen, had worked tirelessly to renovate the house. Max saw the gleaming new windows, the rust-free wrought iron furniture in the gardens, and the immaculate terraces. He hadn't seen his home this nice in forever. Tears formed at the corner of his eyes.

"What's the matter," Isobel asked.

"The house is beautiful," Max said. Isobel put her head on his shoulder and then, after a small hug, reached up to kiss Max. They shared a tender moment, and then Isobel broke the lip lock. She said, "Come on, the clan is waiting for us."

The couple strolled to the door. Max pulled the door open, presenting Isobel to his family beyond.

The crowd inside clapped loudly in applause. Max saw that Meg and Andrew were leading the cheers, and Hector and Kate were in the upper balcony, marshaling the cheers there. May appeared from the crowd. She looked younger than when Max arrived. She wore an elegant gown that must have been in vogue in the capital.

"Welcome, Isobel, soon-to-be niece," May said. The gathered Frasers clapped again.

"As the closest Fraser woman to the late Lady Fraser, I welcome you to our clan," May said, "you have charmed our marquess and charmed us all. May I be the first to say we all feel blessed to have you as our soon-to-be relation?"

The gathered clapped loudly. May then motioned Meg and Devanna forward. The ladies had a pair of blindfolds.

"Now, Max, please step forward," May said. The Frasers again cheered. Cormac appeared, looking unhappy at this duty.

"Now, Max and Isobel, we will blindfold you and send you to

your secret hideaways. As you all know, our tradition is that a bride and a groom cannot see each other before the wedding. As Felgenlanders, we ensure this by hiding the bride and groom away. Our customs ensure no bad luck or evil can find the bride and groom before their wedding. Now the blindfolds," May said. Devanna handed her blindfold to Cormac. Meg and Devanna, as married women, then blindfolded Isobel, and Max watched the women lead her off to another part of the house. Cormac, dragging his feet at his conscription, put the blindfold over Max's eyes when Isobel was out of sight.

"Come on, lad," Cormac said, and he placed Max's hands on each of his shoulders, "This is all a stupid female thing anyway."

Cormac grumbled as he led Max out of the house and to Max's secret location. Blindfolded, Max wasn't sure why the huntsman was so annoyed. They entered the huntsman's cottage. Once they arrived, Max took off his blindfold. Max then realized why Cormac was so grumpy. Max would stay in his cottage until the morning of the wedding. Cormac was giving up his bed to Max.

"Cormac, I can't take your house, even for a night," Max said.

"The deal is done, laddie," Cormac said, "if you're feeling poorly over the situation, don't. 'Vanna and I will be staying in your nice new bed. We can talk about making that permanent tomorrow if you take a fancy to the cottage."

Max smiled and said, "I suppose there is no chance of me leaving the cottage tonight?"

"Nope," Cormac said, "However, I did come prepared. 'Vanna caught me sneaking out a bottle of the reserve. She was worried you'd be hung over tomorrow, and someone would say the wedding didn't count as you were not in sound mind."

"That's wise but a little silly. I'm an Assaultman. I can handle my liquor," Max said.

"I know, lad," Cormac said, pulling out a small flask, "as I said, I came prepared. The flask will be a nice nightcap."

Cormac pulled out two glasses and poured two fingers of whisky into the glasses, draining the contents of the small flask.

"To long life and health of you and Isobel," Cormac said, lifting his glass in a salute and draining the contents.

"Hear, hear," Max said, pulling the glass to his lips and drinking the whisky. The smoky peat and oak flavor hit the back of Max's mouth. Within moments, a warm fire engulfed Max's body.

"Now, I'm off," Cormac said, "Vanna has a ton of chores for me, all for tomorrow. No leaving, or you'll get me in trouble."

"Aye, Cormac," Max said, "thanks for everything."

The huntsman nodded, a small tear in the corner of his eye, "Aye, lad, see you in the morning."

Cormac put his glass in the sink and went out the front door, shutting the cottage behind him.

Max looked around and noticed small things that announced Devanna's presence in the cottage. A small Celtic cross hung in the kitchen. There were some wildflowers in a vase in the bedroom and a picture of her daughter and son-in-law and their children. Max stripped out of his full plaid and jacket. He pulled the wool socks off and was in an undershirt and underwear. He looked for his morning jacket and trousers for the ceremony. Cormac, Hector, or some other relation had hung his wedding costume prominently on the back of Cormac's bedroom door.

Max moved to the bedroom, pulled back the covers, crawled in, and pulled a sheet over him. The bed was not as good as Max's current mattress or the new one he and Isobel ordered—a king-sized bed they would share after tomorrow's ceremony. Max yawned. The whisky was relaxing him, and he settled back to let his mind rest. He noted the alarm on the side of the bed and, after pushing some buttons, saw that the alarm registered eight hundred. That would give him an hour to get ready. His mind drifted until he remembered

Ewan saying he would have a special guest. Max mused over who that would be until he drifted asleep.

When Max awoke, he glanced at the alarm. The clock read seven fifty-nine. He had a minute before he needed to get up. As he sat up, the alarm cried out. He shut off the klaxon and went to the cottage's small washroom. He showered, checked his cheeks for stubble, and styled his hair. After a few minutes of teasing his locks, he called his job good enough and went to get dressed. He put on an undershirt and underpants. He then dressed in gray trousers and black socks and, before buttoning his trousers, put on a white dress shirt, tucking the tails into his pants. After a few moments, he was presentable and put on his shoes. He then pulled out the tartan tie. The tie bore a Fraser tartan and would be the only spot of color in his uniform today. After three attempts, Max finally had the tie knotted where he wanted it. Max then turned and put on the morning jacket and his top hat.

Max looked into the mirror, nodded, and said, "I'm not the best-dressed man, but far from the worst-dressed man in Gilbraith-on-Heather today."

He then exited the cottage, looking out over the part of the estate with the parking area.

Three dropships were coming in low across the horizon. Max paused, tracked the craft, and said, "I wonder where those dropships are going?"

He continued to watch as the dropships got closer and closer. As Max watched, he realized their destination was the Bonnie Dundee. Max wondered if the dropships were attached to the special guest Ewan had mentioned.

Max decided to move towards the house. He pulled out his pocket watch, an heirloom of his father's. The time read eight twenty-seven. As he strode towards the Bonnie Dundee, the dropships came down in the parking area. Two squads of

Assaultmen poured out of each dropship and formed a perimeter around the house. Max hesitated, standing by the main entrance and waiting. The rear hatch of the third dropship opened, and a middle-aged man and woman stepped out. Max looked at the couple. He was sure they were not the protector and patroness since Max could see that the man had hair on his head. Max was about to pull the handle to the door when the door opened. Cormac poked his head out. He was similarly dressed to Max and looked surprised to see Max.

"What's going on?" Cormac asked.

"Dunno," Max said. Both men stood there as the man and the woman approached. The couple climbed the small stairs from the parking area only a few meters from the entryway.

Max looked at the man. His appearance was familiar, but Max couldn't place him. He waited for the man and the woman to get closer.

"Welcome to the Bonnie Dundee," Cormac said formally.

"Thank you. Please summon the marquess and tell him that Grand Duke Alasdair Campbell and Lady Margrethe Campbell have arrived on behalf of the protector," the man said.

Max tried not to laugh as Cormac said, "His grace, the marquess is right here, your grace."

Max strode forward, "Welcome to the Bonnie Dundee, your grace," he said and then realized with whom he was speaking. He added, "You look very lively for a dead man, sir."

"Please, Maximilian, call me Alasdair," the Campbell said, "and as to the rumors of my death, you should never believe anything you read in the papers or see over video."

"Aye, Alasdair, what brings you here?" Max asked.

"Why, you do, Maximilian. I'm here as a representative of the protector for your marriage," Alasdair said, "Although I would have preferred to come as your liege, but that's another matter."

"Please then, sir, this way," Max said.

"No need for sirs here, Maximilian," Alasdair replied, "we're all peers here, now. As a peer and on behalf of our liege, I wanted to thank you for the work with Lamia. When I heard your voice calling out the flash message about the Ultra-Violets, I was happy to quell your fears. At the very moment of your message, I was—entertaining—Mammon and his lieutenants. Happily, they did not survive the festivities, and the Union remains strong and ready to seek victory."

Max hadn't thought of the message to the capital until Alasdair mentioned it. Like a flash, Max realized that when he had urgently called for someone in the capital, he hadn't expected to raise Alasdair.

"So then..." Max began to ask.

"Yes, Mammon is dead. Our liege, in recognition, has elevated me to be his Procurator and the General of the Line Guards. With such elevations comes increased responsibility, and those responsibilities often require aid. I expect the Frasers will not forget the many years of vassalage with the Campbells, and we can continue to call you allies?" Alasdair said.

"Of course not. We remember the many years of your patronage," Max said, "and we are always glad to help our allies."

"Excellent, now you're the main show today. Run along, and your man will escort me," Alasdair said.

Max rechecked his pocket watch again. He had ten minutes to get to the chapel. Max entered the manor through the main entrance. Inside the grand corridor, he saw the large gathering of ladies who would escort Isobel to the chapel. He about-faced and went the other way, passing the Campbell and his wife. He turned to the west and headed for the cloakroom entrance. He'd need to make up the time as the chapel was on the other side of the manor, with Isobel and her half of the bridal party in between.

"No big deal," Max said to himself, "all I need to do is borrow one of the dropships, and I can float over the manor and repel down to my spot on the altar."

Max entered the cloakroom and was about to enter the grand corridor when he heard the ladies singing *Màiri Bhàn*. Max turned around again. Isobel and her entourage were blocking his route. Max realized he'd have to chance a route through the gardens. He left the cloakroom and went right through one of the ornamental gardens. He needed to clear the garden, and then he would round the north side of the house to the chapel entrance. Max approached the north corner when the sprinkler system started. Max dodged and weaved through the spray of water. "If my drill sergeant from basic could see me now," Max said as he moved to avoid the sprinklers.

Max skirted the north side of the Bonnie Dundee without any issue and entered the north entrance doors. He ran south through the corridor, turning east to head to the side door to the chapel. Max checked his shoes before he entered. There was no mud. He opened the small side door and entered the chapel.

The Reverend Fraser stood in front of the small altar. Per tradition, the wedding bands sat on two pillows on the altar. Max crossed himself as he entered and took his spot near the priest. Max checked his watch once again. Two minutes remained. Max let out a deep sigh of relief.

"There is no need to be nervous, my son," the priest said, "marriage is a blessed institution."

"Aye, reverend," Max said. Max was about to say something more, but the large organ that took up a wall of the chapel began to play. Max and Isobel flew in a specialist from the capital to ensure the organ was in working order and tuned. Max had felt that was money wasted, as the specialist came in, played some keys, and pronounced the instrument in tune and functional.

The organ music continued until there was a brief pause. The organ began playing Chibetti's *The Dance of Wedding Flowers*. Max would have preferred Purcell, but the Protelani Chibetti was in vogue with brides in the Union, and Isobel was insistent on the piece. Max looked at the doors, waiting. He noticed some older folks in the five pews inside the chapel. Max figured most folks would watch from the large vestibule outside the chapel or via the camera drone feeds.

The doors opened, and Max expected to see Isobel. Instead, Jennie appeared in an aqua-blue dress. Isobel had asked her niece to be in their wedding. Jennie hadn't hesitated in her quick, positive response. Jennie wore a wreath of flowers in her hair and carried a basket of white petals that she tossed on the rugs in the Chapel. Jennie finished her tasks and then curtsied to Max, moving to the left and back to the entrance using the outer side of the pew. Max remembered to remove his top hat and placed it on the communion rail. Isobel had reminded him to grab the hat for pictures after the ceremony.

The doors opened again, and Max prepared to see Isobel, but instead, Meg appeared. She wore an aqua blue dress and a similarly colored fascinator. She came down the aisle bearing a candle—the marriage candle. She handed the candle to the Reverend. Meg then moved to the chapel's side and went down and out. Max tried to look nonchalant, but he was getting impatient. Where was Isobel? The music continued to the allegro, and Max knew Isobel's entrance would be soon.

As the music's tempo increased, the doors opened. At first, all Max could see was Kensie, who wore a much less formal full plaid of ancient Douglas tartan with a Prince Charlie jacket, wool socks, and patent leather dress shoes. He moved forward, and then Max saw her.

Isobel was radiant. She wore a champagne-colored tulle veil on her head and wore a champagne gown with short chiffon sleeves and silk gloves. Max cocked his head, he saw Isobel's blond hair through her veil, but Max couldn't see her face. He began to worry that Isobel had gotten cold feet and she had found a doppelganger to replace her. At that moment, Isobel moved forward, and the light from the stained glass windows penetrated her veil, revealing her immaculately made-up face. Max inwardly told himself to relax and that nothing terrible would happen.

Isobel and Kensie walked down the aisle. Cormac, May, Hector, and Meg trailed them. Kensie stopped at the first pew, pulled a small bag from his sporran, and stepped forward to Max. The bag symbolized Isobel's dowry, and Kensie handed the small bundle to Max and then shook his hand. Kensie then turned and lifted Isobel's veil. Max looked at his bride's face. She held back tears, and Max looked at Kensie and saw he was doing the same.

Isobel stood to Max's left, as was traditional. Max then handed the little bag, the symbol of her dowry, to Isobel. That, too, was a custom in the Sheeplands, as the woman's dowry would become her dower. Isobel placed the small purse into a silk bag she wore from her wrist. She then pulled out a rolled scroll and handed that to Max. The scroll was the symbol of her authority over the Barony of Cairnbahan. Max took the scroll and placed the parchment in an outside pocket. At their union, the barony would no longer be a separate entity. Cairnbahan would come under the marquess's direct control.

Max and Isobel looked toward the priest. The full nuptial service would have included readings, a Eucharistic celebration, and a formal blessing. Instead, Isobel and Max had opted for a nuptial blessing, and the reverend would work from a tailored script.

"Please kneel," the reverend said. Max and Isobel knelt, Meg and Hector, appearing moments before with the two ancient kneelers that belonged to the chapel.

"The Allfather, divine and eternal, created humans male and female, for the Lord created Eve as a helpmate to Adam. Now, in this holy place, where Frasers of the past have made their vows and strengthened our clan, I present to you, Almighty God, Isobel and Max. The couple shall rise and face each other."

Max and Isobel stood and turned to each other. The reverend came to their sides and said, "Your grace, please answer. I do."

Max nodded. The priest then said, "Maximilian Alexander Fraser, do you take Isobel Brigid Douglass to be your wife? Do you promise to be faithful to her in good times and in bad, in sickness and health, to love and cherish her until death parts you?"

Max nodded vigorously and said, "I do!"

A small chuckle rippled through the gathering inside and outside the chapel at Max's eagerness. The reverend smiled, turned to Isobel, and said, "Isobel Brigid Douglas, do you take Maximilian Alexander Fraser as your husband? Do you promise to be faithful to him in good times and in bad, in sickness and health, to love and adore him until death parts you?"

Isobel's eyes flashed in mischief. She hesitantly pursed her lips. Max felt his heart stop. What if she was having second thoughts?

"I do," she said. The gathering outside began to clap. The reverend scowled and said, "The rings, please."

Cormac and May, on command, brought the pillows with the rings. Max picked up Isobel's ring and she Max's. Max looked at the ring in his hand. The platinum band had a large square-cut purple topaz. Max had begged Meg for his mother's actual ring, and after extracting a mountain of promises from Max—some realistic and other fanciful—Meg assented to giving the ring to Max for Isobel.

"Your grace, please place the ring on her grace's hand," the reverend said.

Max placed the ring on the third finger of Isobel's left hand and said, "Isobel, receive this ring as a sign of my love and fidelity. As we were taught by the Prophet, in the name of the Allfather; Jesus, the Son of Man; and the Holy Spirit."

The reverend turned to Isobel and said, "Your grace, please place the ring on his grace's hand."

Isobel presented the thick platinum band. Max could make out the slight imprint of the Fraser and Douglas coats of arms around the band. Isobel had worked with the jeweler in town on the design. The emblems symbolized their union as both people and metaphorically as figureheads of their clans.

Isobel opened Max's left hand, gently placed the ring on his third finger, and said, "Max, receive this ring as a sign of my love and fidelity. As we were taught by the Prophet, in the name of the Allfather; Jesus, the Son of Man; and the Holy Spirit."

The reverend crossed their hands. "What the Allfather has brought together may no one separate. Your grace, you may kiss your bride."

Max leaned in and kissed Isobel. She placed her arms around Max, pulling him in close. The reverend gave them a few minutes but then interrupted. He said, "I present to you, Marquess Maximilian Fraser and Marchioness Isobel Fraser."

They both broke their kiss and turned to the crowd as the vestibule went wild in cheering. When the hall stopped clapping, Max could hear the faint roar of celebration from the village and the bells ringing across the march. Max turned to Isobel and looked into her eyes.

"You are so cute, my husband," Isobel said, eyes flashing with mischief, "you were worried I wasn't crazy enough to say I do."

"Yes, I expected that you would have run away screaming by now," Max said.

"Darling, a Union auditor, spies, and terrorists haven't scared me away. Compared to all that, being married to you will be a walk in the park," the marchioness said.

"Even if the walk is in the rain and fog, my love?" Max asked Isobel.

"This is Stahlburgh. A walk in the park doesn't count if the day is sunny," Isobel said. Max took her hand, and they strode down the aisle and out of the chapel together into the arms of their immediate family, friends, clans, vassals, and kinsfolk.

Epilogue

Isobel stood on the rooftop veranda outside their apartments. The cool October morning was an ominous portend of the cold winter that was near. She wore a long silver silk nightgown and leaned over the ornate rail, coffee in hand. Max walked through the ornate double doors and joined her. They had both returned from an extended honeymoon on Eisenwald, courtesy of their family—who had pooled resources for the vacation.

"Good morning, sweet husband," Isobel said as Max appeared.

"Good morning, darling wife," Max said, "are you trying out your porch? You'll need a parka to stand out here in a few weeks."

"Yes, yes," Isobel said, pulling Max close, "but for now, all I need is your body. The heat will keep me warm."

Max kissed Isobel, and they stood for a long while, lips locked together. He pulled away momentarily and said, "I can't stay with you all day. There is still so much to do."

"Aw," Isobel said, "Here I was weighing whether I wanted to get in a fancy dress and christen the new children's hospital in Cairnbahan or just skip the whole thing and lie in bed with you all day."

"The hospital is today?" Max said, "That won't work. I have a meeting at the spaceport construction site. We're almost done, and there are some last-minute conflicts that I need to resolve. Hector has done his best, but the builders are arguing again. Then there's the volunteers. I was going to supervise the election of officers—which is scheduled for today. I swear I need a clone!"

"We're working on that, and after he or she is born, then seventeen years later, they can help you out. This is why I wanted to stay in bed all day. I'm planning for the future, dear husband."

"You have presented a tempting offer, my sexy wife," Max said, "let me make some calls, and maybe I can postpone most of the events..."

Max continued when a posh hovercar flew up to the Bonnie Dundee. Max's instincts went on high alert, and he said, pointing, "Who the devil is that?"

Isobel looked out and watched as the car approached. The car skidded to a halt on the main front lawn, and the driver's hatch opened.

"Max, Isobel!" shouted Geordie, "Good, you're up! Get decent! Somethings happened!"

Max and Isobel turned and went inside. Max threw a cable knit sweater over his nightshirt and hastily stepped into some cargo pants. He then shuffled forward and shoved his bare feet into a pair of work boots he had left out in the middle of their bedroom—much to the dismay of Isobel. He was heading towards the door when Isobel intercepted him.

"That was fast, dear. Why can't you get ready like that for one of our appearances?" Max asked.

"Oh, my sweet husband," Isobel said, turning the handle to their bedroom door and ending the conversation. Max and Isobel hurried down to the foyer where Geordie stood waiting.

"Geordie," Max said in astonishment, "I thought you were on your honeymoon!"

"We were, but when Gheegee and I saw the news, we flew from our spa resort home. I am surprised no one has told you! The papers, the audios, the vlogs, have been going non-stop for hours," Geordie said, flapping several print papers in his hand.

"What happened, Geordie?" Isobel asked.

"The *Bismarck*! The Terrans shot the transport down over L98-59 Foxtrot! See," the baron said, handing out the papers. Max looked at the headlines, *'USTC Bismark* Lost!', 'Assault and Navy's Initiative Crushed!', and finally, *'Primus* Feared Dead in Failed Attack!' The headlines were all terrible.

"Oh no," Isobel cried as she read, then turning to Max, she said, "Honey, we need to do something!"

"The march is doing our part for the war," Max said.

"Not all of us, old chap," Geordie said grimly.

"What are you talking about, Geordie?" Max asked.

"You two never asked me my unit, and in truth, I never told you," Geordie said.

"I figured you were an infantryman, just like I was," Max said.

"Oh no, this loss is more personal to me than that," Geordie said, "my friend is lost on that rock, and I need to go get him back!"

"Who, the press hadn't released any..." Max said, and then he remembered his night with the protector. His eyes went wide.

"You mean..." Isobel said, coming to the same conclusion.

"Yes," Geordie said, "I served with the *Primus*. At the time, he wasn't that high up in the *Cognatii*. My friend, Heinrich von Machthaber, is lost on that Terran dust ball, and I aim to get him back!"

"That'd make you..." Max said, recalling the *Primus*'s old unit.

"A *Mecha-jaeger Grenadier Assaultman*, a MjGA—former Special Forces, and we never leave our brothers behind," Geordie said, pronouncing the acronym 'mee gah.'

"But your leg?" Max said.

"I've pulled strings. Amazing how the *Primus'* uncle, the Field Marshal of the Assault, was willing to let me return after I talked to him," Geordie said.

"But Gisela..." Isobel began.

"Told me to put my old uniform back on and ride off like the knight-in-painted armor I was... and am. I figured with all that you were up to, the world was taking a back seat. I am happy that I could say goodbye before I left." Geordie said.

Max wanted to say, 'Take me with you' or 'Geordie, I am going too!' but he knew that would never happen. His role now was to protect the home front and keep the home fires burning.

Max reached out, and Geordie grasped his hand and said, "Bring them back, and bring us victory!"

Geordie nodded and said, "Keep an eye on Gheegee and keep the hearth fires burning by the Allfather, and..."

"The Protector of the Union," all three said.

The Felgenlanders will return in…

Protector of the Union

See more details on our publisher's site at https://woodenhookstudios.com!